He smiled. How little they understood! To them, politics was falling asleep on the green benches of the House of Commons, committees, tea with sycophants, decisions about which figures to release and which to hide. But life – and more especially, death . . . to them, such concepts never entered the frame.

And yet that was the stuff of raw politics, real politics. Who we keep and who we discard. Not a question of principles. Any fool could interpret *them*. You weighed up *values*, *cost*. That was your skill. That was the reason you were chosen. Even Ricaud had realised it. In his own way.

The need to take expensive decisions.

All in all it wasn't a bad thing they'd done – agree on the assassination of a small and insignificant president in a republic most people had never heard of.

In this instance, it was clearly the right thing to do.

Tim Sebastian was born in London in 1952 and is the author of six previous novels. For ten years he reported for the BBC, mainly from Eastern Europe. He now lives in London, where he divides his time between writing and broadcasting.

By the same author

The Spy in Question
Spy Shadow
Saviour's Gate
Exit Berlin
Last Rights
Special Relations

WAR DANCE

Tim Sebastian

ORION

To Caroline

An Orion paperback
First published in Great Britain by Orion in 1995
This paperback edition published in 1996 by Orion Books Ltd,
Orion House, 5 Upper St Martin's Lane, London WC2H 9EA

Copyright © 1995 Tim Sebastian

A CIP catalogue record for this book is available
from the British Library

ISBN 0 75280 170 8

Typeset by Deltatype Limited, Ellesmere Port, Cheshire
Printed in Great Britain by Clays Ltd, St Ives plc

Prologue

In the darkened room they sat watching the television screen, waiting for his appearance, wondering about the little things – what he'd wear, the expression on his face, the way he'd hold himself. Of course they knew what he'd say, they knew what he'd come to do.

Now it would take its course.

Jean-Jacques Ricaud was not a popular figure in the French government. No cult following. No mistresses. A solid, rather lifeless minister of defence, armed with nothing more controversial than a wife, who never spoke in public, and two children, who were so discreet as to have been forgotten by everyone, including their parents. Ties by Hermes, shirts from Turnbull & Asser in London, suits from a completely unknown Polish tailor in Montparnasse. But who could hold that against him? He came, not from the usual 'old school' that teaches its children to lie and dissemble among the best and most important families in the land – but from that other more select variety – which observes and cherishes its principles and has, over successive generations, committed itself to justice and decency.

He was, to damn him for all time, an honest man.

Which was why he had called a news conference that morning at the National Assembly to resign.

Of course, they told themselves, they regretted his decision. They had said as much to him at the meeting.

But if he couldn't accept the collective, international will, then it would be better for him to step aside voluntarily. It would be un-clever to resist.

And should he, either by intention or accident, reveal the substance of their discussions, they would be forced to consider their position.

'May I ask what that means?' He had looked at them in turn, raising a single eyebrow.

And when informed, he had simply nodded his head and said 'thank-you', as if someone had offered him the lunch menu.

It was what he'd expected.

Even if he didn't play the game, he knew the rules.

Those were a few of the steps that brought M. Ricaud to the Assembly that morning, with the television cameras in attendance, and much of Europe waiting to find out what he would say.

There was, they could observe later, little to notice about his bearing. The dark blue suit was unruffled, the shoes spotless – only the green, foulard tie offered a plume of unaccustomed colour. More unabashed, more extravagant than was usual for the man. Perhaps, after a dismal career, he would leave in style.

That is what they thought, as they watched him.

At the podium he laid a black leather portfolio beside the lectern, raised his head and looked round at the assembled ranks.

'I have a short statement to make, but I shall not be answering questions.'

He reached down and took a gulp from a glass of water.

'Ladies and gentlemen, at eight o'clock this morning I telephoned the Prime Minister and told him I no longer felt able to continue in office. I stressed to him that this was a personal matter, in no way connected with the policies of the government. I greatly admire his leadership, and the direction in which he has taken our country and I wish him every success in the future. Mine is a . . .'

Ricaud broke off and reached again for the glass of water.

But his hand travelled instead to the black portfolio, as if it contained a document to which he wished to refer.

And only now does he hesitate. The eyes moving rapidly around the room. A gentle hush of concern.

'You must forgive me ladies and gentlemen . . . a difficult decision. I'm sure . . .'

He licks his lips, swallows, reaches down again. Only this time his hand goes inside the portfolio, and as they were all to affirm many times over, it was hard to reconstruct the immediate sequence of events.

You kept thinking, they said, that a government minister, on National Television, couldn't seriously be removing a revolver from his case, inserting the barrel rapidly into his mouth, and pulling the trigger. A calm, thought-out movement, practised you might think. Quick, but not hasty. Something so planned and so evil, something to send you crying away into a dark corner that the world is mad and the people possessed, and there is no salvation to hope for, from now until the end of time.

And there, in front of you, the head of Jean-Jacques Ricaud is blown apart in a cascading shower of blood and tissue. Half-severed, half-splintered, punched away from his body.

Throughout the great hall there are cries of horror and indignation. The camera is moving in all directions. People stand rigid in fear. Some have covered their eyes in disgust. Several are weeping.

You would hope never in your life to witness . . . never to hear tell of such a thing.

And yet no one leaves. Except the minister.

In his place he has left his blood, daubed like the worst excesses of post-modernism, on the white and gold wall behind the lectern.

And there, on the floor, is his body.

Inside the darkened room one of the men gets up and switches off the television.

For a brief moment, before the main lights come on, there is absolute silence. There is a sense of quiet satisfaction.

3

Chapter One

'*Guilty conscience, boy?*'
   Amesbury could still hear the voice, decades ago, at the bloody British boarding school.

They had always known when he had a secret. He used to shift on his chair from one buttock to another, as the blood coursed up his neck and into his cheeks, quite out of control.

Still happened, of course, only the years of free-flowing sherry had given his face a permanently florid hue, so the blushing was harder to spot.

Always happened, though, when the guilt came on. The knowledge that you had deliberately done wrong. And it didn't matter how you explained it away, with the two other ministers lounging around the table, preened and pampered. It sat there pungent and accusing in the centre of the room.

First time he'd had a journey like this one, slipping unannounced out of London, stealing away to Switzerland, and not a single member of the fag-dragging political press loafing behind.

Each of the men at the table had slipped the leash, sold his department an even bigger load of cock than usual, lied and prevaricated in the name of National Security, and then flown here to Geneva.

Here by the lake, with the mountains breathing over their shoulder.

Here with the guilt. Past and future.

★

'So we're agreed.' The Secretary of State gazed into the middle distance, over the heads of his two companions, through to the woods behind the house. It wasn't the kind of meeting where you looked anyone in the eye. Not one for the photo albums. Do it and leave. That was the size of it.

Amesbury shrugged. 'Agreement is putting it too strongly. Acceptance is a better word.'

'Oh come on my dear fellow – a bit late for scruples, I'd have said. We do it, or we don't do it. Those are the only options.'

Amesbury shook his head. 'We've already chosen the option. We decided on one course. Monsieur Ricaud decided on another.'

'You will make the arrangements?'

'I will make the arrangements. We are in the best position to do that.'

'You have someone in mind to carry this out?'

'Don't be ridiculous. I don't make a habit of associating with people like that . . .'

'But you know where to find such a person.'

Amesbury caught the American's eye and held it. 'We all know that, don't we Drew? We all know that.'

'Let's not quarrel.'

They both turned to the man who had spoken. Dmitry Kallin, the Russian Defence Minister, Oxford-educated, Mafia-nurtured, probably bought and paid for so many times, thought Amesbury, that he no longer knew who the hell he was working for. Like so many of them.

'Given the position of our governments there is one other consideration.' Kallin coughed into a handkerchief. 'We would need certain rather concrete assurances from whoever you chose, that he won't talk.'

The American Secretary of State sighed deeply and wearily and gazed around the table. 'He *won't* talk, will he?'

Amesbury sat completely still. 'Everyone talks to someone. In the end.'

The Secretary of State offered the general valediction, probably because he wanted to get away first, had further to travel, thought he was a cut above the rest.

'We did a remarkable thing, today . . .'

'Yes we did.'

'But of course.'

'Absolutely, my dear fellow.'

The echoes rolled round the table.

And then they rose slowly to their feet, gathering pens and paper, making their way to the electronic shredder by the door. 'Everything, please, Excellencies. Even your tickets. It is necessary, you understand, of course . . .'

The language of gentlemen, for the practitioners of folly and deceit.

'Guilty conscience, boy?'

Dmitry put an arm round his shoulders. Dmitry, known as Russia's 'sympathy minister', for the easy charm and the culture, even though his function allowed little room for either.

He gestured towards the sofa. Amesbury couldn't help thinking how exquisite was the tie, how uncreased the suit, how light one really travels, when one travels without a conscience.

'It's a pity Ricaud could not have understood what we decided today.'

Dmitry smiled. 'I think he did an honourable thing.'

Amesbury shook his head. The man was insufferably pompous. 'He did a realistic thing. He knew we would have made arrangements for him.'

Dmitry spread open his palms. In that single instant the subject had changed. 'You promised me some of your famous grouse when I next come to England.'

'I shall shoot it for you myself.'

The Russian's smile contracted. 'Till then, my friend.'

'Till then.'

★

Outside, the sun dazzled on the lake. The steamers were sailing in force. The world was on a Sunday outing.

Only these men would depart by different routes and at different times. No mass exodus with blaring sirens and police motorcades. No statements or interviews, or silly handshakes caught by a flashbulb. This meeting, more than any other, had never happened.

Amesbury went back inside and waited in the library. He felt somehow lighter, easier, as if his conscience had gone to sit somewhere else.

In a while they would take him in an unmarked freight truck, over the Swiss border into France, car all the way to Marignane airport outside Marseilles, dark glasses, and a hat that he hated.

But it didn't take much to become someone else. You are, he told himself, the person you make yourself out to be. Put a value on your face and the chances are most people will accept it.

Just remember which face it is.

For a moment he wondered what some of his colleagues would say if they had attended the meeting.

'Went too far, old fellow. Sacrificed your principles. Should have said no. Should have got up and left. The PM would have backed you when you got home.'

He smiled. How little they understood! To them, politics was falling asleep on the green benches of the House of Commons, committees, tea with sycophants, decisions about which figures to release and which to hide. But life – and more especially, death . . . to them, such concepts never entered the frame.

And yet that was the stuff of raw politics, real politics. Who we keep and who we discard. Not a question of principles. Any fool could interpret *them*. You weighed up *values*, *cost*. That was your skill. That was the reason you were chosen. Even Ricaud had realised it. In his own way.

The need to take expensive decisions.

All in all it wasn't a bad thing that they'd done – agree on

7

the assassination of a small and insignificant president in a republic most people had never heard of.

In this instance, it was clearly the right thing to do.

Chapter Two

Brigadier Peter Hensham drove to Hereford to put the plan together.

Hensham was the man of first refusal.

The preferred instrument for something a little delicate, a little out of the ordinary. For something that could start to smell if it went bad.

The Minister had used him before.

He had left London at five that morning, knowing the drive would be quick, knowing he'd find the man where he wanted him. There wouldn't be too many people around, in the old sixties offices, housing the largest accountancy firm in the town, guarded through the hours of night by the capable hands of Jimmy McIlvane.

Honest to a fault, our Jimmy.

An honest killer.

Put him beside a pint of McEwans. Slide a scotch into his hand, let him spend the evening with comrades who'd survived intact, or half-intact. Pete the Teeth, The Chocolate Mouse, the fellow they all called 'Splash' because his helicopter had come down in the sea beside the Falklands. Put him with men like that – and he was a charmer.

Well, not a charmer, but a party guy. Slapping backs, muttering to himself about 'his boys', little in-jokes, from little 'in'-operations, known only to the old and the bold, where Jimmy had earned his stripes.

They never lost contact with Jimmy. They, being the

regular Army – the one he'd served all those years back. The Henshams.

Word had gone round that even though Jimmy had been caught with his cock in the custard, he could still be used. With care. You could bung the fellow a couple of hundred quid, give him an address, make sure he could read it, and send him on his way.

The hits were always clean and quiet.

Jimmy didn't talk about his work because he didn't want to. And no one else did either.

Jimmy would be perfect.

Hensham had to knock hard on the front door. The wicked old bastard was having a kip or a crap, he decided.

Only it didn't do to underestimate him.

He always got the work done. Always did what he promised. There weren't many delivery boys as good as that.

They exchanged the barest greetings. No surprise on Jimmy's face.

His life was made up of surprise meetings. People sought Jimmy out from all parts of the world to put a team together, to topple a government, shoot a terrorist, defence or attack, on the side of the angels or the devils, if anyone could disentangle it and work that out.

And he didn't much care.

Quietly, methodically, he made two cups of tea on the small gas ring, stirred in the milk and sugar and listened hard.

Five minutes went by before he asked his first question.

'Why does it have to be a British operation?'

'No questions Jimmy. You know the way it's played.'

'Who is it then?'

'President of a little place you haven't heard of.'

'Oh I see. That's alright then. Just the president.'

'We're the only ones who have access to him. He stays in his residence all day. Terrified of being assassinated. He trusts us for Chrissake. He was educated in Britain. We're going to throw him a party.'

'Good for you.'

'Don't knock it, Jimmy. Be a pretty good send-off, I expect. Plenty to drink, of course. Taxpayers' money.'

'Yeah, like fuck.'

'Are you in or out?'

'I don't know. Why should I have anything against this bloody president?'

'Who gives a shit if you do or not? It's money. That's all. Plenty of it.'

'How much?'

'Twenty grand. Usual procedures. Anywhere you want. Any currency.'

'I don't do assassinations.'

'What about Belfast?'

'Fuck you.' Jimmy turned away and stared round the bleak, freezing lobby. 'They were terrorists. That was war. And you know it. This isn't like that.'

'Twenty grand Jimmy.'

Hensham finished his tea and left this time by the rear door, straight into the car park with the dawn coming up fast over the town.

Jimmy watched him go. Why could he never say no? Each job was more dangerous than the last. More sensitive, more open to betrayal.

At the end of the day, whose bullet-ridden body was supposed to be found? Yours or theirs?

He didn't like this one.

But as Hensham drove away, the time for pulling out had passed.

Jimmy picked up the phone and made three calls. He booked a midday flight to Berlin and cancelled his shift for the next few nights.

Chapter Three

There is a bar, they told Thomas Blake.

There's always a bar.

It's down a street in the Lichtenberg section of East Berlin. Miserable, arse-wrenching place, full of tumble-down mansions and barking dogs. But you'll find it.

He always did.

When you see him, take it slow. Don't push him. He's in a bad state. Nervous.

We're all nervous. That doesn't go away. Just tell me how I recognise him.

You know him. You've known him for a long time.

Colonel Thomas Blake. Forty-two years old and long stopped counting. When you're in the army you're encouraged to reduce things to the bare necessities.

Blake on leave, he had thought. Blake with family – wife Sarah, daughter Veronica, son Charles, on a weekend away in Berlin, western side. All so bloody normal, until the phone goes in the hotel. And some old contact from way back yanks the chain and your gut starts shuddering the way you'd told it never to do again.

'I won't be long.'

They look across the table as if he hasn't spoken. Charles reading, Veronica dreaming, Sarah shaking her head.

'The last time you said that, it was six months.'

'There was a war going on. Remember?'

'And it had to be yours.'

'Look, we're on holiday.'

'We were.'

He'd be back by the evening, he told her, and they'd go out to dinner – just the two of them. The kids had met some people. So God knew where they'd be off to.

And then they'd talk. 'OK?'

She shrugged – and inside so did he.

As if talking would somehow mend the holes in the years.

In a way, he decided, it was probably better not to talk. After this many years of marriage you needed some illusions. You needed to kid yourself that it was better than it really had been, that you hadn't gone away for a year in the middle, that there really hadn't been nights when she had cried, and threatened to put her hand through the glass kitchen door, and you had done nothing to help her.

In a marriage, you needed to affirm with absolute conviction that night was day, and black was white – and reach an understanding that both of you would accept the truth of it.

Only she couldn't. Not anymore.

He left the table and found a taxi in the street. The great united city of Berlin was packed out with shoppers. But the driver seemed to hack through them, as if cutting away at the undergrowth.

Crossing eastwards, the cars thinned out and the rain came softly and the buildings lapsed back into decay. You could tell the history of the place had an attitude. A bad one. Nazis first, then Communists – worse than all the others because they had believed it would work; believed society should be like that. A pain in *everyone's* arse.

For many years to come this would remain East Berlin, whatever they called it.

The bar was a few steps below street level. Blake could see it from the taxi – the cheap neon sign outside, the dismal lighting from within. A place to get through an evening. If he could.

'Want me to wait?' The driver didn't look round, just threw the words into the back.

'No.'

'You won't get another car round here.'

'I said no.'

Down the steps and Blake entered the bar, full of dark mahogany, dim candle lights on the walls, a barmaid – just too old to be one – who's seen it all before and doesn't want to see you. A thick slice of suburban, German depression. In a corner a group of middle-aged couples were well into the moaner's routine . . . but there was no one to meet him.

He ordered a beer, scanning the faces carefully, hoping the drunks wouldn't start singing, wondering when the man would come.

Every rendezvous is late. Blake knew that. They watch you go in, let you get settled, then make sure you've come alone.

For a moment, he wished he was armed. Two tours of duty in the city and he knew all about its heart and its hospitality. Knew about the neo-Nazis and the drug cartels, the Russian crime groups, the Colombians, the low-life that had crawled out from under Europe's stone, when the stone got moved.

Berlin had them all, in their savage glory.

Here, they had always said, you're never more than a street away from a bullet.

Friendly Berlin.

Yes, sure.

Because the undertakers are always smiling.

He came from the back of the room, behind the drinks counter, where no entrance or exit had been apparent. And Blake knew him without even studying the face. No disguise. Just the set of the face was enough, and the long, loping walk, and the hand, flat and cold – a killer's hand, never a lover's hand.

Jimmy McIlvane.

Made somewhere in Scotland, fifty years earlier. Exported, war after war, and on to the next.

Jimmy was a mercenary.

Dead or alive, he was therefore lousy news.

'You look different out of uniform.' He eyed Blake up and down.

'So do you.'

It was the first time he'd seen Jimmy out of his battle fatigues, wrapped in a cheap, grey suit that fastened round the waist, but nowhere else. The thing was made for someone who didn't have Jimmy's outsize chest, his biceps, the legs like short, stubby trees; made for a normal man, which Jimmy never had been.

Blake ordered another beer and looked around the café.

Jimmy never came alone.

Even behind the lines in Bosnia he had always travelled with a friend. Insurance, or maybe reassurance, when you work for a side that has no loyalties or allies, that will shoot its own people in order to blame atrocities on its enemies. That was far too much uncertainty for one man to carry alone.

Blake had met him first on a patrol near Tuzla. He had come out of nowhere down the side of a mountain to warn the British patrol that there were landmines ahead of them.

It had saved dozens of lives.

'Why did you do that . . . ?' Blake had asked him much later in their acquaintance. 'Didn't have to. Wasn't your job. Now they'll go looking for an informer.'

Jimmy had shrugged, the way he might have shrugged off the rest of the world, shrugged off his country.

'I owed you people a favour.'

'Why?'

'Tell you one day.'

But he never had. Instead he had appeared at odd intervals throughout Blake's tour of duty, turning up with bits of information, insights – all of them correct.

Jimmy never lied.

15

And when you're a killer, Blake reflected, you don't need to lie.

What you do speaks for you. Not what you say.

'I don't have time for a beer . . .'

And it was a different Jimmy sitting that night in the bar in East Berlin.

'I needed to talk to you . . . needed some advice . . .' He looked round and Blake thought he caught a glance, exchanged with the barmaid.

'They want me to kill someone . . .'

'They always do, Jimmy. It's your job.'

'Don't be funny, Mr Blake.' He always called him mister, wasn't good with ranks. 'This is different. Bigger. Something I haven't done before.' He picked up the beer glass and drank fast. 'When I've killed people, it's been like wartime. You know . . . they're shooting at you, and you've just got to be faster and better. That's soldiering . . .'

'And this?'

'This is assassination.'

They both released their breath at the same time.

'Then don't do it, Jimmy.'

'Too late, Mr Blake. It's past that. Once they told me the name of the target, there was no backing out. That's how it's done. I shouldn't have let it get that far . . .'

'What did they say . . . exactly, Jimmy?'

'Said I'd . . . Oh Jesus . . .'

Quite suddenly the barmaid appears behind him, whispering urgently, and Blake can see the words settling on Jimmy's face, see the fear inject into his eyes, watch them begin to move as he works out the odds.

'Have to go . . .' The giant, steel body half out of the chair, and the effect is like a building on the move . . . Jimmy, sending a shock wave through the bar, as he frees himself from the tables and coats around him . . .

'Who's they, Jimmy? Who are they? Quickly . . .'

'I can't. Mr Blake. It's a fix. I can't.'

He ducks down behind the bar, through the door at the

16

back, and there is only the tremor of a frightened man, moving very rapidly into the night.

As Blake looks round, the barmaid is already clearing away the glass, wiping all traces of the man and his drink.

'You saw nothing. Nobody was here. *Verstanden?*'

'I've been alone all evening.'

Even as he said the words, he could feel the sudden, cold draught, as the three uniformed police appeared in the open doorway, sub-machine guns in their hands, and the expression of utter indifference that real thugs so often reserve for their victims.

Chapter Four

'Your name?'

'Blake, Colonel. British Army.'

'What were you doing there?'

'Drinking.'

'Why?'

'I was thirsty.'

'Why there? Berlin has many bars.'

'Happy memories . . .'

'You have happy memories in this city . . . ?' The eyes opened wide behind the metal-rim spectacles.

'Girlfriend . . . gone now.'

'So you come here to celebrate her memory?'

'More or less.'

'You are a sentimental man, Herr Blake.'

'Colonel Blake. I'm a colonel in the British Army.'

'It must be a very . . . sentimental army.' The eyes narrowed. 'Funny . . . but that was not my impression of it.'

Blake didn't move. It was clear they weren't police. Too unrehearsed, too ragged, uniforms new and uncreased. More likely Special Services – the kind of wholly deniable little unit that all governments maintain. Killers, thieves, kept on a lead until their owners tell them to go fetch.

They had herded the docile Germans from the bar, thrown a few dilatory questions at them. But it was him they wanted. In the back of the van, down to an unmarked building. Some habits they never grow out of.

'I want to call the British Embassy.'

'That won't be necessary if you co-operate.'

'It's my right.'

'But of course, Herr Blake. You shall enjoy all your rights.' The man got up from the chair, prim, precise, the bald head glinting in the neon light. He went over and stood behind Blake.

'You were seen talking to a man in the bar. Who was he?'

'He didn't give me a name. Men talk to other men in bars . . .'

'What was the conversation?'

'Sex.'

'I see.'

'The man was buying or selling?'

'Neither. The conversation was very general . . .'

In the room next door, a figure in a grey woollen coat reached over to the wall and faded out the sound of the interrogation.

He could still see Blake through the two-way mirror, but there was no point listening any longer. They would learn nothing from him.

His colleague, younger, sleaker, raised an eyebrow.

'He met McIlvane and they talked. We know that, whether he admits it or not.'

'So what?'

'So security's breached.'

'That's your assumption. We don't know if they had time to talk . . .'

'And if they did . . . ?'

'Facts. That's what we provide. Not suppositions or hypotheses. Leave that to the politicians. Besides, you want Hensham asking why the hell Jimmy was allowed to slip surveillance in the first place? You want to admit to that?'

'The Russians had it right . . . You have a man, you have a problem. You have no man – no problem.' He raised his eyebrows and nodded at Blake, sitting the other side of the screen. 'We should kill him.'

'Not a chance.' The senior officer sniffed loudly, drew out his handkerchief and blew his nose. Always did the same thing when the subject of death came up.

She was asleep when he let himself into the room, but she stirred instantly.

'I'm sorry Sarah. I got pulled in by . . .'

'Thanks for dinner.' She rolled onto her side, away from him. 'Just the two of us, and we'll talk. I know. Something came up.'

'Listen . . .'

'To what?'

'I was pulled in by the local police, questioned for two hours . . . some kind of anti-terrorist action . . .'

She didn't reply.

'Sarah . . . I . . .' Something inside him wanted to go over to her, take her hand, hold her close, but he couldn't move. There'd been too many times like that. Too many times when he had talked in one direction and she in another. And suddenly there's a wall between you, and it's too much trouble to scale it. And by the time you look over the top, there's nothing left on the other side.

'The children were very upset.'

'I'm sorry.'

'They needed you.'

He undressed without turning on the light, lifted the sheets and found a cold space at the side. Their legs collided momentarily, but both moved away.

If you stop touching, he thought, then it's almost impossible to get it back.

Each day the relationship is defined by the day before. If you don't touch yesterday, why touch today, or tomorrow? And suddenly it had been months, a year even. And that part of you had died.

I'm always saying sorry, he thought. Sorry for the kids, sorry for what I said, or didn't. I should record a tape and repeat it a hundred times.

'Look, Sarah. I've tried. I don't know what else I can do.'

'Go to sleep.'

'I thought you wanted to talk.'

'I did. Now I don't.'

'Why?'

'Just leave it. OK?'

Blake stared up into the darkness above them.

What happened to us?

Nothing happened. That's the problem. Nothing very good or very bad.

Marriage had been like a patient, lying in bed at the side of the room. They'd known he was there, but they'd never really looked after him. Hadn't fed him, hardly even talked to him or bothered to check his vital signs.

And then one night they had looked more closely and discovered he'd died.

Quite unnoticed and without any fuss at all.

And you didn't even realise.

Good heavens. What a terrible shame. And yet you can't bring him back. Not once you know.

For a while they both lay awake, in silence, on different sides of the world.

Chapter Five

It didn't often happen that the Minister's tray was empty. Three-fifteen on a Friday. No papers to shift. No scapegoats to be found or blooded. No departmental rivalries to referee. He got up and peered through the window down onto Whitehall.

They were cleaning the Foreign Office. Scaffolding and tarpaulins draped across it like shrouds. And the real dirt was inside the building, in the vaults where no one would ever get to it. So clean away, boys, he whispered to himself, clean away.

Tomorrow was Saturday. But it wasn't going to be quiet. He had planned the day with meticulous detail. He would be out in the village when the phone call came. Late afternoon. Better that way, let the panic reach him, as he went about his weekend business, shopping in the supermarket, chatting with the constituents.

Let the big car drive up with a screech, let the orderly dash out and pull him aside, let him open the coded message – and then make the big decision.

Right, he'd say. Get me back to London. Quickest route. And they'd bring in a helicopter from Brize Norton, big red Sea King, and he'd be talking to the PM by radio, and the whole panoply of a state emergency would come into force. A situation room, guards on the office door. Red files, red faces, alarms, contingencies, the whole bloody great machine would start panting and sweating . . . and all because . . .

Yes.

All because the president of a little republic in southern Europe was going to die. Had to die. And everyone else had agreed.

Of course when he'd come back from Switzerland he had talked it over with the PM.

Had to be done. No way round. The Russians were stampeding everyone.

'Quite,' the PM had said.

Was that 'quite right'? Or 'I quite understand'? Or something non-committal, that might, on the slippery, sliding scale of diplo-speak signify anything from 'how nice' to a clearing of the throat?

Dear, dear PM.

Master of the no-statement, the no-decision. So busy ensuring deniability that he was barely there at all.

The Minister went back to his desk. After twenty years in politics he had encountered the full range of truth substitutes – the blind alleys, the commissions, the investigations that sank under the weight of their own paper.

More often than not, the cover-up was worse than the original misdemeanour. But you couldn't admit to it. You couldn't come clean and say . . . 'Sorry, dear friends, dear voters. We fucked up. Sorry, mistake.' No, no, no. The important thing was . . . 'Circumstances had changed . . .' 'Objective world conditions were dictating . . .' 'Errors had been set in motion when the Opposition was in government . . .' You could tell any story, climb into any hole, as long as you never admitted the truth.

The Minister took out his fountain pen and began writing.

He was too old to change the system. In any case the system had moulded him, made him what he was, enabled him to do what he had to.

Carefully, thoughtfully, he wrote out a letter of condolence on the death of a man who was still alive.

At least for a few hours longer.

The British Ambassador in Skopje was never a great one for celebrating his birthday.

Somehow he felt that, after sixty, the event had lost its shine. All the jokes about the hair you didn't have, and the stomach you did, and the future that was all behind you, if only you could stretch your head back that far . . .

And yet this year, he had been told to celebrate. Properly. Royally. Hire the bloody main hotel, old boy, The Grand, invite the President . . .

You have to be joking.

But London wanted the President.

Head of South European department would also be along for the ride. And his deputy. Even a bloody typist, as if they expected to do some real business.

A big bloody deal, Mitchell. That's what London wanted. And they'd be sending a photographer to record the whole ghastly event in tasteless colour.

Why?

We're players these days, old man. Up the profile a bit. Don't want to leave it all to the French, do we?

Bloody birthday. Crates of undrinkable Riesling. Couldn't even get it cold because the hotel fridge had broken down. All the buggers out from London – Club Class, of course – moaning and wanting to know what had been fixed. Fixed? Nothing had been fixed. They were all too busy trying to stave off a civil war. Sorry, sir. They all sent their apologies. Be at the party, though . . .

Bloody, bloody hell.

And then they wanted the whole thing planned out minute by minute – that's what the typists were for. Mix and mingle, three minutes past six; step up to the podium, twenty past; greeting and words of welcome etc, etc . . .

Strange but after that . . . Outside on the steps of the hotel, one more photo-call with President and Head of South European section – as if they wouldn't all have died of boredom by the time that came round.

18.55. That was the allotted time.
For everyone.

Mitchell had been congratulating himself. Well, who wouldn't? The President had gone out of his way to be friendly. Head of South Europe had done a passable job, even learned some small talk off by heart, so that they hadn't all had to hop around with embarrassment, checking their cuffs.

The Riesling had flowed, though he couldn't help noticing the number of people drinking mineral water. And then at the appointed time, he'd had a nod from his secretary, and started ushering them to the cars. Out through the foyer. President waving. Give him his hat, cold wind out there. Where's the photographer? Thank Christ. Through the great glass doors and he can stand right by the Peugeot. Beige thing. Where is South Europe? Get him there for the picture, bloody man. Can't keep the President waiting.

OK? Right! Yes, Mr President, just turn this way.

And then the explosive freezes them all. The wall of heat and shock and violence that slams into their faces.

Only Mitchell can't accept what he sees in front of him. The President, red all over his coat, face contorted, South Europe sunk to the ground and the screams coming from the office typist who's run forward out of nowhere. Police have drawn their guns.

Doesn't make sense. No way to behave at a reception . . . everyone in the wrong place, scuttling around as if . . . No, no please God in heaven, don't let this happen to me, here on my birthday, damning me for all time . . .

Make him get up, make him stop lying there, without moving – all the bodyguards standing over him.

Why weren't they protecting him?

There's a long, terrible, jerking moan from the man's private secretary . . .

No one is doing anything . . . they all run and shout, or

like South Europe, lie cowering under someone else. Miserable little skunk.

Because it's all over.

There's a siren close to, getting louder all the time, enough to wake the de . .

Oh God, police scattering, first shots . . . Christ they're firing, they've seen something.

And then nothing, just anger. Just the desolation. The wind swooping down from the mountains to see what had happened.

A hard, sniping wind.

Across the street people stand lost to the world around them. Eyes open, mouth open. No sound coming forth.

Mitchell shakes his head over and over again and the tears pour down his cheeks onto the suit he had pressed specially for the day, and the flower in his buttonhole, and the order of ceremonies that he would have kept on his mantelpiece for years to come, as a souvenir of something that went right.

It was over – that day and for evermore.

He stood there, muttering the words again and again, until the police told him to leave.

Her Majesty's Secretary of State for Defence is doing the rounds of the supermarket, pushing the little cart, loaded with chocolate biscuits and bananas, stopping to wave and chat, and mouth a 'hello' at people of his parish, who he pretends to remember, but cannot for the life of him actually do so.

God – the effort of it.

Frightful people.

He kept looking at his watch, wondering how long it would be.

Needed some more butter. A little of the orange marmalade, perhaps. Sausages? Always a good standby. Did it all himself now that Gwen had died.

'Shop closing in ten minutes, sir.'

'So it is.'

And it's an hour later in South-Central Europe, and fifteen degrees colder. For anyone who wants to know . . .

'There we are.' Up goes the basket, out come the treats. Love those chocolate things . . . and all the rest. Thank God for food, rich and fattening. Can't be doing with all this faddy, slimline nonsense.

'Hallo Mrs . . . uh yes. Course I remember you.'

An elderly spinster simpers by the sweet shelves.

'That's right, the thing at Christmas. Wouldn't have missed it for the world.' He frowns as she speaks. 'Oh dear, how distressing for you, still I'm sure the doctors are doing all they can. What? Yes I know . . .'

'Thirteen pounds twelve p, please.'

'Right-oh.'

And there's the car almost exactly on cue. Black, polished – man in uniform at the wheel. Looks just like a bloody hearse. The orderly hurries, flustered, into the shop.

It was real. They actually did it.

Probably happened while he'd been hoovering the stairs. Cleaning woman never did them properly. One of the Saturday chores, don't you know . . . ?

'I'm sorry to bother you, Secretary of State . . .'

'That's alright. Thought it was too peaceful to last.'

He grinned the practised, constituency grin. Ah, the problems of the world! But someone had to cope with them, didn't they?

Sarah, I know who killed him.

They're all around the television set. Charles and Veronica wondering what it's about, hoping the news won't cut into the movie.

'Please come into the kitchen a moment.'

'What?'

'Shut the door. I tell you I know who killed him. I met him in Berlin two nights ago . . .'

'What difference does it make? He's dead now. It doesn't matter who pulled the trigger.'

27

'Listen to me. Hundreds of thousands of people may die because of what happened today.'

'But what are you going to do? Who are you going to tell?'

'That's just it. I . . . I can't tell anyone. It's too dangerous. Besides, I don't know who I can trust.'

'Blake.'

It was close to dawn when the phone rang.

'You're moving . . .'

'What?'

'I said, you're moving. Whole regiment. Into Skopje. Blue beret – UN command. Fucking balloon's about to go up. You're booked on the afternoon flight. The rest, as soon as we can get them there.'

'I told you; I had enough in Bosnia. I'm not doing it again.'

'You've been requested. They . . .'

'They? Who the fuck are *they*?'

'The people who decide which ditch you shit in, which part of your ugly face gets spattered in blood, which bodies you get to bury. Who cares who "they" are? Your views have been noted, Colonel.'

'I have to leave in the morning, Sarah.'

'You already left. Don't come back this time. I mean it Tom.'

Chapter Six

In Washington the American Secretary of State swallowed six pink and white pills and returned them to the desk drawer. He hadn't felt well for months. And the trip to Geneva seemed to have unsettled his stomach.

Sometimes, like now, he thought he could feel the lump in his abdomen, stretching itself, coming alive. But of course it was too deep for that.

Yet he could certainly feel the dagger. Spasms – wild, uncontrolled, sometimes breathtaking, shaking him the way a wild animal shakes its victims, picking him up in its teeth, biting deep into him.

Only the pills were wonderful. The pills could halt a runaway train; tame any pain and convert it into the kind of manageable ache that he'd endured for years – and hardly even noticed, thinking it would go away.

Thinking wrong.

Harrison Drew didn't believe in regret. His mother had taught him that.

Taught him to fight only the battles he could win. Taught him to use what he had. The way she, herself, had done.

So the cancer had fired his mind, even as it was engulfing his body.

He could cover a day's work in an hour, a week's work in a day. He consumed paper. Consumed problems. Hurled decisions at them in a way that Washington bureaucracy could scarcely have imagined.

Meetings were cancelled as the participants sat down at

the table. Advisers were cut off in mid-sentence and dismissed. Foreign envoys were made to wait and sent home without an audience.

For Drew, in his flamboyant brown suits, his bow ties, his coughing echoing down the corridor ahead of him, was a man who seemed to care for no one. Least of all himself.

As for his wife, she had long ago retreated to the house in the Shenandoah valley, from which she made brief sorties to be mocked and abused by her husband at cocktail parties.

He served, as do all cabinet members, at the pleasure of the US President. Not that it was much of a pleasure for either of them.

But Drew was well aware of his function – to keep foreign policy quiet, uncontroversial and, most of all, somewhere else.

If he couldn't deliver victories he was to deliver peace and silence. Which meant keeping the Balkans in the background. The President had no wish to be confronted by killings on the network news, reports of refugees, pressure groups, and all the attendant problems of an insoluble issue.

There wasn't a policy, Drew reflected, so there had to be accommodations.

'You're a deal-maker,' the President had told him. 'Make a deal on this one. I don't want to be bothered by all this kind of stuff.'

And so Drew had done it – and brought the moaning, recalcitrant allies with him. Not bad for a day out in Geneva – even if the pain had been excruciating.

Now there was just the insurance. Probably the most vital part of the whole deal.

He got up for a moment and leant across the desk. Sometimes the strangest angles would ease the ache in his abdomen. Five, ten minutes he half-lay there, until the pills began to take effect.

Insurance. You always had to keep someone in reserve. If one of the ducks went astray, or refused to quack on demand – there had to be a substitute. Or a persuader.

30

And insurance went in layers. When you had one slice, you went and took out another.

Couldn't be too careful in Washington.

He had aphorisms for everything, he realised. Potted philosophies –the kind he'd been fed by evangelists in the Midwest who had known it all and felt obliged to pass it on.

'If a sparrow farted,' he once confided to his wife, 'my parents knew what it meant, knew that it signified one of life's magical mysteries. Nothing could ever happen without some fucking, great significance attached to it. All my life I've tried shaking it off.'

Drew sat back in his chair. By now the ache had become just a distant murmur, the far-away rumble of a train in a tunnel. He could live with that.

When it came, the phone call was exactly on time – but the information left him puzzled and angry.

The hit had been carried out in Skopje as arranged.

But the assassin had gone astray, missed the reception they'd arranged for him, branched out on his own.

Trust the Brits! They had supplied the name. They had vouched for the man. Jesus Christ!

From the desk drawer he took a notebook and leafed through it for a number. Now he would make his own arrangements, secure his own insurance, the way he always did.

Duty dictated it.

He could see the woman quite clearly in his mind. She had the kind of smile that could wrap around your shoulders like a blanket, keeping you warm and happy. She was fun, she was laughter. She was the woman you follow home in a crowd, the woman you run down platforms to catch a glimpse of – and then brag about to friends and strangers and anyone who'll listen.

Even when you knew she was utterly and completely false.

And that's what he really loved about her. Really

31

admired. The expert, cultured duplicity that lay hidden under the layers of warmth and sincerity. Whenever she chose, she could unsheathe it in an instant, sliding its stiletto point into the victim who would love her still, even as she put out his life.

To Drew she was all but family – the daughter of an old schoolfriend, an old army colleague. He had held her at her christening – and that had been the last time anyone had heard her cry.

Later, he reflected, she had repaid the favour. She had done well for Harrison Drew. Tough, ruthless, violent when necessary – but always unbelievably charming.

She was his to use as a last resort. The ultimate failsafe. For the time when all the others had gone.

As the Washington day made the turn into evening, he pulled the telephone towards him, dialled her employer in New York, and suggested it was time she went travelling.

Chapter Seven

Tom Blake flew in, the way he always had. Half-briefed, half-frightened, the sweat breaking out at intervals on his forehead and down his spine. It wasn't fear of the unknown, he told himself. Not here. In the Balkans it was fear of the known. The cruelty and barbarism, well outside normal human parameters.

His companion was a suitcase jammed tight with underwear and pullovers, a small collection of music tapes – piano concertos, some jazz. Only there was never time to listen. And when he listened he fell asleep.

You can walk into a command, but you have to think yourself into it first.

Whatever the mood, whatever junk you're carrying in your head.

He shut his eyes.

Only the children had come out to see him off. Veronica holding so tight round his neck . . .

'What's happening with you and Mum?'

'Nothing. It's OK.'

Soldiers' parting words for the last two thousand years.

'Don't tell me that, Dad. What is it?'

'Look it's nothing, OK? We'll talk when I get back.'

Cop-out, Tom.

'When will that be?'

'Soon, love.'

'Promise?'

'I promise.'

It's only the words she wants to hear. She knows it's a lie.
'Charley.'
'Yes, Dad.'
'Look after your mum, OK?'
And he's looking at the ground, holding onto my arm. This isn't a life I've given them. Any of them.

He had peered up to the bedroom window, just to see if Sarah were there. Not this time. 'I mean it,' she had said. And maybe, after all, she finally did.

So went the suitcase of Colonel Tom Blake to Macedonia.

On the plane, he was crammed between two halves of an American television crew, who spent the flight filling in expenses forms and making up names for the hospitality bills.

And this could be a war we're going to?

A war about expenses.

He'd love to try it on the Brigadier . . .

'Here we are, sir. I've kept receipts . . . where possible. Dinner with a couple of warlords. Can't mention their names for security reasons.'

'What's the bill?'

'Two carbonated chickens, sir. They were largely incinerated by a mortar, so we didn't need to add anything for service. Went and picked up the bits ourselves. As you'll see, it's only a nominal sum.'

He dozed for a while, waking suddenly to find a woman in her mid-thirties standing in the aisle, talking to the crew. Had to be the reporter – and yet the charm was subtle, not aggressive. The voice measured and quiet – not the agonised foghorn so many seemed to have cultivated. Blake was struck by the freshness of her complexion, the minimal make-up, the involvement and interest in her eyes. A twenty-year-old at heart, he thought. A little explorer.

She hadn't done late nights, this one. Probably never done a war. She was used to sleeping in good hotel rooms, good beds, probably with carefully chosen, suntanned arms around her, and a thick wallet by the bed.

34

Steady, he told himself. Put the jealous Brit back in his box. She's beautiful and she belongs to someone. That's all . . .

But he couldn't help staring at the unmarked, cream face – the blonde hair, cut short and waved back, as if she were saying: 'I spend my time on other things.' A can-do American, fixing details about the things they'd film, the places they'd go, calls to New York.

'I'm sorry to talk across you,' she grinned at Blake. Relaxed and friendly. It was more greeting than apology. 'Are you part of the war?' The face inclined slightly to the left.

'Didn't know there was one.'

'People are saying it's really serious . . .'

He smiled. 'I know – anything's possible here.'

'Your face looks familiar. I thought I recognised you from somewhere.'

'Isn't that what I should be saying to you?'

A smile shared.

That tiny moment when the eyes connect and hold.

'I should get back to my seat.' She glances up the aisle. 'Nice meeting you.'

Is that what we did?

The cameraman turns round unashamedly to watch her bottom as she walks away.

'Cute kid, that one.' He says it as if he owns her.

'What's her name?'

'Geralyn Lang . . . don't even think about it, buddy.'

Blake shifted his whole body and looked straight at the man's chin, as if aiming his fist. 'Do you have something else to get on with?'

'You . . .'

'Steady, my friend.' Very quiet. Fingers tightening on the man's arm.

The American's eyes seemed to measure Blake's shoulders, two sizes larger than his own. He took a moment to add it up. It didn't seem to come out in his favour.

As the plane flew south across Serbia, Blake looked away towards the window. You couldn't see any lights or large cities. Any places of supreme beauty or value.

But they would fight for it – the way they always did in the Balkans.

They'd kill for the ground they walked on, and for the air they breathed.

And me? He shook his head. I'm squabbling over a woman I only just met.

He chuckled to himself, but he couldn't help the shiver, like the brush of a sharp blade, as they landed in the semi-darkness of Skopje.

Chapter Eight

Against the best expectations, Jimmy McIlvane had never reached the getaway car, for the simple reason he had never intended to.

Born suspicious, that Jimmy.

But then he had good cause.

You didn't observe twenty-six years of institutionalised treachery, in armies from Mozambique to Malaya, without realising that your own side is more dangerous than all the others.

They had waited for him in a side street off the Ulica Branca, with the tall grey houses, and the lines of straggly washing hanging out the upstairs windows. Two kind men, provided so thoughtfully by his employers; and he had pictured the nerve-jangling dash through the streets; the helicopter, some six kilometres outside the city, the low, fast clatter across the mountains into Serbia, under the radar, with no time for interceptors to be scrambled.

So well-executed.

Yes, that was the word.

And there in a wood, as the children's poem used to begin, he'd find an aircraft hangar, or a hut, or a barn – empty but for the man who would kill him, and the body that he would provide.

Well done, Jimmy. Good job back there. We'll send money to your dependents. Not that you have any. We'll make donations to your favourite charity. We'll pay out to the Scottish National Party, to the People's Dispensary for

Sick Animals, to the old people's home opposite the miserable, tossed-on slum in Glasgow where you used to live. We're not ungenerous, you know.

But you can't go home.

He had pictured the scene in its simple, straightforward entirety. Which was why he had left the getaway car where it was; why he had used plastic explosive instead of the Armalite rifle they had given him; why he had exploded it by radio from his room in the Grand Hotel, overlooking the entrance.

He had even made sure he was talking to the receptionist as he transmitted the command to the detonator.

That was Jimmy all over. The details. Not the plan. The little things that could help you escape – or fuck you into the ground.

And he wasn't ready for that.

When it was all over, when he'd eaten, he made his way down to the hotel foyer and cast a professional eye over the damage. The blown-out windows, the shards of glass on the street outside. The remains of the car with its wheels and its chassis blown out from under it. Children had come to gawp, a few peasants, scratching their head, eyes vacant. *What do these people say to themselves?* A bomb makes them all reflect, makes them remember that it's such a short journey from here to there, that you can make it anytime, that you'll never know in advance, and probably won't know after.

Plenty to think about with a bomb.

It wasn't a bad job. Very little in the way of collateral damage. Focused, effective. Two or three casualties at most.

He was getting good, he told himself. Getting good in his old age.

Of course Jimmy hadn't celebrated a birthday since his father had beaten him up on his sixteenth, broken his nose, and he had walked out of the house and never returned. Deep down he remembered he'd be fifty in a week's time. That was bloody old in this business.

He went back upstairs and checked his papers. New passport from New Zealand, business cards, name of a company that had made leather into shoes. A home address that really did exist, even the picture of a girl in a bright green dress, who had gone into a photo booth, but hadn't had time to await the results.

Jimmy had picked them up, just as he picked up most things in his life. Never sure when he would need them.

In his briefcase was a selection of a dozen currencies. Most major, some minor – Egyptian pounds, Zambian kwachas, Turkish lire – still convertible, but harder to trace. When he needed to transfer, he would fly to Dubai, visit the second floor of a shop in the town centre and deal with one of the Hawala bankers. The network of Asian financiers who would order money in one country and have it delivered by their own people in the next. Just a phone call. No wire reports, no paper. They would simply hand you half a photograph or a ticket, and you would receive the other half on delivery. You paid when the deal was clinched – and they *always* delivered. It was a criminal system based on absolute trust – operating for centuries, completely impenetrable to law enforcement of any kind.

Jimmy liked that. Your money went into a black hole – and only you could get it out. Over the years he had secreted plenty of cash in countries where they didn't ask questions, didn't want to know their clients, weren't at all concerned if you threw your assets around or went out and laundered them. Most would provide a basin and a bar of soap and do it for you.

To him the world was one big con trick, and you had to find the people to deal you in.

The rule was simple: always make it more expensive for them to cheat you than help you.

For a while he lay on his bed and wished there were four legs instead of two. It wasn't that killing turned him on, although he'd seen plenty for whom it did. But even when his mind forgot about women, his hands wouldn't. They remembered all too well the softness of skin, the swell of the hip or the breast, the plateau of the stomach, the steep slope into dreams.

He shook his head. No good thinking like that.

The memory was twenty years old, same age as the girl who had given it to him. Probably.

On a warm beach in the Indian Ocean, with the moon the size of a cartwheel, she told him she'd wait forever. He could go off and fight his wars in whatever land he chose – and she would be there to comfort and love him when he returned.

The difference was their ages. She was at the age when she'd say that. He was at the age when he believed it.

Looking back on it, he concluded she must have waited – all of three days.

When he finally did return, ten months later, she was about to give birth to someone else's child, having acquired someone else's ring, a shack, a mother-in-law, and a man called husband.

'Sorry Jimmy.'

Say it again.

'Sorry Jimmy.'

Life's chorus for him.

Went on and on, recited each time by a different voice.

I'm sorry Jimmy. We're sorry, Jimmy. So very sorry, old man.

He sat up on the bed and waited till the memories left him alone.

Stay here, he thought. Sit quiet, rest.

An hour later he turned on the hotel radio. The endless martial music and the funeral dirges told him he had, after all, hit his target.

Chapter Nine

Depending on lunch, it was either very difficult or well nigh impossible to stay awake in the afternoon.

That day the Minister had proved unequal to the task. At four-thirty Big Ben woke him like a distant alarm clock, his neck stiff, mouth dry, hand for some reason stuck down the front of his trousers. Old boarding-school habit. Playing at home.

He sat up. The winter day had grown stale and the office heating was set too high.

Thank Christ, no one had been in – none of the nauseating private secretaries who never needed sleep, none of the little swots with their pressed shirts, and pressed faces, all beaming with zeal and commitment.

And the bloody Minister slept at his chair, finger on the pulse.

He phoned through to his secretary, Miss Lancing.

'I was just about to call you, sir. Brigadier Hensham is here for the four-thirty.'

Bloody man was probably standing right beside her.

'Oh God, wheel him in.'

Anthony Amesbury, Secretary of State for Defence, rose stiffly, tucked in the wayward tails of his shirt and stroked his zip to make sure it was fastened. You couldn't be too careful.

'Peter, how nice to see you.'

'Bad time?'

'No worse than all the others. Come in, come in. Drop of something? No? Tea'll be on its way, I 'spect.'

Amesbury returned to the desk. 'So how are our boys in the field?'

'They're alright. Some of them not so pleased to be wearing the light blue . . .'

'Poor lambs – we must get them something in sugar pink next time.' His mouth turned down at the edges. 'Anyway, now that Blake is there, things seem to be looking pretty good, mmm? Quite the little media star, isn't he?'

'Don't worry, I'm watching him.'

Amesbury looked nonplussed. 'What I said wasn't a criticism, Peter. Far from it. We're delighted with him. He's precise, witty, urbane . . .'

'But he doesn't like orders.'

Amesbury returned to his desk. 'Do any of us? Dammit, the man's almost a national hero. Speaks his mind, stands up to the bully boys . . .'

'And bends the rules . . .'

'What makes you say that?'

'Just a few rumours . . .'

'Don't listen, if I were you. Let me put it this way. Blake's the acceptable face of peacekeeping, at a time when we need one. More troops going in, more money being spent. Lousy job, lousy role, but he gives it credence. Good on television, gives good interviews, says the right things.'

'So it doesn't matter what he does . . .'

'There's always a gap, Peter. Or hadn't you noticed? He gets away with it. In politics that's called first prize, top of the class, scholarship to the next wholly deniable escapade. He looks good. Frankly, with the state we're in in the polls, he's the best thing we have.'

'I'm still going to watch him.'

'You can watch, but don't touch. I'm serious about this one. So's the PM. I'm afraid all our pensions are up for grabs this time.'

Miss Lancing knocked at the door and brought in a teapot on a tray and a pile of turkey sandwiches. Amesbury couldn't help thinking it was probably the same turkey he'd eaten last time, preserved in a mausoleum, usual formaldehyde sauce.

'Now then.' He rubbed his hands together, and reached for a carefully sculpted square of bread. 'I spoke to UNPROFOR in Skopje about an hour ago. They say everything's quiet for the moment. Plenty of "woe is me" at the President's er . . . passing. Politicians scurrying around. But as for actually . . .'

'Doing anything . . . ?' Hensham leaned forward.

'Oh, no. No doing. I'm glad to say.' He swallowed the sandwich and licked his lips. 'None of that. Not yet. Of course, the script is fairly well-defined. Nobody *does* anything at all for a few days.'

Amesbury reached for another sandwich, opened it and frowned at the meagre slice of turkey that rested within.

'And then some compliant politician suggests the friendly neighbours in Serbia might like to come in and help keep order . . .'

'We went over this before, Peter.' Amesbury's voice had acquired a tinge of annoyance. Teacher had to explain again. 'We're talking about an agreement that'll prevent massive destruction, loss of life and a full Balkan war. Yes, the Serbs'll go in. Yes, they'll carve up a tiny little state that in an ideal world should be allowed to live peacefully and independently, instead of being shat on by its neighbours . . .'

'But . . .'

'Hear me out, Peter. I'll only say this once. The Balkans isn't that ideal world. Never has been. It's a hell-hole full of hatreds and enmities that we can scarcely even imagine. There was no other way to avoid massive bloodshed. The Serbs made it clear they'd take the country by any means – and they know as well as you do that the international community can't co-ordinate a fart in a bottle, let alone any resistance. Not after Bosnia. Besides, the Russians said they'd side with Belgrade. We didn't have a choice.'

'So they gave you an ultimatum.'

'Exactly. Allow them to carve up Macedonia or face a Balkan war and an international crisis that would split the UN from arse to tit for decades to come. In other words, the biggest fucking crisis since World War Two.'

'What about the other powers – Bulgaria, Albania, Turkey?'

'All poor countries.'

'So we're paying them?'

'Paying off, I think, is the term.'

Hensham got up, walked as far as the drinks cabinet, then returned to his seat.

'Something troubling you Peter?'

'As a matter of fact, Minister, something *is* troubling me. Remember, I was the one who fixed this deal. I hired McIlvane to do the job.'

'I'd rather no names, Peter.' Amesbury looked uncomfortably down the length of his nose. 'Just make your point and let's get on with it.'

'Well he's gone missing. He was supposed to have been met and disposed of.'

'And?'

'He slipped the leash. Disappeared. Christ knows where.'

'Then you'd better pray, Peter.' The Secretary of State for Defence sat perfectly still. 'Pray that he disappears for good.'

They had a light supper at the Reform Club. Amesbury wasn't in a mood to talk shop, began joking with the Filipino waitresses, then the waiters. The joking was borderline. Flirting, more like. Didn't seem to matter which sex.

Dinner over, they climbed the wide, red-carpeted staircase to the balustrade and coffee.

'Talk about more pleasant things, shall we?'

Only Hensham knew that was danger. He had watched the Minister soften up his victims before, and then eat them

44

with a knife and fork. Now that his wife had died, and taken her friends and her hobbies and her dinner parties with her, he shafted people for pure pleasure.

Hensham fetched the coffee cups and placed one beside him.

'Kind of you, Peter.'

'Pleasure, Minister.'

'Old place has changed a bit since we first started coming here.'

'For the better I think. Women members for a start.'

'Ah, yes.' Amesbury took a sip of the coffee. 'Wanted to talk to you about that.'

'Indeed?'

'Blake's wife, as it happens. 'Tractive little creature. Met her myself, at one of those do's.'

'Indeed.'

'You keep saying that Peter. The point is . . . how's she doing? Sarah, isn't it?'

'She's fine.'

'You know that, do you?'

'I make it my business to know these things. He's one of my men. Could affect his operational capability . . .'

'Bollocks.'

'I beg your pardon.'

'You used to go out with her, didn't you?'

Hensham didn't move. He was conscious of holding his cup a little tighter.

Amesbury smiled. 'It's always nice to keep up with old friends. Course it is. Like to do that myself. But you're not keeping too close an eye on her, are you?'

'I resent that.'

'Lots of people resent the things I say. Glad they do, really. Means things get done. Point is . . .' he raised both eyebrows . . . 'we don't want anything spoiling this man's image. Alright, I don't give a fuck what he does, but I damn well give a fuck what he looks like. Never know who could be hanging round the house. Could be very awkward, if you were seen to be visiting too often. Clear?'

Hensham stood up. 'Thank you for dinner, Minister.'

'I asked if you were clear about all this?'

'I heard every word.'

'I'm so pleased.' Amesbury smiled again and stayed where he was. 'Been a great pleasure. Can't remember when I've enjoyed myself so much.'

Chapter Ten

They met Blake on the tarmac at Skopje airport – a lieutenant, a captain, the liaison officer, who had almost been killed a dozen times, shuttling between the front lines in Bosnia. They stood in a dark semicircle, hands behind their backs, badges glinting on the caps – the men he had requested that morning as a matter of supreme and unavoidable urgency. Because he wouldn't go in without them. Not here.

Even in the darkness he could see the lines on the faces, the vacancy in the eyes. When you see enough killing, he thought, it squeezes the warmth from your heart. Your life is reduced to the basics of survival. And they had all lived in that world, all the men who stood there, fists clenched, shedding normality, bracing for the madness to come.

No one smiled. They knew why they had come – and it wasn't for that.

Blake turned away for a moment as another jet swooped onto the runway. The commercial airlines had laid on extra flights, knowing the military would soon take over Air Traffic Control – and they wouldn't get in again. Not till whatever was going to happen had happened. And who would want to come then?

They shook hands in silence, took his bags, led him over to the white Land-Rover labelled UN. Some of the other passengers turned and stared, sensing that he must be important, the man in a blue anorak who had flown in with them across the mountains.

In the distance he could make out the American television team, and the wavy, blonde hair of Geralyn Lang.

Nice to meet you.

With the life-hungry smile and the wide-open eyes and all the dreams to play for . . .

He would watch out for her. Especially if the war came. Wouldn't be able to help himself. He would need to find a little piece of warmth and beauty.

It had been that way in Bosnia. Almost that way. An aid worker from one of the refugee organisations, late twenties, beautiful and motivated, as only people can be inside the danger zone.

He remembered the pretty legs, the excited eyes, the bosom inside the flak jacket – but above all the single-minded drive of war that can turn the light on in a human being, direct them, stimulate them as never before. It was a drug and she was a drug and he had stopped taking them together just in time.

Blake recalled what he had told himself at the time, persuaded himself that he had a family at home, and two kids – and he didn't want to become the latest in a long line of male clichés abroad. The man who jumped everything that moved, because he was lonely and insecure and it was there to be taken.

What did his friends say? 'You fuck girls at twenty, women at thirty and problems at forty.'

But this time was different. Sarah had pushed him out. And now he would need that comfort. Even a fantasy to warm him in his sleeping bag, on a cold floor, in a strange country, where people might seek to kill him.

The blonde hair disappeared into the terminal.

Only he would see Miss Geralyn Lang again. He'd make sure of it.

There was little to catch his eye as they drove the highway into Skopje. Inkjet clouds had spread out over the hillsides, merging into the darkness, as it rolled in from the east.

Winding down the window he could smell the dampness from the Vardar river, that flowed down from the mountains north of the city, and drummed purposefully into Greece, then out into the Aegean.

Only the river was allowed south. The border was closed. All the borders were closed. And tiny Macedonia wasn't so much landlocked as shut in a cupboard under the stairs, while all the neighbours sat in the front room working out what to pinch. To the north, across the mountains, lay Serbia, to the west Albania and Kosovo, to the east Bulgaria.

They all proclaimed their friendship and sympathy, were standing by to help, wanted their brethren in Macedonia to know they could count on support.

The last thing the brethren wanted.

And the first thing they feared.

Timeo Danaos et dona ferentes . . .

I fear the Greeks and all who bear gifts.

Truer today than the Romans could ever have realised.

'The rest of the team you asked for has arrived, sir.' The captain spoke. Twenty-six years old, a built-in frown, a man who had cried once when he had driven into a massacre near Mostar. Cried like a baby, Blake recalled. And never cried again. Nor would he. You were marked in this business. Life-changing, character-forming. There were plenty of grand ways of describing what happened to people who saw what the captain had seen. Only they're never the same again.

'You didn't want the UNPROFOR headquarters, sir.'

Statement, not question.

'We commandeered the old refugee camp at Dare Bombol. It's up in the hills. Only a few of the inmates left. Either too old or too young to get out in the rush. Bit bemused when we showed up – but the kids seem to like it.'

Through the city centre and the traffic closed in around them, and the rain came sheeting on the windscreen. Blake could see a jumble of lights and faces along the grey streets –

Dame Grueva, the parliament, its drenched, red flag curled up sadly outside the President's office. The dead President. In the distance a siren wailed and raged, neither approaching, nor moving further away, hemmed in by the immovable cars and trucks.

'Place is like a car park.' The captain mopped the windscreen with a rag. 'Thousands are heading for the borders, even though they're closed. Some even going north into Serbia where they think it's safer. You can't forget . . .' He stopped himself, and there was silence inside the Land-Rover, apart from the beat of the rain.

'It's going to be as bad as Bosnia, isn't it? Just wanted to know, sir.'

Blake could see only the back of the man's head, but he could feel the others looking at him. You didn't lie to these people because they all knew the truth. All seen it, all lived it. Out there on the fringes of life, where there's no safety or comfort.

'I don't know what it'll be like,' he told them. 'No one does, for sure. All the signs say it'll be much worse, much more brutal . . .'

'And our mission?'

'Keep the peace and . . .'

'I meant our real mission, sir.'

The captain turned round and stared into the darkened cabin.

'That's why *you're* here. Same as last time.'

When he closed his eyes, he could see it all. That time a year ago in the middle of the Bosnian hills, when the 'mission' had turned on him. The day when he had given up just bending the rules and begun obliterating them.

What had they said . . .? 'You're a peacekeeper, Tom. Don't forget it. No prizes for any basket-loads of bodies. Not on your watch. Keep it cool and calm, and the service will put you in a glass case and we'll salute every time we pass. Otherwise . . .'

Brigadier Peter Hensham with that load of crap.

Only Hensham hadn't seen the events that day. Hadn't been watching from the hillside as the gunmen drove into the village just before three in the dark grey light of the winter afternoon; hadn't heard the shots and the screams; hadn't seen the sixteen-year-old chased out in his underpants and hacked with a Bowie knife, his arms cut off above the wrists; hadn't seen that clear as day through the Zeiss 8x30s, as the others stood around and fucking laughed. Keep the peace, keep the peace, keep the peace, Hensham . . .

That's when he'd ordered them out, got the boys into the Warriors, fast, watched them rev down into the gulley, just the eight of them, the patrol he'd picked, men who could use their hands, and didn't overuse their mouths.

Ten minutes they'd been gone. It wouldn't take them much longer.

He could hear gunfire in the woods above the village. Turn them round, boys, turn them round . . . don't shoot them in the back, for God's sake . . . because later they can tell . . .

And then he climbed into the army Land-Rover and headed in slowly along the main road.

It was a tiny farming community – non-religious, non-threatening – a few barns, six or seven houses. Most of the men and women would have lived there since birth. Probably never even crossed the river. Never done anything to invite the fate that had called on them.

He pulled off the road beside the largest house and, even as he did so, he could hear the screams. Not like any he had heard before. Inhuman, somehow. They came in waves, half-choking, half-grating, echoing out over the tiny hamlet.

For a moment he stood listening in shock.

And that's something, isn't it, Tom? When the cries of the wounded can stop you in full flight . . . you, with the lump of rock on the left side of your chest . . .

He started to run, drawing the Browning as he did so, checking there was a bullet in the breech . . .

Not the house . . . the barn beyond.

The snarl of a dog . . . only it's chained up. Through the paddock. First body, male. Dead, because only the dead lie that way. Only the dead look as though they never lived.

Second corpse, older, slumped over the fence, half the head has gone . . .

Through the washing, blowing there on the line . . . bright colours, socks and shorts and stockings . . .

And now you can see her . . . it's a mother holding her child.

Odd how the mind decides what it's going to see before the eyes can get there . . .

Because this time it was wrong. There's no child . . . no child there, as the sickness begins to rise in his throat and the one eye of a young, young girl turns and stares at him . . .

He wants to look away, but the flow of blood won't let him.

And the eye is pleading with him, and the mouth has nothing but the scream of an animal . . .

She wants to die and she wants me to kill her . . .

Nothing but blood, with the stomach giving way, and the army rations heading fast up his throat . . .

Are you going to do what she wants?

Do it, in God's name man, do it, do it, do it . . .

'Colonel Blake, sir . . .'

The sergeant appears at his elbow.

'Let me through, sir. Please.' The fist closes on his arm, like the bite of a Doberman.

And the sergeant is on the ground beside her. In his hand the hypodermic, the pack of field dressings. He hadn't forgotten the first-aid briefings . . . 'thing about wounds . . . it's either awfully simple or simply awful.'

No need to ask which this was.

'Knocked her out, sir.' The sergeant rose to his feet.

'Chopper's on its way. No one else alive, far as we can tell . . .'

The moment of madness has passed.

When he looks round, they're all behind him. All eight of them. The faces are flushed, they're panting, they're filthy, cheeks scratched by bark and branch. But the eyes are at peace. So, once again, he didn't have to ask, and they didn't have to tell.

It was sorted.

Something a little closer to justice.

Two guards opened the gate and the Land-Rover heaved onto the uneven cobbles. It was a narrow lane between terraced houses, that opened into a courtyard, the schoolhouse over to the left, the valley and the lights of the city beyond.

Soldiers were on the move with boxes and silver cases – the communications equipment that would let them pretend they were informing – and let others pretend they were deciding. Half the radio traffic was meaningless, thought Blake – dross about food supplies and troop levels. If you had nothing better to do you filled the airwaves. If you wanted to be a soldier you went out and did something.

As he got out of the Land-Rover his eye was caught by the movement of a swing in front of the main building. Closer to, he could see a tiny figure attached to it and hear the creaking as it rocked backwards and forwards in the rain and the darkness.

'Name's Sergio, sir. Romany boy. Gypsy . . .' One of the other officers had come up behind him.

Blake went over to the boy. He could see the thick black hair was drenched, so was the pullover, the ragged trousers. But the smile had instant warmth.

'You want to come in out of the rain?'

Sergio shook his head. 'No speak English.' And then he laughed. 'What name you?'

'Tom.'

'Goodnight Tom.'

'Sergio.'

The boy's smile came again, but he didn't stop swinging. Not then. Not even two hours later when Blake finished the first of his meetings, lay down on the horse-hair mattress and tried to sleep.

An hour later he awoke suddenly, not knowing why. He got up and peered through the window. It was too far to see the boy's expression, the rain was surging down the glass. But there was a sound coming from the courtyard and it wasn't the creaking of the swing or the tapping of the rain. It sounded as if the child were laughing. Only that, he concluded, was impossible.

Chapter Eleven

Nobody could ever tell you, hand on heart, what exactly Brigadier Peter Hensham did.

Not that he appeared a mystery. You could place the voice accurately to within a couple of hundred yards of the Brompton Oratory, the shirts to within a tiny segment of Jermyn Street, the manner to a handful of dreadful country schools where they succeed in dehumanising the average eight-year-old, by the time he reaches thirteen.

But none of it told you how he spent his days.

Hensham was tall, and much better looking than his peers would have wished. The grey hair was too full, the voice too loud, the skin just too thick. His secretary, Debbi, told a friend he had missed being a real human by a couple of thousand light years, and only landed on the planet by mistake.

For now there was little sign he had formed any meaningful attachments – least of all to his wife. He bought no flowers, sent no chocolates, accepted only a few invitations and sent even fewer of his own. According to Debbi he seemed to hold his personal life at arm's length – as if it wasn't quite suitable or nice, or belonged in fact to someone else.

There was, she surmised correctly, at least one unburied body under his bed and probably another inside. A thought that made her giggle from time to time as she typed her way through the day.

After dinner with the Minister, Hensham had returned to

his weekday flat in Baker Street and done something he had refrained from doing for many years.

He opened the whisky bottle and poured three tumblers in quick succession – trying to anaesthetise the thought of Sarah Blake.

It had been typical of Amesbury to stick a lance into the wound and then worry it.

The man was quite insufferable. Arrogant, opinionated, but, at the same time, highly effective. And in this case – right.

He held the glass up to the light and stared through it. On the other side the face of Sarah Blake shone back at him – Keegan, as she had been all those years ago. Sarah Keegan, the brightest linguist of the year at London University. Best boobs, too. They'd all agreed on that. And hadn't Hensham been the lucky one, eh? Went out with her before any of the others had stopped drooling, moved in with her, thought he was going steady and permanent, blue skies all the way to the future.

'Yes, well . . .' He put down the glass, thought for a moment, then made his way to the door.

He was drunk. He knew that. Otherwise he wouldn't have been able to do it.

'Christ, Peter.'

Hensham leaned against the porch, hands in his pockets, stupid lopsided grin, hadn't bothered with the doorbell, just shouted until she'd come down.

'You've woken up half the bloody neighbourhood . . .'

'Sorry Sarah.'

'And the kids . . .'

'I said I'm sorry.'

'You'd better come in.' She drew the dressing gown more tightly around her. He could see Veronica leaning down from the landing.

'Who is it, Mum?'

'Someone from your father's work.'

'Is he all right?'

Sarah turned to Hensham. 'Well is he? You tell her what you've come for . . .'

'He's fine. Really.'

She looked up at Veronica. 'See, he's fine. Go to bed, my sweet. It's OK. I'll be up soon.'

Hensham trailed her into the sitting room, trying to stand straight while she shut the door behind him.

'I'm not going to offer you a drink. You've had plenty.'

'I didn't come for a drink . . .'

'Oh . . .'

'I came to see if you're alright.'

She shook her head, went over to the sideboard and poured herself a whisky. 'I think I'm the one who needs a drink, after hearing that . . .'

'What d'you mean?' He made a rough landing into the middle of the sofa.

'God's sake, Peter. When was the last time you bothered about me being alright? All through Bosnia when Tom was away . . . oh what the hell? No reason why you should've, I suppose, but a little encouragement would've been nice.'

'I should have done more.'

'What is this? *Mea culpa* time?'

'People change . . .'

'Oh for Christ's sake. Has Hazel thrown you out again? Maybe Amesbury's smacked your bottom. What did you come for?'

'I still miss you, Sarah.'

'I don't believe this.' She shook her head. 'You and I finished all this crap, nearly twenty years ago. The age of my children, Peter. That's how long ago you and I split up and you turn up out of the blue, with Tom away in bloody Macedonia, to tell me you miss me . . .? I may have been born at night, but it wasn't last night.'

'You sure I can't have a drink?'

She got up reluctantly, and he could see the dressing

gown come slightly apart. It was clear she was wearing nothing beneath it.

'Don't look at me like that Peter. That's finished too, in case you hadn't realised.'

'It used to be really something – you know that don't you?'

'So did Stonehenge . . . Look Peter, I'm going to call you a cab.'

'Remember, Rome . . .?'

'I don't want to remember . . .' But he could see her eyes soften, hear the breath released in a tiny lump, deep down in her throat.

'Are you alright, Sarah?'

'Why shouldn't I be?'

'I suppose I meant you and Tom.'

'What d'you want me to say? That things are lousy, that we're at each other's throats, that I want a divorce . . . that suit you?'

'If it's true.'

She shook her head. 'It's more complicated than that.'

'I can listen.' He laughed. 'In my state that's about all I can do.'

'Another time, Peter.'

'Tomorrow. Lunch.' His face seemed to clear. 'We'll go to Langans, have some fun.'

'I . . .'

She was going to turn him down. Really. But in that moment she tried to remember the last time someone had invited her on the spur of the moment to a nice restaurant, with a piercing blue light in their eye and the embers of passion still there in the fireplace . . .

Only she couldn't.

In Skopje it was 2.30 a.m. when Jimmy McIlvane left the Grand Hotel. He would leave for good in a couple of days. To somewhere else with problems. For now there were still plenty of police on the streets, cars racing day and night with lights and sirens, men in uniform muttering urgently into radios. And yet it was a sure sign they'd had no inspiration. The sirens were just for show.

Jimmy didn't have far to go.

Even in the trouble zones, especially in the trouble zones, the cat bars still flourish – gaudy little graveyards, where the un-dead go to it. Lip gloss and high heels – the business of the night. Any night, every night – same in all the towns. A cat is a cat is a cat – or some other piece of wisdom someone had imparted. War? They didn't care about war. They loved war. It was the biggest kick of all. Made an orgasm seem like the second coming, his mate used to say.

Only nuclear annihilation could rid the world of the cat bars. Maybe not even that.

Cosmos. There it was. Right behind the hotel. One more red-carpeted salon, one more revolving shiny ball with the refracted colour lights, one more set of Marlboro-dragging, under-age pixies – like a used-car market, parked next to each other, polished and shiny, more miles on the clock than they'd ever admit.

Blonde cats, mostly. All legs and trippy little feet on the dance floor, while outside the bloody world fucked *itself*, and they went on counting off the tricks. Hundred a time. Dollars up front. Like a slot machine.

Not again, he thought. Not again.

Alright. Just once.

He got up and made his way to the low sofa, where a selection of the daubed and dangerous sat around.

The man in the red velvet stall watched with satisfaction as Jimmy jumped through the hoop.

The 'shall I, shan't I, what the hell?' routine. He'd seen them all do it.

Man on his own.

Sooner or later you could draw him to the honey pot.

Just take the lid off and push his head inside.

Jimmy didn't take long. Wanted to. When he paid over the

money he thought he'd get the hour, or the better part of it. But she was tired, she said, wanted to get home, do the laundry, wake the kids up for school. Which wasn't exactly helpful. Nor was . . . 'You gonna finish soon, darling?'

Nothing worse than lousy sex. Hated that. Preyed on his mind. God, the ultimate insult when even the whores were giving up on him.

So he was biting angry when he left, up the stairs, out into the alley beside the concrete shopping centre, his body shouting frustration and failure.

Inside, of course, he was running away, same as he always had.

And that's when they got him.

Chapter Twelve

The hand was like a cattle prod, coming at him out of a long tunnel, jabbing at his shoulder . . . so you move in fast, kick at the face or the chest, get close under the guard, with the index and third fingers out there rigid, questing for the eyes. And you can kill in a single bland instant, long, long before you ever have time to think what you're doing and who you're doing it to. At the end of this road there's technique and reaction – and a body on the ground. And it's either yours or theirs.

One half-second longer and he would have struck the sergeant, standing in pale, grey light, above him, the hand shaking his arm . . .

'Sir . . .'

'Yes, OK . . .'

'Bad news, I'm afraid . . .'

'Yes I know, I know.'

Ah yes, yes, of course. The only kind of news there is. The only reason I'm here. And for just a few weeks I'd forgotten the damaged, dented nights, the pace of a crisis, the way it *feels*.

Forgotten the way it takes over and runs you, turning your stomach a hundred times a day, when you fear the worst, and it's even worse than that.

Compelling is the word. All your senses engaged and screaming.

They met in the office he had commandeered, once belonging to the headmaster, once painted, with a dead plant still sitting in the corner, resembling a little the old man himself, the filing cabinet, ransacked before he left.

Young Tito looked down from the wall in white naval uniform, on a day that was sunny.

Blake couldn't help noticing the rain now sponging down the grimy windows, the damp wet cloud that sat around them on the hillside.

Taking the floor was Major English, papers in hand, moustache, teacher-type, to those he fooled. The foxy fellow from Hartley Wintney on the A30, with the sweet, wet wife and the handicapped daughter, who used to help out at the village fetes and organise 'bowling for the pig' . . . and he could kill very well when he wanted to. When the options ran out.

They'd all discovered that about themselves back in Bosnia.

A bitter, bitter discovery, never to be unlearned . . . For English, for Captain Tillier and Sergeant Brock. He looked around at the sleep-sodden faces, woken far too early . . .

After Bosnia, of course, they'd all gone back to England trying to forget the capability to kill.

Taken steps to forget it – filled their time with the kids, the family life, the pub, theatres and concerts. Didn't sit rocking from side to side late at night, thinking, didn't watch the TV pictures, just prayed to God Almighty that they would never, ever, ever put a boot back into the Balkans.

'Serbs crossed the border two thousand yards west of Tabernovce . . .' he could hear English almost in the distance . . . 'simply drove up the main road, turned off into the fields and drove over. Latest count: fifteen tanks, three brigades. Not the crack sort, border louts mostly. Just drove past our observation post – Echo 52 – as if it wasn't there . . .'

Switch on, Tom Blake.

'And the Americans . . .?'

'Kids, of course. Just two months since they got seconded

to UNPROFOR, most of them still think they're in Greece. Anyway they started a major panic, yelled into every radio they could find, about Commies and geeks. Couple of them wanted to throw away the blue berets, take a few assault rifles and do a bit of damage . . .'

He stopped, and they all looked at each other.

'I see . . . and now?'

'Serbs are holding at a village about two miles inside. Best guess: this isn't an invasion, it's a rights assertion mission. They go in and dare us to throw them out. When we do they turn it into a full-scale invasion. It's an attempt to suck us in . . .'

'London told?'

'Same time as we woke you. Response was "proceed with utmost caution. Advise developments."'

'Fuckers.' Blake grimaced. 'Who's up there now?'

'Norwegian commander and about five hundred bleating Americans . . .'

'Right, let's get going.'

They went out into the courtyard. English lowered his voice. 'I've ordered up a couple of platoons, sir, three Saracens. Just a little back-up. After all they *have* bloody well invaded.'

'It's a try-on. I think you're right. Take a couple of armoured personnel carriers as well.' Blake shivered a little in the cold courtyard. 'We never got anywhere by going in light.'

Minutes later the convoy was lumbering down the cobbled drive, between the low houses, up to the guarded gate.

'Wait a minute . . .' Blake drew in his breath. Ahead of them, it wasn't the guard emerging to open up, but a tiny little figure in ragged, dark blue trousers.

'Bloody hell, it's the kid . . .'

'He likes to do it . . .' The captain leant forward.

'Doesn't he ever sleep?'

'Couple hours here and there.'

He wound down the window. 'Hey Sergio. No swing, uh?'

The boy opened the gate wide and approached the Land-Rover.

'You take me with you, Tom?' The little head craned upwards, eyes dark and alive.

'I thought you didn't speak English!'

'I no speak.' The boy laughed. 'You take me?'

'Next time.'

'Promise?'

'No.'

'Promise?' He went and stood in front of the vehicle.

'OK, OK.' He grimaced and Sergio gave an exaggerated bow, standing aside, letting the convoy pass.

Blake couldn't help reflecting that he'd been in the country less than a day, and he was already making promises he couldn't keep.

Wasn't a good sign.

Chapter Thirteen

They picked up the international radio stations as the convoy drove north to the border – BBC, Voice of America, pumping out alarm and foreboding, ready-canned for instant consumption.

The world didn't like what it was seeing – but had no instant answers.

'Need for restraint,' said all the pundits. 'Avoid exacerbating the situation.'

Blake made a face. In the old days when one country invaded another, you fought back and your allies came to help. Now you were supposed to exercise restraint. Can't react too harshly, old boy. I mean they've only taken a little piece of your country, not the whole thing. Be reasonable after all. Not worth starting a bloody war over is it?

Voice of the appeasers.

Such a lot of bullshit.

Inside the Land-Rover they could monitor other more sensitive transmissions. The great flagpole on the bonnet was an aerial linked to a single-sideband transceiver, and as the sergeant moved the dial they could hear other UN organisations shouting at each other through the ionosphere, trying to reach the unreachable.

Where were all the officials in all the high-rise blocks? What the bloody hell were they doing? Governments, bureaucrats, executives –they're supposed to lie in their baskets and wait to be summoned. Only they're not there today. Gone fishing or pissing on the one day they're needed.

This is why we did what we did in Bosnia.

You couldn't sit waiting for people to flaunt their ignorance in fancy meetings, with gold pens and gold embossed notepads. That was group masturbation, institutionalised, refined into an art form. And every year thousands of people in little wars around the world died during the jerk-off season at the General Assembly in New York – when the whole great tower of Babel threw itself a three-month lunch party in the cause of international understanding.

The curse of the world is not the decisions taken, Blake reflected, it's the decisions shelved, bought off, side-stepped.

It's the great, uncharted ocean of inactivity that afflicts all our international organisations, which can't agree on the colour of the bloody ashtrays, let alone a human crisis.

That's why I do what I do.

As he peered out into the blanket gloom Blake could see the road south, blocked solid. Cars and buses inched their way along, crammed and lopsided, some of them so weighed down they scraped the road.

Trucks carried little armies of the departing – children still holding satchels, women and babies, a few men with sticks and rifles – faces expressionless, minds sheltering deep inside bedraggled bodies.

In the grey light you could make out the carts and horses, their breath steaming into the morning chill. The country had nowhere to go, and yet it was on the move.

Blake had seen those expressions before among refugees. When you don't know where you're going tomorrow, or the next day, or next month, your impetus to live shuts down. People need to see a future, people need roofs, people need meals. They need to believe that they won't be beaten and robbed and violated. Only these faces had no such belief.

English shook his head at the window. 'In two hours there'll be tailbacks on every road or dirt-track out of this country. Some'll make it, either to Greece or Albania, maybe Bulgaria. But my guess is those countries will bring out the troops and force them back. Macedonia's going to be corked up . . .'

'And squeezed tighter than a ferret's backside.'

'What then, I wonder?' English wiped the condensation from the windscreen.

'Ah, well then it gets interesting. Then someone will engineer a major accident or another assassination and that will give 'em all the excuse they need to come in. Breakdown of civil order, they'll say, need to protect our own nationals, stop it spilling over the border. That's my guess.'

'Thing about these places . . .' It was Captain Tillier who spoke, his voice hardly audible above the grinding, mistreated Land-Rover. 'To us it's just a name or a piece of land – to them it's a blood feud. Doesn't matter if they've lived in the place all their lives – call it a war, call it a struggle for national rights, and they'll go next door and garrotte the woman they took to the flicks last night. Not even a second thought.' He looked straight at Blake.

'I don't feel part of that, sir. Don't want to be part of it. If that's the human race, I'd like to think I belonged to something else.' He closed his eyes and sat very still, as the Land-Rover groaned on.

It starts with a roadblock.

Blake remembered the one in Bosnia.

They set them up to tell you they're in control. Sometimes they're bluffing. They have a roadblock and nothing else. A few guns, plenty of cheek, and if they can turn you back they've won.

The thugs and the warlords thought they could walk all over the UN – and mostly, they could.

Word had got around that the UN didn't fight back, waited for orders from New York, rolled out its armoured cars and its blue berets for no other purpose than to provide target practice for the local population. Very considerate. A rare treat in these parts. How often did you come across an army you could piss about till kingdom come?

He had seen it that day in Bosnia almost two years before on the approach to Gorazde.

The roadblock had been manned by semi-uniformed, unshaven Serbs who had ignored his greeting, poked a rifle through the car window and demanded he get out and put his hands up.

He hadn't expected it that time.

They don't tell you that in staff college. They prepare you for a world where war has rules, and the rules get observed. Don't prepare you to be half-diplomat, half-patsy, everybody's favourite fuckabout.

He had got out of the car, feeling the anger racing up his spine, and as the man had grinned he had kicked him hard, straight between the legs – a kick that came out of nowhere, hard, fast and very low. And suddenly the grin had gone and so had the man, and the other Serbs were shouldering their rifles, hunting for their pistols – the moment of confusion before the killing that would surely begin . . .

But the shot had stopped them all, echoing out over the pass, silencing the groaning, moaning thug on the ground. Blake had looked round to see a much younger Major English, his Browning 9mm drawn and another shot already in the chamber, and this time pointed directly at the Serb officer.

'I'm a nervous man who wants to kill you.' The voice was very steady. 'Do you understand English?'

And then he repeated it very slowly. 'I want to kill you.'

The man nodded his understanding.

'You know who we are?' English's gun didn't move, lined up as it was on the man's chest.

'I asked if you know who we are.'

'UN.' Just a growl in response.

'Wrong my friend. We're British Army, understand. Army of Great Britain and Northern Ireland. Got it?'

'Yes.'

'Don't forget that. Don't think that just because we wear

light blue hats we're some sort of bloody fashion parade.'
The gun described an arc towards the other soldiers.

'Tell them to drop their weapons, or I'll make a very small hole in your head . . .'

The man gabbled at speed. Blake could see the understanding spread over their faces. The guns weren't just dropped, they were thrown down in a hurry.

'Now get up and fuck off out of my sight. Follow?'

'Yes, follow.'

Blake remembered the major turning round after they had gone and throwing up into a bush.

'You did a very brave thing, John.'

English shook his head, and there was fear in the eyes and the pallid, sweating skin. 'I did a very risky thing.'

'You've been here long enough to know what you're doing. More than I can say.'

'I could have got us killed.'

'That's the business.' Blake had stretched out his hand and English had hesitated for a moment, then taken it.

Now some fifteen months on he could see the roadblock, a few hundred yards ahead, and it had all returned to him.

'What do you want to do, sir?' The sergeant turned to Blake.

'I think you know the answer to that.'

Steady, Blake. Don't go in heavy. He could feel his muscles tense, the sweat on the back of his neck, pulse starting to take off . . .

Take it easy, man. If you start heavy, you've got no room for manoeuvre, no fall-back. You're a British officer, not the animal in a bullfight.

Grade it. Calm first, then tighten the pressure. This is an army that's just invaded its neighbour. They enjoy doing this. They would like nothing more than to make an example of you. Just the way you'd like to make one of them.

You're not so different. You're just on the other side.

There had to be twenty of them at the edge of the road. Well-armed, some lounging, the rest very focused, interested. Two armoured cars had been drawn up beside a machine-gun emplacement, surrounded by sandbags.

The message was clear enough. They were staying.

Blake looked round the faces in the Land-Rover.

'We're going to insist on going through, right to where the border was a few hours ago. We have to reach the observation post.'

Even as he spoke three guards emerged from the Serb position, hands raised like traffic police, forcing the sergeant to brake hard.

An officer, late twenties, approached Blake's side of the Land-Rover. The uniform was spotless, pressed, the boots shone in the sunshine.

'Good morning, gentlemen.' Blake noted the easy, unaccented English. 'What can I do for you?'

'You can dismantle your roadblock and cart it back into Serbia. If you need help we'll happily assist you.' Blake's smile had cemented in place. Let the man make of it what he wanted.

'I'm afraid that's not possible.'

'Oh?'

An expression of mock regret built itself into the young officer's face. 'We are here at the request of the Macedonian authorities. Our job is to assist in maintaining order.'

'Who exactly asked you to be here?'

'I have my orders, colonel.'

'And I have mine.' Blake's smile hadn't faltered. 'My orders are to move along this road freely and to visit our observation posts along the border. I would remind you this is an internationally recognised border . . .'

'I'm sorry, that's not possible.'

'I see.' Blake got out of the Land-Rover. 'Why don't you and I take a little walk together?' He gestured to the man to follow him and they left the road, falling into step along the hillside.

70

'Cigarette?'

The Serb shook his head.

'Where did you learn your English . . .?'

'London School of Economics.'

'Ah, yes.' Blake grinned. 'What year?'

'Eighty. Year Tito died.'

'Quite.' Blake nodded as if deep in thought. 'Also happened to be the year Iranian terrorists seized hostages inside their London embassy . . . maybe you saw . . .'

'I remember.'

'What you won't remember is that I was part of the SAS team that retook the building . . .' The voice was light, conversational. 'You probably won't remember either there was all that controversy at the time about us having orders to take no prisoners, people saying we just went in and executed the terrorists even though some of them surrendered . . .'

'I . . .'

'Well it was perfectly true . . .' Blake's smile had broadened. 'That's what we did do. Just a little pop with the Heckler and Koch – and it was all over. Saved the taxpayers a lot of money, and all that nonsense of trials, and the possibility of more reprisals . . . Well it was for the best, really. Stood me in good stead, I must say . . .'

They had stopped in their tracks and somehow the bonhomie had blown away in the wind.

He had seized the Serb's attention. Now he had to hold it.

'Let's take this situation shall we, sonny? Don't mind me calling you sonny, do you? Most UN commanders would salute you, say "We quite understand about the roadblock", turn their armoured cars round and piss off. But I'm not going to.'

'But these are your orders.'

'How do you know?'

'We were briefed on how UN forces operate. You are not authorised to confront us. Therefore you will do as I say and leave the area.'

Blake's smile returned like a danger beacon.

'Have you ever seen the weapons we're issued?' Calmly, easily, he unbuckled his holster and took out his pistol. The officer frowned, but he was puzzled by the conversational tone. He didn't feel threatened. Blake studied the gun with detached interest. 'It's a Browning nine millimetre, twelve shots, packs a very effective, accurate punch within about thirty yards.'

Casually his right hand closed over the pistol grip and without any warning he lowered the muzzle and shot the Serb in the foot.

Chapter Fourteen

By that time Jimmy McIlvane was waking up in a room he didn't recognise – largely because he couldn't see it.

His eyes had swollen badly after the beating and his chest, arms and back were encased in a wall of pain. They had hit him when he was face down, and gone on long after he had lost consciousness.

But it hadn't been a scientific punch-up. After years of being done over, Jimmy knew the difference.

In fact the only thing he still wondered about was whether it was better to be attacked by a professional who could target and maximise the pain, or just the normal ignorant thug, who simply lashed out at the things he could see.

Perhaps, he reasoned, it didn't matter much either way.

The results were remarkably similar.

As he sat on the bed he recalled the lightning hit outside the club. Bloody club. Bloody frustrating whore . . .

He had assumed by the van they had shoved him into that these were police, or special forces, that his own lovable paymasters had after all managed to give him away . . . and that a ditch by the Vardar had already been prepared to receive him. Then and for all time.

The beating had reinforced that view.

But the unexpected twist of still finding himself alive was difficult to explain away.

Jimmy could look at it all quite dispassionately.

The body would mend – maybe a little more bent or crooked than before. Anyone could fix up the nose, and teeth. Wasn't as if he was entering any beauty contests. Not in the near future.

The only question was why.

Half the day was to go by before he found out.

Jimmy had dozed off in the afternoon. It wasn't the lunch, because they hadn't given him any, but the fatigue and the cold and the body's general wish to withdraw its labour.

He was annoyed at waking, and for a few seconds was puzzled as to why he had.

Gradually he could see the figure sitting by the wall. The scum was in suit and glistening tie – a prick in pants, a dandy sitting arrogantly on a metal chair, watching him with very little interest.

'Mr McIlvane?'

Greeting. Not question.

'Thank you for coming.'

'You shithead.'

The figure removed a cigarette from his jacket pocket and lit it. 'Maybe you do something for us.'

'I know what I want to do for you.'

'No too many choices, Mr McIlvane.'

'Why the fuck should I . . .?'

'You're now in a portion of the country that's been rightfully renamed South Serbia.'

'What's that to me?'

'I have job for you. You do job, time to time . . .' he removed the cigarette. A little cloud of smoke hung immovable between them.

Jimmy grinned. 'Nice way to hold interviews.'

'It was mistake . . .'

'Then I'll go home . . .'

'One of our people recognised you from a while back. Said you violent man, Mr McIlvane. Very violent. So he did what he did. In case, uh? . . .' The voice ran out of road. 'I punish him. We sorry.'

Jimmy stood up.

The man rose too. 'May I offer you a drink? We have doctor here who should perhaps examine you. My name is Kiro.'

He held out his hand.

At the back of Jimmy's mind, a tiny signal switched off the automatic response, conditioned over many years.

Without it, Jimmy would have taken the hand, flattened it against his chest, and broken all five fingers, by dropping to the ground.

This time he shook the offering and gave it back to its owner intact . . .

Later, he would snap it off at the wrist, if that became necessary.

They had done their homework on Jimmy. Knew all about the whore from the club. For a while they considered getting him another, just to soften him up, but concluded correctly that he had gone off to hide in the sexual undergrowth, and wouldn't make another sortie in that direction for some time to come.

So they gave him the booze instead. Rum, mostly. First with the coke and then without.

Let the alcohol dull the pain and the wits, enough to get him to sleep.

There was in fact a doctor in the house but he had no intention of seeing Jimmy.

And Jimmy's doctor was the bottle.

He would drink their drink, he told himself, and in the morning he'd be on his way. Maybe they'd pay him for the damaged face. He'd insist on it. One way or another.

A few of the soldiers kept him company, with broken English, nods and gestures. So he didn't notice Kiro come back in, pull up a chair and start pouring again into his glass.

'You OK Jimmy?'

Jimmy surveyed him with the kind of genuine contempt that real drunks always reserve for the sober. He ignored the full glass in front of him and raised the bottle by the neck.

'I want you to think about the work we could offer you.'

'I'm leaving.'

'Good work, Jimmy. Good money.' Kiro patted him on the back.

'How good?'

'Ten thousand US. Any currency you want it in. We're not short of money.'

'What about my face?' He ran a hand painfully over his cheeks. ''Nother five for my face.'

'Sure, Jimmy. No problem. You get your face fixed up. But then you start moving on this job.'

Jimmy burped and his head swayed from side to side.

Kiro moved closer. 'Want you to hit a refugee camp . . .'

'Don't do women and children. Leave that to you.'

'We don't do them either. The refugees have all gone. It's an army base now. Pricks from the UN. Legitimate target in war. Hit it Jimmy.' Kiro grinned and his eyes opened wide. 'Blow the fucking place up.'

Chapter Fifteen

Geralyn Lang took the road north with a sense of mounting excitement. She hadn't flown into a trouble zone before, hadn't experienced a major foreign assignment. But she knew it was her.

At twenty-eight years old, she had no illusions about why the network had chosen her. They wanted looks – pretty hair, nice voice, women who carried the feelgood factor around with them, meaning in the blunt parlance of the TV boardrooms that they would be 'darned good to feel'. Nothing else seemed to matter.

Over the last year the company had cut a swathe through the old reporters' ranks, shafting, hacking, easing out all the ones who wouldn't go quietly.

'They can buy three of you, for the price of someone who knows something,' a departing correspondent had told her. 'Don't imagine they're investing in your brains – unless you put 'em in your bra this morning.'

She had laughed at him.

True she had no experience abroad, but she had trained hard. Her first job had been with Channel Nine in Washington DC, where you covered the crack alleys of the South-East, the three-a-night murder bag, and hold-ups on the Beltway.

It hadn't exactly changed the world, but she knew she'd done well.

She could write quickly, talk fluently, and smile people into imparting with information. So when 'Mr

Washington', as she called him, requested her to fill in for a year at the London bureau, she went out and bought three suitcases that same afternoon, rented her flat that same night, and transferred her car to her sister by lunchtime the next day.

Mr Washington liked that.

The network liked that too.

So with everyone happy, they drove her to Dulles Airport in a limo, with a Business Class ticket to London and the kind of memorable parting words for which newsrooms around the world have become famous.

'Don't fuck up, Geralyn. You only get one chance like this.'

In fact, by the time the British Airways 747 splashed onto a damp runway at Heathrow next morning, she already had another. A television crew was there to meet her – with a sheaf of faxes and agency reports, another air ticket and a crisis in southern Europe to 'get her arse down to'.

She hadn't slept for nearly forty-eight hours.

Hadn't, truth to tell, known much about Macedonia.

Hadn't had time to be scared.

Until now.

The rented minivan was stacked with television equipment, the crew dozed, Geralyn sat up front with the driver and interpreter. There were only thirty-five kms to the border – if there was still a border – but with each minute her anxiety rose.

She had never seen people pick up their lives and run, never seen the calmness of fear.

Shouting, she knew. Screaming. The agony of the bereaved. But this was different.

Just the stillness of the traffic lines, heading south, into a new day, guaranteed worse than the one before.

Her eye was caught by a woman in a motorcycle side-car, two small puppies in her arms, plastic bags and clothes stuffed in around her.

No one inside the cars was talking. Whole families, whole communities, rendered wordless by the invasion of their country.

And yet it wasn't her war, her battle. She had a job to do. For a moment she closed her eyes, letting the tiredness take over.

Sleep would be wonderful.

Jesus, God.

Something made her sit up.

And then she saw it.

Just specks in the distance through the windscreen. A convoy in white, soldiers . . . something in the way they were standing.

The driver had seen it too and started to brake.

'Go on,' she told him. 'Chip, get the camera.' She reached round to the seat behind her. 'Hey, I think we got ourselves some work.'

Closer now and she could see the two groups – UN and Serb – had to be. Macedonia didn't have an army, not to speak of, and the reports that morning said they had stayed at home.

Fifty yards away she told the driver to stop.

'God,' the word just slipped through her lips.

They were standing some way apart from each other and guns weren't shouldered.

Look again Geralyn.

Someone was on the ground. She could hear the shouts, a couple of people around him, white box, could be . . .

She didn't think. 'Let's go . . .'

As she ran ahead of the crew, she could see some of the faces turning towards her, guns swinging round, young kids, mostly, told to kill the enemy, whatever size or sex it came in, whether weak or powerful, young or old. A threat was a threat was a threat . . . only they weren't sure about this one.

'Wait a minute . . .'

Fifteen yards away she stopped, seeing the UN officer, bending over the man on the ground, the pistol still in his hand. And again that silence, when reason has ended, she thought, and the killing is about to begin. Only once had she seen it – a standoff in the long, hot Washington summer, with two men pointing guns at each, ignoring the taunts of the crowd – and both had fired at the same time . . .

'What's going on?' she called out. 'This is American television.'

She sensed the cameraman beside her.

For a second no one answered.

And then, quite abruptly, the UN officer put away his pistol and turned towards her.

'Just a terrible accident, that's all. Gun went off by itself. My fault. Lucky it's only a leg wound – here, take a look.'

She came forward, the camera still with her.

'Is that true?' She looked down to the man on the ground. 'Is that true what he says . . .?'

He had quietened a little, but the face was still contorted with pain.

'It's true . . .'

'I've offered our medical facilities.' The UN officer shrugged. 'But they seem to have their own.' He turned towards his troops. 'Now we have to be moving up to the border . . .'

And it was only then that she recognised him. The man on the flight to Skopje, sitting between her crew, the one she had seen getting into a UN Land-Rover at the airport.

They moved to one side. Behind him she could see the tension begin to seep away. The Serbs were shouldering their rifles, holstering the pistols; the UN did the same. Slowly at first, each movement balanced, controlled.

'We met on the plane,' she told Blake.

'I know. I remember.'

'I had no idea who you were . . .'

'We don't always come pre-packaged in uniform.'

'What happened just now?'

He looked around, checking to see if the cameraman was nearby. He wasn't.

'You can't use this.'

'Then don't tell me.'

He grinned.

'That's much easier. Good day, Miss Lang.'

'Wait a minute . . .'

'I don't have a minute.' The grin went away. 'In case you missed it, Serbia has invaded this country, and I have to get up to what once passed for the border.'

He turned and walked towards the Land-Rover. There were smiles and handshakes from the team, 'well done, sirs', one or two patted him on the back.

'Bloody good, sir.' The sergeant opened the passenger door to him. 'Test of bloody wills. And you won. Christ, I've never seen anything like it – plugging the little shit in the foot. Bloody wonderful, sir.'

They drove slowly on, skirting the barriers, watched by angry, sullen faces, guns still held ready. They weren't going to forget the incident. That's what the eyes were telling him.

English bent towards him and whispered in his ear: 'What would you have done if that reporter hadn't come along?'

Blake shook his head. 'Would have been OK.' He smiled. 'I think. The Serb had to say it was an accident. If it got out that a Brit had put one over on him intentionally . . . he'd never have lived it down. Anyway – had to do something. Couldn't just turn meekly round and go home.'

'Gonna pay for my trousers to be cleaned?'

'Do it for you.'

'If I were you,' English grinned, 'I'd buy that lady reporter dinner. Shouldn't be too much of a hardship.'

He snorted. 'Bloody woman! Why is it that war zones always bring out the amateurs?'

When he looked back, Geralyn Lang was staring after the convoy, but she was too far away for him to read the

81

embarrassment and anger on her face. And if he had, he wouldn't have minded. She'd behaved like an asshole cub reporter. 'Is it true? What really happened? I want to talk.'

Was this supposed to be a war zone or a fucking debating club?

Asshole. That's exactly what she was.

And she thought the same about him.

Chapter Sixteen

'I'm going to see an old friend for lunch. That's all.'

'Is it a man?' Veronica raised an eyebrow. For a fifteen-year-old, Sarah thought, she had a highly developed sense of intrigue.

'Can't I have any secrets, darling?'

'I only asked if it was a man.'

'Why?'

'Well . . .'

'I'm going to have lunch, child – not run away from home.'

'How do we know that?'

'Oh, do be reasonable.' She looked at her watch. 'I'm going to miss my train.'

'He'll wait, Mum. You're supposed to make them hang around.'

'That so?'

'That way they're hungrier . . .'

'I'm quite hungry myself.' She could feel herself blushing. 'Now if it's all right with you, I want my lunch. OK?'

God! It seemed to her every conversation was like an obstacle course. Tom had been just the same. Always asked questions, as if to collect little pieces of trivia, but never listened to the answers . . . 'What did you do today?' . . . 'Oh, nothing much, blew up the barracks at Woolwich . . .' She recalled standing in the kitchen saying it. 'Really,' he'd replied, staring out at the garden, hearing nothing. 'See anyone?' . . . 'Only a few bodies.' . . . 'Great!'

Sarah had really missed conversation with interested people. The art of speech was so commonplace, so essential – and yet, in their lives, so bloody dead!

No wonder she had accepted Peter's invitation. Well, not exactly accepted. Just not refused. There had been more interest in his eyes than Tom had exhibited for the last fifteen years. And not just interest, either, she thought. Lust as well. She toyed with the word. Sounded foreign. Strange. Wonderful, even.

She called out 'bye' to Veronica and slammed the front door on her inhibitions.

At least that's what she imagined.

She was late, flustered, clothes seemed too tight, too new, even her shoes were creaking.

Had it been that long, since the last outing?

He saw her first, rising up among all the faces. Smart man, elegant . . . eyes that could really hold you. Close or at a distance.

Peter didn't talk to you, she recalled suddenly. He engaged you, made you part of his aura, found out which of your doors were open and went through them. Then he would find the ones that were closed, and pick the locks.

Always like that, Peter Hensham.

Even at university, he had been so very focused. You didn't just go out with him, you got sucked into a world of late-night feasts, phone calls at odd hours, touching and playing, fast cars – a life of unbelievable intensity, for as long as you could take it.

Peter Hensham had been habit-forming, all those years ago. And probably still was.

She stepped towards the table, hand on his shoulder as he bent to kiss her.

Just once. He didn't have the suburban habit of pecking away like a parrot for half an hour. .

One kiss, for now.

'Drink?'

'God, yes.'

'They'll bring some champagne in a moment.'

She laughed, half in the present, half in the past.

'Supposing I'd wanted mineral water?'

'Actually they're bringing that as well.'

'Did you go and order the meal at the same time?'

The eyes looked hard across the table and went in.

'Decided to leave that in your hands. Why don't you choose for both of us?'

Outbid, she thought. The way it always had been.

When they had clinked glasses, he sat back and smiled. She still liked the way he looked. The perma-tan, the blue eyes, the black hair, greying fast.

'I meant what I said the other night, Sarah.'

'The bit where you talked to the dog . . ? I see.' She laughed. 'How could you mean it? You can't even remember what you said.'

'I remember the bit where I said I'd missed you.'

'Really?'

'I remember talking about Rome – and the holiday we had there. Kind of honeymoon . . .'

She didn't move.

'I remember pretty much everything that happened between us . . .'

'After all this time?'

'And most of all I remember being dumped for Tom.'

She picked up the champagne glass and stared at the bubbles. 'Yes I suppose you would.'

'I've never really understood why you did that.'

'I told you.'

'I know you did. But understanding is something else.' He gazed round the restaurant. At every table there seemed to be men lunching elegant women; hoping, he felt sure, that lunch would turn into dinner, dinner into bed, bed into dreamland – before starting again. Is that what he wanted?

'Tom was the quiet side of my life, Peter. He was the sure

85

side. Always there, always consistent. He drew the part of me that needed constancy, a family, the house, the dog . . . you were never that.'

'I could've been.'

'I don't think so.'

'And now that you've had your family?'

She snorted. 'Sometimes it feels as though the family's had me. You probably don't know what it's like. You and Hazel never . . .'

'No. We never did . . .'

'I didn't mean it like that. It's just you feel sometimes like a sponge that everyone's squeezed out. Your time, your energy, your understanding – never mind being . . .' She shook her head. 'But you don't want to hear any of this.'

'And where does Tom fit in?'

'Wish I knew . . .' She stopped, but he didn't fill the silence, just waited for her to go on, as he knew she would. 'He's still my husband, but I don't know that we're going to live together anymore. I asked him not to come back. Don't know what he'll do. You know Tom as well as I do.'

'I went to school with him, Sarah. But none of us really knew him. Other than the strength. The confidence to do what he thought was right. And that's what it is . . . just confidence. Tom is capable of anything – the sublime, the ridiculous – any number of combinations in between. He's very tough – and very unpredictable.'

'Look Peter . . .'

'I really didn't want to talk about Tom. Not today. But it sort of came up. I want you to know I'm here if you need anything . . .'

'I'm fine. Really.'

Tom was a full stop in the conversation. They both knew that.

When they got outside, the sky had thickened into a darker grey, some of the cars had switched on their sidelights, the day seemed prepared to finish early. But not Peter.

'Little stroll? It's still pretty mild.'

'I ought to get home soon.'

They crossed over to Green Park and she fell in beside him. The air was a step away from cold, but she needed it. There was some clearing out to be done in the head, she told herself. Had to straighten out some priorities, put things back on course. Get a grip.

Funny how you repeat all the clichés of life that you've hated since childhood.

And yet they're always right there beside you, she realised.

I don't want to become one myself.

Tom had always said that.

'What's going to happen in Macedonia, Peter?'

The question caught him off-guard – the first time that day.

He made a face. 'Not much. I expect the Serbs will move out again when things quieten down . . .'

'What makes you say that?'

'Just a hunch. I don't think this is Bosnia again. We've all learned lessons from that.'

'Hmm. Be the first time we'd done that . . .' She shrugged. 'Hardly what the international community's become known for . . . learning lessons.'

'We can't have another bloodbath, Sarah.'

'Who says? Try telling that to the Serbs, now that they've moved in.'

'People are jittery. There's been an assassination . . .'

'Oh, so if someone decides to rub out our dear Prime Minister, we should expect to see French paratroops on Beachy Head? Just because everyone's a bit jittery? Sounds odd to me, Peter . . .'

'The Balkans are different.'

'You all say that.'

They walked on for a while, as the people spilled out of their offices and hurried towards the underground.

He turned and smiled at her. 'Still got the old debating skills, I see.'

'I like to keep up with things. Besides the children ask questions, and they've got plenty of opinions. Just because I wash underpants, doesn't mean I'm brain-dead.'

'I know that . . .'

She smiled. 'I didn't mean to sound aggressive. Just fed up with meaningless conversations. People spend so much of their lives just . . . well, swimming in jelly. "Hi, how are you, what's up . . . ?" Nice to talk about real things for a while . . .'

Somehow she had led them in a circle, back towards Piccadilly and the station.

But he stopped suddenly, as if uncertain what to say.

'I want to see you again, Sarah.'

'No, my dear. It's been lovely, but it wouldn't be right.'

'We'll go and have dinner, Saturday.'

'Listen to me . . .' She realised his arm had snaked inside her own.

'I *am* listening. I know how hungry you'll be by Saturday . . .'

'No, Peter.'

'Pick you up at your station. Seven-thirty.'

It wasn't till she boarded the train home, sitting in the compartment by herself, feeling the draught under the door, that she looked out of the window.

The countryside was in darkness, the lights streaked into one another. Easy to turn off your mind when you travel so quickly. Easier to ignore your conscience. Just watch the pictures go by.

And then she caught sight of her own reflection in the glass. Why in God's name was she grinning?

Seven-thirty. Next Saturday.

That was it.

All right, Peter Hensham, she told herself. You're on.

Chapter Seventeen

Soon after nine that night Amesbury slipped away from the House of Commons, caught a taxi, and checked in the back window to make sure no one had seen him. It was easy. The bodyguards always waited outside, and that night he had told them the House would be sitting late. 'Probably midnight, Alfred, old boy. Have a good dinner. No hurry.'

It had always been one of his favourite pastimes – sloping off, hiding, delighting in the fact that not a soul in the world knew where he was. That was the joy of the Commons. For all the television cameras, for all the microphones and reporters, you could still get away for a couple of hours, and no one would know. Even inside the place you could lose yourself in some committee, some lounge, some armchair. In the lavatories if you were desperate.

As the car took him along the Embankment into the Docklands, he suddenly felt uneasy.

Reaching for his wallet, he began to search the compartments for cash. Only ten pounds, for Christ's sake! Bloody Secretary of State for Defence! Supposing the taxi cost more!! How was he to get back without his chauffeur and all the lackeys in tow?

They were turning into the back streets now, winding close to the Limehouse Link. Amesbury could see large, deserted warehouses, broken up by scattered modern developments, a long narrow road, the huge tower of Canary Wharf, closer than he'd ever seen it, jutting out of the rooftops, much larger than he had imagined.

As he pulled down the window he could smell the river and hear it restless and agitated, just a few feet away.

Over a slip bridge now, slowly, the cab driver peering around for signs, but seeing none. A pub came into view, a block of flats.

'Shoulder of Mutton Alley, you said.' The man's tone was accusatory. He wasn't going to take the blame if they couldn't find it. Customer's fault. That was the rule.

'Wait. I think you just passed it.'

'Who says?'

The cab stopped, like a large black beetle, lit up in the darkness. There was a white block of flats on the left, a row of terraces across the street.

'Go back about twenty yards.'

Amesbury had been right. The sign was there, but the road looked less than promising. Just the side of the block, and a fence of boards, with building works beyond.

'What number?'

'Fifteen.'

'There isn't one.' The driver grinned with satisfaction.

'Oh God . . .'

And then as he wondered what to do, the face appeared beside him out of the darkness.

'My dear chap . . .' Dmitry, his Russian counterpart, stood beside the cab, in dinner jacket and overcoat with velvet collar, looking anything but the Kremlin's Defence Minister.

'I couldn't find the number . . .' Amesbury said dejectedly.

'Of course not, my friend.'

He paid off the driver and they waited till the cab had slunk away down the street.

'Wonderful city you have here. Full of dark, how you say, hidey-holes.' Dmitry was showing off.

'Where are we going?'

'Just round the corner. Marvellous place. Apartment, owned by some of my friends . . .'

'I see.'

They began to walk across the street, down into a square. Amesbury could see the sign on a pub . . . 'The House They Left Behind.'

He felt like the minister left behind.

'Who are these friends, Dmitry?'

'Businessmen. That's all.'

'Why did you want to meet here? This isn't the usual procedure.'

'I was not aware we had one.'

'It's what we agreed in Switzerland, for God's sake. If the thing started to go wrong for some reason, then we would gather at the same place – all of us – and take steps to repair it. Or am I mistaken?'

Dmitry had stopped at the front door of what looked like a converted warehouse. He pulled a plastic card from his pocket and ran it through a metal housing on the wall. The main door opened silently in front of them.

'You're not mistaken, my friend. I merely wished to take some steps, *before* things went wrong. A minor problem, that's all. But we should not take all this too seriously.'

A lift door opened in front of them. Amesbury felt a sense of quiet luxury, bare flagstones, polished wood, a few giant indoor plants. Understated.

'My friends have bought the building . . .'

'Of course.'

Who are you dealing with, Amesbury?

And yet his curiosity led him into the lift, up to the sixth floor, out onto the penthouse terrace that overlooked the river.

In the darkness he could make out the sweep of the north bank, round the Isle of Dogs, and away east towards Greenwich. A freighter with two green lights chugged almost invisibly below them. In the distance he could hear the ducks calling to each other, the constant rustling of the tide, the presence of a huge city, far away.

Dmitry stood beside him, hand on the guardrail.

'Drink?'

'A small orange juice.'

'As you wish.'

When he returned, Amesbury had become impatient.

'I need to get back to the House.'

'Then I will call a car.'

'You mentioned a problem . . .'

'Please don't get upset my friend.' Dmitry's hand brushed his shoulder. Amesbury tried not to flinch. He'd grown up in an environment where men didn't touch each other. Well, not unless . . . 'You have a new man out in Skopje. Commander of your peacekeeping contingent. Name of Blake.'

'What of it? Blake's a good man. Best we have. Decisive, articulate. People believe in him. They saw him on television so much during the Bosnian thing, he's almost as well known as the bloody Prime Minister.'

'I think you should find someone else.'

'What are you talking about?'

'Our associates think he might interfere.'

'I repeat, Dmitry, he's necessary for the credibility of the operation. If he's there, people will believe it.'

'If he's there, he might wreck it.'

'I doubt that.'

'Your doubts, my friend, might not be sufficient to convince everyone concerned.'

Amesbury turned away from the river. 'I'll say this one more time, and only one more time. Leave Blake alone. The British public will be reassured if they know he's there. It's . . .' he raised a single eyebrow, 'it's the decision of Her Majesty's Government.'

There was silence for a moment. The wind picked up, ruffling Amesbury's fine white hair. Behind him the lights at the summit of Canary Wharf went out, as if the building had entered a black hole.

'All right, my friend, we'll talk no more of this.' Dmitry shrugged, and then the smile of welcome, the public smile, returned. 'Come inside, come inside, finish your drink and we'll talk about grouse shooting instead.'

They sat on the sofa, and for the second time that evening Amesbury was startled.

A young man in white shirt and black trousers, his dark hair slicked tight against the scalp, entered the room with a tray of drinks and laid it on the coffee table. A single lock of hair curled on the forehead. Amesbury could see the man was heavily made-up. A boy, almost. No more than twenty.

'Thank you, Andrei . . .' Dmitry grinned at him.

'Andrei's from Moscow. Come here to improve his English.'

'I see.'

Andrei smiled cautiously, as if he hadn't understood the introduction. As he moved his head a small, tight pony-tail became visible, tied with a silver band.

'A-nother drink?' He turned to Amesbury.

'Thank you, no. I have to be going.'

'I will call a taxi, then?'

'That would be very kind.'

The young man had been kneeling beside the coffee table, but now he rose up, in a straight line, like a dart. A body in peak physical condition. Perfect muscular control. Perfect balance. Clearly doing more than English.

When he had left the room, Dmitry patted the sides of the sofa and sighed.

'You know I always miss Russia, when I am away from her.'

Amesbury gestured to the door. 'But at least you have company.'

'Things are not always what they seem, my friend. Andrei, it is true, looks after me, both here and in Moscow. He is my bodyguard. He also takes care of problems, if they should arise.'

'Oh?'

'Problems like Colonel Tom Blake.' The smile returned suddenly. 'I'm so sorry, my friend. We weren't going to talk anymore about him, were we? Do please forgive me.'

Chapter Eighteen

As Blake watched from the border observation post, the sun burned a hole through the clouds, and ran a spotlight over the hills. Nothing moved.

The quietest of invasions. A few tanks, a few thousand men – and they had simply ploughed across the fields, three miles inside a sovereign, foreign country. No fighting, no firing. Just swept past the UN's glorious protection force as if it were a traffic light.

Some of the invading units had even stuck up their middle fingers at the blue berets. The big fuck-off from Serbia. And to the outside world . . . 'We're just a neighbour helping out. Nothing to worry about. They asked us to come in. Did we do something wrong?'

But you had only to look at the exodus south. The people knew what it meant. The stream of families, tearing up their lives and chucking away what they couldn't carry. You couldn't fool *them*.

Blake handed back the binoculars to the US sergeant.

'Doesn't seem real, sir.' The man saluted.

'Does to me. I've seen their artwork already.' Blake saluted back.

'There was nothing we could do. Our orders . . .'

'Your orders are crap, Sergeant. We all know that. Under the circumstances you did what you had to do. Don't rule out the possibility that you might have to ignore your orders at some point . . .'

'I don't understand, sir.'

'Yes you do. You have a duty to ignore or countermand what you know to be dangerous and inaccurate orders. Do I make myself clear?'

'Yes sir.' He shook his head. 'No sir.'

'In my command, Sergeant, we fight back. Is that understood? We're not in the business of cheek-turning. Tried that. And while we turned our cheeks, they shot the balls off teenagers in the next valley. You're still with me, I hope. Don't go away . . .'

'My orders are to observe and report . . .'

'Your orders are to behave as soldiers, Sergeant. You see something going on, you act on it. Call me if necessary. Understood?' He turned to go, but seemed to change his mind. 'One more thing. I don't intend to let these new borders become permanent.'

'Yes sir.'

'I intend to get reinforcements up here. I intend to have the international borders respected, and lastly I intend to have this invasion force out of here. Tell your men, Sergeant.'

They saw him off the premises, as he told it later. The Blackhawk helicopter, they said. There to evacuate the post. If he'd like to make use of it . . . ? Yes, he would like that. And, as he whispered to English, it was as much to prevent any possible evacuation as to get home to Skopje in time for supper.

They were silent as they drove from the airfield to Dare Bombol.

First shot fired. First challenge. He knew they would mark him, the way they had done in Bosnia. No one would be told to kill him. Too dangerous. Too risky. But if he walked in front of a stray bullet, then there'd be medals all around. Drinks, prizes. Weekend by the sea.

He shook his head. That was about the size of it.

When they reached the camp he found Sergio banging a gypsy drum, swinging from side to side as the sun disappeared behind him.

The boy stopped and smiled when Blake approached.

'You like music?'

'Where did you get the drum?'

A tremor in the big, black eyes.

'Was drum of my Daddy. He always say . . . When I die, Sergio, this will be your drum. Now he's dead. Is mine, no?'

'Yes.'

He sat with the boy for a while, as the soldiers went inside, and the dinner was readied in the kitchens, and the life of the British encampment wound down around them.

'How did your father die, Sergio?'

'Don't know. Soldiers – they came, took him away. Many men in the village. No one came back. Mother said to me – all dead. Don't know why.'

The voice had become matter-of-fact, unemotional. The boy had put time and distance between himself and his father.

'You have Daddy, Tom?'

Blake nodded. 'Old man now. Lives by the sea. Mother's dead.'

The big eyes narrowed. It was as if death had given them common ground. The boy was a man in all but size.

'What do you want to do now, Sergio? What about school?'

'No school. Need money.'

'How?'

'Play drum in town. Cousin . . . I have cousin, he plays . . .' Sergio gestured with his fingers.

'Accordion, you mean?'

'Maybe.'

Blake turned round and looked towards the kitchen. 'You want to come and have some food?'

Sergio laughed. 'Your food very bad.' He shook his head. 'I eat today . . . no yesterday. Big pain.' He pointed to his stomach. 'You be careful. Bad food, they give you. You get same thing.'

Blake smiled and offered his hand. The boy took it and held it tight.

'Tell me if you change your mind.'

He watched him return to the swing, his fingers flicking and tapping at the surface of the tiny drum, and his eyes half-closed as if the rhythms were filling his mind.

It was good to have the boy there. He was cheerful, human, and above all disconnected from the routines of soldiery. So different from his son Charley, back in England. Fine boy, strong boy, and yet the product of a structured system of schools and exams and competitions. Life for him was a ladder with even rungs. The days went by and you climbed a little, and if something went wrong you fell back and started again.

If something went wrong in Sergio's life, your father was taken out and killed by a bunch of stranger-thugs.

And all you got was a drum in compensation – and licence to busk in a war zone.

Sergio could smile at a fate like that. Which in Tom Blake's eyes made him someone pretty special.

Much later, with the darkness of the forest around him, he made the call through to London. They sat on odd chairs and boxes, watching him – English with his pipe, Captain Tillier, Sergeant Brock.

He told the Ministry what he'd seen and what he needed – more arms, reinforcements, the will to do something. Told them they had a window of opportunity to roll back the invasion. All they needed was to play it very tough. Show an example. While there was still time.

When he had finished, he replaced the satellite phone and stared at each of them in turn.

'My comments have been noted.'

English continued puffing on his pipe, letting the smoke gather around him. The others sat staring at the floor.

'So they're going to let it happen again . . .' Sergeant Brock was watching a cockroach sashay across the bare boards. 'I think I'm ready this time.'

Blake looked around the other faces. 'We did it in Bosnia . . .'

'In a way I hoped it was over. Sort of put it away in my mind, sir. Thought . . . that's gone now. Bloody awful time. Now we can get on with our lives. Only it's not like that. The job's still out there. Gotta be done.'

The room had become very still. The single lightbulb burning from an old cheap lamp on the table.

'Everyone I talked to about it said . . . isn't it terrible the fighting, the killing – and it was, course it was . . .'

'Sergeant . . .' Blake was about to stop him, but English laid a hand on his shoulder.

'But somehow we did good, sir. We made a difference.' He smiled and shook his head. 'When I was at school, sir, we had one of them really old atlases, with half the bloody world marked pink. And I remember the teacher – silly old bugger, he was – saying . . . "Look at that, Brock. Half the world is pink – and the other half is jungle. The British have reclaimed it and civilised it." ' He shifted on the chair and rubbed a hand across his eyes. 'I know it's not really like that. I've been around a bit, travelled and that. But the teacher was right in one way. It is jungle out there. And if you don't reclaim some of it – then people get killed and the animals take over. And that's why I wanted to come. Don't know why I'm telling you all this.'

'There's no harm.' Blake didn't move. 'Talk if you want.'

'Before I joined the Army, I was a bit of a thug. Maybe you knew that. Went to some of the football matches, beat up a few people. Boredom I suppose. Never got caught though. Nearly was . . . but I always got away. Mum made me join the Army and I thought, OK . . . could be a laugh. Beat up a few people and get paid for it. Been a bit like that, hasn't it?' He grinned. 'I don't regret any of it. And when I go to sleep I don't see the faces of the people who died. I see the ones we saved. And that's not a bad thing, is it?'

English removed his pipe. 'Brock's right. But we wouldn't have come back if it hadn't been for you. That's not bull, my friend, or sentimental claptrap. We're a team and we'll do the bloody job.'

Tillier got up and boiled a saucepan on the tiny electric ring. He spooned instant coffee into the mugs. Funny, he said, how you can get hooked on lousy coffee. The ritual. Cup in hand. Finger up bum. Mind all over the place.

'We're all going to leave the Army when this is over,' he said quietly. 'We talked about it on the way out. You didn't have to say anything. We know what's got to be done. I've got a wife back in England. So's John.' He nodded to English. 'But if necessary we'll do what has to be done. Take all the risks. Like Brock said . . . has to be done.' He took a sip of coffee and grinned. 'Bloody awful isn't it? Just the way Mum used to make it.' And then the smile was gone and he looked hard at Blake. 'We're quite prepared not to go home at all. If that's what it takes.'

He got up. They followed him with their eyes but didn't speak.

'Just wanted you to know, sir. That's all.'

Chapter Nineteen

Three hundred yards away, Jimmy McIlvane watched the lights go out in the camp at Dare Bombol.

'You saw? You saw?'

Kiro stood next to him in the forest, Kiro the ugly, he called him, with the brand new army-surplus uniform, boots polished, blacking on his face, silly fucker all round, trying to be a soldier.

'I come with you,' he'd said. 'You show me, Jimmy. You're the expert.'

So they had gone up there, soon after nightfall. Stolen an old Zastava with Macedonian plates, joined the traffic. Kiro had brought with him a captain called Dimitar, aged about thirty, nervous and sullen. Jimmy knew the type. He wouldn't like being hauled along to see how a foreigner did it. Professional pride. The man was sweating a lot, said nothing and Jimmy knew better than to ask. You can't ever be certain what kind of baggage a soldier carries in his head, so you leave it alone, unless he wants to tell you. That was the rule.

They had pulled the car off the road and Jimmy had covered most of it with branches. The map told him they had a three-mile walk, but the map had been drawn by someone who'd never done it. Five miles, he reckoned. No paths. No signposts. Just the compass and your instincts. A map never saved anyone's life.

So they had crawled and climbed northwards up into the hills, the long way round, because you never knew what precautions they would take. Except that this was the UN – and they were short of soldiers, short of equipment. Half an army for half the time. Biggest joke in the Balkans. Some said . . . the only joke. It was clear they'd be badly protected.

All the way up there Kiro had moaned. 'This dirty route, Jimmy. We go another way, no?'

'No.'

'Why?'

'Because I say so.' In his head, he added the words . . . pompous, useless prick. The time would come when he'd say them. For now he'd just get on with it. 'You hire me to do a job, we do it my way. Understood?'

But Kiro had only puffed and panted and said nothing. Not even to the captain.

Doesn't he ever speak?' Jimmy had asked Kiro.

'He speaks when I tell him.' They had stood for a moment in the clearing, catching their breath. 'And right now I don't tell him. He's made many mistakes. I not pleased with him. Not pleased at all.'

Jimmy looked at the man. Despite the climb, his face seemed cold. Cold and sweaty. Sick. Deep inside. It was too dark to see the eyes, but they didn't make contact. He wasn't engaged, wasn't motivated.

From his rucksack Jimmy took a bottle of water and gulped down a mouthful. Kiro grabbed it from him and did the same, but made no move to pass it to the captain.

Jimmy pointed a finger. 'Give him some.'

Kiro shook his head. 'I don't feed dogs.'

'Fucking give him some. Otherwise he'll dehydrate and slow us down. Got it? It's like cars . . . you don't fill up the tank, they don't go – uh?'

Kiro threw the bottle to the ground, watching as the man grasped it, fumbling it to his mouth, drinking greedily. Without a word he handed it back to Jimmy. The eyes held for a moment, long enough for Jimmy to read the fear. Something in this man was terrified. But he didn't know why – and no one was going to tell him.

As he looked down at the camp, through the trees, he couldn't help admiring the British Army. Everything so quiet and ordered you'd think it was a bloody school parade. All the routines observed. Vehicles bumper to bumper. Kit stowed and covered. Discipline in the details. 'Hundred and ten fucking per cent, McIlvane.' He could still hear the voice of the sergeant, bellowing into his ear, a thousand miles away in a place called Aldershot, three or four lives ago, when he had joined.

And he'd learned it – and been grateful for it. Had it shoved down his throat on every rain-sodden parade ground from Hong Kong Island to Berlin to Yemen, where the blood flowed more freely than the sweat. Good times, they'd been, for a while. Only ever for a while.

Hadn't been the Army's fault, Jimmy had gone freelance. He just couldn't stay civil long enough to hold down the job. And that too, had set the pattern with every job and every command.

In the end he would piss them all off, and the time would arrive when he'd need to move on.

One day, of course, there wouldn't be any armies left to employ him. And then what? Maybe he'd do it for them – and put a bullet in his own head.

Better that, than to give some public-school thug the satisfaction, because he was too old and too tired to go on running . . .

Don't think so much, he told himself. Just get on with it.

When the lights went out in the camp he had stayed very still, puzzled by the distant sound of creaking metal. For a while, he couldn't place it, couldn't work it out. In the end he picked out the boy in the night-sights, tiny thing in baggy trousers, like a rag-doll, drumming and swinging, swinging and drumming . . .

'What the hell . . . ?' Kiro's pungent aftershave arrived downwind.

'Just a kid.'

'What's he doing there?'

'How the fuck should I know? Want me to go down and ask?' Kiro got stupider as the night wore on.

'How much longer we have to stay?'

'Till I see what I have to see.'

'You very difficult man, Jimmy. Very difficult.'

'Then call off the wedding.' Jimmy grinned. 'Just pay for the honeymoon.'

He settled himself on his front on the damp ground, oblivious to the discomfort, watching for something he'd missed, something that could trip him in the darkness.

An hour later, they changed the guard. One a.m. A dog began barking far away down the hillside. He could feel moisture oozing down his face so he knew the slow winter drizzle had started again. If you listened hard it was like the sound of tiny footsteps over the leaves.

He looked over his shoulder but couldn't see the captain or Kiro. They were probably sheltering and arguing. Their problem, Jimmy. This is yours. The camp and how to blow it up – nothing else.

Another hour, he thought. You could already see the patterns. The blank spots. All too easy to go in and lay explosives. Near to the generator. Near to the dormitories, around the vehicles. Three men, he reckoned. And ten lucky minutes. It was all you'd need.

And if it looked easy – you knew that it wasn't. You would have to find the closed-circuit cameras. Find the dogs. Take them out quickly and quietly – anyone who got in the way.

And then he heard the scuffling beside him. A shout, the sound of running . . .

'What the fucking . . . ?'

And Jimmy could move so quickly when he had to. Fast turnaround on all fours, back into the cover of the trees. Voices, a shout – more scuffling. Jesus. And almost automatically he was reaching for the gun that he knew he didn't have. Kiro had it. That was it. Kiro had insisted. He was the only one armed.

On his feet now, was Jimmy, sliding ahead, seeing by the moon, from tree to tree. Shadow to shadow.

Nothing.

He scuffed his leg on a rock . . . but Jimmy doesn't cry out. Jimmy doesn't feel pain. Just the sense that it's all going wrong.

And then the moon half-exits the clouds, and twenty yards away he can see them on the ground. Kiro above the captain, pinning his arms with his fat knees, the fist rising and falling time and again, in the damp forest, middle of the night, where it makes no sense of any kind.

Jimmy lunges at Kiro, pulls him off. 'What's the matter with you . . . ?'

'Don't need to answer to you.' He points downwards at the squirming face . . . Jimmy can see the blood, bubbling up, meaning that he's probably coughing it – and that's a bad sign. One of the many. But that one is really bad.

'Leave him. He needs a doctor. Now.'

'He tried to escape. Tomorrow he faces trial. But he tried to escape . . . so guilty.' Kiro was panting out the words. 'I kill him for that.'

'What's he done?'

'He traitor. Who cares what he's done?'

'How d'you know?'

'He warned a Macedonian family – a very bad man – that we were looking for him. He very corrupt, cheated us out of many millions. This pig warned him before we got there. He's gone. No one knows where. A traitor, see . . .' Kiro got off and smiled. And then a thought seemed to strike him.

'You kill him Jimmy. I'm the commanding officer. You kill him. It is . . . sentence of the court.'

'You can't do this Kiro.'

'I am commander. I do what I wish.'

'He gets a trial, man. Everyone gets a trial.'

'I just tried him. Here in the wood. I tried him and he's guilty. Verdict's in.'

'Procedures, Kiro. Fucking procedures . . .'

And Kiro is taking the Beretta 9mm from his waistband. 'I said . . . you do it Jimmy.'

'Bollocks, I don't kill people like this.'

'Take the gun, Jimmy. Take it . . .'

'Don't be stupid. I'm going back.'

As he turns away he can hear it, the round sliding, spring-loaded, into the breech, and the finger of fear, like an old, old enemy walking over him. And he knows, the way Jimmy always knows, that the train has begun to move and something quite unstoppable is on its way . . .

'Jimmy.' Kiro's shriek coming at him out of the trees.

Walk. Fucking walk Jimmy. Don't turn round. Only he won't let himself go on. Swinging round, he can see Kiro, the gun pointed at the captain's head, two shapes cast and joined by the moonlight.

Too late, Jimmy. Years too late.

And he watches the scarecrow figure shudder in the impact, falling lifeless away, with the lines severed, control gone, snatched away by the dark.

Say it Jimmy.

But from this point on there are no warnings, no shouts, no entreaties of any kind.

Death by murder. Death by injustice.

And Jimmy has seen it with his own eyes.

How many have you seen? The men going down, the women crying and scattering, children caught in crossfire. How many Jimmy? And why does this one so upset you? What's the difference between the killing you do, and the killing you saw?

Jimmy McIlvane turns away and walks down the hillside, through the trees, back to the car, carrying the questions with him.

'What's the difference between you and me Jimmy?'

'I'll tell you, you miserable shit. I kill – as part of a job. It's a distressing job. A sad job. I'm a sad human being, got

105

it? Known that for a long time. Sad and sorry. But what I do is for a cause. Maybe not mine, but it's someone's cause. Who's to say if it's right or wrong? They pay me to do the dirty work – and I do it. Quickly, cleanly. If there's a reason – or if I have no choice.'

Kiro had started to clap.

'But you – you fucking do it for kicks, to show what a big guy you are, in your flashy kit, with the badges on the wrong way round. You think you're such a professional. I've seen more professionalism from circus animals. You're a coward who can pull a trigger . . .'

'And you, Jimmy. You're a coward who can't.'

Kiro sat in the car and pointed the gun at Jimmy's head.

'When you've done the job, Mr Jimmy, get out of here – quickly. Very quickly. I might remember some of the things you have said. And sometimes when I remember, I get angry.' The lazy, overweight voice, seemed to slow to a standstill. 'Then I not very nice to be around. You got me?'

Jimmy stared into the darkness and said nothing.

Chapter Twenty

Sergio woke him when it was still dark.

'What is it little fellow?'

'Morning, Tom.'

'Doesn't look like it.' There was no sky to see through the dirty window pane and the pre-dawn cold had seeped into the sleeping bag alongside him.

'Visitor, Tom.' The dark eyes gleamed at him.

'Who?'

'Don't know. Lady!'

'Lady! You must be joking. Why didn't someone come and tell me?'

'I come.'

'Jesus, Sergio . . .' And then he smiled at the boy. 'You might as well run the bloody camp. No one else is. Where is she?'

'Outside. Swings.'

She was standing with her back to him, huddled in a blue parka, looking out over the camp, watching the early routine swing into action, the soldiers' drill. But he instantly recognized the blonde hair and couldn't help the involuntary jolt.

'Miss Lang?'

She turned round, startled. 'Colonel Blake, I . . .' The head inclined to the left. He could see fresh colour in the cheeks. 'I came to say I was sorry.'

'For what?'

'For being obnoxious the other day, out by the border. I

107

behaved like Miss High School Reporter on first assignment. Worst of the worst. I apologise . . .'

He couldn't help smiling. 'Do you always apologise this early in the morning?'

She returned the smile, but the colour stayed where it was. 'Mostly I don't need to.' She bit into her bottom lip. 'At least in the mornings.'

'Can I offer you breakfast?'

'Is it edible?'

Leading her into the makeshift mess was like showing off your first girlfriend at school, he thought, watching the heads turn, the muttered comments of appreciation. Standard female entrance into male-dominated world.

She took a tray, heaping it with eggs and sausages – a bowl of porridge.

They sat at the end of a long bench. English and Tillier made a point of leaving them alone.

He watched her wiggle out of the parka, and survey the plate in front of her.

'So this is what keeps the British Army afloat.'

He grinned. 'This is what's sinking it. Who knows the battles we might have won if they'd improved the food?'

'You look pretty fit.'

He glanced up, surprised by the cheeky expression, the raised eyebrows, daring him to react. There was a sense of fun in Geralyn Lang. That much was already apparent.

'Where's the camera crew today? I thought you people were chained together for life.'

'We divorced.' She gulped a mouthful of egg. 'I wanted to make peace with you by myself. They'll meet me in an hour or so. Besides, they were tired. We were out late last night by the border . . .'

'How did it look?'

'Quiet. Deceptively so. Too many people falling over themselves to tell us . . . we're here to assist a neighbour – a friend – that kind of thing . . .'

'What do you think they're waiting for?'

108

'Hey, wait a minute.' She pushed away the plate and finished her mouthful. 'I'm the one asking the questions.'

He laughed aloud.

'No, I mean it . . .' She shook her head, still smiling. 'What do *you* think they're waiting for?'

'I think they're waiting for the West to throw them out.'

'And will the West do that?'

'Is this a private conversation we're having?'

Again the raised eyebrows. 'Very.'

'No, is the plain answer. The West can't even agree which plastic bag to piss in. This place has been bought and sold.'

'How do you know that?'

'I know the way they operate.'

English laid a hand on his shoulder and bent down close to his ear.

'Signal just in. Think you should see this.'

He got up. 'Would you excuse me for a moment?'

His concern seemed to have communicated itself to her.

'What is it?'

'Be right back.'

Inside the radio room, he read the message through twice and handed it back.

'This is from the US base, Echo 81, right?'

'Yes sir.'

'Damn.' He turned to English. 'John, we have to get moving. Get the boys on the road. I'll take the helicopter up and have a look. Meet you along the road.'

'Right.'

He ran back into the mess. A buzzer had gone off in the courtyard. The last of the men was clearing the room. Geralyn Lang was standing up, pulling on the parka.

'We have to go.' He put a hand to her shoulder. 'I'm sorry. I wish there was time to stay and talk.'

'What is it?'

'Not sure. Movements near the border.'

'I'll come with you.'

'You can't . . .'

109

'Listen, just a moment.' And her own hand fastened over his. 'I think I should. Really. It's important.'

Odd, he reflected later, that you could punctuate a time of panic and action with a moment of intimacy. But that's what she did.

If she had told him it was the people's right to know, or that he had a duty to the press, or any crap of that kind, he'd have walked her to the gate.

But she had said simply – intimately – that she thought it was important. And he couldn't deny that.

As she strapped herself in, he told her the little he knew.

'Seems to have turned nasty. They've moved into a village called Trajica, about ten miles inside the border, started herding the people into groups at gunpoint – by religion, we think. They've brought in some buses. We may be seeing some kind of ethnic cleansing going on. Can't afford to wait on this one.'

The Puma shuddered into the wind and he glanced back again to see her removing a tiny Hi-8 camera from her parka.

'You've thought of everything.'

She touched his shoulder, readily, easily, as if the precedent had been established.

'Not by a long chalk, Colonel.'

Beside him, Blake could see the pilot, checking dials, pretending he hadn't heard.

It was good that Charley and Veronica had gone out for the day. So Sarah had time to herself, to lie in the bath, and imagine the evening with Peter Hensham.

When the water went cold she ran the hot tap again and travelled the full range of options.

She wouldn't turn up.

She *would* turn up – but she'd tell him the date was off.

They'd go out, have dinner and she'd leave early.

And then the other one . . . he'd kiss her in the car, and she wouldn't get home until very, very late.

She lay for a long time, under the warm water, playing with the bubbles, thinking of that one.

While she dressed, she told herself to grow up. Married women – the kind she knew – didn't do THAT sort of thing. Only she could name the ones who did.

As for the rest? Well, the rest were good Army types, at home with G & T in one hand and a bloody bazooka in the other, dehumanised, desensitised, marching the kids to school through the rubble, luxuriating in cordite as if it were Chanel No 5, loving every goddam minute as the fighting man's female appendage.

She thought of them all as she dressed. Sarah Jones, putting the kids to bed with Milly, Molly Mandy, born ready-indoctrinated into the right wing of the Tory party; Philippa Carr, driving her Morris Minor as if it were a hockey stick; Belinda Farley, loud and awful, still behaving like the bloody Brigadier's spoilt daughter, instead of the Captain's wife.

What a team! And how would they be spending Saturday night, while the *chaps* were off on their patriotic duty?

One would be on the phone with daddy, asking him to write a cheque so that she'd feel better. Another would cry half the night into a sherry bottle, not really knowing why; and the third, she well knew, would lie down in her dressing gown, open the little bedside drawer, take out the long, pink piece of plastic, and drive herself to distraction – because no one else ever had.

And she, Sarah Blake, wasn't going to join that lot. She would bloody well go out and have some fun.

She went to the chest of drawers and chose the skimpy black panties from the bottom of the pile. That said something didn't it? Hadn't worn them in a decade.

The clock on the wall showed 10 a.m., so there was a whole day to decide what else to wear. She giggled to herself. Assuming she *would* wear something else.

'There it is . . .'

Blake could see the farming village of Trajica in the distance. 'Take her round to the north and come in across the hills. They might just think it's one of theirs if we arrive from that direction.'

The pilot made a face. A gale had come up from the mountains and the helicopter wasn't enjoying it.

'I'm gonna turn her into the wind. Bit difficult to manoeuvre. Not a bad idea to take off the side panels. We won't get battered so much.'

Between them they wrenched back the doors and the pilot began a wide arc to the north. 'Hate to mention this, but our speed isn't that great. We're a bloody big target, if they want to use and abuse us.'

Blake nodded. 'Just once. Fast as you like. But I have to see it.'

He turned back to Geralyn. 'Want to get out?'

Her eye never left the camera viewfinder. 'Bullshit.' He could see her smiling, teeth chattering in the wind. 'But thanks anyway.'

The clouds were low as they turned in south, the mountains behind them. Far below, Blake could see convoys of military transporters, backed up on the Serb side of the border, manned and in formation. Through binoculars, he picked out fresh gun emplacements – anti-aircraft mostly, but there was field artillery as well – very little of it hidden from view. This was not an army expecting major resistance. No sign of air support. No forward helicopter patrols.

It was like a kid on his first date – feeling his way up the girl's leg, waiting for her to brush him aside, gearing up for the second advance.

A mile ahead, he could make out Trajica – a series of fields and farm buildings, flat country, with the Vardar flowing by to the east, tall trees along the banks, acacia bushes – gentle arable land, inhabited by gentle people. At least it had been.

'I'm going in about two hundred feet.'

Blake raised his thumb.

Involuntarily he curled forward, as if to present a smaller target. The helicopter banked abruptly and he saw Geralyn Lang shift position, the camera still to her eye.

Over the fields now – first of the farm buildings. His eyes scanned left and right. Nothing. A crossroads. The rail-track. Where for Christ's sake were the people? Another few seconds and they'd be through and out.

'You'll have to go in again, lower. Over there towards the silo.' He pointed to a modern aluminium structure.

The pilot shook his head. 'You didn't hear it, did you?'

'What?'

'Someone took a few shots at us from the ground.'

'I didn't see anyone.'

'Wouldn't be a good idea . . .'

'We have to take a look . . .'

In the driving wind, the helicopter banked again, lower this time. The cold seemed to batter them like a stick.

Slower now as they approached the silo. Probably grain storage. No sign of anyone. No bloody sign . . .

It was Geralyn Lang who saw it first, jabbing him in the shoulder, pointing down to the western end of the structure. And then he saw it too. A door had opened and a figure was running out, young, long hair – Jesus, a girl – faster now, streaking across the field, running the way only the desperate can run . . . but now there were two men in the scene, fifteen, twenty yards behind her . . .

'Get down there, man.'

He could see the pilot stamp on the foot pedals, changing the thrust of the tail rotor, swinging the machine around.

One of the men had crouched on the ground, gun in hand, right arm stretched forward . . .

The other turned towards the helicopter, calmly took a rifle from his shoulder.

'We have to get out of here . . .' the pilot was shouting.

'Wait!'

'There's no time.' He jammed the pitch column forward, dipping the nose, building speed.

'Jesus Christ.'

He could see it even as they had turned into the wind. Saw the girl go down – a little, stick figure in the grass now, the man still kneeling, right arm pointed forward. You can't just turn away. Can't leave it. Can't pretend it's not happening.

'Christ, dammit!

'We have to go back.' Blake turned in the seat, struggling to see below.

'We're unarmed, sir. And we have a civilian on board.' The voice was suddenly very quiet.

Blake nodded.

'Get our controllers on the radio. Find out the position of the patrol. We'll rendezvous with them.'

Silence, except for the wind. And inside his head he could see the scene again and again – the girl's dash from the barn, the men who had gunned her down. God alone knew how many others were there.

Five minutes later, they circled the small British convoy and landed beside it.

So absorbed was he that Blake had not even looked behind him to the rear seat. Only when he climbed out, did he see the cold, frightened face of Geralyn Lang, smeared by tears, crying silently and out of control.

Chapter Twenty-one

Sarah arrived early at the station, angry for doing so, half-hoping he wouldn't come at all. She walked back down the main streets, staring disinterestedly at the shops, but they were closing – and she caught sight of her reflection in the windows, awkward and nervous. Too tarty in the short black dress, too much make-up. Everyone's little bimbo. She should never have said yes.

Only she hadn't. Had she?

He'd said it for her.

As she walked, the streets emptied around her. Only the pubs were open. Maybe they could just have a quick drink and leave it there.

She pictured herself, walking home disappointed, to a night with the television.

No, she'd bloody well go out and have a good time. And then she'd push him away if he started anything. She walked on purposefully, mind made up.

Even so it was a scary feeling. When you were twenty, she reasoned, you kissed everyone, and it meant nothing.

At thirty-eight, though, with two kids and a husband – you didn't kiss anyone, unless it meant *something*. And if you took that route, as an Army wife, you could be heading for outer darkness. Any leak would mean instant banishment from the regimental coffee mornings. Ritual shunning at the parades. No Christmas card from the padre. An end to Sunday sherries in the officers' mess. The full range of punitive sanctions.

Of course it wasn't her fault that Peter Hensham had been the best lover of all. Urgent, intense. Bright and warm, like a clear summer's day. It wasn't Tom's fault that he'd always been more of a wet afternoon – something to get through and dry off as quickly as you could. But she couldn't help recalling the difference. Not anymore.

Heading back to the station she was undecided whether it would be worse to be touched or not touched.

After all, if it was over with Tom, why not?

If.

'Sarah.'

She turned suddenly in surprise. Surely he'd come by train – wasn't that the reason people met at stations?

But no – as she looked beyond him, she saw the shiny, pencil-shaped Jaguar parked by the station entrance. And she knew it was his.

Two kisses, like tiny heartbeats, on the same cheek.

Style, Peter Hensham.

'Shall we go then?'

'I . . . Maybe we should just go and have a drink. There's a pub down the road.'

'Let's just have a drink at the restaurant.'

'Peter . . .'

'You look wonderful, Sarah . . .' And the hand had led her over to the car, and she didn't want to make a scene, she wanted an evening out. Nothing more. A meal. A drive in the Jag. Surely that wasn't too much to ask!

They took the country road to Farnham, and Sarah couldn't help luxuriating in the drive, the tight leather interior, the long bonnet, with the engine singing and whining, couldn't help remembering what a girlfriend had said about a man with a Jag all those years ago. 'Might as well ride on his dick. It'll come to the same thing.'

'Why are you smiling?'

Peter didn't miss anything.

'Just a distant memory.'

'I like those too.'

As he changed gear his hand diverted briefly to touch hers.

Just reassurance, she thought. Don't read too much into it.

Only the hand stayed where it was.

Blake almost lifted Geralyn out of the helicopter. She wiped her eyes.

'I'm sorry. I'm really sorry.'

'Don't be. You saw something horrendous. Everyone reacts the same way.'

English saluted. Tillier, Brock stood by the convoy. There were no longer just the Saracens they'd had in Bosnia. These were the latest Warrior armoured cars, with the additional protective plating. More important to Blake were the 30mm Rarden cannons capable of firing high-explosive and armour-piercing shells up to about two thousand metres. Six of them, in the white UN colours, pulled up by the side of the road. He had asked for them specially. Each had been equipped with the Hughes Chain gun, which fired 7.62mm linked-ball ammunition.

Defensive, they'd said in London. Best defensive weapon in the business.

Bloody nonsense, he'd thought. These were wagons, meant for travelling. You didn't circle them and sit in the middle while the enemy shot your balls off. You went out in pursuit, stuck the cannon up his arse, and blasted the shit out of him. That's what the Warrior was for.

Blake glanced round the faces. They had to move quickly.

'Sergeant Brock, please arrange for Miss Lang to be escorted back to Skopje.'

'Colonel . . .'

'I'm sorry, Miss Lang. The tour ends here.'

'I deserve to see the outcome, after what we witnessed.'

'Probably. But not this time. I'm sorry.'

'What are you going to do?'

'Get there as fast as we can.' He turned and started to walk towards the Warrior, then seemed to change his mind.

'I'm sorry Geralyn. Really. Talk to you when we get back. Sergeant . . .'

Brock held out his hand, leading her towards a Land-Rover.

He looked at English. 'Let's get moving.'

They cut engines, a half-mile from Trajica. Three men in khaki fatigues crossed into the fields, smoothly, silently, keeping close to the ground. The light had worsened and Blake could see a mist moving south towards them from the mountains. It would give them cover.

'No other UN personnel in the area. I checked.' Tillier got down from the Warrior. 'Give it five minutes, sir.'

'We can't afford to give it any longer. They murdered a woman in full view of us, not caring whether we saw it or not.'

He peered down the road, but the metal silo was out of sight, about 500 yards from the bend. Around them clung the stillness of a late winter afternoon; the country felt damp and sad.

For a moment, they stood silent, listening.

'Odd.' Blake shivered involuntarily. 'No sign of anyone. The American report said buses, troops. Where the hell are they? Too bloody silent.'

'Want me to ask the Yanks?' Tillier picked up the microphone, but Blake's hand covered it instantly.

'I don't want anyone knowing we're here until we've cleared the sector.' He raised an eyebrow. 'For obvious reasons.'

And then the radio bleeped into life inside the Warrior.

Tillier disappeared for a moment inside the machine, emerging seconds later. 'Recce team, sir. They've been right up the side of the thing, couldn't penetrate, but they've got listening gear, and there are definitely voices. Child crying. Man's voice. Seemed to be telling them to shut up. They don't know what to make of it.'

'Right Captain. Let's have the platoon. You and I'll go in. John . . .?'

English nodded.

'If we get into trouble, bring in the Warriors.'

'Why don't *I* lead on this one?'

Blake grinned. 'You'd show me up.' He patted English's shoulder. 'You do the next one.'

The mist had thickened perceptibly as they moved across the fields. Fast and quiet. This team. The one's he'd asked for. Brock and Tillier and the seven or eight others who would always keep their mouth shut. Because they wanted to do it.

And whatever uniform you wear, he thought, this is why you join. To crawl across a soggy, pissed-on field, when you're wet and cold, and target for a hostile gun. You can tell yourself later it's the cause. When you're back at the club, looking at it through a crystal glass of Scotch. But when you're down there, it's something else. Your own will to survive and win. No one in their right minds would do the stupid, bloody job for someone else. You do it for yourself.

Two fields away now, and he could see the silo. Grey, ordinary – lousy place to . . .

One side entrance and a main loading door . . . that's what the recce team had said. No windows.

Get in further. What the hell were they doing in there? Waiting? No busing, no killing.

And then they heard the single shot. Was it? The first moment of denial. Tell yourself you got it wrong. Tell yourself there was nothing. Dead sound, thick. Another. Jesus. Then two more, muffled, but shockingly audible from inside the silo.

Blake doesn't remember giving the order to go. Just recalls the headlong, animal stampede across the fields. The recce team, armed and positioned by the side door – two flattened against the wall, one already kicking it in.

Decisions are out of your hands now. You're into

119

reflexes. And some very stark questions. Are you quick enough, clever enough? Can you shoot straighter . . . ?

Fifty yards away, he sees three men – as if blown out of the loading entrance, scattering wildly, dashing headlong towards the mist . . .

Down you go.

Blake sinking to one knee, Browning Hi-Power in his hand. The killing machine of choice. Favourite among Her Majesty's best, hired to gun people down on Saturday afternoons in foreign fields.

The three men at the edge of his vision.

'I'll get 'em . . .' Tillier and a corporal giving chase.

'Get down!'

And in the instant they dropped, his finger tightened on the trigger, and the gun spat into action. Choosing the dead. All by itself.

Chapter Twenty-two

She was wrong about the kiss. He didn't kiss her after dinner.

He kissed her before.

'Engine's not quite right . . .' as he pulled into a lay-by and for about three seconds she believed him, until his mouth crossed the tiny distance between them and pinned itself to hers.

'God, Peter!'

'Been a long time, Sarah.'

'There was no need to swallow me. I'd have come quietly.' She giggled. 'I didn't mean that.'

To cover her embarrassment, she wound down the window and let the cold air flood in.

'Dear God . . .' and she still didn't know whether to be pleased or upset. It was just funny the way you remembered people's mouths. All so different. And she really hadn't kissed anyone's for so long.

'I take it we *are* going to have some dinner, somewhere . . .'

He switched the engine on again and she settled back, inhaling deeply, watching the long bonnet ease itself into the Saturday night traffic.

Riding on his dick, indeed.

The kiss had been nice. But she didn't want to make a decision on *that* one. Not tonight.

★

There is always silence when you've killed. Or maybe there isn't. Maybe it just feels as though there should be.

Tom Blake got up off his knee, and slipped the safety catch back on the Browning.

Tillier was there, beside him. In that moment so were English and Brock.

'Everyone inside is fine, Tom. Not a single one injured or hurt.'

'What?' He spun round, the disbelief searing across his face. 'I don't get it. We heard the shooting for Christ's sake!'

English shook his head. 'I don't get it either. The only ones dead are the ones you shot. Makes no sense at all.'

'What about the girl I saw from the helicopter?'

'No trace. Everyone accounted for.'

'And the men who ran out?'

'Unarmed. Doesn't seem to be any reason. We'd better talk to the villagers and straighten this out.'

As he turned round again they were coming out of the barn. An old woman emerged with a sergeant's arm around her, weeping silently, a blanket spread across her shoulders.

Did I dream the shootings. What in the name of God went on here?

And there were those with the blank faces he remembered so well from Bosnia. The light still shone in the eyes, but the owners no longer lived there. Faced with terror, the minds had simply fled to a corner or a backwater, or a shadow from where they might or might not return. You never knew.

Around them all, the mist was drawing in, cutting off the rest of the world.

I don't believe this. Any of it.

The exhilaration of the chase had gone. Now there was just the clearing up. Not like a party – piling the plates and glasses. Here, you cleared up the people who'd attended.

And then as he watched, Blake saw a figure walking towards them across the fields.

His hand moved to the gun . . .

Brock's voice right beside him. 'UN sir. Don't know where they came from. Russian commander – Norwegian troops. Just this moment came through on the radio, otherwise we'd have started shooting holes in the buggers.'

Blake stood where he was, aware that his men had formed a semicircle around him.

'Colonel Blake?'

The words thrown at him across the field. Only now he could see the light blue beret.

'You are?'

The shape acquired a face, but it wasn't smiling, wasn't open for greetings.

'Colonel Yevgeny Luzhkov. United Nations . . .'

'Ah yes. So nice that we're all on the same side.'

'Are we?' The Russian halted a few feet in front of him, and looked around at the activity. A big man, built solid like a hillside.

'What happened here?'

'We're investigating that.'

'My impressions are not good.'

Blake noticed two of the Norwegian soldiers had fallen in beside their commander. The guns pointed to the ground, but they were held ready, not at ease. This wasn't a friendly visit.

He exchanged a glance with English. The major had reached the same conclusion.

'If you'll forgive me, Colonel . . .' Blake's smile was like thin ice. 'We have work to do here.'

'You're aware, Colonel, of the Rules of Engagement.'

'I'm aware that it's none of your business.'

'On the contrary, Colonel. I am mandated by the Security Council, to monitor observance of those rules by our forces.'

'Since when?'

'Three days ago.'

'My answer's the same, Colonel Luzhkov. I have work to do. If you'll excuse me . . .'

'I shall be making my own report on this incident.'

Blake smiled. 'You must have seen a lot of it through the mist.'

'Enough.'

'Then you're indeed a remarkable man, Colonel. Good day . . .'

'My men will be examining the bodies.'

Blake's hand tightened on the Browning. 'The hell they will. Not unless you return with written authorisation from the Security Council. Clear?'

The Russian opened his mouth, but closed it again without speaking. The movement seemed to indicate he had taken a decision.

Dinner was the culinary event she had expected. Salmon in pastry, artichokes and mushrooms, caressed by sauces she hadn't tasted and couldn't make, exciting the tongue, melting one into another.

No hurry as she looked round the panelled dining room of the country hotel, candlelight against the faces, conversation for couples only, soft and whispered.

The whole room seemed to be indulging in foreplay – batting eyelids, moist lips, touching fingers.

For a moment she wanted to laugh. It wasn't a licenced restaurant, as the sign proclaimed. It was a licenced clip joint. Come dessert and half the men would be groping the stockinged legs beneath the tables. There wouldn't be a dry crotch in the house.

Dear oh dear, she thought. Am I too old for all this? And then she looked over to Peter. I'm not too old at all, she told herself. In fact . . .

He refilled her glass from the sweating bottle in the ice bucket.

'I notice you're not refusing a top-up.'

'Should I?'

'Of course not. Just seems you've changed.'

'To be honest, Peter, I don't know who the hell I am these

days. I did. I was wife, mother, and I picked up the clothes from the bathroom floor. That defined me. Now I'm having dinner in . . .' she looked round and smiled . . . 'a whorehouse that just happens to serve food.' She smiled. 'And I love it. So you tell me who I am.'

He got up. 'Will you excuse me a moment?'

Sarah nodded, watching him walk out of frame, resting her head on her elbows, letting the wine take care of the doubts.

Had she been running her hand along his thigh, the way some women in the room were behaving, she might have felt the pager vibrating on his belt, might have worried, might have suspected that life was about to sit up and bite the evening in the arse. But she didn't . . .

Nor did she know that Peter Hensham went out and telephoned the Secretary of State for Defence at home – who told him in uncompromising terms to 'propel' himself back to London. A report from Macedonia was 'burning holes in bums' from Brussels to Brooklyn. And he had better have some constructive suggestions.

Christ! The first fucking evening in decades when he could have had some warmth and some fun – and it was all being carted off to hell.

Why?

Because of Sarah's bloody husband.

The four of them sat in his makeshift bedroom at Dare Bombol. Testimony and papers on the trestle table between them.

Tillier got up. Since he spoke Serbo-Croat, he had done most of the interviews with the villagers.

'This is the story, the way it was given to me. Apparently Serbs came along late afternoon, told everyone they were being evacuated for their safety. Buses would be there in a while. They could come back the next day. But for now there were terrorists in the area. Meanwhile they should wait in the silo. All lovey, lovey. Nothing to worry about. Besides it was raining and they could do with the shelter.'

'Just three Serbs?'

'Yes – but, the villagers all say they had radio contact with another unit. They were told what to do. Told to sit tight, until late afternoon.'

'And then?'

'And then it made no sense. They were told by radio to empty their weapons in the air, leave them and get moving. Never mind about the villagers. Just leave the guns and get out of there.'

'I don't understand.' Brock shivered in the draught.

'Seems they were ordered to rush out and be killed.'

'But why?'

'To set us up.' It was English who spoke. 'I'm afraid that's what it looks like. Bit too convenient, the whole thing, with the Russian officer just happening to be there.'

'But how could they have known we'd be in the area? What about the Americans? They made the original call. So they must have spotted something.'

English stared straight at him. 'They didn't make the call. They've checked their records and they can't find one. Someone made the call for them.'

He got up and walked to the door. 'This was an arranged marriage. We were meant to shoot them. And the UN was meant to see it happen.' He raised an eyebrow. 'We've been had.'

An hour later Tom Blake made the call from the camp at Dare Bombol, using the satellite phone, hearing the familiar tones of the Aldershot exchange.

Someone had told him once that families give you strength and support in times of trouble – and he supposed this was one of them.

The day I killed three men.

It was Veronica who answered.

'Dad, what are you doing, calling . . . ?'

'I'm in the room next door . . .'

'Don't tease me like that . . . how are you? I was worried, all the reports. When are you going to be on television?'

He tried to laugh. 'Don't know.'

'Well make it soon. I told my friends to watch out for you.'

Watch out for the man who kills.

'How's Charley?'

'Gone to the rugby match.'

Life in monosyllables.

'Everything OK, love?'

'When are you coming home?'

'Soon as I can. Definitely before Christmas.'

Soldier's diary, he thought. Everything you really want to do is three months away.

'Will you be back for my concert?'

'I'll try.'

'I'm playing the Chopin you like.'

'That's great, love.'

You don't have any idea what your dad did today . . .

'Is your mum there?'

'She's out.'

Ah! Different tone of voice. Not a simple answer, that one.

'All right love, take care. I'll call again soon.'

'Don't worry, Dad.'

Strange thing to say.

'Bye.'

'Bye.'

For a few moments Blake sat quite still in the room, wondering what he felt about Sarah's night out.

When you set it against the rest of the day, it hardly seemed worthy of note.

Besides, if he were being totally honest, he wasn't sure if it mattered or not.

Chapter Twenty-three

'Peter . . . what's going on?'

'I told you.' He slammed the car into first, letting the car scream out into the darkened country. 'There's some sort of flap in London. They beeped me while I was in the bathroom.'

'But what? Why won't you tell me something?'

'I don't know myself, really. For Christ's sake Sarah, you of all people should understand. After all you're a . . .'

'Go on, say it . . .'

'I'm sorry. I didn't mean that. I'm really sorry.' He offered his hand in the half-lit cockpit, but she didn't take it.

' "An Army wife . . ." That's what you were going to say. Wasn't it? Well you're damned right I'm an Army wife. So just drop me here and I'll get back in my box. After all I've had my five minutes out, even got half a dinner, this time. Of course I didn't get the regulation, rapid-fire fuck, so I suppose it must be serious. But thanks, Peter. Thanks for putting it all in context.'

'Sarah . . . I . . .'

'Just stop the car.'

'I can't. It's the middle of nowhere. I'm taking you home.'

'I don't want you to.'

They didn't speak for the next forty minutes, well past the signs for Aldershot, time for her to cry a little in silence, and then 'pull herself together'.

It's the training, she thought. You get used to the

128

disappointments, rammed down your throat. Stupid to think that this time might have been . . .

Might have been what?

'Don't drive right up. Stop here.'

'Sarah, I'm so sorry. I'll call you as soon as I find out what's going on.'

'Don't.'

He leaned across, trying to take her hand. 'We have something . . . you and I. Still. Even after all the years.'

'If that was something, I don't want it.'

'Won't be like that, I promise.'

'Go Peter. Goodbye.'

She turned and walked away, trying hard to find the kind of medium-happy face that the children would expect from her.

Veronica was right there in the hall as she opened the door, waiting, it seemed, scalpel in hand.

'Dad called.'

First incision.

'How is he?'

'Tired. There was something on the news – an American report. Seems there's been some killing.'

'Go to bed, darling.'

'Did you have a nice evening?'

Second incision. Deeper.

'No, not really.'

Hensham went straight to the Minister's flat. Amesbury was a little overdressed, he thought – yellow cardigan, check shirt with cravat, dark corduroys. Preened and combed. There was something effeminate about the fellow, that he hadn't noticed before.

Probably a dirty old man, thought Hensham. Or once was. Or wanted to be.

And yet he was very controlled. He wasn't the type to let a few, nasty little peccadilloes ruin a career.

He would play with people out in the open – figuratively

129

of course – and get his kicks that way. Set them up, then turn on them. If he couldn't bugger them, he'd knife them instead.

You would have to be oh so careful with Amesbury.

'Come in, come in. Sorry to ruin your evening.'

Bollocks. Hensham could see it was the only pleasure the man derived.

He waited for Amesbury to speak.

'Don't have much more than what I told you on the phone. Report's started fucking up everyone's Saturday in New York. All the politicians torn out of their mistresses' arms. And accusations flying that Blake went over the top. Shot down three men in cold blood, another one in the foot. Literally. And everyone wants him out.'

He gestured Hensham towards a rickety Queen Anne chair. The flat was spotless, but the air was stale and old.

'What's Blake reported?'

'The bare bones, as I told you. He's still debriefing some of the hostages. Trouble started because the UN had a Russian monitoring team in the area. Apparently the commander's screaming that Blake's a dangerous killer. He's also trying to rake up stuff about Bosnia.'

'I mentioned that might be a problem . . .'

Hensham could see the raised eyebrow across the desk and he knew he'd made a mistake.

'I'm buggered if the Russians are going to dictate who commands our forces. Besides the PM wants Blake there. Is that understood?'

The minister picked up the crystal glass on the desk beside him and sipped the whisky. 'Let's be quite clear about this – Blake is a peacekeeper. I want some peace from him. I want him there. I want him on television – the symbol of our concern and our commitment. And leave it at that. A symbol, Peter. Nothing less. And certainly nothing more. Bodies and peacekeepers don't go together.'

'And if it's too late?'

'We won't think along those lines, just now.' Amesbury

stood up. 'Bottle it and get rid of it. I want Blake out there trumpeting the effectiveness of our operation . . .'

'While the Serbs take whole villages hostage . . .'

'He shot dead three unarmed men. There'll be no more shootings.' The voice was very quiet.

'The whole thing stinks.'

There are times when the truth just stands there and looks you up and down.

Amesbury turned and led the way to the front door. 'Get out there, Peter. Warn him. There are no more chances on this one.'

They didn't shake hands and Hensham was glad to get back into the cold.

For a while he sat in the car, looking up at the window, seeing the occasional shadow as Amesbury moved around the flat.

The man couldn't have it both ways. Couldn't sell the country to the Serbs and still claim Britain was protecting it.

He didn't give a fuck about Blake, but the policy – if that's what it was – would flush them all down the nearest drain.

'Don't do that to me again, Dmitry. Don't ever set up my man again. You understand?'

'Believe me, my friend. It was a mistake. The local commanders, you know how it is – everyone on edge. They went too far. People are nervous.'

'It was a deliberate attempt to compromise my officer.'

'I give you my word it won't happen again.'

Amesbury could hear a rustle on the line from Moscow. It was as if the wind were blowing through an open window. About as transient as Dmitry's word.

'We have given instructions that everything is to be cooled down, my friend. Politically, it is going just as we planned. Serb deputies are stirring up support in the parliament, business is being encouraged between the two communities . . .'

Amesbury had a vision of a Serb businessman holding a

gun to the head of his new-found partner, and making him an irresistible offer.

'I'm so pleased to hear that.'

'So don't worry my friend. Quiet and peaceful from now on.' The smile oozed all the way from Moscow.

'I'm grateful for your assurances.'

'Goodnight my friend. Don't forget my grouse.'

'As if I would.'

Amesbury replaced the receiver.

If Dmitry didn't keep his word, there'd be a lot more shooting than just a bloody grouse.

Chapter Twenty-four

The rain had set in along the hillside where Kiro had established headquarters. Once a hunting lodge for the Communist Party bosses, it was now, Jimmy decided, a pigsty. A pigsty full of weapons – and a pigsty full of pigs.

Three days since the boys had gone in and seized the place from its current tenants – a collection of tired, Orthodox priests who had been using it as a rest home. Terrified their gold watches and Western cars would be stolen, they had fled without even token resistance, muttering prayers and crossing themselves in an outbreak of unseemly panic.

Now, the lodge served as the training ground for the special hit teams, and it was clear why Kiro had chosen it. A sheer drop on two sides to the valley, and a single access road through rough, open country. All along the track, army units had dug in at regular intervals, but close to the house the fortifications were even more impressive. Armoured cars, bunkers, ringed by sandbags, artillery positions – and four T-62 tanks. The old Russian warhorses, now under new management.

Under Jimmy's direction they had planned the hit with unaccustomed professional zeal, building a mock-up of the UN camp – the perimeter fence, the main buildings within. 'You fucking do this properly,' he had told the blank, uncomprehending faces, 'or we're not doing it at all.'

The team was a ragbag. He knew it, they knew it. A little crew of lorry drivers and farmers, who'd spent their

Saturday nights beating each other up in bars and roadside cafés and now did it in uniform.

Some were cunning but totally impractical. They stood silhouetted in doorways offering themselves to be shot.

Others were quicker on their feet – but couldn't remember the group they were in: who was clearance, who was support?

Then came the linguistic crisis. They had to practise the codenames in English – simple words, chosen by Jimmy for ease of pronunciation. At least he thought they were. But half the time he couldn't understand what they said back to him. So in the end it grew to resemble a children's game. The operation was called 'dog'. The objective was 'cat'. Blake was 'sheep'.

And Jimmy didn't know whether to beat their skulls in or carry their satchels.

In the end he decided there were four who would make it. Tall, hard bastards, they were. But quick and agile. And motivated, although he had no idea why. They could memorise the drills, they were quiet. And they seemed to want to kill, without a thought for their victims. No baggage inside the head. Baggage on your back, or in your hands. The mind free to press the button.

But where were the crack units? he had asked Kiro. Where were the special forces from the old Yugoslav army, the men who had trained Libyans and Syrians, and all manner of the so-called non-aligned during the Cold War?

And Kiro had shrugged.

He had what he had.

They had told him the commando units were needed elsewhere. He wasn't going to get them. End of story.

It would be, they insisted, 'a slice of cake!'

In the end, of course, the training improved them all.

They responded well when you shouted at them, threatened them, told them you'd go after their mothers and sisters, and axe their little brothers, if they didn't get their miserable fucking act together.

134

And that was the language they understood.

Jimmy had heard that in some East European armies – like the Russian – commanders were expected to 'lose' a few men in the cause of discipline.

If not lose, then 'waste' them, simply to enforce the diktat from above.

The reasoning was that if you shot people, you were serious. If you patted them on the back and upped their rations, you were a fool.

He well remembered watching the Polish army impose martial law back in the early 80s. They had kept the ranks so cold, and so hungry, that they had no inclination at all to question orders. Either they sat by braziers on the street corners, trying desperately to keep warm. Or they did as they were told, as fast as possible, in the hope of a better meal.

When Jimmy cut the rations, things started to happen.

And Kiro loved it.

Fat as two pigs himself, he relished the spectacle of his subordinates suffering hunger pains, and would clap his hands with delight, as a miserly ration of bread and biscuits was handed round to the disgruntled men.

But they got the message.

Jimmy made sure of that. If you were going to mount an operation – even with donkeys – you made sure that the donkeys could take the weight.

The dress rehearsal had gone well.

Eight of them, cutting into the perimeter fence, dropping two guards, running quiet and like hell itself to the dormitory buildings, and then down the rows with silenced bullets, picking them off as you went.

Of course the cardboard cutouts didn't shoot back, didn't have ears, hadn't been trained by the British Army, but Jimmy didn't dwell on that.

There'd be plenty of time to shit themselves later on. Jimmy surveyed the estate and concluded they had thought of most things. A makeshift helicopter pad for supplies.

Commanding views. Rough, difficult terrain. Standard military encampment. And when you thought about it, nothing much had changed over a thousand years of military tradition.

To control an area, you found yourself a high place, sat on it and fired at anyone who came near. They weren't that stupid, after all.

For a while he watched the fat, puffy clouds slither across the sky. From here, he guessed, the old Party slobs would have ridden out on their placid, Valium-fed horses, to shoot boar or deer, already tethered to the trees to make sure no one missed.

Kiro was simply a man in the Party mould. When the time was right he too would roll out of here and claim his prize, only returning for the occasional weekend of relaxation or debauchery. Or both.

Jimmy had seen it happen the world over. From Glasgow to Yemen to the Northwest Frontier and the heartland of Asia. The slobs always got what they came for.

And they always used people like him.

'Well, Mr Jimmy, you like my place?'

He didn't turn round immediately, didn't want to acknowledge Kiro as the man giving the orders.

But even as the Serb approached, Jimmy could see the anger in his face. The eyes were pinched, resentful. The face flushed despite the cold wind.

Kiro clenched his teeth and put his fist against Jimmy's ear.

'What's the matter Kiro – haven't killed anyone today?'

The fist withdrew a foot and slammed into the side of Jimmy's head, but Jimmy stood his ground.

'Maybe I kill you, then.' Kiro's fat body shook from the effort of the punch.

'Not a chance, mate.'

'You piss me off, Jimmy.'

'Oh yeah.'

'You piss me off, something bad.'

'I can walk out of here any fucking time . . .'

'You walk – and I kill you, Jimmy. Promise. No joke.'

The pain in Jimmy's head began to dissipate. He wanted to rub his temple but he wouldn't give Kiro the satisfaction. The man's mood was even lousier than normal. Something had gone badly wrong.

'When am I supposed to hit the camp?'

'Don't ask questions. I tell you when, got it?'

Jimmy grinned. 'So we do it when you get the go-ahead, huh?'

'Fuck you! I don't need go-ahead.'

'So let's do it.'

'I swear it Jimmy, I fucking kill you!' And then as his fist rose again, the anger seemed quite suddenly to disappear. Kiro, the little boy, was standing there. Kiro who wanted to be friends. Kiro who hadn't been allowed to go out and play.

Jimmy had seen Kiros before. Men like guard dogs. Half the time they didn't know whether to bite your legs off or jump up and lick your face. Animals.

'Listen. I'm sorry about your face, Jimmy. We have drink. OK?' He patted the Scotsman's battered features. 'We go inside.'

They took the stairs to Kiro's quarters. A large bed dominated a room the size of a swimming pool. Dirty clothes lay all around it. Rugs had been dotted across the bare boards. Empty bottles, mostly broken, were stacked in the fireplace. The smell was terrible.

'Tell you what, Jimmy. You want a woman?'

Jimmy shook his head.

'I got some coming here tonight.'

'Party, huh?'

Kiro opened the window and took a couple of beer bottles from the window sill – nature's fridge.

'You know my problem . . .' He slithered onto a rug at the end of the bed and gestured for Jimmy to do the same. 'Belgrade is my problem. The bastards there, who say to

me: "Go here Kiro, make a war here, do some shooting."
Then "Stop Kiro, keep it quiet Kiro, don't make a fuss.
Leave it to us. This is big. This is international. We handle
all that. You pull the trigger when we say . . . OK?" '

Kiro unscrewed the beer bottle with filthy fingers. 'Now
they tell me: "Wait" – and you know what I tell *them*? I tell
them . . . *you* fucking wait. I was chosen to take over here,
in a week. One week, huh? One week and Kiro to be in
charge. Administrator. Nice name, huh? So they got no
right telling me to wait.'

'What do your friends tell you?'

'Friends? You kidding, Jimmy. You think I discuss it
with anyone here? Why you think I tell you?' He laughed
and took a mouthful of beer. Outside Jimmy could see the
clouds darken. By nightfall there'd be a full-scale storm.

Kiro leaned against the bed. 'You can trust no one in my
position. My commanders? All of them belong to Belgrade.
They watch me – I watch them. From time to time I make
some examples. Shoot one – like the guy in the forest. Or I
beat someone up. Understand me, Jimmy - this is
necessary. Otherwise . . .' His hand described a circle in
the air. 'Otherwise they try to fuck with Kiro. It's true.' The
head nodded for emphasis. 'This I know.'

They drank for a while in silence and Jimmy knew there
was more to come. Kiro wasn't a deep man. But he could see
the different emotions flashing across his face, like surges of
lightning – scowls, grimaces, even some tears. The full Slav
repertoire was being rehearsed in silence.

At dusk he got up.

'I tell you Jimmy, I'm an unhappy man today.'

Jimmy said nothing.

'This is personal now. Before, it was war. My country.
My nation. But now is personal.'

'Why?'

'One of my brothers. Dusan – younger brother. He was
shot yesterday. I heard this morning.'

Jimmy nodded, but he wouldn't commiserate.

'Shot by a fucking UN bastard.' The tears began their descent down the pock-marked slopes of Kiro's face. 'He wasn't even armed. Shot down by pig in blue hat.'

A warning sign appeared in front of Jimmy's eyes. 'What was the commander's name?'

'Who cares what his name. I kill him first of all. Me – Kiro. I do it with my hands.'

'And then the camp?'

'Yes, my friend.' And suddenly the old Kiro was back. And the eyes were dark and pinched, and the jaw set in concrete. 'His name is Blake. Fucker from England. Where you come from.'

Jimmy didn't move. Not a muscle. But his mind was working fast – and in turmoil.

Chapter Twenty-five

It was after two a.m. when Hensham rang her. The voice was slow and tired but he knew she wasn't sleeping. She would be busy regretting the evening; regretting the smart dress, the washed hair and all the trouble of 'icing the cake', as she used to call it. And she didn't want to speak to him.

'You're pushing your luck, Peter. Can't you afford a watch.'

'I need to talk.'

'Done that, thank you. Goodbye.'

'Wait Sarah. I'm flying in to Skopje tomorrow.'

And her silence had been the open door he had wanted.

Just over an hour later, with the first lights in the sky, beyond the even rows of Aldershot chimneys, he walked up the garden path and knocked on the door.

'This is the last time, Peter. Anyone'd think you were bloody Father Christmas, the hours you keep.'

He noticed she was fully dressed this time. There wasn't going to be any peeking inside the bathrobe. Sarah was not in the mood.

She led him into the kitchen and shut the door carefully.

'Why are you going?'

'Been some trouble. Three Serbs shot . . .'

'So?'

'People are making a fuss about it.'

She had been about to make coffee, but she changed her mind. 'Talk Peter. You didn't come here to lament a few bodies. What happened?'

He looked around the kitchen. On the wall were some old children's pictures, a handful of school pictures, a couple of holiday souvenirs, mugs and stickers. No one got rich in the army, killing for their country.

'Seems Tom might have shot them.'

'That's what he's there for. He's a bloody soldier isn't he?'

'Not when he wears the blue beret. He's a peacekeeper. Peacekeepers aren't supposed to shoot people. We're funny like that.'

Sarah sniffed and sat down on a stool. 'If that's what he did – he had his reasons. I have plenty of quarrels with Tom but the way he did his job wasn't one of them. He always went the extra mile – you know that.'

Hensham looked at the cups on the dresser and smiled. 'Am I going to get that coffee?'

Her expression softened, and she boiled the water, not looking at him, spooning the instant coffee, fetching the milk from the fridge.

'I should really be the one to apologise to you.' She came back and perched on the stool. 'Flouncing off up the street . . . Haven't done that since school, when mum told me I couldn't go to the dance. I'm sorry, Peter. I really wasn't expecting lights and an orchestra, I just thought this would be one evening – where I was the one that mattered most. It was stupid and selfish . . .'

'Sarah, you . . .'

'I'm lonely, you see. Bloody lonely. And when I look back I've been lonely for years. All the broken nights, broken weeks, broken months. And they don't mend, that's the awful thing. They don't come back again. It's time lost. Because when you see each other, you can't just pretend there hasn't been this huge gap in your lives – when you've done things and he's done things – and you haven't done anything together. Christ, Peter!' She picked up the coffee cup and replaced it without drinking. 'So what do you do? You try to get to know each other all over again. And just when that has a chance of working – he goes away.'

She stopped for a moment and the neon light began buzzing over the sink, and the kitchen clock ticked on regardless as if nothing she'd said made any difference.

'Anyway you didn't want to hear all this.'

'Yes I did. I told you I'd come back.'

She smiled and pushed his cup between them as if to erect a small safety barrier. 'Don't be nice to me Peter. I might behave badly. Just drink your coffee. The children are upstairs . . .'

'Are they asleep?'

'Yes . . . and so am I, practically.'

He took two sips of coffee. 'I'll leave you then . . .' But he stayed where he was. And suddenly, it seemed the clock was counting down, not just ticking into the future.

'Well then . . .' She pursed her lips.

'Right. OK.'

'You alright to drive?'

'No.'

She grinned. 'Yes you are. I've only given you coffee.'

He got down off the chair and walked one and a half steps to stand with his body touching hers. Knees touching, her breasts against his chest. His hands on her arms. And slowly the lights come on, in the silence of the kitchen, with the clock and the buzzing neon light.

First the kiss on the hair as he bent her head towards him, then the head, then the cheek. Three kisses because God, they say, loves the Trinity.

Only God has nothing to do here.

Her mouth was half open. Lips moist and fresh like a flower after the rain. No waiting time with Sarah. No warm-ups. If she wanted you, then you knew about it.

'Can we go somewhere else?'

'No! I told you – the children are upstairs.'

'So?'

'Just kiss me.'

And as he kisses her, his hands are slipping under her pullover, under the blue denim shirt, up the stomach with the inverted tummy button, inch by inch, everything to climb for, just the way it used to be, the soft wall of her breast, the weight balanced in his hands, full, fashioned – and the nipples larger and harder, and more urgent against him . . .

'You have to stop, Peter.'

'I can't.'

'Not with the children here.'

'But . . .'

He moves back an inch, but his hands are still under her shirt.

'Peter. Not here. Not in this house. I can't and I shouldn't.'

He pulls away and stands there.

'When you come back.' Her face is flushed and her breathing is coming like hooves on a racetrack.

He can see she's crossed the line.

'When I come back then.'

'Yes. I promise.'

They didn't speak again, both thinking it would have been better if she hadn't turned it into a promise.

Promises were like privileges, he thought, as he drove back to London. Like rights. Like agreements.

They had a habit of being withdrawn.

Chapter Twenty-six

Blake faced the reporters and cameras – and knew he had to lie to them with total and unshakeable conviction. They deserved nothing less – and nothing less would do the job. And yet he couldn't help searching the faces for Geralyn Lang – for the warm spot.

Most of the journalists he remembered from Bosnia. The gold-diggers, the bullet-dodgers, the pundits who knew it all.

To them you were just a door they would pass through. You opened easily or else they battered until you did.

You made copy – or you possessed no value.

Of course there were exceptions, but Blake knew better than to treat them as friends.

He had mastered the eight-second soundbite; he could show passion and anger; he sometimes gave them the pictures they wanted. So they came to him.

But they weren't interested in the truth, so what the hell did it matter if he lied?

He had to for Christ's sake.

'This is what happened.' He stared out into the television lights, unable to focus on anyone at all. 'I'll say it once and then we have to get out on patrol.

'All forty villagers from Trajica were herded into a barn, and guarded by three plainclothes soldiers – possibly security agents. We don't yet know their identity . . .'

Clear, concise. Keep it that way.

'Four-forty-two, we heard shooting from the barn. We

hurried to investigate. As we approached, three men in battle fatigues emerged, firing wildly. We were forced to fire in self-defence. Any loss of life is regrettable to a peace-keeping force. In this instance we had no choice.'

'You could have fired low.' The voice sounded Australian.

'I could have.' Blake tried not to let the contempt show. 'But people who are hit low can go on firing. I made the determination to take them out, based on our rules of engagement. Self-defence. The regulations are quite clear.'

'What weapons were they firing?'

'Machine pistols. Two of them. The third had an AK47 assault rifle.'

Lie. Go on. More.

'These weapons are standard issue to the Serbian army.'

'You said you heard shooting in the barn – but no one was hurt. Were you mistaken?'

Was I?

'No. But so far I'm at a loss to explain the shooting. The villagers have told us the men were given an order by radio and began firing at the roof. I've no explanation for this.'

'What about reports that you saw a lady shot down when you were patrolling by helicopter.'

'Perfectly true.'

'You could have imagined that too, couldn't you?' And now he could place the voice. Not Australian. But the sanctimonious whine of south London.

He was about to answer, when he saw the blonde hair move and heard the voice at the same time.

'He didn't imagine it. I saw it too.'

Geralyn Lang emerged from the sidelines, like the US cavalry, he thought. Just in time.

They had other things on their mind than guarding Jimmy that night. When dusk came they sat him in the kitchens with the men who had killed a sheep, and were going to cook it for the party, they said, winking, nodding, jerking their fists up and down.

That kind of party, thought Jimmy.

But his own mind was somewhere else. Why did it have to be Blake commanding the UN? Of all the people in the world. Anyone else and he could have blown the place sky high with not a qualm in the world. Anyone.

But he couldn't kill Blake.

You didn't do that kind of thing. Not even a mercenary – not a gun for hire. Not the little shit with an Armalite rifle and a box of gelignite, sold to the highest bidder. Not me, he thought. Not in a thousand years.

Blake had been his commander. He had deserved his loyalty and got it. He had put him on his back and carried him out of a minefield in Cyprus, with the bullets kicking into the sandy strip, his thigh torn open by shrapnel, and all the world screaming and shouting and dying around him.

And you didn't blow up someone who had done that for you.

Never.

He looked around at the soldiers, wondering what to do next. Some of them would be going into town first. They'd hit the clubs that were still open, the bars and discos, see if they could drum up a little interest, and a little talent. And what they couldn't drum up, they'd drag or buy, or threaten.

It didn't shock Jimmy. He hadn't ever done it himself. But that's what armies did.

'Why not let me come into town with you?'

'Uh?' The captain spoke English like a gorilla. Plenty of feeling, but no vocabulary.

'Me. Town. Tonight.' Jimmy did a passable imitation of the jerking wrist.

But the man shook his head.

'Kiro say no. You stay. We bring for you.' He said something in Serbo-Croat and the others began laughing, chanting and singing a little ditty at his expense, slapping his back.

Jimmy hoped the time would soon come when he could

break all their necks. It would be a distinct pleasure, slamming them first with the butt of a rifle, chopping at the carotid, forcing their heads up their unwashed arseholes, as far as they'd stretch.

Christ, he'd enjoy it when it happened.

But for now he had to get out.

He approached the captain. 'You tell Kiro, Jimmy wants to go into town, or there's no fucking operation tomorrow. Got it?'

The gorilla looked stunned. He stared round the men to see if anyone had understood this outburst.

There was a moment while the brain seemed to engage, but not a lot happened. And then he reached for Jimmy with a hand the size of a bread loaf, and marched him upstairs to the main bedroom.

Kiro had been asleep in his clothes, half on the bed, half off it, his face like a wild garden.

'Fuck you Jimmy. I sleep. Fuck you too,' he told the captain. 'What is it with you pricks?'

'I want to go into town with the others.'

'No. Too dangerous. They see your face, they shoot you. All the UN fuckers around. No way.'

'Then there'll be no operation tomorrow.'

Kiro visibly weighed up his options, sitting up on the bed, lowering his eyes, examining Jimmy, with a view to causing serious damage between his legs.

The captain said something, but it clearly wasn't to Kiro's liking, for he got up without warning, striking the man on the head, and following it quickly with a kick to the crotch at a speed that amazed Jimmy. Kiro was a fat pig. But the pig could move.

From deep down in the captain's throat came a moan of pain, as he slid to his knees on the bare boards.

'The fucker tries to tell me what to do.' Kiro pointed a forefinger at him. 'Me! Kiro. Tells me to be more careful.'

He jerked his head at the fallen gorilla, who raised himself in evident pain, and limped out into the corridor.

'You come with me Jimmy. Uh? We go into town, see what's to find, yuh? You and me.'

In his mind Jimmy checked that Kiro was still at the top of the list – the list of those he would kill with a smile on his face and a light heart, when the opportunity came his way.

'I want to know who set this up. And I want to hit them.' Blake had gathered them in his room straight after the press conference.

'So get out tonight. Go in civvies. Hit the restaurants and bars: find out what you can. If I were you, try the girlie bars – shouldn't be a hardship. Put some money around. I want the whispers. I want to know who's the warlord calling the shots round here. Hell of a performance they staged in Trajica. If we don't hit back, they'll screw us again, badly.'

'Do we go armed?' English put away the pipe.

'Not this time. If there are any fights, try to avoid them. The weapons could be a disadvantage in a crowd. I'd come with you – but my face might not be a help. A lot of them see Western television on satellite.'

When he came out into the courtyard he could see Geralyn Lang had stayed behind. She was standing by the swings, pushing Sergio, as he battered his drum, and the sun slunk away over the hills.

'Is this woman a nuisance to you?' He smiled at the boy, but then came close to her, laying a hand on her shoulder. 'Thanks for coming to my rescue back there.'

'I have a small confession.'

'Oh?'

'The film I shot from the helicopter didn't come out. What did I tell you about a kid reporter on first assignment?'

'That's OK.'

'No, it's not.' She picked up a stick and threw it into the woods.

Blake watched her. 'How did I do, back there?'

'You did good, colonel.'

'Tom.'

148

'Colonel Tom.' She grinned.

He liked the way she played with him. In the distance the boy began wailing and singing – the little voice of southern Europe, an endless, wandering lyric full of different sounds and rhythms.

'Was it true?' The question thumped him in the stomach, winding him, with the force of surprise.

He breathed deeply. 'Why do you ask?'

'You asked me . . .'

'I meant . . . did it look OK, that's all . . .'

'It looked fine. Very precise. No room for doubt of any kind. I didn't mean that I doubted *you*. It was just such an extraordinary thing. Almost as if they came out wanting to be shot.'

Relax, Tom. Get the breathing back under control.

'I just keep thinking there has to be more to it.'

'If you find out what it is – let me know.'

They took it in turns to push the boy. After a while Blake chased him round the courtyard, missing him each time, watching him scamper away into the forest.

'You're too fast, Sergio.'

The boy smiled. 'You too slow.' And then his eyes took on another look, as they walked back to the swing.

'You like her, Tom?' The tone was conspiratorial. Sergio knew about such things.

'Of course I do.'

He broke away and ran up to her. 'Hey miss – he in love with you, you know that? Tom in love.'

'God, Sergio, you . . .'

He could feel himself blushing, his own cheeks giving him away.

She just stood there, grinning, the blonde hair swept back, the skin perfect, her clothes hugging her, the way he would have wanted to himself – close about her hips and breasts, close to straining, but well within the bounds of taste. She was obvious if you were watching – but not blatant.

149

They sat on the single bench. Imperceptibly Sergio's drumbeat had altered into a new more complex rhythm.

'You have kids, Tom?'

'Two. Boy and girl.'

'Does a wife go with them . . . ?'

'She did.'

'I'm sorry, I didn't mean to ask.'

He grinned. 'Yes you did. What about you?'

'I have a friend back in Washington. Had – is a better word. We don't see each other too much these days. I think he's too well-connected. Too many fancy lunches and power dinners . . .'

'D'you have family . . . ?'

'Not any more. My dad was a helicopter pilot in Vietnam. Did three tours. Loved flying. It was his whole life. When I was seventeen he paid for me to join a club and then taught me to fly as well. Said it was the last gift he could give me.'

'Did you enjoy it?'

'Loved it. Loved the feel of the machine. The way it seemed to break all the rules of aerodynamics. I used to take my friends flying. Made me very popular.'

'I bet.' Blake was about to speak again, but stopped. Her expression had darkened visibly. 'What happened to your father . . . ?'

'He was flying into a tiny airport in Virginia, going to see some friends for the weekend, when he crashed into the woodland near the Shenandoah. Clear-blue sky. Perfect conditions. Nobody shooting at him. No war. I never found out why. The accident investigators said there was nothing wrong with the helicopter . . . and the post mortem showed nothing. But he wouldn't have crashed for no reason, would he?'

'I guess not.'

'I've never flown a helicopter since then. Ridden in one, sure. But never piloted. Just lost the desire . . . Anyway . . .' She looked over to Sergio and seemed to slam the chapter shut. The boy had stopped swinging and was watching them, beating ever faster on the drum.

'He's quite a kid, that one . . .' She waved at him.

'Geralyn, why did you wait behind today?'

'I wanted to talk. I don't know why, Tom.' She shrugged. 'I'll have to go soon. We're going to satellite the piece . . .'

'I'm glad you stayed. There isn't much time to get to know anyone in this kind of situation.'

'Is it lonely?'

'Wrong word really. No time to be lonely. Too many people. Too much going on. But inside, just before you shut your eyes and sleep, there's a part that's lonely. But what the hell – you get used to it.' He stood up. 'I'll take you back into town if you want. Grand Hotel?'

She nodded. 'Thanks . . . you know I just wanted to say . . .'

'What?'

'I wasn't questioning your account of things back there. I'm just amazed at it all. Please don't think anything else.'

She stood up and the dying sun caught her hair, weaving it with red and gold.

It was impossible to disbelieve her. She was too beautiful. Too finely constructed, too genuine.

And way too good to be true, said a voice deep inside him, that he didn't want to hear.

Chapter Twenty-seven

From the polished confines of his leather armchair, Amesbury looked hard into Blake's face on the television news and knew he was lying.

He smiled to himself. The man did it so well and with such conviction. When the army had finished with him, a career in politics positively beckoned. There were junior ministers by the dozen, as well as the cabinet veterans who would kill for a little of that conviction, that gravitas. That 'bottom', as they used to call it at school – where bottoms had featured so large.

Yes, he told himself. All in all, a satisfactory performance. Of course Blake had gone too far, shot from the hip, or wherever it was one shot from. Only maybe, after all, that hadn't been a bad thing. Just once. Just to tell everyone the Brits couldn't be buggered around.

But now there'd have to be some quiet. Some time for diplomacy and negotiation. That was the way it worked. Conferences in Paris, perhaps. Emergency sessions in Trieste. Black cars entering the UN late at night. It was important to create the aura of negotiation – while all the participants would do would be to get pissed, watch videos and go to sleep.

Because the deal was already done.

Done that sunny day in Geneva by all the great and noble powers.

Signed, sealed – and now at last to be bloody well delivered.

As for Blake, there would be a little carping in the left-wing press about the Trajica incident, but the heavies would leave him alone.

'He's the hero we all wanted,' a newspaper editor had told him, some time back. 'We want to believe in someone who's strong, who gets things done – but hasn't lost touch with the human race in the process. That's your man.'

Bollocks, thought Amesbury. But if that's what people believed, then all to the good.

He was about to switch off the television when he caught an item from Washington and, staring straight out at him, the features of a very Russian minister.

What the hell was Dmitry doing in the States? And why hadn't he known about it?

Christ! The bloody man was standing silk-suited, in camel overcoat beside his Pentagon counterpart, while Harrison Drew, the Secretary of State, coughed out his guts at the edge of the picture, as he always did.

The talk seemed to involve some nonsense about routine co-operation. And Dmitry was smiling his best airline-hostess smile – stroking and ogling the microphone. Any closer, thought Amesbury, and he'd be sucking it off.

'We are co-operating on a broad range of issues. This is a sign of the times. Sign of new understanding between our two countries.'

And what did that mean?

Leaning back in the chair, he couldn't help feeling cheated. It had been like catching sight of your girlfriend, out with another man.

Not that he harboured feelings of that kind for Dmitry. Good God no.

All the same it was galling. Throughout the Cold War the Americans had been playing off one ally against the other, now they were at it again. Like a bloody bedroom farce. Every time you opened a cupboard door, someone was standing there who should have been somewhere else.

Gone was the common interest, the common enemy. The trust that had held everyone together.

Now it might suit them to be friendly this week, but what about the next?

He got up and switched off the television, struck by the complete silence around him. The carriage clock had stopped on the mantelpiece because he'd forgotten to wind it – something the old girl would not have been at all pleased about, if she'd been alive.

Wouldn't have been very pleased about the deal in the Balkans either, he reflected. Not that he would have told her.

And yet it would have been nice to have someone around if the thing went wrong.

And that, he realised, was the reason Dmitry had gone to Washington.

Contingency planning.

Tying up the ends.

Working out who to blame, and who would take responsibility if the cat leaned out of the bag and started to talk.

And he knew exactly who they'd want to blame, did Amesbury.

Chapter Twenty-eight

Tillier and English hunted well together: the young captain with fluent Serbo-Croat, and the older teacher-figure, whose outlook on life came from years of gentle study, interrupted by bouts of extreme violence. The one, he often said, made the other tolerable. You studied man's ideals – and you met him in the places where he fell short. English wasn't interested in trivia.

They began across the river in the Turkish section. Tillier was amazed at the normality of the early evening bustle, the crowds in the main square by the footbridge, the flower sellers huddled by their paraffin lamps, the Vardar, flowing strong and fast beside them.

Another half-hour and they'd lose sight of the hills beyond Skopje. But the presence was there in the dark.

Most of the city was exactly thirty-four years old: devastated by the shattering cruelty of a ten-minute earth-quake in the early sixties, rebuilt without money or art.

Perhaps that was why it went about its business as if there had never been an invasion. Nature had already called and left its card – instant and total destruction, from the blocks of flats, to the kiosks, to the schools and the hospitals, and the pavements you stood on.

The Serbs could do no worse.

They ate dinner in a small restaurant, where a singer in a black sequin dress half-whispered into the microphone, draping her arms across the men who passed by.

Tillier caught her eye for a moment, but she seemed to

toss him aside. The song was all she was paid for. A song and a whisper. If you wanted romance, she seemed to say, then you should choose another time.

When she had finished he went up to her, told her how much he'd enjoyed it. And she looked at him, as if she had heard all the lines like that, and didn't want to hear them again.

But he talked of music and travel, of England, of songs he had learned – and his eyes held hers, instead of dropping to her bosom and her waist, and roaming all over her, the way she expected.

'Bad time,' he said, and she nodded. 'You want a drink?'

Reluctantly she slid over to the table where a glass of red wine arrived to meet her, easing the chatter. In the corner English just went on smiling away, not wishing to interrupt.

And then, quite casually, he asked her if the Serbs ever came out to eat. As she laughed he could feel the eyes of the patrons turning towards him, the conversation trickling away.

'We avoid them, and you want to find them!' She giggled. 'No baby, they don't come here. They don't want to eat and drink and dance like you and me . . . they want . . . uh, who cares?'

She stood up and sang again – but she wouldn't look at him, wouldn't hold his eyes.

After two numbers she stopped quite suddenly, bowed for a moment of applause and walked away as if she had tired of the evening, lost interest in the customers. English paid the bill. It was after ten, but the patrons kept on coming.

Even as they left, their table was occupied by a group in dark grey suits. The war merchants, thought Tillier. Because war is business. War makes money. Even if you blew up the streets and firebombed the shops, the business would flourish. Someone would have to rebuild the street and shops. Someone would smuggle, where once they traded. Countries might fall to their invaders, but business would get up and walk away.

They headed through the dark streets towards the city wall. As they crossed the footbridge, the singer fell into step beside him, a dark leather coat over her dress, the make-up gone. Tillier gasped in surprise.

'Don't go asking more questions.' Her eyes flicked towards him. 'They're all around here. This is the Balkans. Nobody knows who is who. There were some Serbs in the restaurant. I don't know what you do, but if you go on like that you won't be doing much of anything.' She took a quick look behind, as if searching for a companion. 'Go away baby. Go away . . . come back in ten years' time, and buy me champagne.'

She laughed.

They had reached the middle of the bridge, and the noise of the water was loud and urgent beneath the wooden slats.

'Where do they hang out?' Tillier didn't look at her.

'You're crazy. You don't listen to what I say.'

'I listen but I need to find them.'

'Go to the Cosmos, behind the Grand Hotel. Some of them pick up girls there. Now I go. Don't look at me, don't do anything. Just walk on, OK?' She smiled. 'Next time baby, you get a kiss from Marta. That's me. Go!'

'Where can I find you?'

'You crazy boy, you don't find me. And you don't look for me either. And you know something . . .'

'What?'

'You never saw me. OK? Never in your life.'

Kiro had taken three bodyguards with him, but there were others around the city that Jimmy knew nothing about. Others who went out looking for information from their contacts and informers. They listened and paid. Paid and listened.

'Sit the fuck down, Jimmy.'

Inside the Cosmos Kiro was in expansive mood. 'We have wine and champagne – and big plates of pussy.' He howled with laughter. A girl with long black hair straddled his knees, stroking his beard. 'You see how much they like us here, Jimmy. Now, maybe you believe what I say. They wanted us to come, uh?' He cupped the girl's breast inside her small tight costume. 'She wants me to come, too.' And he laughed again, as the disco opened up around them like a cannon, drowning him out.

In the strobe lighting Jimmy could see people moving along the side of the room, shadow-people who lived in the half-light, doing deals and buying people. Others sat still at the tables, the higher ranks, removed from the chaos around them, but ready to advise and persuade if needed.

When the lights came on again he took in the expensive suits, gold watches and chains.

They were the other end of the business. The people who march in just behind the soldiers. The people who stay behind when the soldiers have gone.

A few of them glanced at his battered face. The women glanced and looked away. Others wondered who he had upset. And then they looked at Kiro and didn't wonder anymore.

Jimmy sat very still, knowing he didn't have long. Inside his trouser pocket was a note he had scribbled in the kitchen. The warning to Blake. Now he needed a messenger. A little bird to deliver.

Drinks came. Sweet champagne, warm and frothy. The girl spilt it down her chin and began to giggle.

He leaned over, tapped Kiro on the shoulder and pointed. 'I want one like her!'

'Uh?' Kiro's face split open into a grin. 'You? You even know how to do it Jimmy?'

'I said I wanted one . . .'

Kiro muttered something to the girl on his lap. She called to a friend of hers, a long, lanky woman, short-haired, blonde – no smiles or wiles, a take-me-as-I-am kind of tart, thought Jimmy. She came and stood sullenly by the table as Kiro outlined the deal.

'You want this one?' He dug a hand into his pocket. 'I give you. Birthday present, Jimmy.'

158

'Thanks.'

'You go upstairs with her . . .' He grinned and patted the dark-haired girl with delight. 'Don't forget: you must take off pants first – not after . . .' and he exploded in laughter, shaking himself up and down, slapping the girl on the thigh.

The blonde caught Jimmy's eye, but the expression didn't change. She didn't speak.

Into a corridor now, as she shuffled ahead of him. Bare plaster walls. A staircase – broken glass on the flagstones. A single light bulb – and all the romance you could ever wish for . . .

She pushed open a door at the top of the stairs. Piece of carpet on the floor, an old cushion, patterned and ragged. A sheet rolled up in the corner.

She gestured to his belt and slid the shift over her body. Beneath it she was naked. Cruelly naked, thought Jimmy. Thin, cold, with all the seductive quality of a moonrock. About eighteen, he guessed, and so very far away from the world where the young are supposed to live.

'Speak English?' They stood under the lightbulb. She was totally without inhibition.

'Of course.'

'I don't want sex . . .'

She just stood staring.

'I want you to take a message to someone.'

'Why?'

'Because it's important.'

She sighed as if the word conjured up a memory.

He picked up the dress from the floor where she had dropped it, and she took it from him, slipping it back over her head, but somehow still naked. Jimmy couldn't help thinking of the cold, skeletal body beneath the fabric.

From his pocket, he took the note. 'Do you know the camp at Dare Bombol?'

She nodded.

'Take this. Give it in at the gate. That's all you have to do. Here's the money. Will you do it?'

The head moved imperceptibly.

'Tell me you'll do it.'

'I do it.'

Once she had crossed the footbridge, Marta headed east along the embankment. The crowds were thinning out as the temperature plummeted and at times the wind seemed to claw at the leather coat, catching and scratching. She tightened the silk scarf. About a mile ahead was the row of apartment blocks where she lived, among the cheap, rusted cars and scrawny curtains. Only the church offered hope – the church with the lighted cross.

She shouldn't have looked round.

The glimpse over the shoulder.

The three men thirty yards behind.

She knew they were nothing to do with her, but it made you think, made you nervous.

After all, the country had been invaded. Times weren't normal. People weren't normal. Strange things happened.

She came to the roundabout, crossed into the centre, where the traffic had died.

The streetlights peered down cold and blue.

Look again.

And still they were there.

But that was good. Three strong men. They could help if something happened. If a drunk appeared. Or an attacker. Three men was a good thing.

On the other side of the roundabout she quickened her step. Cold was the wind.

She hummed a little as she went.

Words of a song.

> You my love, man of my dreams.
> You're the one – or so it seemed.

Quicker down the street.

No one there. No one with me. Marta, you're fine. Everything's fine. Why do you worry, why do you fret?

160

Think, think, think. In time to the steps, moving so fast behind.

Past a block now.

And there was the Saviour's symbol.

The church rising up, dead ahead. The cross like a beacon. The light shining out for all to see. Light of the world. Light of my life. Let my cry come unto thee.

No harm could reach her now.

Not by a church.

Not with a cross to guide, and a cross to support.

She turned again. Just a hurried look.

Relief surged inside her.

The men had gone. Gone, of course. Just three men, who were walking home.

Fine, Marta. Fine, fine, fine.

Nearly home. Nearly home.

Footsteps past the church. And she'll walk up the steps, cross herself. Give thanks. Thanks for the safe walk home. For the day tomorrow. For the night that's past.

Up the steps.

Marta and the song.

Marta and the prayer.

Rounding the side. A shiver from the cold.

Late, very late. And she's tired.

Just a short prayer.

One more look behind.

Only this is the one, she shouldn't have done.

For all she sees is the hand. The hand reaching for her neck, the rope in the air. Her head forced upward, upward, eyes towards the cross.

All she sees is the lighted cross, the message of hope and comfort, protection for the weak. The symbol of life everlasting – even as she steps towards it.

Chapter Twenty-nine

When Jimmy sat down he could see who they were.
Not their names or their ranks.

But he knew their origin.

British Army was stamped on the faces. The set of the
jaw. The way they walked. The traces of self-conscious Brit
that no training can erase.

When you'd been one of them, you knew.

'What you want, Jimmy? You don't look happy. Was it
no good for you?'

Leering, Kiro sets down his glass and stands up, taking
the girl by the hand. 'I got my own business. You wait.' He
nods to the bodyguards around him.

In the corner Jimmy can see two girls descending on the
British, bottoms parked with exquisite care on the arms of
their chairs. Plenty of teeth and hands and 'hallo darlings' –
he knows the routine.

In other times he might have strolled over to talk to them
– man to man, soldier to soldier. But he no longer belongs to
their army – and wouldn't want to again. He has sent them a
warning. The most he can do. And with that, the debt is
paid.

Five minutes later and Kiro emerges from the side door,
angry and in a hurry.

He beckons to the guards, who scoop Jimmy between
them, and hurry to the exit.

Something badly wrong.

They assemble in the car park, the cold squeezing down

on them, the city deserted. Kiro paces up and down beside his Toyota Landcruiser, his pride and joy, while they stand in a group – the six or seven of them – watching his anger boil.

And a split-second before it happened Jimmy knew, watching the man dig deep into his tunic, produce a piece of paper – Jimmy's piece of paper – and march towards him, violence in every moment.

He stands in front of Jimmy, and removes his pistol. The guards take a step away. They have watched this scene before.

'You are the most stupid of fuckers, my friend. You know this.' He pushes the paper in Jimmy's face. 'A little warning, huh. Little warning to old friends.' He crumples the paper, smearing it over Jimmy's face, forcing open his mouth, ramming it inside. 'I should kill you for this, Jimmy. You know I can do it, uh?' And, as so often with Kiro, the anger has gone, to be replaced by a controlled determination.

'But you have work to do Jimmy. So I let you work.'

He half-turned. 'And when the work is done, we settle accounts. OK? Yours and mine.'

And the half-turn was for a reason as Kiro shifted weight on the balls of his feet, stepped to the side and delivered a kick straight, hard and powerful into Jimmy's stomach. As the head went down his fist battered the left cheekbone, tearing open the scar tissue, peeling it away in ridges, letting the blood flow freely.

English had noticed how thin she was, the girl with the short blonde hair.

But she looked different now.

She wore a smile and a golden necklace that she hadn't possessed when the evening began.

He bought her a Curaçao cocktail, and began to traverse the chat-up routes. First time in Skopje; cold, cold winter; nice place you have here.

Yes, yes darling. Buy me another drink.

And then after lots of winking, and oh such little strokes of the hand, here and there, he asked if she would be interested in earning some money.

Yes, she said. And the lights seemed to pick out the heavy gold chain around her neck, as it gleamed in the semi-darkness, asking for more.

'We go now,' she smiled.

'We don't go.'

She sipped her drink, waiting for a new suggestion, weighing the angles.

'The big man with the beard, who left just a little while ago . . . who was he?'

And she wasn't in the slightest hesitant or scared, sitting on the arm of the chair, as the nightclub danced around her.

'His name is Kiro.'

'I see.' English looked around. 'And who is Kiro?'

'Serbian commander. Lives in the hills by Tabernovce. He'll be the new administrator in this region.'

English raised an eyebrow, as if only mildly interested. 'Thank you for that, my dear.'

She smiled, the way she must have smiled as a child, playful, innocent, with the years stretching ahead of her like so many summer days.

'You're welcome,' she replied and then giggled. 'He asked me to tell you.'

They drove back in silence to the camp at Dare Bombol, keeping to the side roads, well away from the refugees. To the north, clouds had moved in during the darkness, weeping gently over the countryside. There were isolated farmhouses and tiny smallholdings and when they climbed the hill, they could see the city, left behind in a damp mist that hung immovable, like a sullen mood.

'Marta was right.' Tillier punched the Land-Rover down into second gear. 'You never know who's who in this place. We come in from outside, knowing nothing about the

Balkans. Peacekeeping?' he snorted. 'We don't even know who's fighting. Don't know the friendships, the alliances, the clans, the religions. Nothing. And none of it breaks down the way it should. It's unfathomable. Like a great web, sewn together by centuries of hatred and nationalism – and now torn apart by unbelievable brutality. But which bits fit where? How to put it back together? God alone knows that.'

'So what should we do?'

'Like Brock said . . . you try to reclaim a bit of the jungle. Go into the forest, take down a few of the big trees, and hope the others'll get the idea. That's all you can do . . . oh Jesus!'

He had turned off the main road towards the camp, and now he braked furiously as the headlights picked up a dark shape on the road, a bundle, a bag, a piece of kit, fallen from a truck . .

'What the . . . ?'

They climbed down from the Land-Rover, hit suddenly by the damp coldness of the hillside, but neither moved forward. In the yellow headlights lay an old rug, once patterned, now filthy, rolled and tied with string, as if to be offered for sale.

And yet it was left so exactly in the middle of the road, with the rain coursing beside it among the stones and mud. So carefully positioned.

'God almighty . . .' Tillier moved first.

'Wait.' English stood in his way. 'Could be booby-trapped. We don't know what it is. Give me the torch from inside.'

He took it from Tillier and bent down in the mud peering into the ends – first one, then the other. He was quiet and unemotional, kneeling there as the rain and the cold dug at him.

Opening his coat, he produced a pocket knife and cut the string holding the rug together. And as he unrolled it, they could see first the legs, then the leather jacket, then the face of a woman streaked with lipstick, a cord still round her neck, cutting deep into the skin, where it had killed her.

'Go sit in the car.' English leaned forward and closed the eyes, that were staring into the headlights.

'It's Marta, isn't it?'

'I know. Go sit inside. Only needs one of us.'

Tillier got back into the driver's seat, feeling his hands begin to shake, watching the major go about his business.

He checked the body, searched the pockets and at one point he saw him cleaning her face with his handkerchief, smoothing back the lank, clammy hair. An act so out of place in the aftermath of murder.

In the end he wrapped her in the rug again, lifted the bundle and put it in the back of the Land-Rover.

He slid into the passenger seat. 'Go on, drive.'

'Christ, Major. I can't believe they . . .'

'I said drive. This was for us. They killed her to show what they can do.'

The Land-Rover bumped down the track towards the camp gate. 'We killed her, Major. If I hadn't spoken to her, she'd be alive now.'

English was silent for a moment, staring straight ahead into the darkness.

Chapter Thirty

Blake hadn't meant to break the rules. Not this time.

He had dropped Geralyn Lang at the Grand Hotel, touched her shoulder, shrugged the way soldiers do, at what might have been and could have been – and walked away without so much as a goodnight kiss.

What an idiot!

Left her smile hanging in the lobby while every nerve had screamed at him to hold her tight and refuse to let her go. But he had.

And then he had driven away to a small restaurant nearby, eaten a passable dinner on his own and convinced himself to do the decent thing and return to the camp. Commanding officers don't get nights off, don't go hanging round pretty girls, don't make fools of themselves, where others can see.

His resolve lasted until the city suburbs, where the lights dwindled away out into the country, and the rutted roads disappeared into darkness. He pulled over. Suddenly the thought of a blown-up camp-bed on the floor of an office, and a mug of warm, dark piss, labelled coffee, wasn't so attractive after all – so he turned the car round and headed back to the Grand Hotel, where they tell you the room numbers without question, and you just get into the lift and walk along the corridor and knock at her door.

Bloody hell, is this what I'm really doing?

And she stands there in sweat pants and pullover, the make-up gone, but the face even lovelier without it. Cool and poised, she is, and 'perfect' is the word that comes to mind.

There is no trace of surprise.

'Come in, Tom.'

He falters for a moment. 'Thanks. You don't seem surprised to see me.'

'Should I be?'

'Probably. Am I that obvious?'

He sits on the bed and she pours him a whisky from a duty-free bottle.

The room smells of her, the indent of her head is on the pillow. Her clothes and belts and shoes lie in some kind of disordered pattern around the room. There's a jewel box, a purse, a radio. She has not travelled light. But this is Geralyn's place. At home to visitors. Come after midnight, stay till dawn . . .

But it doesn't say that at all.

It's a young, high-powered professional lady. And this is her temporary home. And if it's beautiful, then it's because she is.

She sits down on the bed beside him, one leg crossed.

'Tom.'

It's a voice that's going to want answers.

'Think about what you want.'

'How do you mean?'

'Do you want a journey or a stop-over?'

'I'm sorry . . .'

'Listen Tom, I've had it with stop-overs. And I'm sick of being like Christmas – coming once a year. Now I want to know there's something to go to. A road to travel – and not just by myself. Think about it, please. I know you've just ended one journey, so you may not want to start another. But that's where I'm headed.'

'I hear what you say.'

'But . . . ?'

'But nothing. You've given me something to think about.'

'Maybe you didn't want that.'

'Time I did, Geralyn.'

She stood up. 'I wasn't looking for instant answers.'

'I feel I've just been sprayed from the hillside by a very accurate machine gun.' He grinned.

'I'll take that as a compliment.'

'Goodnight, Geralyn.'

She closed the door behind him and smiled.

If she had let him into bed, she reasoned, she could have held him, caressed him, owned him, maybe for the night – but not much longer. Not a man like Tom Blake.

Let him stay outside the door a little longer.

And then, given time, she would end up possessing him completely.

Before getting into bed, she made a call to Washington, recited the lines of a poem to a silent recording machine, then fell asleep.

The evening had not prepared him for Marta's body, for the empty pallor of her face as the medical officer explored the ending of her life.

'Not a great mystery,' he declared. 'The rope marks round the neck pretty much tell it. Unfortunately . . .' he made a face, 'there was quite a bit of work on her before they finished. Want the details?'

'Spare me.' Blake turned away and went back outside, glad of the sudden chill of dawn.

The little boy stood waiting for him, ragged blue trousers flapping in the cold, a single tear frozen to his cheek.

'I see her come in, Tom.'

'Don't think about it.'

'Makes me think about my daddy. I not see him. Not after men came to our village.'

'I know.'

'You think he look the same as her?'

'No Sergio. Here . . .' and on impulse he bent down and

169

picked the boy up, staggered by the lightness of him, hugging the little shape against his shoulder. 'Don't think about that. You have to think about the future.'

'What is the future?'

'I don't know.'

'Where I go?'

'I don't know that either.'

'So how I think about future?'

Blake set the boy down and put an arm round his shoulders. 'One day – soon, I hope – the war will end. And you and your mother will return to your village. That's what I'm working for. That's why I'm here.'

In the darkness the big black eyes were wide open, watching him.

'I'll do my best for you, Sergio. I promise. I'll do what I can.'

'Where you think my daddy gone?'

'Somewhere better.'

The boy smiled. 'That's OK then, uh? That's OK.'

Blake watched him go off back to his mother's room. Then he climbed the stairs to the camp-bed, in the cold bare office that looked out over the hillside.

He had an image of the man who had killed Marta – an image of the man who had killed Sergio's father.

One day soon he would meet him and return the favour.

Chapter Thirty-one

Next morning they ferried Sergio into town in the back of a UN Land-Rover, as they did most days when he 'went about his business'.

They dropped him at the grey, concrete shopping centre behind the Grand Hotel, his drum in his hand and his blue, baggy trousers flapping in the breeze, and he waved them goodbye till they were out of sight.

Someone had lent him a parka, but he refused to wear it – said he didn't feel the cold.

And yet on the bitterest of days his teeth would chatter, the nose would run, and the wind could squeeze tears from those sharp, black eyes.

His one concession to comfort was a rolled newspaper which he carried beneath his pullover, and as he reached his normal corner, between a jeweller's and a shoe shop, he pulled it out and sat crosslegged on it – and began to ply the business of the day.

When his hands were cold, it took a few minutes to bring forth the rhythms, but in a little while he was tapping and flicking the drum, crooning high-pitched, tremulous notes, and the covered walkway echoed to the bittersweet Romany music, to the culture of a thousand wanderers, and a little boy on a winter morning.

A few of the passers-by dropped money at his feet. Pennies, mostly, and among them a couple of near-worthless, worn-out notes. But after an hour he reckoned he had bought his tea-break – the entry ticket to the café three doors down, where he would solemnly purchase a hot, creamy mug of chocolate, counting the money out onto the kitchen table, while discussing the world's most pressing problems with Darka, the waitress.

It was a comfortable daily ritual, and when there was nothing else to be done he would buy himself two cups in the morning and afternoon, and then wait for the ride home. Business had its ups and downs, he reckoned. Some weeks would inevitably be better than others.

And yet, what he really looked for each day was the busker's jackpot – a benefactor. More often than not, it would be a lady, passing by, unable to ignore the plight of a tiny victim, or an old man, who kept 'thousands' under his mattress, and had a conscience about a long-lost son, a conscience Sergio found all too easy to trigger.

If treated right, such people would take him gently by the arm, sit him in the café and order him plates stacked with food, cakes by the truckload, drinks till he could drink no more, and pocket money delivered with solemn instructions that it be spent only on a coat or shoes.

These were the people he watched out for. After all, he told himself, there was little point in being cold and bedraggled if no one took notice.

Only this morning, it seemed, no one did.

After an hour of penny-dropping, Sergio thought he was ready for a major performance. As he played the drum his eyes gazed trance-like to the ceiling, tears tumbled onto his cheeks, and he moaned and shuddered a little, as if lost in the grip of some unimaginable trauma.

There was, of course, only so long he could keep it up. And Sergio, having contrived to froth a little at the mouth, was fast running out of additions to his act.

In desperation he opened his eyes again, only to find a lady with short blonde hair and pale, cold skin, kneeling inches from his face, examining him in considerable detail.

'Uh,' he exclaimed.

She didn't respond.

Sergio looked around quickly, came out of his trance, and attempted to size her up. She didn't look in a much better state than he was. The jeans were frayed and old, the woollen coat had been ripped along the left shoulder – but it was in the eyes that he recognised the aimlessness and loneliness of a street person. She wasn't a gypsy. That much was clear straight away. But the two of them were cut from similar cloth.

'Are you all right?' She spoke quietly in Serbo-Croat.

'Of course. Are you?'

She grinned her yellow teeth at him, and rose to her feet. Despite being ten years older than Sergio, she was substantially thinner. She stood for a moment looking round the dismal arcade, her body bent and gaunt, like a winter tree.

'I'll buy you a hot drink.'

Sergio nodded and smiled. 'Maybe I buy you one as well.'

Inside the café he nodded proudly to the owner and ushered his new-found friend to a table in the window.

'It's OK. They know me here.' He rubbed his hands together, and called out to the waitress, as if it was the kind of thing he did every day, instead of fetching his own cup from the kitchen and drinking it there for half-price.

Darka went over to him and smiled. 'Who's your companion, Sergio?'

He opened his mouth to say something, but she spoke first.

'Valentina, I'm a student.'

'Your face is familiar. Been here long?'

'I have friends in Skopje. So I visit from time to time.'

'Ah, what it is to study!' Darka blushed. 'You want coffee?'

'Yes, coffee is good . . . and . . .' She glanced towards Sergio.

'Sergio will have a chocolate, won't you Sergio?' Darka patted him on the shoulder. 'He's one of our best clients.'

The boy smiled happily across the table. 'So you been here before, uh?'

'Maybe once.' The colour had returned to her cheeks.

Sergio examined her again. She was young but she was old at the same time. That's what the streets did for you. It was always the way.

'What you study?'

'Buildings. I look at different buildings in the town, and compare their structures.'

Sergio stared blankly and made a face. 'I see. It sounds . . .'

'Very boring!' She laughed. 'I know, sometimes I think the same.'

Darka set the tray down on the table, handed the chocolate to Sergio, but left the coffee where it was. The owner had told her where Valentina came from – and she didn't like it. Girls from the Cosmos club were not welcome in her café. That sort of thing wasn't right or proper. And what was she doing with Sergio?

'So what you going to study today?' The boy stirred his chocolate with a straw.

'Today's difficult. I wanted to visit some buildings, but many are closed because of the troubles.'

'That's too bad.'

'I was thinking maybe I go up to Dare Bombol – look at some of the places there.'

Sergio's eyes flashed. 'But that's where I live, up there. The old school. You know, the one that's a camp.'

'You live there? My God, it's one of the buildings I want to study.'

'Then you must come and see it with me.' His face fell for a moment. 'But I think it's a problem, maybe . . .'

'Why?'

'Army. The Army is there. They not want visitors.'

Valentina shrugged. 'That's a shame.' She sipped her coffee and stared out of the window. The wind had driven away most of the shoppers. There would be little business done today.

She turned to Sergio as if an idea had suddenly taken root. 'Would you do something for me?'

174

The boy grinned. 'Sure.'

'Would you help me draw a little plan of the building – just to help me out?'

'Why not?'

Of course, thought Valentina, it was lucky the little tyke had such a good memory. Lucky he could fill in the location of the guardhouse. He also knew where the communications were stored, the weapons, the commissary – his attention to detail, she had to admit, was phenomenal.

After a while, she realised she'd run out of good will. The waitress had recognised her; so had some of the customers. But that was only because they were dirty bastards themselves, who came into the club looking for anything they could find to grope and snivel at.

She took one final look at the little diagram. 'So where do they sleep, all these soldiers? There aren't enough bedrooms, are there . . ?'

'No, no, no –' Sergio wanted to be as exact as possible. 'Most of the men sleep in these corridors . . .' he pointed with his straw. 'And some of the officers . . . Tillier, here, Blake here, English . . .'

'You sure Blake sleeps there?'

Sergio looked hurt. 'Of course I know where he sleeps. He's my friend.' He took out the pencil and marked the spot with a big red cross.

Valentina smiled and bought him another cup of chocolate.

Chapter Thirty-two

Brigadier Peter Hensham arrived in the early hours of the morning, bringing yesterday's papers from London and a lousy mood.

And he too wanted to see the body.

Of course, there was nothing – no, less than nothing – that Hensham could do either to advance the investigation or pronounce on the cause of death. But he insisted on pushing his way in, up the stairs to the sick bay, along the corridor to the makeshift morgue.

Blake felt strangely protective towards Marta, and embarrassed for her as the man peered down at her naked corpse, pointing out the wounds with his gloved finger as if no one else had spotted them, screwing up his eyes, sighing loudly. It was like a second-rate politician, touring the sights, feigning interest and concern – understanding nothing.

'Nasty business.'

Blake nodded. *Penetrating insights as well.*

'You think it was this fellow Kiro – one of the commanders in the Tabernovce region.'

'That's what my people tell me.'

'Well unfortunately, he isn't our concern.' There was a shrug and a final glance at the body – as if it was all just the way of the world.

'So what exactly is our fucking concern then . . .' Blake could feel the anger launching itself deep inside him, 'sir?'

Hensham turned round in his crisp uniform, and his

shiny-glass shoes – a man who had washed and spent the night in another place –and took in the expectant faces of the medical officer, Tillier and English standing in the corner.

'We'll talk about this outside.'

For a while, though, they said nothing, standing bad-tempered in the courtyard, as the foul, grey morning swirled in around them.

'I'll get to the point, Blake. We may not get along – and quite frankly we've no reason to. But after all the years we've disliked each other, I'd rather say this to your face than have it passed down the system. You follow me?'

'No. Say what?'

'For a peacekeeper you seem to have too many damn bodies following you around. Know what I mean? First Bosnia, now here. I pick up the rumours, you see. I listen to the way the bloody wind is blowing . . .'

'That's always been your strong point.'

'I'll ignore that, Colonel. Fact is . . .' he sniffed as if the air was somehow not to his liking, 'you're finally running out of road. Oh, you can play the bloody TV personality on *News At Ten*, and have the Yanks eating out of your hands, but your star isn't exactly rising back home. Plenty of murmurings and mutterings . . .'

'Always are in girls' schools.'

Hensham sniffed again. 'I don't care what happened in Trajica, with the villagers in the barn. I don't care if you were set up, as you seem to think, or if you just fucked up, as seems to me much more likely. No more bodies, Colonel, and in case you're wondering, that's not just an order from me, to be pissed on and have darts thrown at it – it comes from the Prime Minister and the Cabinet Office. No bodies. Understood? No shooting. I want fucking peace on earth – and some fucking peacekeeping in this region. And if we have to walk over your crappy, second-rate carcass to get it – we will.'

Blake grinned for the first time that day.

'I love poetry.' He turned and faced Hensham head-on.

177

'And I thought your arrival was going to make it such a bloody, dull day.'

They put on a face for the rest of the day, touring the camp, visiting the forward bases, Hensham insisting on being flown right over the Serb units, as he jotted his observations in a little notebook.

It was only when they said goodbye at the airport that evening that Blake made his pitch.

'I'll say this once, because I want to, not because there's even the remotest chance you'll listen to it . . .'

'Don't push the insubordination, Blake.'

'We have a chance here. Listen to me Brigadier. The invasion is still in its early hours. The Serbs don't really know what they're doing. They've brought in a few units, and run them a few kilometres down the road – and that's it. That's the invasion.' He shook his head. 'They're testing the water. They reckoned that once the President was topped, the place would be a soft touch – and it was. But my point is this . . .' He glanced at Hensham, staring at his watch, impatience in every gesture. 'Get the go-ahead and we can kick the bastards out – once and for all. This one doesn't have to fall. Not like the others. Listen to me . . . they're just waiting for us to react.'

'I have to go.'

Blake opened his mouth, but then closed it again.

'That's all very interesting, I'm sure.' Hensham picked up his bag. 'But there's only one thing you have to concentrate on. You keep the fucking peace. Even if you're shot at, bombed, blown up, or castrated over a camp-fire. OK? Peace. That's what we want.'

'Whatever the price?'

'You said it, Colonel. If there's another body turning up in this sector, I'll come looking for *yours*. Got it?'

The plane took off to the northwest, and Hensham sat back

watching the last shards of sunset, rubbed out by the black clouds, bringing rain.

After all these years it had felt so good sticking it up Blake's arse.

What a pompous, arrogant prick he'd been at university. With his trendy, loud friends and their endless drunken parties. How Sarah could ever have . . . ? But that was over. And now the marriage was over too. There should never have been one in the first place.

In a little while he'd bring the bastard down. Screw him at work – and then screw his wife for all the world to see.

Such a treat! Blake on his knees.

Chapter Thirty-three

'Hallo, Sarah . . .'
      'God, it's you!'
'I wanted to speak to the kids, is that all right?'
'How . . . how are you there?'
'Fine. Well, not fine at all, really. Usual fuck-up.'
The satellite line was so perfect, so clear. You could hear
every ounce of hurt. Every jagged piece of regret. Every
layer of defence. Strong and clear. No secrets on this phone
line. A few old feelings laid out in a small pile – because
there weren't many left.
'They're out, I'm sorry. Charley's playing in a school
concert. Veronica's on a date – well sort of. Only someone
from round the corner.'
'Are they alright?' .
'Usual colds, that sort of thing. Veronica's a bit
chesty . . .'
'Tell them I called, will you?'
'Do you need anything . . . ?'
I just want to be sure.
'Sarah . . .'
'What?'
'Have you been thinking about things?'
'Of course I have.'
'And?'
Just tell me.
'What do you want from me, Tom?'
'I want to know where I stand.'

'I thought we'd had this conversation already . . .'

So leave it there, can't you? She's said it all. Don't make her kick you in the face, because that'll hurt.

'Did you mean what you said about not coming back?'

'Tom, listen to me: what's going to change between us? What can you put into this marriage today, that you couldn't put in yesterday?'

'What about you?'

'I *could* put something new into it. I really could – but I don't think I want to. Not anymore.'

He couldn't find an answer to that. Not one that he wouldn't regret later, when the remorse set in.

As it surely would.

'Look after yourself Tom. The children talk about you a lot. You're important to them, whatever happens with you and me.'

He couldn't bring himself to say goodbye. Just hung up the phone, wondering what he had really wanted to hear.

Maybe the sound of the door slamming – or the creaking of a door, still open.

Now he knew.

He walked back into the courtyard, and the wind seemed to pick itself up when it saw him, gusting off the hillside, howling at the trees.

He tried to imagine Sarah in the kitchen, looking down at the phone, Sarah in the bedroom, Sarah with the kids, Sarah in the arms of someone else. But the image wouldn't form.

Instead, as he stared towards the city, he seemed to glimpse the blonde hair of Geralyn Lang, spun in the dying sunlight, and he thought he could taste the lips that had offered him a journey.

'Get up Jimmy.'

'Sleeping.'

'We move.'

He braced himself on the thin, flat board, in the corridor,

waiting for the kick in the guts – but it didn't come.

Instead Kiro was there, with the men in dark blue night fatigues, bulletproof vests, blackened faces. The men he had trained.

A mug of coffee was pushed into his hand.

'Ten minutes, Jimmy.'

And for once he didn't feel like laughing at Kiro. This time the man was dressed right. Sidearms, the MP5 Heckler & Koch, grenades, flares. They all had their little arsenal, primed and ready to go. Ten, twelve of them. Silent, tensed. Professional.

'Your call Jimmy. Your night out.'

'I know. Why not warn me?'

'You're a soldier, right? Always ready, uh? You done the practice. You don't need no more.'

His own kit had been laid out on a chair in the kitchen, arms on the table, ammunition. Medical kit. Although among the twelve he could see the medical officer, his right eyelid flapping out of control, like the wings on a fly.

Let him shit himself, thought Jimmy. Why should he be different?

Take on the British Army and everyone should shit themselves. And he ought to know.

'I want to check all the weapons.' He made them open the holdalls, take out each one under the kitchen's neon light. Uzis, Ingrams, AR15s, 9mm pistols, M60s – rifle grenades if you needed them.

Just in case, Staff McIlvane. That's what they'd always told him.

'*Don't stint on the weapons, you ugly little crud. You don't find carpenters going to work leaving half their tools at home. So you don't find soldiers going into battle half-fucking-kitted out. Only the dead ones.*'

Good words. Really good.

'Alright, pack it up again.'

And now he could feel it, alright. Like an extra pump pushing the blood round, boosting it to all the corners.

Christ, there was nothing like it. An evening out with the lads, even this bunch of idiots, a chase, some killing, some shooting – and the largest bloody stake of all, lying out there on the table to be won or lost.

Your life.

He herded them out to the Land-Rovers, pleased that the clouds had moved closer in, keeping out the moonlight, with no sign of a breeze.

Perfect weather to kill by.

Tom Blake sat in his room at Dare Bombol and felt like the headmaster of a boarding school who had put the top classes to bed. 'Back to the dormitory, fellows. Lights out in half an hour. No talking.'

And then in the morning the bloody great bell would go off and the prefects would shout: 'Hands off cocks and into socks.'

Institutions always had rhymes for things. Because that's the way they controlled your mind.

He could recall his time in the Paras, sitting in the C-130s droning and shuddering at a thousand feet for the quick drop-in, reciting the litany:

> Head well forward –
> Shoulders round –
> Feet together –
> Watch the ground.

And so it went. If you did it right. And if you didn't you'd float all the way down, with your hand wrenching at your dick, and a ploughed, foreign field getting ready to ram its way up your arse.

Such stark choices in the Army.

Do it this way, or get killed.

Follow tradition. Follow orders. Do the decent thing.

He was about to get into his sleeping bag when he realised what he wanted.

Around him was the camp. Outside the camp was the

sprawling mess of the Balkans. In the Grand Hotel was Geralyn Lang, promising him a journey, holding out a ticket, getting ready to leave. And he bloody well wanted to go with her. All the way. Wherever it went.

So it didn't take long to pull his clothes back on and slide into one of the Land-Rovers, coaxing it down the track to the gatehouse.

For once he was glad there was no sign of Sergio. The boy never seemed to sleep at all, swinging and drumming all hours of the day and night. Let him rest.

From inside his box the corporal stared out at Blake with the complete incomprehension of a man who had once worked the minicabs and was trying hard to look like a soldier.

Blake slid back the window. 'I'm on the radio if anyone needs me. No need to inform the Watch or the Operations Room. I'll be in town for an hour or so.'

The corporal saluted, opened the gate and stood watching the Rover's rear lights bump their way to the main road and disappear down the hill.

He could tell with that unerring minicabber's instinct for unlikely stories that it was all extremely irregular. But this was the Colonel, the CO. This was an irregular man. The one person, they said, who could bring it off in the Balkans, if any fucker could. So you didn't mess around with him.

In fact, he told himself, in his heart of hearts he would cheerfully go to the wall for Tom Blake. And if Blake wanted a tart in town for a half-hour, let him have one, for God's sake.

He, Lance-corporal Edwin Tolhurst, from Peeling Road, Dalston, East London, would keep his bloody mouth shut and make sure everyone else did the same.

Silence in the bus, when you're on your way.

Jimmy and the troupe.

An old covered truck to take them. That's all it was. And they sat on the floor with the bags between their legs, and the guns held very still.

He had calculated they had twenty kilometres to go, round the hillside to the north of Dare Bombol, then on foot through the forests – the way it had happened when Kiro had shot his own man.

The march would take thirty-five minutes. By ten to four they should be at the perimeter fence.

Five to four, they would do it.

Jimmy was superstitious about going in on the hour.

Five to sounded better.

God knew why.

Through the tiny window with the piercing draught, Sergio had watched Blake leave, his breath misting on the filthy glass. He didn't know where he was going, nor did it seem important.

Blake was a soldier and soldiers fought.

But he might be tired when he returned, might need food and drink, so Sergio would prepare it for him. Sergio would look after his friend Tom.

The boy pulled on his shirt, pullover, and the ragged blue trousers, and went out into the cold, taking his drum with him.

From the guardhouse Lance-corporal Tolhurst saw him head down the track to the main courtyard but took no notice. Sergio was a fixture. Like a dog or cat, to be fed and petted and played with. He was the camp mascot. No one interfered with him, he simply got on with his business.

Inside the canteen, Sergio pulled out bread and jam, and cut it skilfully into a sandwich. The fridge held orange juice and milk.

He chose milk, because he preferred it himself, then he placed the plate and glass on a tray, put his drum under his arm and climbed the stairs to Blake's room.

The door was open so he stepped inside, laid the tray on the camp-bed, and looked around. There wasn't much to see. A selection of tunics and battledresses suspended on hangers, boots, the cap with the regimental badge. Sergio ran his finger over it, and polished it on his jersey.

And then he looked at the food, and couldn't help the avalanche of hunger that seemed to engulf him. The sandwich lasted less than a minute, followed closely by the glass of milk. It tasted wonderful. Pure and wonderful.

Of course he'd have to go downstairs and get Blake a fresh supply. But for a moment or two he'd just lie on the bed, and steady himself. After all, the room was warmer, better insulated than his own. The bed was untold luxury, the sleeping bag new and inviting.

He didn't even know that he had closed his eyes.

Chapter Thirty-four

It was clear she wore nothing beneath the thin cotton dressing gown, for as she moved he could see the swell of her breasts rocking gently beneath the fabric. When she leaned towards the bedroom light her whole body appeared in silhouette, curved and sculpted.

'Geralyn . . . ?'

She grinned. 'Tell me you left a book behind, or forgot your glasses – and that's why you came.'

'I left a book behind and. . .'

And somehow her mouth had walked over to him, quite by itself. She kissed him just a second before he knew it would happen, holding long enough for him to taste her, but then broke away again, and sat on the bed, smiling, letting him stand awkward, still in his gloves, still with the cold on his face and clothes.

'What does that mean?'

'I kissed you, Tom.' The smile didn't falter. 'Does everything have to have a meaning?' She lay back against the pillows.

'No. But you were the one who talked about a journey.'

'And your journey seems to consist of coming here, late at night, uninvited.'

'I like the view from your window.'

'And I like the view from yours.' The smile faltered at the edge. 'But we can't always have what we want. Besides, what are you offering?'

'I didn't think I had to make offers, just to go out with someone.'

'But you don't want to go out . . .' she laughed. 'You want to stay in.' She patted the bed. 'Do take your gloves off and come and sit down. How rude of me not to ask you sooner.'

'So . . .'

'So where are the chocolates you bought me?'

'I ate them on the way.'

'And the flowers?'

'Seemed a shame to pick them.'

He knew he felt something, but the pressure on his knee was so slight that he had to look down to make sure.

'So it seems I'll have to pick my own. What about the night on the town?'

'First town we get to – promise.'

'And the night?'

He glanced towards the window. 'Looks pretty dark to me.'

There should always be a dance, he thought. If there's no dance, there's no music. A dance to set the rhythm.

'So, Colonel Blake . . .' The hand had been travelling in large circles; now it seemed to move more quickly, more directly. She had leaned forward from the pillows, the bedside light behind, her body rested on her right arm. Just a few inches away the dressing gown had slipped apart and a full, soft breast hung there, proud and unsupported, with a mind and presence of its own, revealed as if by accident – and only her smile said it wasn't.

'There's one thing you can do for me . . .'

'I had several in mind.'

She leaned over his lap and pulled the tiny radio receiver from his pocket. 'You can turn *that* off.'

'Dammit, Hensham, what did the bloody man say?'

'He didn't say anything, Secretary of State. He listened.'

'With comprehension, I trust.'

'I made it very clear.'

'Let's hope you did. For the first time we're out of the headlines tonight – see that? – thanks to a bloody football crowd going mad in Germany and killing six people. Only bit of good news there's been since this thing began.'

'I think we're alright, sir. I really do.'

Amesbury hung up and nodded his head at the water-colour on the wall. A flock of damp-looking sheep were grazing peacefully in a field, as the rainclouds gathered over the hills behind them. One of his colleagues had dubbed it 'MPs on day out in the country.' But he liked it. And perhaps it was a pretty accurate symbol after all.

He got up and went round the room fidgeting, as Gwen used to call it, re-positioning the ornaments, trying to make sure in his mind that everything had been squared away. Every dog was in its basket. Everyone who needed to be pressured or intimidated had been. The finger was firmly in the dyke.

At the sideboard he stopped, removed a glass and poured a decent-sized whisky.

He wasn't nervous, he told himself. He was just faced with the unusual phenomenon of things going right. Blake had been chastened, Hensham had done the business. For his part even that snake Dmitry had promised to keep the warlords quiet. Now with the publicity spotlight on the thugs in Germany, the Serbs could move quietly behind the scenes, put their own people in place, make the deals – and above all do it peacefully.

After all, that's what the bloody thing was supposed to be about.

Somewhere along the way, Hensham decided, Tom Blake had lost himself.

And the file had missed it.

He leafed through the buff folder, marked 'Secret and Confidential', with all the symbols that are never explained to anyone outside the system – and even to most of those who are in it.

189

Christmas trees, if your politics were left of centre. Ladders if you'd come up from the ranks. Hearts – that was a good one, thought Hensham – if you had a personal problem or a broken marriage.

Blake's record had begun at Sandhurst, and they had marked him early. There's always one to watch in the group. Every year they arrive, coming out of pubescence, shaking off the acne, chins still light and fresh. But in there, among those fine public-school accents, there's a stag. One who knows he's better than the others, prouder, fitter. Half-way between a stag and a pig. The one who possesses the arrogance of youth and the wisdom of age, passed down to him or picked up from God knows where. The officer – the class, the bearing, the ability to decide and order. The one who'll never be too pissed to walk home, never get too angry that he can't control himself, never lose the training or the judgment that the Army has invested in him.

Blake was the stag.

Hensham read the file with mounting anger. It was all there. And he'd hated Blake for it – even then.

One by one they had lined up to praise him. Instructors, CSMs, RSMs, the ranks themselves – they had all judged him special. But they'd all missed something. The little piece of Tom Blake that he'd kept for himself.

Yes, he'd served the Army. Yes, he was committed, involved, dedicated, ruthless. But deep inside him he had kept his views to himself. That square of the planet on which we all place ourselves was out of sight with Blake and no one knew where it was. No one could be sure. Until he'd gone to Bosnia.

Odd though, how they'd all kept so silent around him. Blake inspired such fierce loyalty, such respect, that when they had tried investigating the rumours, it had been like questing blindfold through a cemetery.

Plenty of bodies – but no one to talk. The regiment shut tight around him.

And out in the field were the other corpses that kept on

190

turning up around him and his unit. And with them, the clearest of clear impressions that this was a man who was fighting back.

Peacekeeper? Not this one, thought Hensham. Never this one. The reflexes were all wrong. The breaking-point was too low. The mind and the conscience were too connected. It was the mind of a freelance.

And look at the background: the charm, the 'rough diamond' approach, the young life moulded in a cocktail party, surrounded by money and manners – until the old man had finally used up the one and squandered the other, and then died in the shame of it.

A family breaking-point. It was there if you wanted to read it. Only no one had.

Such a long way from the steady, smug household of the Henshams, ruled by Dad, with his gold watch and cast-iron values. Minor public school. Prefect at seventeen. Nose in the library while all the others were out in their Triumph Spitfires with long wavy aerials.

Religious principles on the outside, yet hiding all the shoulder-chips inside. Bitterness about lost promotions, bitterness about status and achievement.

There's always going to be someone better than you, Hensham's dad would say.

But why did it have to be Blake? And why did he have to care so fucking much about it?

It was an hour later that he picked up the phone.

'It's good of you to ring, Peter.'

'Sarah.'

'I'd like a night in, if that's alright.'

'Absolutely fine.'

'I just want to get things straight in my mind. I know I made you a promise. I haven't forgotten that, and I'm not changing my mind. In fact I haven't thought about much else for the last forty-eight hours.'

'Take all the time you want, Sarah.'

'You're very good to me.'
'I want you – you know that.'
'I know.'

Chapter Thirty-five

The cold was a steel claw that came at them out of the forest, cutting into their faces, clutching at their eyes.

Tomorrow, for sure, the snow would come, carpeting the trees, obscuring their tracks, sleeting down across the mountains to freeze the country where it lay. In the early hours of dawn, with the roads and passes paralysed, they would slip away to the mountain base, and watch the storm close in. But Jimmy knew that not all of them would see it.

The compass led them north and the pace was good. A dozen of them, single file, a dark little convoy through the night. Jimmy in front, Kiro at the rear – and the sound of the boots on the forest floor, over the bracken, through the bushes, across a frozen stream.

At times, from the undergrowth, an animal or a bird would scuttle away in fear. Their ground invaded, violated.

Jimmy took a quiet look back, following the line that snaked behind him. They were tough bastards. That much he knew from the training. Between them there was no love lost. They were hard, competitive, well aware that if they made good on this one there would be rewards, and more operations, more prestige.

There are some human beings, thought Jimmy, who live normal lives for years and years until you open a door inside them that they never knew was there. And then they'll kill anyone you choose – anytime.

Only you can never again shut the door. They've looked

through into the room beyond and they like what's inside. They're killers for life, because you made them that way.

Those were the men he had with him.

He looked at his watch and called a halt. A five-minute rest had been built into the schedule. They needed water, breathing space. No one said anything as they unclipped the bottles from their belt and let the ice-cold liquid fall into their mouths. A couple removed their black cap-comforters and wiped their mouths.

'We on time, huh?' Kiro appeared beside him, breathless, grinning.

He nodded.

The Serb looked round to make sure no one was listening.

'When we reach the fence, I tell you what we do.'

'Like fuck you will. We know what we're doing. We set the explosives and pull out. That's it.'

'We can blow the place up, anytime.'

'Listen, Kiro. We trained for this. Hours on end. Days on end. That's what these idiots know how to do. Nothing else. Don't piss on it before we even get there.' He looked at his watch. 'Now let's move. I want this show on time.'

Kiro shrugged and returned to the back of the line. In his tunic he held the diagram that the gypsy boy had drawn, in return for a simple cup of chocolate. But he wasn't going to tell Jimmy about that. Not yet.

Lance-corporal Edwin Tolhurst was a great believer in military discipline. Twice a year when he returned home to Dalston on leave he would bore his relatives silly with tales of the rigid and immovable regulations that governed Army life.

Not that he objected. On the contrary, he believed the rules had served their purpose. The British Army, he maintained, was at the cutting edge of military strategy. The tightest and most highly motivated force the world had ever seen.

And he was proud to be part of it.

194

'And I expect, dear,' his mother would reply, 'that they're just as proud to have you with them.'

Quite how Lance-corporal Tolhurst reconciled his views on discipline with the bottle of whisky standing between his feet that night is not a matter of public record.

And yet, a little tot had done him no discernible damage as a cabbie in the East End.

Here too it would simply help to steady his nerves, during a long watch.

After all, the country was technically in a war zone. Tens of thousands of refugees were on the march. Things were tense and unpredictable – and his own responsibilities, truly awesome.

He took another swig from the bottle, a little more than he'd meant to, giggled and replaced it between his legs.

Yes – 'awesome' was a good word to describe his job. He'd use it when he got back to Dalston and told his friends in the pub what he'd been up to.

In fact he was enjoying the thought immensely when he looked at his watch and noticed it was seven minutes to four. Almost time for a good scratch of the nuts, a wander along the fence, and what his mates referred to as a 'Dingo's Breakfast' – a piss and a good look round.

He sighed deeply and took a final swig of the bottle.

That night Captain James Tillier had found it hard to sleep. The sight of Marta's body had unnerved him, more than he expected.

Nameless bodies were alright, faceless ones even better. They went with the job. But it was a different matter when they'd been talking to you a couple of hours before. Bright, pert, funny – and now very deceased.

For a while he turned on the light and watched a cockroach amble across the wall. The room was cold, dirty, functional – and even the semi-clad photos of his girlfriend that he'd stuck strategically beside the bed did little to comfort him.

In all probability, he reflected, she was bonking one of his mates at that very moment, after failing for the tenth time to remember the name of the place he was actually in.

'I keep telling you,' he'd said on their last evening together in the bar. 'It's called bloody Macedonia.'

And wasn't that the truth?'

Thirty yards from the fence, Jimmy McIlvane slithered onto his stomach, and motioned for the others to do the same. A pile of bracken separated them from the barbed wire, a six-foot-high perimeter barrier, with concrete stanchions every fifteen yards. No electric current, though, no infra-red trip-wires or cameras. He'd already made certain of that.

Jesus Christ, they were casual. Put a blue beret on them and they seemed to think they were a fucking protected species. British Army! Not the same when he'd been part of it.

He felt a touch on his arm, and Kiro beckoned him back into the trees.

'What?'

'We make it simple Jimmy. Very simple.'

'It's simple already – these assholes couldn't handle anything that wasn't.'

'I want Blake. That's all.'

'Oh sure.'

'Easy my friend. Easy. I know where he is.' Kiro tapped his blackened nose. 'The address . . .' He winked and nodded his head up and down, reached inside his battle-dress and took out a folded scrap of paper. 'This is where Mr Blake live.'

Kneeling on the ground, he removed a tiny flashlight and shone it on the diagram.

'Look – first floor, above the canteen, upstairs, three doors along. Mark with the red X. Good, huh?'

'Fuck you Kiro.'

Kiro giggled. 'Just you and me Jimmy. You wake him up,

like pretty little nurse in the middle of the night, come to stroke his face – and I do the business. I want him to see me when he dies.'

Perhaps it was the effect of the whisky, but Lance-corporal Tolhurst's mood had altered radically when he came out of the guardhouse and made his way towards the central courtyard.

For one thing, he shouldn't have been on his own, that night. Little Johnny Field, private, and miserable arse-wipe, second class, had taken it into his head to get a stomach-ache about ten-thirty, slunk off to his bed, he had, pretending he was too ill to stand his watch. Lying basket!

Of course they should have replaced him. That was the rule. But the little bugger had said he might feel better later, so they had left it open. Besides, the Sergeant insisted, Tolhurst could manage perfectly well on his own. If the hordes appeared at the gate, all he needed to do was wave his handbag at them and they'd run back into the trees.

Bloody cheek!

Into the courtyard now. Just a pale blue nightlight against the canteen wall, the darkness of thick cloud, stuck to the hillside.

A night without redemption, this one. As the CSM used to say.

Along the fence now, and the dew had already frozen on the grass. Cold as a sparrow's arse.

A thousand miles southeast of Dalston.

In the trees, the birds had fallen silent – and the wind that normally moaned and charged and agitated seemed strangely at peace.

He stood still for a moment, looking round, and then rubbed his eyes and breathed the cold air deeply, filling his lungs, trying to clear the whisky from his breath. Another few minutes and he'd go back inside. Wasn't worth doing the whole fence. Didn't need a soldier to catch rabbits.

When he opened his eyes though, he found himself

staring straight through the fence at the curious blackened face of Jimmy McIlvane.

Alarmed and paralysed by fear, he instantly forgot everything the Army had ever taught him, and muttered in a thin voice: 'Who the bloody hell are you?'

It was at that point that Jimmy shot him through the forehead with a silenced bullet from the MP5.

They had cut the wire without difficulty, an easy square segment like a cat flap, the lower section prised right out of the freezing ground. Four inside, four out . . . and the other four with him and Kiro to cover the doors. That was the plan – covering fire from the perimeter if needed. The men in a straight line outside the fence. No shooting till the order – and only to cover withdrawal.

Had they got it, Jimmy wondered?

Too late if they hadn't.

Silence as they ran – close to the buildings where they could. Jimmy leading, Kiro right beside him, the others turned outwards watching the edges. Full-circle cover.

And he couldn't help the thrill of the chase, the thrill of the kill.

Just the power in your hands. The tiny trigger-pull, translating order into action. Quick and slick and clean. And he was running on air.

Halt at the stairs. Take stock. Turn 360. Clear.

So far the men in position. He could hear Kiro next to him, breathing like a train. Unfit bastard.

Up the stairs now, with Messrs Heckler & Koch for company, feeling good, really good.

And Blake?

Well he'd tried to warn him, hadn't he? And that was the debt.

Now he'd have to take his chances.

Tillier had dozed fitfully while the cockroach continued its long march to the floor, crossed the boards and climbed the wooden bedframe.

Reaching the summit, it quested for a moment in thin air and, for reasons best known to itself, dived into space, landing on Tillier's left cheek.

'Fucking hell . . .' He stirred violently, swiped the insect onto the floor and sat bolt upright in bed, aghast at the unwarranted attack. There wasn't a moment of peace or safety in the bloody country. Couldn't even have a kip without the animal kingdom marching over you.

He took a look out the window. The dawn was still a long way off. Nothing but the trees and the dark shapes and shadows of night.

Hell would be this quiet, he thought, this much fun.

And then one of the shapes moved.

'Fucking hell,' he whispered again. Only this time he moved fast to the holster beside his bed.

When he looked again, the Browning 9mm was in his hand.

Jimmy on the balls of his feet, light-headed, fast along the corridor. *Ea-sy. Ea-sy.* The chant in his mind – like the shouts from a football crowd, and the shout from the ranks when the enemy's in sight. *Ea-sy. Ea-sy.* And now the blood's up, every muscle keyed, connected, whole fucking body on standby, to do the business. Nothing can stop you. That's what you're told. Whatever the odds.

Checking as he ran. The MP5 hot in his hand. Little killer, you. Little killer. Who's behind, who's outside? Count the doors, count the bloody doors.

This one. And in the semi-darkness of the corridor, he stops, Kiro beside him.

'Wait.' The little word hissed into the night.

Jimmy peering into his face, half-blue from the night-light, half black. And in that second he knows the man has lost it. Bottle gone. Nerve shot to hell. Voice a whisper wracked with fear.

'You do it, Jimmy. You do it.'

Fucking coward.

Kiro stepping back, leaning against the wall. The stop-watch on hold.

So do it. If you have to. If there's no choice. Do it and get it done. For the hundredth time in your life. Just shoot the bastard who's in there, whoever it is, and walk away. You don't have time for this.

Jimmy raises the Heckler & Koch and kicks out hard towards the door.

Tillier has thrown on trousers, pullover. Running the length of the corridor out into the cold.

But there's no one.

What had he seen?

Maybe the kid swinging in the old playground.

No kid.

He checks the Browning. Safety off. Twelve bullets in the magazine. Twelve tries.

Too cold for this. One quick look round. The clouds heavy on the hillside in the middle of nowhere.

What about the fence?

Fence is fine.

And he stands for a moment, as the wind chops at the trees, his body in perfect silhouette against the off-white wall.

Only the sound hits him.

The sound of a silenced bullet, cutting through the air, an inch from his cheek, smashing into the brickwork, with a slipstream of heat and violence that is hard to quantify.

Christ! By the fence.

He drops to one knee, the Browning outstretched, rigid in his grasp – and the triple thump as three bullets hit the airwaves, heading for the black shape that had sought to kill him.

Jimmy heard the gun even as his foot lashed out at the door.

So he couldn't have stopped.

Couldn't have foreseen the speed of it all.

Inside the room – pitch darkness. Curtains pulled.

Killing is full of snapshots – and suddenly this is one of them.

One moment there's darkness – and then, from nowhere, two eyes dead ahead, straight out of hell.

Eyes you'll go on seeing years later.

Blake's eyes.

And Jimmy's hand comes up so fast, so automatic, the way he's been trained – like a machine – and he fires without thinking.

Because it's him or me.

Always him or me.

And the bullet is on course for the point between those eyes, so you know it's him.

The eyes have gone.

Back into the dark.

Just another kill, Jimmy.

In the split second that follows he hears more shooting in the distance, but it's the here and now that bothers him. Something not quite right in this room.

'C'mon Jimmy, you done it. Get out of here.' Kiro frantic by the door.

'Top of the stairs. Secure it. Don't go down.'

Orders. Decisions. Snapshots. This is his world.

Outside, they've all woken now. Bloody shooting match. But it doesn't matter.

Something wrong here. The cry as the bullet went home. The silence.

Jesus, God what is this?

He moves forward slowly, eyes accustomed to the dark. Only he knows the stillness of death. Like no other stillness. The primeval sense of one departed.

You know they have gone and you have dispatched them.

From his tunic Jimmy takes the penlight, and shines the narrow beam onto the bed.

And you think you've seen most things, he told himself. You want to believe that. You want to believe that no face can spook you, no death, no manner of dying.

But you'd be wrong, wrong, wrong.

The little boy is lying back on the pillow, a tiny drum under his arm, and the hole punched between his open, sightless eyes.

Dear God of all soldiers.

Jimmy.

No time.

I'm sorry.

And the dying and chasing has ended in a truckle bed.

You got a kid, Jimmy. Unarmed. Not even ten years old.

'Jimmy!'

Kiro at the door.

'Fuck's sake Jimmy. Move it.'

Leave him. No more to be done.

Run. That's what you're good at. Run.

Into the corridor, three steps, four, maybe to the top of the stairs.

And outside, through the filthy windows, the shooting has intensified.

'We not make it this way.' Kiro's hand like a block across the stairway.

And Jimmy can see it now.

Outside, below them, a whole British platoon is up and out. A line of them set up and firing from the canteen below. Shots coming back from the fence. He shoves Kiro's hand to the side.

'Don't be fucking stupid, Jimmy. We never get out this way.'

'Those are my men. I trained them. I can't leave them like that.'

'Then you die with them.'

In the blue half-light on a hillside, draped with clouds, that's the choice.

Chapter Thirty-six

Tillier felt sure that one of the three bullets had hit home. Too dark to see. Too far away to know. But something tells you.

You get your own intuition.

He had crawled rapidly away from the white wall. There was camouflage from the dustbins at the side, but no cover.

And now they were firing indiscriminately, as he pinned himself to the frozen ground, head right down.

Christ, where was everyone?

But it only seemed long. Woken by the noise, he could hear shouts from inside the dormitory blocks, the sound of boots on the floor. Hurry it up for Christ's sake. Bullets all around him.

Good sign to hear them. Bloody good sign. Cos you never hear the one that gets *you*.

And then the glass shattered on the downstairs windows, and the heavy rifle and machine-gun fire of his own people broke out above his head.

Only there was English's voice – dead calm, steady as a rock. A voice you could hang by over a precipice and it wouldn't let you down. Nothing would shake that voice, under any circumstances.

'Got you covered, James. Slither ten yards to your left, head down, that's it.'

Calm. So bloody calm. Might have been directing traffic in Basingstoke.

Not fighting your life out on a Balkan hillside.

Training. Mental attitude.

As he crawled, Tillier was aware they had redirected the fire away from him so he could get out behind the building. That's what he needed. Breathing space. Heart going like bloody crazy. Must have been more worried than he thought.

He stepped into the darkness behind the canteen, and leaned against the wall.

He didn't even hear the rustle behind him, didn't feel the sudden displacement of air, in fact felt nothing at all.

He was thanking God for English and the rest of the crowd, so trained, so organised – and that voice, coming at him like a lifeline, telling him where to go.

Those were your real mates – people who could pull you out of the pot, even when the bloody natives were dancing around it.

Beyond the building, the rifle fire had become more sporadic. That meant the attackers were seriously depleted.

He stood quite still, breathing deeply, waiting for his heart to stop pounding.

What the hell had they been after? And why hadn't they run? When the shot had missed him, why hadn't they turned right round and fled into the forest? No way they could have taken on the entire platoon. Not in a lifetime.

He shook his head.

Oh Christ. A tiny light seemed to switch on deep inside. Christ almighty. What it meant was that they already had someone in the camp, someone they were covering. A hit squad, an explosives team. . . ?

James Tillier, captain, once of the Green Jackets, aged just twenty-seven, was a second away from turning, when Kiro's bullet smashed into the back of his head, spattering his life across the back of the building.

'You're a fucking coward.'

'Get out Jimmy. Cut the fucking fence. Get out.'

Only the last thing Jimmy wanted to do was run with this

bastard. The man who couldn't shoot a British officer face on, bottled out, except when offered the back of someone's head.

Easy target that one. Anybody can blow the back of a head off. No problem.

And Kiro already had the cutters in his hand, slicing through the barbed wire, pulling and swearing as the teeth cut into his wrists.

'We can't leave the men.'

'Fuck the men!'

A true commander, he thought. And what about his own attitude, standing waiting for his escape route, as the men he'd trained were systematically shot down by better soldiers than they could ever have been?

Where the hell was his own honour?

'Go. Go on.' Kiro pulling and scrabbling at the wire, not caring at the blood pouring from his wrists. 'Run, Chrissake.' And his huge bulk forcing itself through, as the wire cut his tunic into ribbons and gouged the skin off his back. But he didn't care. The momentum and the pain simply carried him through.

Jimmy following.

You too Jimmy. Just the same. Your night out. And wasn't this one to remember?

Sprinting the forty yards to the forest. And now it's the long way across the brow of the hill. And you'd better watch the compass on this one.

Two minutes maybe. Three.

Suddenly all he can hear are the footsteps crashing over the ground, tortured breathing, the rattle from the guns . . . and there's silence back at the camp. Which means it's over. The men had given up, or bought it. And these men would have died, rather than be taken. Didn't know anything about fuck-all, but they had a sense of honour. Gave a good account of themselves. The best you can say about a soldier.

He ran on, following the bastard Kiro, loafing, swaying through the trees, grunting as he ran.

And Jimmy was sick, right through to the sad, misshapen lump in his chest that passed for a heart.

English took only one of them alive, gesturing the man to lie flat on the ground, kicking his legs apart, hands behind his back, face in the grass.

All around him his colleagues were lying in the bright arclight, their bodies doused and smeared in blood, the bullets stitched across their heads and tunics.

Brock verified they were dead.

And then, as the survivor was handcuffed, the two of them moved fast and soundless up the stairs towards Blake's room, not a word passing between them, both hit by the same foreboding.

Door open, but the room is dark, and the cold air is flooding through from the broken window.

That's where they went.

Softly now, step by step into the room because whatever was here has passed. The wind says so. There are only the pieces to sift through. And if they got Blake they got him.

Across the bed the little boy lies straight on his back, looking up to them with motionless black eyes. In the crook of his arm he's still holding his drum. The light isn't working, but English has a flashlamp, and there is only a single hole in the forehead, to tell how his story ended. A young forehead, punched through by a nine-shot automatic, made in a country he'd never heard of, by people he never knew existed, in a world that should never have touched him – not like that.

Brock leans forward and closes Sergio's eyes. 'My sister has a boy same as that.'

English has managed to get the electrics working, and in the harsh bright light he sees the empty tray and the empty glass of milk on the floor beside the bed. And he knows what happened.

'Find out if the gate logged the CO out anytime tonight. I'm going to make sure James's OK.'

English heads back down the stairs and out into the frozen courtyard.

The men have started mopping up. Body bags for the dead. First aid for two of the British soldiers, hit by flying glass.

There is a low chatter and a few grins and jokes. They don't make a thing out of dying. Dying is simply what happens when the job goes badly.

If you're a shopkeeper, you get burgled, or your business falls apart. If you're a soldier someone scrapes your brains off a hillside.

Different stakes. That's all.

And even with the philosophy imprinted in his mind, English is unduly upset to find Tillier's body behind the canteen, with the blasted head. He doesn't need to feel for a pulse, just as he didn't need to feel for Sergio's.

To look at him, his face is without expression. Bodies don't faze him. He can't cry, can't get emotional.

Instead he sits down in the mud beside Tillier, just to share a moment or two before it's over.

In the past he wondered whether anything would ever upset him, get to him, reduce him to tears.

And the funny thing is that it's the trivial things that can do it.

When he was a teacher the anger would build and build inside him: if the boys worked badly, if they came in late, if their homework was sloppy. If he had to wait in line at a shop.

And yet he could pick his way through a pile of mutilated bodies on a battlefield without a care in the world.

Thoughts that came to him as he sat beside the body, half blown-away in the cold.

He kept thinking they'd have a whip-round for Tillier's girlfriend, something to show they all cared, even if they didn't know how to.

What was her name? Charlotte, Charley – a pretty, giggly creature, who wanted nothing more than to have a good time with the guy she fancied she loved. Didn't know a thing about war. She was into carrier bags in Sainsburys, hairdos, make-up, and fending off mum, who kept thinking 'the fellow' ought to declare his intentions.

Why should she be hit with a dead boyfriend?

She didn't deserve that.

It was always the families and friends who were the real undefended, he thought.

Soldiers are armed. They have a chance.

The families have nothing. No protection at all.

He remembered the way Tillier had laughed at the girl, that last night in the mess, telling her:

'It's called Mac-e-don-ia. Bloody Macedonia.' But she was too drunk to get it.

Only now she'd remember for all time.

Chapter Thirty-seven

As they emerged from the forest, the snow began falling in thick tufts from the cloud base and the silence seemed to echo around them. No sign of dawn. No lightness in the east. A hard and bitter night still clung to the mountains.

He'd been amazed that Kiro had kept up, wheezing and grunting through the trees. And yet fear would have driven him on. The fear of cowards who only shoot from behind, who back away from the fights that matter.

In a thicket, already sprinkled with snow, the truck was waiting, the driver and two guards, sitting expectant, babbling excitedly at Kiro. But as Jimmy watched them the expressions dissolved and melted away, the mouths fell silent. No passengers to wait for. No victorious comrades. No wine and women and celebration. Suddenly, the soldier game had ceased being fun and the players weren't coming home.

He climbed under the tarpaulin into the back of the truck, and pulled a sack beneath him, to soften the ride. And when Kiro's bulk slumped down opposite, the machine staggered and groaned onto the road, and the wheels began slipping as it took on the gradient.

This was the last one, Jimmy told himself.

When you shoot kids between the eyes, you have scorned the world and set yourself apart. You have forfeited club membership. The rights and the privileges are withdrawn.

There would be no more.

He closed his eyes for a moment and wiped cold sweat

from his forehead. Even in the semi-darkness he could see his hand was black from the camouflage.

And then the anger took him, burning deep inside. Years-old resentments at the way life had done him down. Because life was to blame. Life gave and life took. And in the end it fucked you where you lay.

In his rage he reached over to Kiro and wrenched at his tunic.

'You've had it now, pal. You think I'm a killer? You haven't met one yet. But you will. I promise you that.'

They had found Lance-corporal Edwin Tolhurst, kneeling beside the fence.

When the bullet hit him, they reckoned, he would have sunk to his knees, and fallen against the barbed wire, which had continued to prop him up, until rigor mortis had taken over and stiffened him where he was.

They examined the gatehouse logs, but there were no clues there. All comings and goings to be noted. Especially the CO. That was the rule.

Only the rule had been broken.

Blake was out. And the log was blank.

They tried the radio. Called for twenty minutes. But only the static came back.

By which time English was in the Land-Rover on his way into Skopje.

Of course he should have thought of it first thing. Plain as a Sunday virgin where the man had gone.

And bloody lucky for him that he had.

'I should have gone hours ago.'

The velvet skin stirred against him. He could still taste her, still breathe her.

You switched on all the lights, Geralyn Lang, room by room, step by step.

It's as if you've been here with me before.

Cupping her head, he lifted it from his chest and kissed the closed eyes.

'I'm off . . .'

She stopped him with her mouth – soft and open, using tooth and tongue, the blonde hair wild across her face, and her eyes tight shut.

'If they close their eyes – means they love you.'

The old teenage saying.

And if their eyes were open, they wanted your money.

Not much of that.

He got up, and pulled on his clothes in the darkness, but suddenly her hands were round his waist, roaming, probing, teasing him.

'You can't just come and go.' She giggled. 'Well, you can come, but you can't leave straight afterwards.'

He pulled her round in front of him, kissing her hair, her face and eyes.

'Why must you go?'

'You know why, Geralyn.'

'I know why,' she repeated softly, slipping out of his grasp, moving back towards the bed. She switched on the light, pulling the covers across her . . .

'Don't do that. I want to see you.'

She grinned. 'Enough for the first date. I want those chocolates and flowers before you see anymore. I want some serious spoiling and flattery. You haven't done well on that front.'

'How about the other fronts?'

'Advancing well.' She laughed. 'Not that you encountered much resistance. Next time I'll have to put up more of a fight.'

'Good.'

He climbed onto the bed, pulled down the sheet and kissed each breast, hearing her giggle as she tried to push him away.

'Hey, buddy, you gotta pay up front, if you want more.'

'What's the rate?'

'More than a soldier can afford.'

'How about three times a night?'

'Sold.' She pulled the covers up over her breasts. 'Now you can stop drooling all over me. Remember what I said though, flowers and chocolates, or you can go back to using your right hand.'

'You drive a hard bargain.'

'Call that thing a bargain?' She pulled his head down and kissed him.

There was real warmth to feel, he thought. Warmth you could cash in on a cold night in a hostile world.

And then he was out in the corridor, striding towards the landing, and the warmth died that same instant, as English stepped from the lift, death in his eyes and on his clothes, and in the set of his shoulders. Death, instant and un-adorned. Blake had seen it in the man so many times before.

He was sorry for Tolhurst. Bloody sorry for Tillier. The man had been a loyal soldier and comrade. Gone the extra mile. Extra ten miles. Gone willingly and repeatedly and way beyond any proper, legitimate order would have taken him. A solid, straightforward man – kept his life simple. Chose blacks and whites for colours, because they were easier to deal with. But you don't weep for other soldiers. That was the code. And they don't weep for you. You sell off the kit, and you have a laugh and a fond farewell, because, as the Lord might see fit, you could well be joining them before much time passed.

But Sergio was so very different.

He could hear the screams from the boy's mother as they entered the camp, the snow falling hard around them – a winter-white shroud to freeze the dead and the living.

As he got out of the Land-Rover Blake was struck by the beauty of the trees and the fresh blood beneath them.

Beauty without meaning or value, when a child has died there.

And I told you to think of the future, Sergio.

Told you one day you'd go home.
But you didn't believe me.
Looked up at me with the head inclined and the big black eyes
that knew more than I did.
And you were right.

At the top of the stairs, in the cramped, single room that the little family shared, a mother cradled her dead son, his face wet and washed with her tears, a bandage across the wound, and the little eyes shut tight.

And that was proof, if any were needed, that reality is a sour and wicked distortion, and the world a sorrier place than the poets could ever render it.

'I wanted . . .'

She turned for a moment. But she couldn't see him and didn't want to.

Grief shuts out the world, he thought, and I have no place beside her dead son.

He couldn't help noticing the boy's arm still clasping his father's drum.

Now there was no one to inherit it.

The drum had died with Sergio.

For a moment he thought of the motionless swing and the silent courtyard outside. Of course the activity would go on. Soldiers running, shouting, hurrying to the canteen. The body of the place would continue to function, as function it must. The camp would clear the dead, soak off the blood, wash away the tears.

But the little heart had gone.

Chapter Thirty-eight

Every army has its mechanism for notifying death. In wartime it's a telegram, otherwise it's the army personnel officers who get called out, day and night like the devil's own messengers – 'black coats', as they're sometimes dubbed – to deliver the news.

The lousiest job in the whole lousy world, they say. Because there's no way to do it well.

From the satellite telephone Blake called the regimental Headquarters and woke up the system.

In Aldershot, Captain Harry Phillips picked up the phone by his bed – soft-spoken, businesslike. He had his lists and his routine, knew what to do, knew what to say. Never knew though, he admitted, how anyone would take it.

Like everybody in Army life, the bereaved fell into categories: the quiet and tearful, the shocked and the desperate. He would go personally to Tillier's family, he said, because they had a house nearby; and a colleague in London would drive out to the East End, where Tolhurst had lived. Be there by dawn. Leave it to us, sir. We'll take care of it.

'I always call,' Blake told him.

'If you wouldn't mind waiting until we've had a word first, sir. Break the news in person. We'll give you a bell, let you know when it's done.'

'Tillier had a girlfriend. Someone should see her too.'

'I'll find out from the parents, sir. I'm sorry this has happened. Very sorry, sir.'

Sorry.

It was still dark when the telephone rang again. And he realised that he hadn't been to sleep, hadn't felt tired, hadn't even noticed the passage of time, staring up at the fly-blown, cracked ceiling, examining faces that he wouldn't see again.

'I've been out there, sir, spoken to the parents and the girlfriend.' Phillips' voice had lost the twang of confidence.

'How did they take it?'

'Badly. Very badly. Tolhurst's lot were very quiet, according to Lieutenant Richardson. He just telephoned me. I think they'd all appreciate your call, sir. I'll give you the numbers. We'll be thinking later about transporting the bodies home.'

Blake sat up on the bed and steadied himself.

As he went through the list he could picture the scenes. The Tolhursts in the council flat in Dalston, dawn well in across the rooftops, the first light of an appalling day coming in over the back garden. He knew the trains had started because he could hear them in the background. And Tolhurst's father thanked him profusely for calling, and said they had been so proud of the 'boy' and hoped he hadn't suffered, and the nice man had told them what would happen now – and it wasn't till then that the voice died away. Blake could hear an old man sobbing into his handkerchief, putting the phone on the side, and he waited and waited until someone else came and picked it up.

'I'm his brother. I'm sorry about Dad. Don't know what else to say. We can't really take none of this in. I thought you might be ringing to say it was a mistake. That Ed was OK, that nothing had happened, after all. But you weren't, were you?'

'I'm very sorry.'

'He loved the Army. Proud, he was. Bloody proud. Talked about nothing else. Bored us all silly, it did. But we listened . . .'

'He was a fine soldier.'

'Was he? I always wondered if he wasn't secretly a piss-artist. But it doesn't matter, does it? He was my brother and it didn't matter what he was.'

Another train rattled past, and Blake could almost feel the tiny kitchen shaking and the plates rattling, and the jangling shattered nerves of the family crammed in around the kettle.

'Why didn't you protect him?'

Question from the heart.

'I wish we had. We can't protect everyone. Your brother died defending the camp. Many more people would have been killed if it hadn't been for him. I know that doesn't help, but he was a very brave man.'

'So what happens now, Mr, I mean, I don't know your rank, I'm sorry . . .'

'Doesn't matter. My name's Tom Blake. How do you mean . . . what happens?'

'Well, do you go after the killers? Is someone going to pay for this? You know – a trial. . . ?'

'We'll investigate and we'll do everything we can. I don't know yet who did this. But I'll find out.'

'And then what?'

'And then we'll try to bring them to justice.'

'Try?'

'Yes.'

There was a pause all the way from the suburb of Dalston in London's East End. But it didn't last long.

'Mr Blake – I don't know much about the Army and politics and all that kind of thing. You could tell me anything, and I'd have to believe it, wouldn't I? We're little people, see. Don't know anyone. Don't know the way these things work. But it seems to me we've paid a high price already, and I want you to be honest with me and give me a straight answer. This family deserves that, don't you think?'

'Go ahead, Mr Tolhurst.'

'Seems to me nobody ever gets justice in wartime. And in wars like this there're always deals. We never get to hear the truth. I just want you to tell me if we'll ever find out what happened, and if the bloke who shot Edwin will ever pay for what he's done.'

You have to tell him.

You have to give him the answer.

He's right when he says they deserve it.

'We're here as peacekeepers, Mr Tolhurst. I've been warned in the strongest possible terms that I'm not to fight back. My orders are to keep the peace, keep things quiet. Turn the other cheek.'

'Orders?'

'I'm afraid so.'

'Well, your orders stink, Mr Blake. And if that's what the Army's going to do after my brother's been shot in the head for them, then the Army stinks as well. Fucking stinks. Do you think that's good enough. Do you?'

'No, Mr Tolhurst, I really don't.'

By the time English knocked on his door, it was seven-thirty, and he had made all the calls he ever wanted to.

Was it good to have telephoned?

Who knows?

In the space of an hour he had covered the full range: the stoicism of the Tilliers, the mad hysteria of the girlfriend, the pinpoint questioning of Tolhurst's brother.

'He went straight to the heart of it.' Blake sat on the bed and shrugged at English. 'As if death somehow cuts out the crap and leaves you with the essentials. He knows. This boy really knows.'

English sat very still.

'We interrogated the Serb – the one who survived.'

'And?'

'You won't like this. Any of it.'

'Tell me.'

'The boys were less than gentle with him.'

'I'll save my pity.'

'He's dead, Tom. They beat him up very badly. I'm

217

sorry. Should never have happened. Feelings were running very high tonight. What with Tillier and Tolhurst – Sergio. That's no excuse. Evidently the man's heart was weaker than anyone thought. Someone took it too far.'

'Someone?'

'You wouldn't expect me to tell you. And I hope you wouldn't ask.' English looked straight at Blake. 'Not after some of the things this regiment has done. Not after these soldiers have put themselves way out on a limb. For you, Tom. Because you asked them to.'

'Jesus, Christ almighty.'

The two men were silent for a while. Outside, the snow had gathered against the corners of the window panes. In just a few hours, the forest around the camp had gone from grey-green to white, and the violence of the dark hours had been buried.

It was Blake who broke the silence. 'We don't kill prisoners, John. We do lots of things we shouldn't do, but we don't kill prisoners.'

'I know.' English shook his head. He was tired, but he never functioned at anything below full par. Full commitment. Everything he had, he used. 'I don't like it either.'

'How'm I supposed to maintain the fucking discipline here, if we start topping prisoners?'

'Won't happen again.'

'It can't. And maybe I should make that clear . . .'

English stood up. 'That's your decision, of course. But I think it'd be a mistake. What happened here went too far. No question. But what we did in Bosnia went too far as well. To the men it's exactly the same thing. Listen to me, Tom. These men would follow you to whatever shithole in the world you took them to. Why? Because they think you get things done. Don't destroy that. If they break the rules, it's because you asked them to, in the first place. You need them to do that. We need them to do that. Now perhaps more than ever.'

'Why?'

218

'That prisoner talked before he died. The target of the raid was you. Nobody else. Just you. Seems one of the fellows you shot at Trajica was a relation of Kiro's. So he came looking to pay you back. His idea. His orders.'

Blake was silent.

'There's more though. The man who trained them was a mercenary. A Scot they all called Jimmy. Big fellow. Liked his booze. But wasn't so keen on the women. Apparently they lifted him one evening outside a club in Skopje. Could be anyone.'

Blake stood up and opened the door for English. In that moment he could see Jimmy' face, just as he'd seen it in the bar in Berlin. The big man, so scared, running for his sad, sorry little half-life, suddenly weighted down with far more knowledge than he wanted. Always happened in the killing business. You ran out of road, crossed the wrong people, did one deal too many, in one alleyway too dark to recognise, got caught in a game you'd never even heard of.

Only if this were Jimmy's work, he'd slot him, the same as a wild animal, gone mad. The man he'd once saved from a minefield. The man he thought he knew.

Better not be Jimmy. Or he'd kill him with his own hands.

'What happened, Tom?'

'Geralyn . . .'

'What? Tell me, for God's sake.'

'Put some film in your camera and get over here. I want this shown.'

Chapter Thirty-nine

A thousand miles north of Skopje, Sarah lay on her bed, and went back over the night before.

Married women don't do what I did, she thought. Don't do it up against the wall, with their skirt rucked up around the waist, breasts snatched out of the bra, knickers half-down, yelling for freedom and all who sail in her.

Don't do that kind of thing in the Army. You're supposed to put a good face on it all. Grin and bear it, old girl.

Bloody hell! She'd certainly grinned and borne it – the weight of his torso pressed hard against her, his pelvis arching up between her thighs, and he'd gone at her like an animal, like no animal before, pent-up and thrilling.

And she'd loved it.

Peter Hensham, the way he used to be. Only more so. Harder. Driven.

He'd wanted to do it again in the bedroom. But she wouldn't let him come in.

Up against the kitchen wall was the right place at the right time. Not this room that she had shared with Tom, the family pictures still on the dressing table, the jugs and pots and post cards that he'd sent from all the war zones and peace zones, and some of the other places he had never officially visited.

That was all they had now – a collection of dusty souvenirs. Maybe that was all they had ever had. But it still wasn't a place for Peter Hensham.

God, he had been ready for it. And so different from the

archetypal soldier, dick hanging out of his khaki trousers, foraging into the bush, with all the artistry of a bloody search and destroy operation.

Peter was someone who could respond and evoke responses in her. Not a tame little ritual of give and take, but each of them seizing greedily from the other. Something close to the brink. Hard to walk away from that after ten years of half-life in the Army, where, as one friend had put it, you couldn't even rely on getting fucked for your birthday.

Peter Hensham had put the capital L back in life.

Idly, she got dressed and went down into the kitchen. The children had gone to school, leaving cereal bowls on the table, magazines and junk mail in a pile, old shoes and books everywhere. Even the television was still on.

And over by the bar was the place they'd done it. She remembered her hands slipping on the Formica cupboards, scrabbling for a hold, one foot anchored, the other parked on the central-heating radiator, the sweat flowing free. What a hell of a performance!

She made coffee and watched the morning news titles. Outside, the day was a cold, grey bag with nothing inside. She'd get her hair done, maybe go to the wine bar, the library . . .

And then she glimpsed Tom's face – just a few inches away on the screen. Tom's eyes staring right into the kitchen where she'd done it. She could see hurt and anger in the set of his jaw, a row of body bags behind him, and a night of killing that had left two of his men dead and a child.

Tom! Christ, Tom!

The pictures showed the bullet holes in his room, the narrow camp-bed, the child's mother, weeping, jumbling words of a language she couldn't understand, no mention of the soldiers' names until the relatives had been informed.

Oh God, Tom.

And then his face again. Grey hair uncombed, same mole on the same cheek, just below those same, same eyes.

Yes, he'd been the target.

Yes, he'd been out of the camp when it happened.

Yes, he was lucky to be alive.

And Sarah Blake couldn't help the tears. Fast and scalding. Tears for the night when he had nearly died – for the night she had broken their faith, up against the kitchen wall, clasping the cupboards.

For a second, when the telephone connection was made, Amesbury had been too angry to talk. God only knew if he'd had a button on his desk, he'd have pressed it and sent them all to . . .

'My dear Anthony . . .' The silky voice from Moscow got in first.

'Don't fuck with me, Dmitry.'

'You are angry.' The voice was like a dog's tongue, licking a slab of meat. 'And I am angry too, Anthony. Please understand this, my friend. I had no knowledge. No conceivable knowledge that such a thing could happen.'

'Who is this Kiro? Who controls him?'

'Belgrade were supposed to keep him in order. I myself expressed doubts when they chose him as administrator for the new territory. But he has some important friends there. This is clear.'

'He'll have to be replaced. I can't have my troops subjected to random attack in what is a clear violation of our agreement. You promised to control the Serbs. You promised a peaceful transition. This is flagrantly and deliberately. . .'

'You're absolutely right, my friend.'

'There'll be an immediate outcry over this; questions in Parliament.'

'I quite understand.'

'How the fuck could you? Your parliament can't even vote itself toilet paper . . .'

'I would remind you . . .'

'I want a meeting in Geneva.'

'Anything, dear fellow.'

'You're a shit, Dmitry,' said Amesbury. But by then he had replaced the receiver.

Jimmy lay on a mattress in the freezing corridor, oblivious to the cold.

He had thought about running. But the tiredness had attacked him, and the will had left him.

Remorse was a foreign commodity, so he didn't recognise it when it came calling.

In front of him, the boy's face kept appearing – too cold and too grey for someone so young. The jagged hole had formed a half-inch above the bridge of the nose, because he had shot him with surgical accuracy, just as he always did, without a flicker of nerve, the arm tight as a clamp, thick as a tree, and the eyes in synch.

Bloody good, Jimmy.

Bloody fine shot.

Champ of the SAS, the Rhodesian Special Branch, the South African Defence Force . . . in each of them he had walked away from the tournaments with every prize monkey they had.

And now he had an extra act in his repertoire. Shooting little boys.

He could hear the last CO he'd had in Angola . . . 'Don't worry, bucko, could have happened to anyone. Laws of the jungle. Think of it this way: the kid would have grown up and blown *your* head to buggery. Uh? Get your mind round that one.'

But that was bullshit.

You could grasp at any old load of dog, and make yourself believe it. Soldiers always did that, telling themselves . . . there was no other way, no choice, no option . . . just because there had been another hideous cock-up, the way it happened in every war and in every unit, and every operation.

Of course Blake would come after him. But that was OK.

And Blake would probably kill him. The man was just as good a shot, he was lighter and quicker, and he would be motivated. That was the requirement. The combination of skill and mental aggression.

Jimmy had the skill, but the mental bit had gone missing.

And yet, even with all that said and done, there would have to be one last job. Final commission. The bloody swan-song he'd promised himself, ever since his beating outside the Cosmo club.

He would strangle Kiro's fat neck and laugh while he did it.

After that he'd lie on his back with his legs in the air, like a dog, digesting its meal.

And Blake could do whatever the fuck he wanted.

Chapter Forty

An Orthodox priest buried Sergio in a tiny wooden coffin, in a shallow grave, salvaged only briefly from the winter. The diggers had complained the ground was too hard and asked for more money. And Blake had taken them aside, stuffed twenty dollars into their hands, and would have beaten them senseless if it hadn't been for the little party standing close by and the grief that seemed to come at him in the wind.

As they stood in a row beside the grave, fresh snow fell in tufts from the clouds across the mountains, covering the priest's beard, dusting the coffin, freezing the mother's tears.

When the service was over, she bent down and laid the boy's drum on the top of the box, because, she said, there was no one else to play it. And if the owner had died, then the drum had died as well.

Besides she would hear him playing from wherever he had gone. Somehow, across the worlds, the sound would reach her.

Together with Brock and English, Blake went over to her, whispering his regrets and sympathies. She looked up into his face and listened, but no one translated. The message was clear, and she could understand all she needed from the cadences in his voice and the cloud in his eyes.

Eventually she took his arm and as they walked slowly back to the camp at Dare Bombol, she talked of Sergio. Several times he caught the boy's name, and the names of towns and regions and mountains, and he knew that she was telling him the story of their life. The gypsies' journey across Europe, the push south from northern Germany, through Austria into the Czech and Slovak lands – the route that the Slavs had migrated centuries earlier.

At times she would smile and laugh, at others the tears broke through the cold to run across her cheeks and down into the camouflage Army scarf he had given her.

A life, richly patterned on the streets and byways of Europe – before the madness had struck them.

Only when they reached the camp did Blake call for the official translator.

'I want you to ask her what she'll do now, and tell her she's welcome to stay. We'll look after her. We'd be honoured if she'd stay.'

For a moment she turned away without replying. But he knew the answer. The cracking, faltering smile spoke for her, the clenched jaw, the eyes that seemed to stare into the distance beyond them. She was already somewhere else.

Two hours later, she emerged from the staircase onto the snow-covered cobbles, with her life reduced to a simple shoulder-bag, her head in a brightly-coloured scarf, the thin body encased in a shapeless black coat.

Blake took the bag from her. 'We'll get you to the station or wherever else you want to go.'

But she shook her head.

'You can't just walk out into the snow like that . . .'

Again, the shake of her head. Only this time, for the first time since Sergio's death, she was smiling with a real and unforced happiness.

They walked her in procession to the gate. Blake and the translator, English, a few of the soldiers, and the Orthodox priest who had yet to be paid for the funeral.

As the barrier lifted, she walked through, waved once, and then shuffled away under the honour guard of snow-capped trees, over the brow of the hill and out of sight, the footsteps small but confident. Long after she had gone they stood watching and listening to see if she would change her mind. But it was as if the countryside had taken her and she had disappeared into the silence.

Blake turned to the priest. 'Why?'

'She couldn't stay where her son had died. That's all she would tell me.'

'Where will she go?'

'She'll walk and walk into the night and then she'll stop.' He paused. 'In a few hours she will die out there, and neither you nor I could have stopped her. She'll die because she wants to.' He turned and stared back towards the camp. 'To her the logic is simple. In death, she believes, she'll find the life of her son. These are not empty words. Not the product of dreams or fantasy. They are true. She said them to me last night. I could not find a way to persuade her otherwise.'

'I'm sorry we failed her.'

The priest raised his arms and shrugged, as if it were the way of the world.

'Maybe you will not fail her, my friend. Maybe when the time comes you will do what must be done.'

Chapter Forty-one

On the plane Amesbury could still hear the Prime Minister's words. Plenty of references to 'your policy, Anthony' and 'the way you wanted to do it' and 'the assurances you gave us'.

The man was a gutless prick. You didn't scuttle the boat, just because you hit a storm. You rode it out, steered round it. Played a little politics.

Only that wasn't the PM's way. 'We wanted peace, Anthony. That's what we were buying with this deal of yours. Us and all the other interested parties. A blissfully quiet, peaceful takeover. No killing, no ethnic cleansing, no refugees all over the bloody television. Now they're stampeding us. Trying to force us to pull our troops out. Doesn't look good, that.'

'I'll sort it, Prime Minister.'

'Hope so, Anthony. Bound to be questions in the House, media stuff. Don't let it get out of hand.'

'You have my assurance on that. The Americans are with us on this one.'

The Prime Minister had gone over to the study window and stared out onto Mountbatten Green. 'No one's with us these days, Anthony. That's what happened after the Cold War. We're all on our own. All of us. Alliances don't mean a piss in the pond. Watch our back, Anthony.'

'I think I . . .'

'What about our man there – Blake? He's not going to fly off the handle on this one, is he?'

'We went out and warned him, just a couple of days ago. He knows what he has to do.'

The Prime Minister had turned and looked Amesbury up and down.

'I wish to hell someone did.'

'Tom, I have to leave for a day or so. Just wanted to call and let you know.'

'Where you going?'

'Paris. Regional meeting of the network's reporters. We have to talk through the coverage, and what the implications are. Usual bullshit, but I have to be there.'

'Bit sudden isn't it, with all the stuff going on here?'

'You and I know that, but they don't. They come from a city where seven people are killed every day. To them it's no big deal.'

'I see.'

She could tell he was disappointed. She smiled into the receiver. 'What shall I bring you back?

'Food.'

'And there was I thinking I'd get some sexy underwear and some perfume and a few other things to send you wild . . .'

'I'm wild already.'

She giggled. 'Think you can stay that way till I get back?'

'You better hope I don't meet any sheep on the hillside.'

'That's disgusting.'

'Don't worry. I only go for the ones that shower regularly.'

She was silent for a moment, changing the mood, letting the laughter subside. 'Will you stay out of trouble, Tom?'

'Would you want me to?'

'Tell me this at least: are you OK?'

'I'm alive. It's getting harder to say that round here.'

Hensham had rung Sarah from a callbox less than a mile away.

229

'I don't have long, darling.'

'For what?'

'Are the children there?'

'I'm not in the mood for that, Peter. You can have a coffee and that's it.'

But he knew her better than that. Three minutes later he was leaning against the doorbell – tie loosened, a single rose clasped in his hand like an entry fee.

'Why the hurry?'

'Meeting in Brussels. Plane leaves at six. I wanted to see you before I left.'

She led him back into the kitchen.

'Peter, I meant what I . . .'

But even as she spoke he was kissing her, taking her face in his hands, sliding his tongue along her lips, until they opened of their own accord, letting him in . . .

He had known her body for twenty years, known the route to take, the switches to throw.

Sarah didn't know how to be cold or moody. Maybe her sex drive had hibernated during the marriage, but it was certainly a light sleeper. Woke in an instant, despite herself, despite the protests that lost themselves in her breathing, in the short, staccato intakes of air. Kissing her, he could already sense the muscles tighting, the wetness . . . .

And then his hands were roaming unrestricted over her breasts, cupping, squeezing lightly. Her eyes shut tight. Lips half-open. The body starting to move in a rhythm of its own.

He needed that response. Needed the sense of possessing her, leading her out of Blake's world and into his own.

That had to be part of it.

Much better to have her half-naked in that kitchen. Not organised and formal in a boring marriage bed. He liked to see the proper little Army housewife with her clothes creased and her make-up smeared, and her legs and arms at all angles.

Control.

Blake's wife. Under his control.

He didn't bother with removing her black, satin panties, or the suspender belt. Just pulled her onto the breakfast table, watching her body squirm with anticipation, hands grasping for the zip on his trousers.

It wasn't her anymore. He knew it in that instant. Lifting her full white buttocks towards him, prising her legs wide apart, her thighs tensing . . .

He didn't love her. Such a shock to realise it.

Perhaps he was even indifferent to her.

He simply wanted to cut into Blake's life wherever he could – damage it, defile it, take it for himself.

When he had gone, she went upstairs to the shower, and ran it hot and then cold, washing away the afternoon.

The day had been a jumble of conflicting pieces: Peter, Tom, the children. Her life. Theirs. None of them fitted.

At the back of her mind she knew she would have to break it – just as she'd known at university, so many years back.

Peter was powerful and compulsive and still deeply habit-forming.

But you couldn't take such a drug for long. One day you would have to come out of it.

He didn't just touch your life, he banged and battered and left his footsteps all across it.

And today? Today something had been different about him. Even in the throes of it she had noticed the change in his mood. Probably work. Pressures of the war. The latest killings. Soldiers could never just leave the dead at the office.

Something was obsessing him, and she knew it wasn't her.

Chapter Forty-two

The meeting was to take place in a bank.

Amesbury looked out of his window and watched the grey and purple storm clouds hurry across Lake Geneva. They reminded him of city commuters, rushing to get home before dark.

Of course the bank was a very private place. A kind of matchmaker bank, where nothing was ever said, but plenty got done. One arm did the weapons deals, the other supplied the finance. One bit dealt with the terrorists, another with governments or drug cartels.

Customer was king. Whatever he wanted.

It was the kind of full-service bank they had all used over the years. So discreet, so self-effacing. Never, even under torture, would they admit to having met you before.

To them, each greeting was a first greeting.

Each goodbye was final.

Until the next.

In ten minutes, Amesbury decided, he would set out across the town on foot, passing by a patisserie or two along the way, lingering over an espresso. A little walk in the grasping wind – to help sharpen his knife.

Over breakfast that morning Hensham had reported his findings as the advance guard. Both the American and Russian had arrived late the previous afternoon, and checked into different hotels, under different names. Harrison Drew into a fleapit in one of the northern suburbs. Dmitry, typically, into the pride and joy of Geneva hotels

– the Grand, with views stretching forever towards the lake and the mountains.

Amesbury snorted as he looked out at the city. According to the ludicrously overpriced 'people' Hensham had hired to do surveillance, the American had spent the entire night coughing up his guts, and waking half the hotel. Only at dawn had he quietened down to receive a young and incredibly beautiful blonde who had stayed for just over an hour, before exiting by the staircase – not the lift.

Proof, it seemed, that the sick old goat could still do a turn when he wanted.

As for Dmitry – that one had long since turned and turned again. Hensham's report stated quite baldly that the Russian was in fact doing exactly what they thought he was doing – sharing a bed with his manservant, Andrei. At six in the morning a chambermaid had blithely thrown open the door of their room to confirm 'they were all over and into each other'. And that, she said, was putting it mildly.

Amesbury's mouth couldn't avoid a grin. Nothing like a little buggery to clear the passages before a difficult meeting.

Of course he wouldn't hold it against the man. How could one, in all honesty, after his own nine years at a country boarding school? All the same it might provide useful ammunition when the general nastiness began. The way it so often did.

The way it would this time.

He pulled on his coat and left the hotel.

As he stepped into the street a few drops of rain leaked disinterestedly onto his head, but he knew the real storm was yet to come.

Unless Dmitry could provide some clear assurances, the whole arrangement would unravel to the point of critical danger.

Already it seemed the Serbs would begin a whole series of terror attacks on Western troops; and then the taps would open, and the blood would begin to flow by the barrel.

Cost: utter humiliation for the major powers.

Hundreds of thousands more people ethnically cleansed and joining the ranks of the permanently dispossessed.

A carbuncle of impotence, clearly visible on the forehead of every government that let it happen.

And, worst of all, his own career in the bloody killing bottle. Christ, he wouldn't be around long enough to fart out loud; long enough to call a taxi to the main gate.

Amesbury stepped under an awning as the rain began beating on the pavements.

He'd been sure he would make it before the cloudburst, but the weather was clearly more treacherous than he'd imagined.

Lesson for the day, he reflected.

The weather was a warning.

As he entered the bank vault Dmitry's aftershave seemed to hit him full in the face. It was sharp and pungent – a full-scale assault on the senses.

There had been the usual extravagant greetings, three Judas kisses on the cheek, and a trite little comment about 'how God loved the Trinity'.

And then the business.

Don't take it all so seriously. Just a handful dead. Let's move on, Anthony. Don't make a big thing out of it.

How are we supposed to move on, if the Serbs start shooting our fucking soldiers?

No reason to shout, my dear fellow. We're all on the same side.

And then there was a moment of a delicious silence while each caught the lie at the same moment – plucking it out of the air as it flew past, savouring its bare-faced, unembarrassed quality.

Harrison Drew watched the two men glaring at each other. Leaning forward, he spread his arms wide in a Christ-like gesture of reconciliation.

'The Serbs have apologised.'

'That's bullshit.' Amesbury's cheeks flushed with colour.

'There'll be no more attacks on UN or British troops in the region.'

'Cock.'

Dmitry blinked several times.

'We have to apply some pressure.' Amesbury looked hard at each of the faces in turn.

Harrison coughed for a few moments, then swallowed half a glass of water.

'What do you suggest. Sanctions? That's like telling an atheist . . . Christmas is going to be a little delayed this year. Who *gives* a fuck?'

He swallowed again. 'Truth is we don't have any levers – except common sense. It's in their interest to do it quietly. And after a period of quarantine when we've stood up on the highest moral pinnacle we can find and pissed down on them, we can all be friends again.' He shrugged. 'Makes sense, doesn't it? No one's gonna back out of the agreement, not them – not anyone in this room.' The left eyebrow climbed. 'Ricaud tried that.'

He was back out in the street, not caring about the rain, playing all the little speeches back in his mind.

And when the agreement goes this high and this private, who polices it? Who keeps to the rules? Who can re-set them?

Only the Majority.

Two against one – if it worked out that way.

Amesbury pulled up his coat collar and felt a tiny shiver.

Cold city.

Always cold when you fight alone.

He recalled the time, years earlier, when he had worked in Downing Street as a prime-ministerial aide. There'd been one of the regular flaps going on – heads rolling all over the place, blood in the Thames. And a private secretary had whispered to him the kind of epithet that sticks in your mind when the games are going wrong; when the lies come back to roost; when you've shat on your own doorstep and there's nowhere else to stand.

Exactly how had he put it? 'At these exalted altitudes, Amesbury, they don't just fuck you for getting it wrong. They fuck you to death.'

'Amesbury has very cold feet.'

'I noticed that too.'

'Cold and slippery. Who knows which way he might slide.'

'The Ricaud syndrome?'

'I think not. He's a fighter. He wouldn't give up like that.'

The US Secretary of State sniffed the air and stared at the woman he had known since her childhood.

He couldn't read her expression. She had the ability to block out completely her thoughts and feelings – although he doubted for the thousandth time whether she really had any.

The combination of beauty and warmth on the outside, and the chill of a cemetery within. It meant you couldn't be at ease in her presence. You never knew if she could suddenly turn . . .

And yet he knew the family so well, been to school with the father, celebrated the birth.

A good family. Tried and trusted New Englanders. And she too was tried and trusted. Never let him down. Never had.

She had listened to the meeting from within the vault, emerging only after the others had left, in blue business suit and white shirt, her blonde hair bouncing in shape – so feminine, he thought, so inviting.

She stood with her back to the wall. The atmosphere seemed to suit her. The smooth steel bars, the polished marble floors, the mahogany banker's desk. No hint of dirt or dust – the room was shut hermetically, so that the real world would have no place there.

It was, he realised, like a tomb – already sealed.

Chapter Forty-three

They talked in whispers, gathered in a semicircle in Blake's room. They were the hard core of the unit – English, Brock, a couple of the others who would carry out the assault. Now that they knew there was no choice.

Blake looked hard at the faces. They were happier than he could remember them. If there had been doubts, they were buried. Quickly and out of sight. For once they had a motive and a cause. And they knew it was right.

Each of them had crossed his line.

That afternoon the news from the city had hastened their decision. Four members of the Macedonian assembly had been found in a car outside the parliament with bullets in their head, and full explanations of how they got there.

They wouldn't make deals; wouldn't see reason; wouldn't vote the way they'd been told to by the new men in town.

'We warned them what would happen,' said the piece of paper stuck grotesquely onto the dead driver's nose. 'It is the will of the people. History will vindicate us, and justice will be ours.'

It was, as Brock so aptly described it, 'a piece of fucking crap'. Below the surface, the quiet invasion was gathering momentum and collecting bodies along the way. And on it would march until enough people had got the idea.

Earlier that day, though, Blake had contacted the other UN commanders, amazed to find they were playing the whole thing down. 'Growing pains', went the approved wisdom. 'Society in transition. Got to be a bit of blood-letting in a place like this. If it doesn't hurt, it isn't doing any good.'

Invasion? What invasion?

He had put down the telephone, feeling the cold finger slide its way gently up his spine. The fix was in. The approved version already in circulation.

English let out his breath noisily. 'Another few days and they'll own the place without even moving a tank.'

Blake emptied his coffee mug. 'So much for the fucking international community. They couldn't give a stuff what we do. Besides, they're counting on the sure and certain knowledge that the UN never does anything.'

'Except for one part of it.'

Blake reached for the mapcase he kept beneath the camp-bed.

He spread a chart on the floor between them and turned to Brock. 'You recce'd this place from the chopper, but you went overland as well, didn't you?'

'Took the traditional route. Donkeys over the hills. So well-trodden, it's like a bloody AA roadmap. The smuggling still goes on. If anything it's stepped up considerably since the Serbs came in. Fifty-litre fuel cans strapped to the animals' sides. Whole convoys of them.'

'How did you and the donkey get on?'

Brock grinned. 'We're getting married next week. That's what happens when you ride on a girl's back long enough.'

They all laughed.

'How close did you get to the Kiro camp?'

'Crossed the main access road within about three hundred yards of the house. Got a lot of hardware dug in. Anti-aircraft mostly. Tanks. Artillery emplacements. But they weren't doing much. Pretty half-hearted bunch. Sitting around, smoking. Not the crack units – that's definite.'

'How many?'

'More than you'd expect. We saw about eighty. Probably twice that number in all. Who knows?'

238

'Did they tell you to piss off?'

'No way. Our guide got talking to them. Joking, shooting the shit. We ended up selling 'em a whole bag of cigarettes and some hooch. Disgusting stuff. Tasted like three weasels had sat around pissing in it. One of the Serbs, though, took a swig and loved it. Said they'd take another batch, next time we were passing.'

Blake caught English's eye, and there was silence in the dreary little room, as they watched the condensation dripping down the window, gathering in a puddle on the floor.

The idea had hit them all in the same moment.

Jimmy McIlvane had never nursed resentments for long. All through his life he had gone out and done something about them. And then they'd disappeared. Whether it was beating up the little runt at school who'd pinched his book, or the bigger runt who'd challenged his supremacy in the street where he lived, or the warder of the prison where he'd done time, whom he eventually mugged in an alley on the way home.

In Jimmy's book, resentments were not there to be nursed.

Only that's what he was doing now.

Inside the cell where they had shut him, he lay on the floor and went over the last, worst twenty-four hours.

Not your fault, Jimmy.

The old refrain came back to him.

Not your fault that the woman ran away from you all those years ago, that the rest of the unit got killed, that an unarmed child with big eyes that happened to shine in the darkness received a bullet straight between them.

Always someone else to blame.

And now it was Kiro.

Only he knew what he had to do.

With his right hand he reached round to his side and tore the flat knife from the patch of skin where he had taped it.

They hadn't even thought to search him.

'Hey! Who's out there?' Jimmy got up stiffly and battered on the wooden door. Twice that day they had let him out to the filthy lavatory with the broken windows. Surely they would let him again.

Not a sound.

'Come on, you bastards.'

The door opened a crack. He could see one eye staring at him.

Not too fast Jimmy.

'It's me for Chrissake. I want a shit.'

'You had shit already.' The voice was young, high-pitched.

Jimmy braced himself ready to force the door.

But in that moment it swung open. In front of him was a soldier he hadn't seen before. Small, wiry, cap pulled down over the face. But he was never going to waste time. Even as he passed through the door, the knife held behind him, he stooped a little, ensuring the right entry point for the blade – hard upwards, under the rib cage, gouging into the heart.

And yet even as his arm swung out, he held the soldier's eyes and knew it was a woman.

Quite enough to deflect the perfect stab.

Jimmy felt the blade strike bone, felt the woman struggle, nails questing for his eyes. She was yelling now, even with his hand on her mouth and the other one stabbing in and out. Five, six times. *Jimmy you fucked it*. Again and again his right hand pounding the knife in up to the hilt, knowing the blade was too short.

And only then did she weaken. Going fast. Sliding away from him. The knife still in her. So small and frail, dying so fast.

But Jimmy didn't feel it anymore. Nothing. No alarm. No disgust. Couldn't feel it after the boy. Even the killing of a woman wouldn't touch him. He'd stepped outside and he knew it.

By the basin he washed the blood from his hands and face.

Now it was Kiro's turn. And as many of the others as he could take with him.

240

Chapter Forty-four

'I'm back, Tom.'
   'I hoped you would be.'
'Want to come round?'
'Any reason why I should?'
She giggled. 'I bought you something in Paris.'
'What makes you think I can be bought. Try again.'
'I have a body that's wet and I don't want to dry myself with a towel. Is that clear enough?'

Twenty minutes later Blake found the door unlocked. The lights in the room had been switched off, but there was a pale blue glow from the streetlamps and the shape on the bed twisted perceptibly as he approached.

She lay half-wrapped in the sheet, one leg outside, one breast naked and pointing. Her whole body arching towards him. There was a sheen to the skin, as if she had covered herself in oil and he stood watching the shadows fall across the bed, making her half-real, half-imagined.

Without warning she pulled him down to her, forcing him onto his back, climbing astride him. He could feel her warmth through his clothes, the heart like an engine, breasts against his chest. Her hands went to his throat, gently at first, massaging, and then there was a sudden flexing of the fingers, and the thumbs were pressing deep. Deep and sudden. His breath seemed to die in his throat. Somewhere an alarm began to scream inside his head, as the fingers pinpointed the artery, closing off the blood supply. Precise, calculated. He'd done it himself. Done it. Done it. Done . . .

'Christ . . .' In a single movement he gripped her by the arms and flung her from him, hard, across the bed, feeling the fingers release him, hearing her yell in surprise.

I don't believe it . . . she was going to . . .

'Tom, what is it?'

His breathing ragged, irregular.

'I don't know. Your hands. Pressing on me . . .'

Was it a mistake? Did he imagine it?

She crawled towards him, lay on her side, next to him, hands stroking his face, her mouth so close. 'It's all right Tom. I'm sorry. I was playing.'

'I know, I know.' But his head wouldn't leave him alone, the buzzing in his ears, his eyesight blurred at the edges. It had been quite deliberate. Quite clinical.

Oh Jesus. Take it steady.

'Tom, you're more upset by things than you've admitted.'

'True.'

In the semi-darkness he could see the whiteness of her teeth, smell her breath, hear her breathing. Inside her was something he hadn't sensed before. That engine. A separate mechanism, divorced from her beauty and warmth. A separate agenda.

Her hand left his cheek and her index finger traced across his lips.

'I was just being playful. You know that.'

'I know.'

But he didn't, he realised.

He didn't know at all.

242

Chapter Forty-five

Dmitry leaned over and straightened the curl on Andrei's forehead.

'We must have you looking your best, mustn't we?'

The young man scowled back.

Dmitry patted his bottom. 'You don't like waiting, do you, little friend?'

'Waiting is not productive.'

'Ah yes, the Communist work ethic. Production. And production at all costs.' He nodded. 'How good it is that we grew up in such a society, where everyone worked so productively, and the results were so staggeringly excellent. Do you know, little friend, that we had the biggest supplies of oil and minerals in the world – and the worst economic performance of any industrialised country, bar none? That is how *productive* we were.'

'Why are you telling me this?'

'Because there is such a thing as productive *waiting*.' He let a moment of silence go by to emphasise the word. 'And this is what we are doing now. Things have not gone badly in Macedonia. Once the President was removed . . .' he luxuriated over the word, 'the local politicians began to see sense. Accommodations were made. So why press on with an invasion if it isn't necessary? The Serbs are prepared to continue their persuading behind the scenes – at least for the moment . . .'

'You have talked to Moscow?'

'But of course.'

'And the British and Americans?'

Dmitry kissed the young man on the cheeks and smoothed the uneven powder on his forehead.

'Plans change, my dear boy. Why upset them needlessly when there is nothing they can do? All of which means . . .' he kissed him again, harder this time . . . 'which means we may be obliged to keep your special talents in reserve for a little while longer.'

'You are teasing me, Dmitry.'

'Until now, little friend, I was not. But it will give me great pleasure to tease you for the rest of the night. Tease you – and, I hope, please you at the same time.'

'What about the British commander – Blake? He was the reason – one of the reasons – that I came here.'

Dmitry sighed with satisfaction. 'Put yourself in Blake's position, Andrei. His camp has been attacked. The little boy he befriends is shot dead – this we can understand very well – and he is in a mood for blood. What would you do?'

Andrei licked his lips. 'I would mount a full-scale attack on Kiro's headquarters.'

'Exactly.'

'And it would wreck the entire agreement reached in Geneva . . .'

'Exactly.' Dmitry grinned, stood up and began unbuttoning his shirt. 'The whole plan is finished. Blake will get rid of Kiro – and then his own side will get rid of him.'

'What do you want me to do?'

'Wait a little, my friend. And in the meantime . . .'

Dmitry took off his shirt and pulled the young man's head down close to him, hungrily, his fingers weaving the slicked, black hair.

Politics and deals were all very well, but the dear, sweet boy was a genius at other things.

Chapter Forty-six

Up the steep path along the hillside and there was no light to guide them. Blake led the way on horseback, as if at the head of a tiny medieval army. Behind him, some twenty men on foot or on donkeys, dressed in old coats and farmers' jackets – as straggly and coarse a bunch as you could hope to meet, coming out of the snow-white night with moonshine to sell.

And yet there was nothing straggly about the three Puma helicopters, brought into the base that afternoon at Dare Bombol, now standing warmed, armed and ready to depart. Their UN insignia had been removed, the white paint blackened and machine-gun mountings had been attached in the old school workshop.

Two had come from the American detachment, who'd been told the British would borrow them for the day and return them serviced.

No argument there.

Among the foreign community the invasion was already being referred to as 'so-called'. After all, hadn't the Serb forces stayed where they were, just three kilometres inside the border? Wasn't it all a fuss about nothing?

That night even the diplomatic cocktail circuit had begun to revive, with Blake receiving his first invitation since arriving in the country. 'Her Britannic Majesty's Ambassador requests the pleasure of Colonel Thomas Blake . . .' and so sorry he was that on this night of all nights, he was otherwise detained.

'Perhaps next week then.' The Ambassador's secretary had breathed optimism down the telephone. 'Things *do* seem to be getting a little more normal round here.'

'Indeed they do,' Blake had smiled. 'Pencil me in for next week.'

'Jolly good. Will do.'

And just three hours later he had set off into the mountains. And it wouldn't be jolly good at all, by the time they found out what he was doing. They'd get his name off that cocktail list faster than silk drawers on a sheep station.

No more Tom Blake, best of the best, officer at large, man of the moment – it would be Blake the traitor, Blake the unholy, Blake who had done something extremely unpleasant on the front lawn that everyone had seen.

He liked the thought of that, as the horse strained its way along the ridge, and the clouds sank lower to hide them.

Once he looked behind, raising his hand to English, virtually unrecognisable in long, shabby coat, and dark woollen cap.

Beneath the garb, he would be carrying his silenced Browning 9mm, as well as the Thompson sub-machine gun, again silenced, because silence was the way in – the only one.

A mile and a half to go, and they would approach the camp as the guide had arranged. Along the single access road, past the sandbags and the T55 tanks, and the lazy bastards trying to keep warm around a camp-fire. They'd be seen as a group of smugglers, nothing more. Come to deliver the goods. People of the night, people of the mountains. Ask no questions – and they'd ask none of you.

Money and booze.

Booze and money.

That's all they'd be expecting.

Jimmy was faster than you'd have thought. Even if the body had expanded, the legs still did the business. Still carried him light and silent when he needed it.

He was lighter now that he had killed again. Killed and slammed the door on life the way it had been. The world was against him and he was against it.

Just the way it had been when he was a boy in Glasgow, all those years before.

His dad, the school, the boys from up the road – all hunting him; all wanting to put their fist through Jimmy's face.

And only the boy and his wits standing between them.

As he ran through the building, he didn't have to plan the future. Just the final job at the end of the line, and then you lie down and kiss it all goodbye. There was, he decided, great relief in doing it this way. No lingering pain. No fireside chats with the conscience. No half-believed, half-whispered prayers to a man with a white beard, who might or might not take you in when you knocked at the door.

When you go, go quickly. That's what they'd always said.

And the journey wasn't optional. It was compulsory. And the journey was now.

Jimmy climbed the stairs from the basement, his body tight against the bare brick walls. He had removed the gun from the woman soldier's body, but it was her stiletto knife that he held in his hand. The knife would get him to Kiro, without any need for permission.

All through his life it had got him things other people hadn't wanted to give.

Silently he eased open the door to the main hall. The lights had been dimmed. Most of the men would be outside on guard, or in the outhouse or the kitchens. The place was unusually quiet.

As he moved to the first landing, he caught sight of his own reflection in the window.

But something else was there as well.

Jimmy glanced up and then looked again. Outside, beyond the house, there seemed to be a thin line of lanterns, moving, swaying in the darkness.

After a few seconds, the line became a procession of animals, and the animals carried human burdens.

247

Of course, he had heard of the smugglers' trains, but this was the first time he had seen one.

A perfect distraction for the apes on guard. Like a mobile shop, delivering the duty-free, and all the little perks of soldiery.

Maybe he'd take a bottle up to Kiro, and smash it on his head.

They came so slowly to the camp. Blake's own horse had been coated up and well-fed, but it still snorted at the cold, still dragged its hooves.

About a half-mile from the access road they had begun waving the lanterns. There should be no surprises for the troops. This was the appointed time, and these were the appointed deliverymen. A few more than expected, but they had brought plentiful supplies – cases of whisky, boxes of cigarettes and cigars, even some champagne . . .

And if he had his way, the bastards would never get to drink it.

Everything depended on their guide to talk them in. Jolly them along. Lull them like babies on their way to bed.

Of course Nico knew what he had to do. Just twenty-two years old, he was used to action. Not that he ever discussed it.

You don't discuss it when a group of bandits enters your home, ties you up and forces you to watch your mother and sisters raped repeatedly before your eyes.

You don't *ever* discuss it.

'There are battles,' he had said once to Blake. 'There are wars. And when you think you've seen them all . . . there are the Balkans.'

So when he was finally driven south, as the thousands before him, Nico had kept the memories, like an old bill in an old jacket pocket, waiting to be paid – waiting for time and opportunity to come together.

To him the British Army was both.

He knew they would open a door through which he and his memories could pass.

Tonight, he had told himself, was his night – and the night of his mother and sisters; a night when that feeling of wholeness could be restored to the family, when the girls would be able to dry their eyes, and Mother would once again deliver herself of that earth-warming smile which seemed to have gone forever.

He had taken a Browning pistol and a couple of knives for himself –and Blake had watched him do it, saying nothing.

If anyone could get them in, Nico could do it. Nico with the charm and the easy manner – and the hatred that would burn a hole in a tank.

As Blake looked on, he saw the boy raise his hand and wave to the Serb contingent.

A few of the men came sleepily towards them, guns raised but not threateningly. They were unwashed, stubbly, numbed by the cold –and yet already there was a glint in the eye.

Nico threw them a couple of boxes of Marlboro, watching the glint grow warmer.

The Serbs bent down in the snow and tore open the wrapping, grabbing out the packets, calling excitedly to each other. Blake began counting . . . *wait till you get at least twenty, thirty if they'll keep coming . . .*

Slowly his men were manoeuvring into that rigid straight line. Always a straight line, because then you can't cross into your own fire. Shoot any angle, as long as it's in front of the line.

Without prompting, the Serbs had begun unloading the boxes from the donkeys. Suddenly a young soldier brought out a bottle of champagne and waved it above his head. And that was the signal for the stampede.

Everywhere you looked there were men in vests and tunics hurrying out of the house, leaving the barricades. And Nico in the middle of them, taking the money, arguing, joking, backslapping.

Blake caught English's eye. They couldn't wait much longer. This was as good as it would get.

249

Nico, get out of there!

A finger of alarm down his back.

'Nico!'

But the fellow wasn't listening.

'Jesus, Christ almighty.'

English must have read his thoughts, because he was already dismounting into the snow, smiling broadly, no hint of urgency, shuffling towards Nico, like an old friend.

His hand went out to the boy's shoulder. But Nico simply glanced round, said something in Serbo-Croat, and jerked his head dismissively.

English beckoned again but the boy was already moving further into the crowd of soldiers. Only just for an instant the eyes seemed to catch English's, and his hands pointed towards his own body. The merest, slightest, most fleeting of gestures, but in that moment the meaning was clear.

Nico was going to shed the first blood.

Nico would give the cue.

Nico was taking over command.

From his horse Blake had seen it as well, and felt the nausea already climbing in his throat.

He looked round to check the men were ready. Nobody moved. The hands were motionless on the reins, just a few centimetres from their weapons.

And then something caught his eye in the distance. Beyond all the faces, silhouetted against the light, he could make out a bulky figure emerging from an upstairs window, climbing onto the balustrade, staring straight out towards him.

Even in the dark it was a memorable figure. The head looked to be the size of a football, stuck on square, wooden shoulders. No sign of a neck. It just stood there, hunched, inanimate. But the threat seemed inbuilt. No man of peace stands with such concentrated hatred and aggression.

He knew it was Kiro.

The two of them would need no introductions.

And even though the creature was at least two hundred yards away, it seemed as though their eyes met and held.

250

You're mine, Blake told him silently. I'll take you my friend. And I'll take you alive.

And that, on instinct perhaps, was when Nico gave his signal.

Jimmy had expected the guard outside Kiro's room.

Far away down the long stone corridor he could see the figure lounging against the wall, hands in the leather jacket, where he kept the arsenal – the 32-calibre Colt, the brass knuckles, the flick-knife. Thug's gear. Not a professional, standing there in suspended animation. And Jimmy felt elated, raising his hand in greeting, fixing on the toothless smile.

Inside him the world had gone quite quiet; the mind filtering out all extraneous sounds, providing only the information he needed. He had a gun and he had a knife, but this time, he reckoned, the pleasure would come from using his hands.

Thirty yards away the guard pushed himself upright off the wall, and turned to face Jimmy.

Shoulders like a brick wall, mind computing only angles and distance. Fifteen stone, he reckoned, of attitude and aggression.

Twenty yards. Give him a hallo, talk, keep his mind moving. He doesn't speak a word of English.

Ten yards. And it's as if Jimmy cocks a trigger inside him.

Wait for the range. Wait for the moment.

Jimmy on the balls of his feet, Jimmy more agile than he'd been in years, Jimmy with all the training of forty years from the grimy streets of Glasgow to the rubble of the Balkans, and he launched himself in a kick he hadn't made in a decade. Jimmy's karate coach would have died of shock, watching the right foot arrow out towards the guard's neck, striking the adam's apple, a searing, blinding kick, with nearly three hundred pounds of McIlvane brutality backing it.

The guard catapults to the floor.

Jimmy on his feet again.

So fast.

So nimble.

No longer thinking. Put back in the groove. Trained and programmed.

Jimmy's boot stamping down hard on the man's face, twisting, scraping, altering the geography.

The right hand flattens in a chop.

And he reaches down leisurely, slams it into the neck, finding the nerve and the artery.

Killing had never been a problem for Jimmy. It was living he couldn't handle.

Chapter Forty-seven

Blake would never forget Nico's signal, given without prelude or warning.

Even in the darkness he glimpsed the boy's hand, flashing out into the crowd of soldiers, fingers clutching the metal shard. One man clawed at his chest. And Nico's stiletto blade has disappeared into the body, right up to the scabbard. The Serb staggered and righted himself – eyes wide open, mouth soundless. An everlasting moment of silence while he stood on the steps between life and death, staring round – with the crowd staring back.

Now Tom . . . Don't wait. Go now.

He nodded almost imperceptibly, but all along the row of soldiers, the eyes took it in.

And already the hands were diving inside the coats, pulling the guns; Brock, English, in single polished movements as if they'd done it all their lives, opening up on a score of ragged soldiers, still unaware what was happening, as the matt black barrels begin to crack and spit and the bullets sort through them . . .

Nico down.

Three beside him.

Blake picks one more with the Browning Hi-power, tool of judgment, great decider . . .

Like hacking through an overgrown field.

Because they've all got to go.

Most of the Serbs were unarmed. Relaxed. Dying there with a bottle in their hands or a new pack of cigarettes.

Dying with smiles at the smugglers' haul.

Dying as they welcomed their benefactors.

Twenty years to grow. A second to die. No time like the present.

And even as they culled the little group around them, Blake and English are dismounting, sprinting for the house, firing as they go, almost unaware that the first of the Puma helicopters is landing around them . . . and the building is theirs to take.

On this, Nico's night out.

When he heard the shooting Jimmy didn't hesitate. Because Jimmy wasn't going to be cheated out of this one. Not this kill. Not the one he'd waited for.

Without even aiming, he shot the lock off the thick wooden door, kicked it open and crouched on the threshold, ready to fire again.

But even as he did so, the laughter came to him from the far corner of the room, loud, brash and raucous, echoing up to the high ceiling, out into the corridor. And in the semi-darkness he saw the man and the bottle, kneeling beside the bed.

Jimmy knew that scene. He had left it behind in Glasgow thirty years earlier, nurtured by the men who spent half their lives in Barlinnie jail, and lived the other half like that.

With a different bottle every night for comfort. A bottle to dream by, a bottle to forget, a bottle to love when the world is a cold, cold place and there's no one to reach out to. A bottleful of excuses for why nothing ever did or would go right.

And there was Kiro, perfect in the mould. Drunken coward that he always had been, killing the ones who couldn't kill back; pissed himself because he finally came up against a real army and didn't know what else to do.

Only Jimmy had no pity for the man. The Kiros of the world were mad dogs, and you shoot mad dogs. You're supposed to. Duty not pleasure. For the good of mankind, the human race, the planet, the environment . . .

'Have drink, Jimmy. Put gun down, have whisky.'

He hadn't been drinking long. But he'd drunk quickly. Jimmy could tell from the frozen jaw and the lolling head. Probably half a bottle straight down. Would have knocked out anyone else. But this man could take it.

Jimmy moved over to Kiro and raised the gun to within an inch of his eyes.

'Time, Kiro. Hear the bell? I promised you this. Now's the time.'

The drunken eyes peered upwards.

'What the fuck Jimmy?'

Eyes a little wider. Something was getting through.

'Hey, what I ever done to you. . . ?'

'It's a long list, friend. Too long. Now you have to pay the bill. Party's over. Everyone's going home. 'Cept you.'

Kiro's eyes began to flash around the room.

'Wait, wait, Jimmy. You want money? Ten thousand bucks. I give you right now. Cash. Twenty. Fuck sake Jimmy. I give you everything I have.'

But Jimmy had talked enough. He took two steps back, checked the magazine, and his hand was as steady as a steel clamp as he brought the muzzle down level to Kiro's temple.

'I want say a prayer, OK, Jimmy?'

'One prayer. Quick version. No fucking time for the Bible.'

English clamped on the helmet with the night vision and shot his way into the darkness of the main hall. When he could no longer see the targets he rolled a grenade gently towards the great staircase, as if it were nothing more serious than a bowling alley, and blew out the windows.

By then most of the soldiers had fled.

Blake had taken three as they hurtled out of the kitchen, running into the bullets, screaming, and going very silent, very quickly.

Entering the hall from the south side, he stepped over the bodies and stood still for a moment, listening. Always take a second, they'd said. Even when the shit's flying, and the buggers are dying. Take a second to think. Could be worth a lifetime. Hillsides are full of people who didn't.

Outside, the last of the Puma helicopters was landing, amid heavy machine-gun fire. He couldn't tell if it was coming from the ground, or the troops in the air. Glancing at his watch he could see they were less than three minutes into the operation, but they needed Kiro.

They took the stairs abreast. English forever turning, searching, watching their backs.

The house was bitterly cold, no different from the hills they had travelled.

Face numb, hands numb, mind switched to minimum sensitivity. All you can feel is the gun.

Onto a landing now, two corridors stretching away left and right. Without contact between them they knew which to take.

Blake went left, feeling his way along the rough wooden boards. There is light from the windows, punched at intervals along the wall. But he takes his time – a slow, silent choreography by such a practised dancer.

At the end of his vision, down past the uneven rusted doors, the cracked plaster, there's a shape on the ground, rigid and immovable as only the dead know how.

And someone has just passed this way to despatch the unwary.

Kiro was fumbling his words, the drunken tongue lolling obscenely from his mouth, as they rose and fell – a jumble of sounds that meant nothing to Jimmy.

As he listened the cold and the fatigue pressed down on him.

Would have been easy to close his eyes. Years since he had. Years since he'd left his mind and his memories somewhere else, and slept clear. Clear and peaceful.

Ten more seconds and he'd finish it. The half-man, half-insect was crawling on the floor in front of him, intoning, rubbing his hands together, dribbling.

256

Five more.

And then the pain and the shock hit him at the same time. A sudden avalanche of agony that shot up from his groin and seemed to pierce his heart. And then he's awash with it, eyes spinning, all defences breached. Shouting . . .

He must have shut his eyes for a second, for when he looked down there was a knife embedded in his left leg, and Kiro struggling to his feet . . .

Jimmy lashed out half-blind, catching him hard on the side of the head, felling him into the filth and bottles.

Jimmy leaned down and pulled out the knife. Immediately the blood began oozing down over the khaki, but it didn't matter. You get so far down the road, leave normal life so far behind you. Blood is just business. It's nothing personal. He raised the pistol and savoured the moment.

'Hold it Jimmy.' Voice from the doorway. Like a jolt from an iron girder.

'I said hold it, Jimmy.' Voice from the past. 'Put the gun down.'

And Jimmy knows that voice without having to turn around.

A grin on his face. 'Mr Blake . . .'

'Colonel – Jimmy. You were never good with ranks.'

'Sorry, Mr Blake.'

'Just drop the gun very slowly. Do it now.'

'Can't, Mr Blake. This one's got to be.'

'You have to. No choice. We'll put him on trial. That's why we're here. We've risked plenty to get this far.'

'Won't happen, Mr Blake. I've seen too much like this. He'll get away with it. Be a deal. Always is. That's why I should finish it now.'

'I'll kill you Jimmy.'

'And I'll kill him first.'

Jimmy turned round to smile at his old commander. Even as he did so, Blake shot him in the shoulder, watching him spin round, wildly, crazily, watching the lamp that had served to light Jimmy's twisted, tortured path go out.

Chapter Forty-eight

Amesbury slept in silk pyjamas, which he had purchased by mail order just three weeks after his wife's death. Of course she would never have allowed them. 'Far too poofy,' she'd have said, and thrown them in the bin.

But the Minister was both delighted and grateful.

Especially grateful they had arrived in a plain, brown wrapper.

Each time he wore them he would execute a low bow in front of the mirror, then stand to admire the red Chinese dragons cavorting across the black silk chest and the black silk bottom.

God, the old girl would have roasted his chestnuts for Christmas!

Especially if she'd looked more closely at the fly, where a kind of priapic griffin was lifting the dragon's tail for a closer look.

Amesbury was pleased with his reflection in the mirror, particularly on the few occasions when he managed to prod an erection into life.

These, of course, were gentlemen's secrets. What one did in the privacy of one's home, or imagined in the gallery of one's mind – that was one's own business.

That was his first thought as the telephone woke him at four a.m. and Peter Hensham came to the door.

Amesbury pulled his dressing gown tight around him, in case a dragon got out.

'Bloody hell, Peter.'

'My thoughts entirely, Secretary of State.'

They went into the kitchen and Amesbury sat pale and tired at the farmhouse table. Conspicuously he omitted to ask Hensham if he wanted anything. He was buggered if he was going to make the bloody man his morning coffee.

But as the brigadier began to speak, he got up and put on the kettle, in an effort to marshal his thoughts.

Try as he might he couldn't help the anger that awoke and began to surge inside him. Not the daily anger. Not the testiness of a minister surrounded by idiots. But an anger, tinged with fear, and garnished with hatred. Hadn't been that way for years. Not a full-blown tantrum, not since school really, when they'd burned his homework as a joke and he'd been caned before the whole class because the teacher thought he'd lied . . .

When Hensham had finished speaking, Amesbury's morning pallor had disappeared and there were angry red patches on his jowls.

He didn't look so gentle anymore. Didn't feel gentle. He was quite unaware that his dressing gown had slipped open and a dragon was leering across the kitchen table.

'Get out there Peter.'

Hensham didn't move.

'And do what?'

'End it.'

'You're going to have to be more specific, Secretary of State. We've done enough on nods and monosyllables over the years. You're going to have to spell it out this time. Sorry.'

'I'm telling you Peter, get Blake out of this place, and the Serb with him. Do it before the whole world knows it's happened.'

'And if he won't give up?'

'Then our valiant officer will have to suffer an accident. The Serb too. This has been agreed.'

'You mean kill them . . .'

'Dammit Peter, are you recording me?'

'Only in my mind, Secretary of State.'

'Listen to me. Blake can't be brought home in disgrace. It's too costly. Worst of all worlds. Utter and total embarrassment. But he can't be allowed to go on with this nonsense either. You say he's insisting on putting this Kiro on trial. There *will* be no trials, Peter. Reconciliation, that's the new agenda. A few buggers get their wrists slapped, and then we're all friends again. Christ, in a couple of years the Queen'll be tripping off to Belgrade to review a bloody honour guard. That's politics, nothing more. Look at China. Look at all the other bloodbaths. Doesn't matter.' He shook his head. 'Only the deal matters. Is it a good one? How long will it hold? What happens when it doesn't? Blake's upset the deal. He has to go.'

'Thank you for being so candid, Secretary of State.'

'Just get rid of the whole thing, Peter. No fuss. Understand?'

It was Veronica who wanted to speak to her father that night. Veronica who wanted to impart all the minor school disasters that had been heaped upon her: a lost place in the swimming team, exam results which had sunk her into the class below and a music competition where the best friend, but not the best player, had walked away with the prize.

And only a father would do.

They had tried the satellite phone direct, which was, in the strictest sense, forbidden.

But the lines were not going through. And then, with Sarah doing the talking, they had got on to the wife of a friendly signals clerk in Aldershot and she had promised to make enquiries.

'Probably just a blip,' said Phyllis Mead. Whatever a blip was.

'Thanks.'

'I'll get back to you,' replied the lazy, disinterested voice, as if she might or might not be bothered, and would in any case expect considerable gratitude.

So they waited, watching the news to see if Dad was flying the flag. But he wasn't. Where was the invasion? Where was the war? Who cared? For Britain it was a quiet Monday evening and the promised treat for Tuesday was a train strike.

And that was all the news for the day.

I could ring Peter Hensham, thought Sarah, and find out if all was well. But she didn't want to. It was time to put some distance between the two of them, some space for thinking. Peter was extraordinary. But Peter was dangerous. That had always been his real name. And now it had gone way too far. She wasn't ready. She would have to talk to him, and make him see reason.

Only, even as the thought came to her, she realised how impossible that would be. The only reason Peter had ever seen was his own.

In the end of course, Sarah knew perfectly well she would have to call him. But not about Blake, and not now.

Across the sitting room Veronica had fallen asleep on the sofa and the television droned on and it was nearly midnight before Phyllis Mead rang back.

'Bit of a flap, really.' The laziness in the voice had disappeared. Phyllis had become half-gossip, half-conspirator. 'Eddie said I shouldn't tell you any of this. But Eddie can be a silly bugger when he wants to be.'

'Any of what?' Sarah held the phone tight against her ear. Veronica had woken instantly.

'Don't know what to make of it really. Nor did Eddie, to be perfectly frank.'

'Please just tell me, Phyllis.'

'It's frightfully odd. Apparently communications have been down with Skopje for a while, and then there was a whole rush of traffic, Eddie said, round about ten tonight. Some kind of movements in the area. But the traffic was mostly in code. "Cosmic", they call it. Highest Nato classification. I shouldn't be saying any of this.'

'What happened Phyllis?'

261

'I don't know what happened. That's what I'm trying to tell you. After all this traffic, it simply stopped. Everything. Eddie's friend was told to shut down the satellite communications. Nothing was to go out. Nothing was to come back.'

'But why?'

'I don't know. No one does. Eddie should have come off shift hours ago, but they're keeping them all on the base. Nobody's being allowed home. Leastways not in Signals.'

'Please find out for me Phyllis.'

'I'm doing my bloody best.'

Sarah replaced the receiver and raised her eyebrows at Veronica.

'What, Mum?'

'They can't get through to your dad. Lines are down.'

'Why?'

'Nobody knows.'

'But something's wrong isn't it?'

She went over to the girl and kissed her cheek. 'I think it may be.'

Hours later she called him from the phone in the bedroom, knowing already that he wasn't there. She counted twenty rings – more than enough to wake the innocent and the sleeping.

Only Hensham was neither.

Chapter Forty-nine

Jimmy lies on the bare mattress, with half a bullet still inside him, sitting way too close to the heart. But he's conscious. He knows Blake is beside him.

'I can't tell you I'm sorry, Jimmy.'

The Scotsman grins with half his mouth, lines of pain running right across his face 'You're an honest man, Mr Blake, but you should've let me kill Kiro.'

'You've killed enough people in your time.'

'This one counted. This one was important.'

'He'll go on trial. That's why we did this.'

Jimmy croaked and the grin reappeared at the side of his mouth. 'Don't make me laugh, Mr Blake. There won't be no trial. And you don't believe it anymore'n I do.'

'Go to sleep. We need to talk later.'

Blake got up and left Jimmy by himself.

Even if he wanted to, there was nothing he could do for him. They had field dressings and morphine. They could dress a wound or bury a body. There wasn't much in between.

Outside the house, English had been herding prisoners towards a makeshift barn. He turned and caught up with Blake.

'Tell me what London said.'

'Not much to tell. I sent the message straight through to Whitehall. Told'em we'd arrested a suspected war criminal. The barest details, that's all. Asked for helicopters to pick up the wounded. And then nothing.'

'What d'you mean?'

'No acknowledgment. No confirmation. Silence. So I sent it again on an emergency frequency. That didn't work either. Brock says the satellite's down. We're not getting through.'

'Christ almighty, Tom.'

Blake nodded. 'For the moment *he's* about all we have going for us.' He pulled out the classified signal – the only message to come through from London – and handed it to English. 'They've closed airspace in the region, and they're warning us not to attempt to fly out. They're going to box us in. That's what they're trying to do. I wouldn't mind betting the satellite was shut down intentionally. And now, as far as the outside world's concerned, we don't exist.'

Through the grimy window he can watch the wounded being dressed, and the bodies laid out along the hillside. Bag by bag, the disposal team passes down the line. The clearers. The tidiers. Macabre in their masks and gloves, sorting through the departed.

Death, thought Blake, can be sickening if you watch it detached. Far less so, if you're out there with your hands dipped in it. And then you're screaming like hell, with the blood and the madness all around you, side by side with the man in black, picking out the victims.

But to watch it cold, to watch the aftermath, is to doubt and question, and calculate the cost.

And there are no answers. Instead, there are moods, where you come in certainty and leave in despair. Where you argue and justify, where sightless eyes stare at you from across the grave, asking you why you did it, and what it was for.

For now though, it was enough to study the flabby landscape of Kiro's face. The eyes of an animal reprieved. The leer that opened up his face like a pumpkin, the sparkle of delight when Jimmy was shot.

Blake had pulled him to his feet, rammed the gun into his

kidneys and warned him he would much enjoy the chance to pull the trigger.

'Course, Mr Blake, you are boss. If you say it, then it's true. Kiro behave good. You see. Then you find out truth. Kiro not such bad man. Trust me, Mr . . .'

He had shut the mouth with the back of his hand, smacking him hard across the jaw, feeling the man reel from the shock.

And when he looked again, there was blood seeping from the mouth. Only the smile was still there.

'Is fine, Mr Blake. Very fine. We talk about all this at the trial. Kiro not worried. No problem. Then you regret this. British soldiers don't beat prisoners. Not nice. Not nice at all. You get me?'

English had manhandled him out of the room, and led him away.

And Blake had worked hard to get back his control. Because just for a moment Kiro had led him to the edge. Scary to think of that. Scary to know that if someone can take you that far, they can also take you further. There's nothing you can't do, when you kill for a living. When you pick up a khaki tunic, and a piece of long, black metal, and go off pumping lead at your fellow human beings and then bury them in the ground in boxes. All for the price of a little house and a four-year-old car, and a Chinese meal on a Saturday night. And now London had put them in quarantine. Turned off their lights and was making them sweat. For the first time he was up against his own side. Why? Why no discussion?

He got up and circled the tiny room.

Keep it under control, Tom Blake.

No pity. No self-doubt. You did what you had to do.

And there aren't any medals for this one.

On the contrary, they'll take your old ones away.

He picked up one of the bottles they'd brought to the camp as contraband, unscrewed the top, and poured for a good five seconds.

You're OK Tom.
You made it.
You're coming through.

By four a.m. that morning Hensham had his team.

They met at the Brown Bear off Commercial Street, where the tarts still prowled the deserted alleys and cul-de-sacs, and the pimps and drug-addicts sat in the dark grey cars, engines running, heaters full blast.

Inside, the landlord, still active, still in the game after his tours in Rhodesia and South Africa, in Yemen and Algeria, made them all hot drinks, doctored with Courvoisier, and told them they were a bunch of arse-holed ragheads and he wouldn't take them to a bloody ball-game, let alone a war.

And they grinned at him when he said that.

Because war was what they did.

There's a ritual at these kinds of meetings. The brown envelopes go round the circle, with a few hundred inside each of them. Expenses, fellahs. And that makes 'em all smile. Some free drinks, a little money in the pocket. Loosens it up, as they say. Gets them in the mood.

Not that they needed much encouragement.

They had all been doing jobs they disliked intensely. Labouring on building sites, mending motorbikes, joining up with old mates to drive minicabs – a bit of debt collection just to keep the fist in. So they were ready.

When Hensham arrived, the talking died away. They knew him of course by reputation, if not from contact. Knew that Hensham took on the jobs that counted – the dark ones, the 'wet' ones. The ones that were never ever spoken about, after they'd happened.

Mouth zipped, boys. They all knew that. If they came home there would be more envelopes to open. And if they didn't, the wives and girlfriends would do it for them.

No one signs pieces of paper. For there are rules, written way back in another time. And no one breaks them except a fool.

'Everyone got a drink?' Hensham looks round the faces. A nod here, a raised eyebrow, a grimace. But they're all different. Every last one of them. No common profile, no distinguishing features unless you look into their eyes. The place where they all live and die. 'Mickey, Teeth, Splash . . .' the genial greetings tossed out to the little gathering.

'Sir . . .'

'Good to see you all. Any questions?'

A ripple of laughter around the bar. Sir is such a joker. So then he tells them.

He gave the men two hours to sort themselves out. To do the home run, kiss the dog, pat the wife or water the plants.

He knew that each of them had something he cherished. Mercenaries aren't drifters, with nothing to fill or enhance their lives. They're not devoid of feeling or affection. It's simply that the furniture of their lives is differently arranged.

Violence is confronted not shunned.

Pleasure is a drink, or a game of football, or a night of passion, enjoyed with double intensity.

And it's the risk that drives them. He had seen it so many times. The men who wanted to give it up and drive trains. Left, drifted, wept at the boredom of it all, and came back to the rifle and the comrades, their heart in perpetual motion somewhere between throat and sphincter.

A couple of them simply made phone calls and spent fifteen fumbled minutes with the tarts beside the all-night café.

Food, sex, booze – life's essentials, grasped and wolfed down, because it's always later than you think.

Hensham stayed in the bar and made sure the transport was ready. The plane out of Northolt, the ammunition and weapons.

He wanted to call Sarah, but something stopped him.

Not a conscience, but just the feeling that if you push fate too far, she'll bite you in the backside. At that point in time, it wasn't what he needed.

Chapter Fifty

Harrison Drew had spent a week without pain. For him, a golden, cloudless week. For Washington, a miserable time of searing, gusting winds and bitter temperatures, when the nation's capital sank into its overheated living room and cowered beside the television. Schools were out. Children stayed home. Lovers and mistresses were stranded apart. The elderly got carted off to hospital. And he couldn't have cared less.

Only now the needle had returned, piercing him deep inside the groin, not an ache or a spasm, but wild, limitless pain with roots and causes, refusing to leave till it had done what it came for.

He grasped the pills and swallowed what he could, his face contorted, his breathing snatched and coarse, as he waited for the drugs to control him. Only each time it took longer. Each time he returned to the world a little weaker, opening his eyes, wiping away cold sweat from his forehead, as if he had completed a terrible journey.

Perhaps the message from London had brought it on, followed as it was by the simpering voice of Anthony Amesbury, assistant chief arsehole to Her Majesty's Government – as he'd dubbed him silently the first time they had met.

Amesbury had been one long promise. He'd sort it, finish it, pretend it had never happened. The team was on its way.

From the window of his house in Georgetown, Drew could see the snow falling, all the way down to M street, where the shops were empty and the streets raked by killer winds.

The weather had been predictable well in advance.

Only the blind ever got surprised.

And yet in Washington it was hard to have eyes in your back passages. In most places you either won or lost. Here you would do both. The stakes were so high, the risks so great, it was impossible to win them all.

Even Reagan had been forced to learn that.

Take policy. Great while it worked, but when it failed, it was hard to see how it was justified in the first place. Like all the grand schemes designed to cure the world of its ills, they only worked for a while. Then, the world went out and fucked itself with something new. Today's friends were invariably tomorrow's embarrassments. Noriega, Marcos – all embraced into the fold, and then needing urgently to be shipped off, or shut up, or shafted. Always the way.

The question most asked in the upper echelons of power was: 'Who the hell authorised that?'

So now all new policies had to come with an all-new ingredient. Built-in deniability. Don't leave home without your shredder. That extra little facet, allowing you to claim you had never seen or heard of it in the whole of your life, and never would have contemplated such a damn fool idea in the first place.

The instincts of fifty years of Washington told him that the agreement was probably at an end.

But it also told him not to dump the whole casket at once. If the Brits could fuck it up, then they would most certainly do so.

He picked up the phone and dialled straight through to Geralyn Lang in Skopje.

'My dear lady.'

She awoke, as always, in an instant.

Had she really been sleeping?

You would never know, Drew realized. Geralyn was an

impenetrable forest. So much going on inside, and all of it out of sight.

He told her what Amesbury had said – in half the time, using single syllables, removing the bullshit qualifications that the Brits always threw in to confuse you.

'I'll be ready,' she replied. 'Just let me know.'

When she replaced the receiver, it was an automatic gesture to lift it again and call Blake at the camp. She wanted to be sure where he was at any hour of the day or night.

Only this was puzzling. The main phone at Dare Bombol was ringing ceaselessly, but no one answered. It was almost as if the place had been cleaned out and abandoned.

But that, surely, was impossible.

Chapter Fifty-one

On the balcony outside Kiro's room the three British soldiers surveyed the compound around the house. The night was agitated, the wind squally, ill at ease.

Blake turned to English. 'Give me the casualties.'

'We've got twenty pretty badly wounded – Jimmy among them. Some of them will die in a few hours.'

'There's nothing I can do. You saw the message. They've closed airspace around us. My guess is a team will come in tonight and attempt to take us out. There's no other reason for the signals blackout.' He shook his head. 'In any case they can't wait too long. Not if they want to keep it quiet. We've crossed their pain threshold.'

'What's our best option, sir?' Brock's question was neutral. No trace of alarm. He just wanted to know.

'We'll stay and fight, if necessary. No alternative, Sergeant. No communications. If the helicopters take off, my sense is they'll be shot down. We're in the middle of an operation that never happened.'

English turned to face him. 'If things go badly you should try to get out. Really, Tom. I'm serious. Whatever way you can. Even if they shoot at the choppers, the Sidewinders can do some damage. Worth a try. Somebody ought to know what happened.'

'We're a team, John. We'll stay as a team.' Blake put a hand on the man's shoulder. 'That's the way it's been.'

He left the two of them in silence and headed for the cellars. Jimmy McIlvane had been given the warmest, dryest of the rooms, but it hadn't helped his condition.

As Blake entered, he could see the man had deteriorated rapidly. The face seemed frozen, with that aura of half-life, half-function, where the body simply gives up and lets it happen. You could consult that face just as you consult a barometer. It was there for anyone to read. The sharp cold weather had set in for good and all the summers were past.

Jimmy, the despatcher, lay stretched out in front of him on the torn uncovered mattress. Jimmy, the decider. Always sending people away down that dark, unknown road, never taking it himself. Until now.

'Are you gonna operate, Mr Blake?' The eyes were still closed, and the body hadn't stirred but the voice was Jimmy. The whisper.

Blake approached the bed and bent down beside him.

'Can't operate. I'm sorry. We're in quarantine Jimmy. You know what that is. This isn't happening. We're out here and they've closed us down.'

'Never trust the fuckers, Mr Blake. Always said that.'

Blake smiled. He let a few moments pass, then drew up a chair. 'Way back in a bar in Berlin, there was a story you were going to tell me, Jimmy. Remember?'

'I remember, Mr Blake.'

'Want to talk about it?'

Jimmy's dry tongue emerged and licked at his dry lips. 'Don't know if I do.'

There was silence for a moment, as the wind battered the outside wall. For a moment the lights flickered, but stayed on.

'I'll bring you some water.'

'Scotch.'

Blake nodded and left the room. Rapidly, he whispered to the corporal outside. 'Get Major English. Tell him to bring the small video camera . . . and a bottle of whisky.'

Inside the room Jimmy had turned onto his back, the eyes still shut.

272

'You were a worried man in Berlin, Jimmy. D'you remember that?'

'Aye.'

'You wanted to back out of the job didn't you?'

Jimmy swallowed, but didn't speak. Outside, the wind attacked again.

'Can I ask you something, Mr Blake?'

'Go ahead.'

'What's in this for me?'

Blake shrugged. 'Name it Jimmy. World cruise. Season ticket at Murrayfield. Sides of smoked salmon . . . all yours if you want it.'

He laughed at that, tried to laugh, till the coughing racked his chest with pain and his body went rigid.

Out of the corner of his eye Blake saw English enter the room with a bottle and glass, then, in total silence, the man slid across to the darkest corner of the room, sat on the floor and took out the video camera.

Blake filled a tumbler, lifted Jimmy's head and poured a few drops into the open mouth.

'I want some money for the boys back home. That's what I want, Mr Blake.'

'What boys?'

'The ones I live with. Ex-mercenaries. People I've looked after. The ones everybody forgot about. Just a round of drinks and a meal, will you do it? Be a way of saying goodbye to them.'

'I'll do it, Jimmy.'

He opened his eyes, and he could see English in the corner, with the camera turning, but he showed no surprise, just lay there putting his mind in order. After a while he took another sip of whisky and told them about the early morning visit of Brigadier Hensham, about the assassination of a president, and about a little boy who was never meant to die.

He must have talked for nearly an hour. Talked as he'd

never talked before. Without excuses. Not blaming life, or its cast who never helped him.

When he'd finished, English turned off the camera, and Blake got up and walked out without a word.

It was just as well Jimmy was going to die. Otherwise he'd have strangled him then and there, on the mattress where he lay.

And then there was no more waiting. Blake knew what he had to do. He couldn't sit still and idle, couldn't let the day take its own course. Someone would have to get through to Skopje.

When it's right, he realised, you never question, never doubt.

Just take the steps. Just do it.

And it was Brock who volunteered well before they asked him.

To make himself feel better he spent a few minutes on the jokes. Grown attached to the donkeys, he told them. Softest thing he'd sat on in weeks. Missus had never been that comfortable. And then the smile went away. 'Piece of piss, sir. Back in no time. See if I'm not.'

Voice of the wideboy.

Blake looked him over, checked his gear. 'When you get into town, head for the Grand. That's where the press are. Get as many as you can. Make them insist on a helicopter. Some might have chartered by now. Also try room 218 – Geralyn Lang, the American. We have to get 'em here before our own friends start arriving.'

'No problem sir. I've been wanting a walk all day.' Brock grinned at them and pointed to the sub-machine gun. 'I've got the Thompson, got a compass, and I'll take a crate of scotch. What more could a man need?'

Blake shook his hand.

A little luck would be in order, he thought. He had listened to the forced confidence, measured it against the odds and was now quite certain in his own mind that Brock would never make it.

Hours later, he handed the tape of Jimmy's confession to English.

'If I don't make it out of here, do what you think best with it.'

'You mean make it public.'

'I can't tell you to do that.'

'What are my choices?'

'I think it should be released. But you may need it to buy your safety. If that's what it takes, don't hesitate. You've got a wife and family. When this is over, you'll go back to them.'

English got up from the chair, smiled and pulled his pipe from his pocket.

'If I'm not mistaken, among all the Army-speak, there's a principle here, isn't there? The family knows that, and they support it. You have my word the tape'll go public. They wouldn't want it any other way.'

Chapter Fifty-two

In the bar, the noise had become grating, overpowering. But Geralyn didn't mind. She enjoyed the attention.

They had all gathered round her – the tv men with the stick-on hair, the dissolute fuzzy-headed photographers, the poor cousins with nothing but a notebook. If there was a view to be had in Skopje, then the common view was that she was it – friendly, touchy, teasey. Possible. The lady reporter was the ultimate lonely man's dream, when the wife and kiddies were shut away in another time zone, and you could safely take your dick for a walk.

But would she come across? That's what they wondered. Worse still, would she come across with someone else?

Questions for the gentlemen of the press, on a boring night in a war that wasn't happening.

As the evening limped on, Geralyn bought a round of drinks and coffees and decided to stay for another hour.

By then they wouldn't even notice they were repeating the same stories. Ever louder. Ever more intense.

A couple of times she went over to the reception desk, dialled the number at Dare Bombol and replaced the receiver. Ten hours since her last attempt. Where the hell was Blake, and all the others?

The moon shied behind the clouds as Brock edged the donkey along the track, buffeted by the wind. Such a thin, fragile animal, so grossly overloaded, and yet it stayed the course. No hesitation. No reluctance.

Ahead of him the route was scrubland that dipped away from the house in a gentle incline southwards. Right direction but far too open and exposed. To the west thick woods offered much greater protection, only there the ground was steep, craggy. And in the darkness, highly dangerous.

As he turned west, the wind pushed him hard towards the trees, and almost immediately, the darkness of the forest closed around him. He shivered for a moment. But there was no place for fear. Kick it quickly, they always said. Kick it before it grabs your nuts and wrenches them off. And then you're no use to man nor beast. Kick the fear and never let it back.

He let the donkey find its way, and soon the animal had picked up the semblance of a path, rocky and hard, running like a slalom course down the hillside, winding and doubling back on itself.

As the gradient sharpened, he dismounted and followed the animal on foot, admiring the beast's persistence, stroking its thick, rough fur.

Every few minutes he would stop the donkey and listen, while the sounds of the forest went on around them.

Perhaps it was the cold that had dulled his mind. Perhaps the moon had tricked his eyes.

Only for one halting second, way down in the valley, he fancied he could see a lamp. And yet, no sooner had his eyes fixed on it, than it was gone.

It had to be a house, maybe a farm, or a woodcutter's cottage. He didn't know the landscape. Anything was possible.

But as he peered through the trees there was nothing. Beside him, the animal snorted and tugged at the reins, anxious to move on.

Once again Brock stood his ground, staring into the trees, every sense on edge. Again the darkness stared back.

After a few moments, he moved on, still watching. But now the ground was falling away beneath his feet, and he had to concentrate hard to stay upright. The donkey, too, had begun to slip and lose its footing.

About thirty yards to the right he could just make out a narrow ledge, cut into the hill below them – a place where they could rest up for a few minutes and take stock. He didn't like unexplained lights that went on and off in the middle of nowhere.

Even before he reached it, though, he could sense danger. The darkness prevented a clear view, but as he moved closer, it looked as though there was the entrance to a cave.

Watch it, boy. Quite involuntarily he felt beneath his coat to the Thompson sub-machine gun, thoughtfully equipped with a silencer.

Good to know it was there.

He hit the ledge hard, falling the last few feet, letting go the reins at the last moment, in case the donkey fell on him. But the animal landed better than he had.

Brock sat on the ground for a few moments. The cave was nothing more than the shadow from the rocks.

In the distance he could hear the birds calling out to each other in the valley. And now the wind had dropped, and the branches, once agitated and nervous, were at peace.

Beside him, the animal was snorting, pawing the ground with its hoof. Brock gave it some sugar from his pocket and stroked it again, but it wouldn't stand still. Pain. Nerves. 'C'mon old fellah. Keep calm. Quiet. Take it easy.'

From inside the saddle pack he took a thermos of tea and poured the boiling liquid into a plastic cup.

Christ, his hands were freezing. He could hardly hold it steady.

No time to hang around. People die on mountains in winter. Move it, Brock. Move, you bastard. Get the fucking job done.

He stowed the thermos and felt better.

By nine that night it was clear to Geralyn Lang who wasn't at the press party.

The diplomats were missing – so too were the UN officials, the administrators, the press officers, the auxiliary staff who would come every night to the watering hole and take their ease. She consulted the doyen of the press corps, a balding, expansive Italian who worked, during his more sober moments, for *Corriere Della Sera*, and was known as 'Dry Martini'.

'Have a drink Geri. I want to get to know you better.'

'You buying?'

He licked his lips. 'You selling?'

'Always.'

He led her through the crowd at the bar to a table at the side, nodded at the two men sitting there, who instantly rose to give up their seats.

'You have influence, I see.' Her clear blue eyes opened wide, as if to draw him in. 'I like that.'

'What can I do for you Geri?'

'Information.'

He grinned. 'Nobody has any.'

'Not even you?'

'People tell me things. Of course they do. But do I believe them?'

'Have you been told anything tonight?'

'Not yet. But the night is surely not over?' He inclined his head.

'Where are all the regulars?'

'I don't know. You mean the UN people? No idea. They have drills. They make plans. And then they have more plans and more drills. They are useless. We should not concern ourselves with them.'

He grinned at her and slowly moved his glass across the table to clink it with hers.

'Who knows what these people do? Last time I was there, they were practising kitchen duties – how to feed themselves during evacuation. The wives were doing needlework classes to prepare for the national emergency, when we will all have to make our own clothes. You laugh, but this is the truth. Listen to me. I've been here two years, OK? Nothing ever goes on here. Even a war they can't do properly. And why should they? Serbs have won. Opposition either frightened or shot dead. They control the place as it is. Who needs a war?'

'Someone thought they did.'

'Sure.' He touched her hand with his little finger. 'And now they've changed their mind.'

At the bottom of the hillside Brock could see the donkey was lame. The animal's hooves and fetlocks had been badly gashed on the rocks. Each step was causing discomfort and pain.

He would have to go forward on foot.

In the distance he could hear the rush of a stream, so he pulled the donkey towards it, thinking to leave the animal tethered, but close to water.

Above his head a large bird launched itself from a branch nearby, squawking wildly. He looked round, but there was nothing. Difficult to hear with the stream close by. As he approached, he could tell it was fast-moving, urgent. Too fast to freeze even in the bitter winter cold. He would leave the animal here, let it fend for itself. There was nothing more he could do.

Ahead of him was perfect cover. A row of bushes that led down to the water's edge. He could tie the animal there. At least it would be out of sight for a while.

Brock opened the saddle bag and gave it the remains of the sugar, patting its cold, stiff fur.

He was about to turn round full circle when he felt the gun between his shoulder blades.

At nine-forty-five the Italian was called to the telephone. He excused himself from Geralyn Lang and didn't return for twenty minutes.

When he sat down again the expansive gestures had gone; so had the teenage lip-licking, and the open-zip expression around the mouth. Something had surprised and shocked Mr Dry Martini.

She ordered him another beer and then raised an eyebrow. 'Do you want to tell me, or shall I call an ambulance?'

He raised the beer to his mouth, but she could see his hand was shaking. 'What is it? Talk to me.'

'Thirty miles from here, close to the Serb border, something has gone wrong. A military accident maybe. I got a call from a friend. He didn't know what it was. But the area is being sealed by UN troops.'

'What for? We have to get out there.'

'Wait, wait. God's sake . . .' The voice was suddenly angry. 'You want to charge off – then I tell you nothing. Not a word . . .'

'OK, OK – I'm sorry.'

'My call was from a friend in the UN Liaison Office. He said he couldn't talk now, but he'd be leaving in an hour or so, then he'd call again. It seems there are special forces in the area. This is not so new. They used them undercover in Bosnia, but something has gone badly wrong.'

Geralyn excused herself for a few minutes, went up to her room and tried a call to the US. But the lines were out of order.

'Fuck you,' she told the receiver.

The balloon was up and flying and everyone was disappearing on her.

Brock turned slowly, carefully, his gut seized with fear. As he did so, the gun was withdrawn and in the darkness he got a glimpse of its owner.

There were two of them, six feet from him, soldiers, but very young. That much was clear, but he didn't recognise the uniform. Night fatigues, special forces. He hadn't seen them before. They wore no badges, no insignia.

The younger man gestured with his pistol. 'Who are you?'

281

English – but it wasn't his language. Brock could have sliced the accent with a knife.

Who the fuck were they? Serb? No, they wouldn't be out here on patrol. Wouldn't need to.

He decided to play the dumb smuggler, gesturing to the box of whisky in the pack slung across the donkey.

As long as they didn't search him . . .

The older man reached for the saddle bag and undid the clasp.

He brought out a bottle of whisky and showed it to his companion.

'Business, huh?' The man laughed, and muttered something to the other. Brock couldn't be sure what it was – Spanish, Italian?

'OK, you come with us to the jeep.'

And that was when he knew what had to be done. If they had transport, then he'd have to take it from them. But the odds weren't good. One of the soldiers would have to be taken out . . .

He pointed at the donkey and waved, as if he planned to mount and say goodbye.

'Uh-huh, if you go, we shoot you.' The younger one raised the pistol.

Brock's hands came up in a stop sign, and he pointed to the bottle of whisky, and made a pouring move, as if to say . . . that's OK. We'll have a drink and then I'll come quietly.

That was the message they got.

For the two grinned at each other and, with no hesitation, turned their attention to the bottle. One of them produced tin mugs while the other began to pour.

They didn't even notice Brock opening his coat. In fact they were about to raise the cup to him, when he shot the youngest one with the silenced sub-machine gun. Not as exact as he'd wanted – three bullets puncturing the face and neck, even as the man turned, cup in hands, as if to toast his departure from the world.

In that instant the other went for his pistol but Brock had already shifted aim.

'You don't have time . . .' His voice steady. 'I'll kill you now . . .'

The soldier stopped in his tracks. Eyes calculating. The moment when life and death stand equally balanced before you.

'Put the fucking gun down.'

He did as he was told.

Keeping his eyes fixed on him, Brock bent down and checked for a pulse on his colleague. But he couldn't find one. The skin seemed cold, as if the winter had already claimed him.

'What you want?'

Brock could see the soldier's hands held in front of him, shuddering out of control. He forced him up against a tree and searched him, removing a titanium knife and a small 32-calibre pistol that he couldn't identify. He pointed to the body.

'Get the clothes off him. Quickly. Get him out of it.' The man didn't move.

Brock turned him round and slammed his fist into the man's jaw. 'I said quickly.'

Immediately the soldier knelt down by the body, scrabbling with the belt and the buttons, hurried jerky movements, teeth chattering in the cold.

As he put on the uniform Brock searched the pockets. They were empty. No papers or identity tags. Classic special forces. If he'd left them both alive they would certainly have pressed the alarm.

Over by the stream, he caught the donkey looking forlornly back at him as if it expected to be next.

But Brock turned away, pushed the soldier in front of him and headed for the jeep.

Every so often he would stick the gun in the man's ribs and stop him, turning 360 degrees, listening, checking.

He realised he no longer felt the cold. Only the tiredness

seemed to gnaw at him. Tiredness, and the fear that you stuff away into the corner of your mind and hope you'll forget.

And now the soldier was leading, and this was the danger time. Did the jeep exist? How many others were in it? Could it pass the roadblocks?

But you can't let the questions take over. You have to be certain you'll make it.

Right up until the time when you don't.

Chapter Fifty-three

The glint of reflected light made him stop, and he rammed the barrel of the Heckler & Koch into the soldier's kidneys. As he peered into the middle distance, the wide jaw of a white Toyota Landcruiser stared back.

'Anyone else there?'

The man shook his head.

'Lie to me and you'll get it first.' Brock pushed him forward. He knew they didn't have long. Two-man patrols seldom strayed far from each other. Most likely there was a line of them, attempting to seal the area at intervals of two or three miles.

Thirty yards from the vehicle, he stopped. 'Get in there and get it started.'

'I don't have keys.' The man's confidence had started to return. Maybe he too thought he had a chance.

'Then crank it.'

The soldier smiled.

Without warning Brock raised his leg and kicked him hard between the legs. He groaned and sank to his knees. As he did so the foot shifted and struck him in the stomach.

'You don't have a choice in this. Get up and start the fucking thing.'

The soldier rolled over and threw up into the snow. 'Move it.' The man rose gingerly to his feet and Brock could see that the smile had gone.

Of course, he thought later, he must have lost his concentration. Maybe he was more exhausted than he had realised. But as if from nowhere the noise seemed to settle over him – the terrible clatter of an attack helicopter, all lights on, a huge, questing, sucking creature, swooping low and slow over the trees, even as they stood paralysed and exposed by the snowy roadside.

'Wave, fucker.' He shouted at the soldier and raised his hand in greeting.

Only all he could think of was that they had found the body and they knew who he was.

And that this beast had come out of the darkness to kill him.

From high up on the mountainside, Blake had spotted the same helicopter. After a few minutes there were two of them, their spotlights trained on the trees, lighting the valley, like two giant insects, sweeping in circles.

So there, if he wanted it, was final proof that the area was being sealed.

And without even the tiniest shadow of doubt, Brock was finished.

Chapter Fifty-four

Geralyn Lang had grown ever more impatient. The Italian was a royal pain in the arse and couldn't be counted on. She would have to make her own arrangements.

Back in her room, she lifted the receiver and tried the camp at Dare Bombol. The phone rang ceaselessly. Damn Blake. Where the hell had they gone? And why had he excluded her?

Hurriedly she flicked through the notes New York had given her before leaving. It was a list of the network's contacts – people they'd used and abused over the years and then thrown away. Most of the time, television's scorched-earth policy meant you could never approach the same contacts twice. Either they had never been paid, or waited months for their money, or been insulted by a sixteen-year-old producer who didn't know any better.

Half-way down the page, though, was the name of a helicopter charter company that had once operated throughout the Balkans. Mainly they would be ex-Air Force pilots, which probably meant ex-Agency, which probably meant they were marked or compromised or generally branded undesirable.

According to the notes, the company appeared to have offices in Belgrade, Athens and Skopje.

But then, she reflected, the list was probably older than she was.

Geralyn picked up the receiver and dialled the Skopje number, without enthusiasm.

The attack helicopter had disappeared rapidly into the darkness, heading back towards the valley, combing and searching. Brock didn't waste time. Pushing the soldier into the driver's seat, he took a glance at the map and ordered him to drive. Once they reached the plain there were plenty of routes into the capital. But for now, there was just a single highway south. And he knew it would be sealed.

As they moved off, the snow began falling again in thick tufts, an almost impenetrable mass lit up by the yellow light from the headlamps. Once, the Toyota skidded badly on a hairpin bend, but the soldier regained control, slamming it into second gear, holding down the speed.

Brock jammed the gun into the man's side. 'Keep going, damn you. This isn't a fucking Sunday drive.'

'Road's slippery. We'll go over the edge.'

Brock lifted his gun so it was back in the man's field of vision.

'If I have to drive, I'll kill you first. Move it.'

For nearly twenty minutes they crawled forward. Only once did they see other traffic – two military supply trucks, painted white with UN insignia, droning past in the opposite direction. Otherwise the snow lay clear and unmarked before them.

From the map it seemed they were some twenty-five miles from Skopje, but the roadblocks would come first.

He turned to the soldier. 'Where are they set up? I want details and locations.'

'They move them around. We don't know. No one tell us.'

Brock said nothing. The man was probably right. But this route, of all routes, would be blocked at specific points.

Staring into the gloom he could see the road begin to climb for the first time. It was no more than a dip but beyond the ridge, he could make out a reddish hue in the sky, which probably meant a village or hamlet, unmarked on the map.

It didn't worry him, but it should have done. At the top of

the rise, the snow gusted straight at them and for a moment he saw nothing at all. And then the world jolted before his eyes. Ahead of them was a village all right. But the place had been ringed by armoured cars and troops in night fatigues, transforming it into a heavily fortified roadblock. As he stared through the windscreen, Brock could make out a communications post, with at least ten men on hand, as well as dogs. There was no way of telling how many more might be out there.

He turned away and swore quietly to himself. He should have known it, should have planned for it, should have taken his chances on foot. Now it was too late to turn round.

Brock lifted his gun and stuck it hard into the soldier's stomach. 'Play it nice and friendly, but keep moving. No games.'

Thirty yards now.

Twenty.

Fifteen.

Funny the way he could hear his mum's voice all those years ago, telling him what a cheeky sod he was, and how the Army was the only thing that would make a man of him. They'll keep you out of bloody trouble, she'd said.

He smiled as the roadblock edged closer.

Keep him out of trouble, eh?

Pity the old girl couldn't see him now.

As he watched, two soldiers stepped in front of the Toyota. One of them – a captain – had his hand raised.

The driver wound down his window.

'You finished in this sector?'

He nodded.

'All you people have to get out of the area now. Where you going – Skopje?'

Again he nodded.

Brock froze. 'Give this guy a lift then.' The captain pointed to a thin, dark figure by the roadside. 'He's sick. Medics think it's appendix. Drop him in town, OK?'

They opened the back of the Landcruiser and the figure

was helped inside. Brock noted he was still heavily armed.

'Right, get going.'

As the driver let in the clutch, Brock glanced back at the roadblock, but the interest in them had passed. The barrier came down again. The soldiers had turned away. Even so his mind was in turmoil. Now there were two of them in the Landcruiser and the odds had shifted against him.

Bad situation. Critical.

Forty yards ahead the road bore left, but he knew they'd never let him make it.

In their position he'd go for it now. Had to. No choice, Brock. No choice. Never any fucking choices. Kill at random. No big deal. Done it once, done it a hundred times. You're only pulling a trigger. It's the gun that does the rest.

He wrenched the pistol away from the driver's side, leaned over the back of the seat and shot the thin, dark soldier in the forehead. Even as he did so, the driver swerved wildly to the left, skidding the wheels, braking harshly. The vehicle slewed round, facing back towards the roadblock. Brock's head hit the windscreen hard. He must have shut his eyes involuntarily from the pain, for he could feel the gun being wrestled from his grasp. Jesus, the man was mad. A series of punches slammed into his face and neck, fingernails were clawing at his eyes. Mad, mad . . . And then his vision cleared and the gun was still in his hand, and he fired at the tortured twisted face just a few inches from him. Seeing death closer than he'd ever done before – the bullet passing straight through the man's left eye, the other opened wide in fright and surprise. Blood spurting at him like an open tap . . . and only the voice inside that said move. Move it Brock, before they come and get you. Move it.

Roughly he dragged the dead soldier onto the passenger side, climbed over him, and shifted the Landcruiser into gear.

In the driving mirror he could see the barrier was still

down, the soldiers turned away, as a helicopter came in to land nearby.

Christ, Brock. Christ Jesus almighty. Blood everywhere. Carnage.

You stop that.

The voice again.

Stop that now. You follow orders. Whatever it takes.

Whatever the cost. Once you start on this game, you never, ever have the luxury of looking back. You drive to Skopje, young Brock – and you do as you're fucking told.

Chapter Fifty-five

It was Hensham's squad that had checked through the
Landcruiser.

They had moved in early that evening and taken over
from a combined US and Italian special force. From now
on no other troops were to be allowed in the sector.
Whatever happened on the hillside that night was to
remain secret.

Along the journey Hensham had made the rules clear
enough. For those who shut up, there was money, and
plenty of it. For the ones who talked, a bullet. Wherever
they went, however far away, in whatever country, he or
someone else would find them. That was a promise and they
should treat it that way. They had entered the land of stark
choices and there was no room for misunderstanding.

At ten he gave them the final briefing.

Of course they were surprised. Among the faces in front
of him he could read disdain, anti-climax, even disappoint-
ment. After all, they had psyched themselves up to land in a
flurry of bullets. A seize-and-destroy operation of the kind
they liked best. And Hensham was telling them to play it
friendly and soft.

'What's the matter, Pete?'

He singled out the wiry, little figure from Teesside, who
was shaking his head in frustration. Pete 'the Teeth' was the
self-appointed commander.

'I thought we was gonna finish the job.'

'Well?'

'So what's all this about talking to them nice and matey-like?'

'That's how we start it, Pete. See if they play ball. See if they accept our offer.'

'And if they don't?'

'Ah, well that's different.'

'How different, sir?'

Hensham paused and looked round the room, as if weighing up the answer in his own mind. 'Then you can kill every one of them you can find. One by one. That suit you?'

Pete grinned and glanced round the other faces, gauging opinions. Thumbs were raised, grins exchanged. After all, there were plenty of debts to be settled with the regular Army. Plenty of slights and insults to be avenged.

The group was happy.

Geralyn Lang replayed the conversation in her mind. The helicopter company had sounded less than fully operational. The first voice had bellowed in an incomprehensible language and cut her off. The second spoke English in a long-lost Brooklyn accent and seemed to fall asleep at the receiver. The third voice was awake and far too precise. They weren't flying. They had no permission. Airspace was closed and the weather was fucking awful.

If she didn't like that – she could write to her congressman.

After a while she decided to return to the bar and pay homage to Mr Dry Martini, but she was angry and frustrated. He still had no precise information. The friend of a friend had let him down and hadn't called back, so there were no hard facts of any kind. Something had gone wrong, somewhere in the north. But what? Christ, it was a lousy place to get things done!

When the knock came on her door, she knew it was the Italian, wanting something on account, the dirty little creep. That was the limit. She'd tell him to . . .

But as she opened the door she found a man, clearly on

293

the outskirts of life – beyond cold, beyond fear or exhaustion. The shell of a man, still alive, but with his lights dimmed and fading.

Looking more closely, she recognised him from the camp at Dare Bombol and, holding open the door, she led him inside and sat beside him, till the warmth of the room had reached his body and he was able to talk.

Under cover of darkness no one saw Hensham make his way to the lead helicopter. No one saw him put a tiny box aboard, stowing it carefully in a locked container beneath the pilot's seat. And no one was there to examine it.

The box contained a tiny receiver with a built-in antenna, capable of picking up a frequency-modulated signal within a range of about two miles. More on a clear day in clear conditions. Less in the mountains.

As for the other contents, they were highly volatile, and, in close proximity to their target, invariably fatal. They carried a brand name that the Czechs have made almost as famous around the world as Coca-Cola.

It's Semtex – and its sole purpose is destruction.

Chapter Fifty-six

Just before midnight Blake did the rounds of the wounded, lying in rows in the main hall, as the wind tore at them through the smashed windows. His men had done their best with field dressings and morphine, but they couldn't prevent the slide.

Strange, he thought, how they always die in the evenings and in the hour before dawn.

As he watched, the regimental padre made his way from bundle to bundle, offering a hand or a prayer, once stooping to close the staring eyes of a young, dead Serb.

Here, there was a quietness about death. An inevitability. No sense of struggle or conflict. The great hall, with its wide staircase and shattered chandelier, was simply the staging post between here and there. The departure lounge. And every so often another passenger got up to leave.

Outside, though, the picture was very different. His own troops had taken over what were once Serb defences – the armoured cars and gun emplacements as well as the makeshift sniper positions on the roof of the main building, the anti-aircraft missile launchers.

The kit was in place. So were the men.

He had talked to them all that evening. Told them what he expected – an assault by other British soldiers, with orders to disarm them, sanitise the entire complex and bury all traces of what had happened. Orders.

'We can't let them do that.'

They had looked back in silence.

'All of us, we've seen too many lives chucked away in the Balkans. Time the war criminals were put on trial. Time we saw a little justice. That's what all this has been about. I know we've been down this road. And I know you all came voluntarily . . .' A chuckle went round the faces. 'Whatever happens now I want to thank you for coming this far.'

The silence was restored.

'I'm sorry it has to come to this.' Blake shrugged and for a moment he looked at his feet. 'But there are mad and ruthless people all over. Trouble is they're on our side too.'

He could see them taking it in.

'Make no mistake. The people who come tonight won't be regulars. They wouldn't dare use them. They'll be killers, paid for and licensed by our masters. I've no doubt at all what kind of people they'll use.'

And then the cliché. 'Good luck to you all.'

As they wandered away he wished he hadn't said that. It was like the First World War generals, ordering their troops to get mown down by going over the trenches. Good luck, fellahs. Jolly good show. *Bloody* good luck if one or two of you get through.

Of course he could end it all now, if he wanted. Surrender the arms, get the wounded seen to. Have them all home by the weekend in the arms of their wives and girlfriends, or down at the pub. But no – he, Tom Blake, wanted a bit of justice. So they had to get shot on a hilltop to make a point. Fucking good job, Blake.

He watched them move away and take up position – except for one man, the sergeant who had stood in for Brock: no more than twenty years old, and almost as round as he was tall.

'Me and the men just wanted to tell you something, sir.'

'Go on.'

'We've all considered our position.'

A finger of doubt touched his arm.

'We'll go with you all the way, sir. Whatever you think we

should do. We trust you to do what's best.' The man saluted and turned on his heel. He had said his piece.

Blake and English exchanged glances.

'British Army.' The major shook his head. 'Articulate buggers, aren't they?'

Blake stared after him. 'I was about to change my mind, tell 'em to chuck it in. I'd take all the blame, and they could go back home to Aldershot and forget about it.'

'I think we're past that point, Tom.'

'Why d'you say that?'

The major fastened his tunic and pulled the cap comforter lower on his forehead. 'Because of what Jimmy told us on the tape. We know who started this. We know who ordered the President's assassination. We know too much. It's as simple as that. Whoever comes tonight doesn't want us going home. Not if he can help it. Not any of us.'

Chapter Fifty-seven

Geralyn Lang is calm now – every contoured, sculpted inch of her – as she sits back in the armchair, toying with a bracelet, feet on the bed. And yet inside her the drumbeat has started. A quite discernible pulse, firm and rapid. There's a climax in sight. She can always sense it.

There are fresh clothes for Brock, borrowed without explanation from the camera crew. And she isn't taking them with her. Not on this trip. Not for anything. From her suitcase she removes the tiny Hi-8. The television tool that doesn't argue, or stop for meal breaks, or demand overtime. All weathers. All conditions.

She asks Brock to wait for her downstairs and calls the Italian in his room.

'I have a story . . .'

'What d'you mean, Geri, my dear? I am the one with the story. No?'

'I'm leaving now. You want to come with me or stay?'

A chuckle at the other end. 'I would come with you anywhere . . .'

'Then get your coat . . .'

'But where?'

'You'll find out.'

'I be there, Geri.'

'I knew you would.'

And there's just one final call long distance to an unlisted number in Washington.

'Where is he?'

'Away from his desk, right now.'

'I need to speak with him. Urgently.'

'I'll leave him a message.'

'Now, I said.'

'I'm afraid that's quite impossible.'

'Why?'

'I'm sorry. I can't help you.'

No answer either at his home. Where are you Harrison Drew? Away from your desk, or away from Washington, on a wholly deniable mission somewhere else?

On her own now, Miss Geralyn Lang.

They had headed deep into the valley, the three grey-green helicopters, without markings of any kind.

On a signal, the noses tipped forward and they began clawing the cold air, rising in sharp and vertical formation, like high-speed elevators on their way to the top of the mountain.

Hensham could see the target looming above them, the cloud barely above the rooftops. No time to land gracefully or pick a position. Just slam the chopper down and do what you have to.

And now the surprise has gone. Three giant rotors, three turbo-charged Pumas screaming in anger as they rise above the sheer cliff, determined to wake half the world. And even before they hit the ground the lead team is out, flattened on the ground, securing the area around the machines. Fifteen seconds, twenty – no more – and they're all in place on the top of a mountain, ready for an order, with the Balkan wind whipped and freezing around them.

Hensham takes a moment to compose himself. Full battle fatigues, all the stripes in place. The combat brigadier, with each of the options covered, and everything to play for.

Just finish it, Peter.

That's all he had to do.

He gets down into the night to find the darkness total. This is the last time Blake will hold the cards. The very last.

As Hensham stands there, a battery of arclights comes on, illuminating the field around him as if it's a stage – and the performance is about to begin.

The airport had long since closed for the night, although during the state of emergency a skeleton staff was employed round the clock in case of unscheduled flights. Tonight, though, the approach road itself had been blocked, a half-mile from the perimeter fence. Geralyn could see the local troops warming themselves beside a makeshift brazier, stamping their feet on the snow. As the minibus drew closer they began waving their guns to warn them away.

She pulled up and looked at her passenger. 'I'll tell them we've fixed a charter . . .'

'It's OK.' Brock leaned forward. 'I have UN papers. We've got access to the airport.' He got out and handed over a document to the nearest soldier. The response was immediate. The man began flapping his arms wildly and shouting at his fellow troops and between them the barrier was lifted. Brock grinned and climbed back inside. 'Something had to go right. If I remember, there's a cargo section to the west of the main building. The last time we unloaded there were a couple of old helicopters parked there.'

'Old helicopters?' The Italian raised his eyebrows. 'What about new helicopters? Maybe this not such a good idea.'

The western section of the airport was in darkness. Two hangars were closed and padlocked. They got out of the minibus. Brock disappeared round the side and was back within seconds.

'You better look at this.'

They followed him to the edge of the hangar.

'Oh, Jesus!' Geralyn couldn't help the exclamation. Parked in front of them there was indeed a helicopter. At least the remains of one. An old beige Huey, eight-seater, once the workhorse of Vietnam – now . . . She looked again. Now God only knew what it was.

She went up to it and pulled off the side panel. At least it wasn't a museum piece. There were plenty of signs of recent life – maps, sunglasses, a couple of plastic coffee cups.

'What do you think?' She turned to Brock.

'Don't know anything about them.'

'You?' She looked hard at the Italian.

He shrugged and turned away, adjusting his silk scarf, tucking it deeper beneath the sheepskin coat.

Brock made a face. 'I don't see too much sign of any pilots.'

Geralyn gave a big sigh, her breath creating a tiny cloud in the freezing night.

'I guess that leaves me then.' She climbed inside and began the pre-flight check.

Brock and the Italian stared after her in complete silence.

'Hensham.'

He heard the voice call out to him, before he saw the figure, emerging from the darkness in the direction of the main buildings.

Blake was immaculate in uniform and light blue beret.

'I might have known it would be you.'

'Greetings, Colonel.'

'What news from London?'

'Come to assess your needs. Didn't know what we'd find here.'

'Took your time.'

'We had to keep it quiet. You didn't make it easy for us.'

'Bullshit, Hensham. What about the wounded? How many do you think have died here since I sent out the message.'

'We did what we could. If you'd kept within your orders you wouldn't be in this position. As it is, we can fly the wounded out in the morning. There are medical teams assembling in Skopje. All we have to do is give the word. As I told you, we've come to assess what you need. You have prisoners, don't you?'

'Of course we do.' Difficult to hear the voices above the wind.

'Let's talk inside, Blake.'

'Let's talk here, Brigadier. I like the fresh air.'

'As you wish.'

The two men stood eyeing each other for a moment, till Blake broke the silence.

'Why did you cut the communications?'

'For Chrissake man, this is sensitive enough. We don't want the world and his dog listening to the traffic . . .'

'So what are you going to tell the world? Uh? What's the approved Whitehall version going to be this time? Been dying to know.'

'Don't push it, Blake. If you come quietly there won't be any need to talk to the world – at least not in detail.'

'There are casualties – on our side as well. The families will have to know . . .' He could see the first snowflakes behind Hensham, blown in on the wind. The Balkans were closing around them. Different rules out here. Different ways of dying.

'The story is this, Blake. You called on the local Serb commander, but unfortunately some of his troops were trigger-happy. They began shooting, you returned fire and there was a regrettable loss of life. Both you and the Serb are to assist with an international enquiry.'

He could see Hensham's men, flat on the snow beside the helicopters, could see their guns pointed straight at him. If they fired he knew that his own troops would cut them to pieces. Or would they? Probably Hensham would withdraw and attack the building with missiles – he wouldn't want the risk of dirt on his trousers. Bloody inconvenient, that sort of thing.

And yet whatever he did, they had come too far to end it like this.

'I can't go along with that, I'm afraid, Hensham.'

He didn't move, just stood there straight and still in the wind. 'I'm sorry you said that, Colonel.'

Perhaps it was only a few seconds before it happened. Perhaps a minute. But the noise of the machine was unmistakable. Both men turned at the same moment, as an old beige Huey swooped above the clifftop and hovered over them, its lights full on and its rotor blades churning the snowflakes, like a beast in fury.

Chapter Fifty-eight

In the special suite at Georgetown Hospital the Secretary of State lay sleeping, guarded by the Secret Service, cared for by no one.

For two days he had been treated for the worsening pain in his abdomen, as the cancer seemed to play with him, taunting him with the ultimate release, then snatching it from his grasp.

And yet, soon after six that evening the hospital had called his office and announced that, for now at least, the worst was over. The pain had relented somewhat. They didn't know how long it would last.

'What about visitors?' his secretary, Miss Blanchet, had asked.

'Out of the question,' came the reply. 'He is not, shall we say, in the most accommodating of moods. It would not be appropriate.'

Miss Blanchet knew perfectly well what that meant. In a less than accommodating mood, Harrison Drew could destroy people with the full force of a cruise missile, whether he was standing up or lying down. And in that state he was better left to his own devices.

Without any hesitation, she picked up the receiver, dialled the Willard Hotel and asked for room 618. Since the line was engaged, and it was already after working hours, she decided to go along in person instead of leaving a message.

Of course, Miss Blanchet had met the Russian Defence

Minister on several occasions, so she knew the extent of his business in Washington. Or thought she did. But it puzzled her greatly that he had arrived in the capital unannounced the day before and had rung her to say he had urgent business with Harrison Drew, whether he was alive or dead, or somewhere between the two. Moreover, she discovered that he had registered in a completely different name from the one bestowed on him by his parents.

All this made her anxious to see him in person and learn the reason for his latest visit.

As it turned out, she arrived just as Dmitry was entering the hotel lobby and was promptly invited for a drink at the circular mahogany bar on the ground floor.

They sat in one of the alcoves, famous for Washington assignations, while Dmitry amused her with tales of wicked, flirtatious Communists and the 'goings-on' in the *ancien régime*.

Miss Blanchet found his humour infectious but although he was a good-looking man, there was something she didn't fancy at all. Perhaps he was a little too sure of himself, too confident. Of course she dealt every day of the week with ruthless men: they weren't subtle, they weren't over-burdened with consciences or doubts. But most of them had their limits – somewhere, way beyond normal and accept-able boundaries. But at least they had them. And Dmitry didn't.

Later, as they got up to leave, he thanked her for coming and kissed her hand.

'Dear lady, I must insist that I see the Secretary of State tomorrow. It's a matter of vital international importance. Further delay would be dangerous and unacceptable.'

In that moment she felt the pressure on her hand, quite a bit stronger than protocol would normally allow, forcing her to pull away sharply and in some distress. And as she looked into his face, she saw an expression that unsettled her, all the way home on the Red Line metro to Shady Grove.

Next morning, while applying her handcream, Miss Blanchet noticed a faint bruise on the side of her hand, where his fingers had clamped tight, with the full and deliberate intention of causing her pain.

Chapter Fifty-nine

'Who the hell are you?' Hensham's voice barked out over the hillside, but no one could hear him above the noise of the rotors, as they sliced and chopped at the wind. Behind him his men took up position, crouching in the snow around the Huey.

'Good evening, good evening. Press party.' The Italian emerged from the cockpit, now in sheepskin coat and fur hat, producing a card from his jacket. 'This lady is from American television. This gentleman is British, and we wish to know who the hell are you, too.' He turned and grinned at everyone, as if pleased he had mastered the vernacular.

In the silence that followed, you could have held the disbelief in your hand. Only Blake stepped forward to make the introductions, telling them to come inside, shooting a glance at Brock to pretend they had never met. As they walked he looked over to Geralyn Lang, but there was no time to talk. As for questions . . . the Italian was making the running.

'Who is senior officer here, please?'

Hensham pushed his way between them. 'We'll explain everything in due course. Just arrived ourselves. Have to tend the wounded first of all. Sure you understand.'

As they entered the main hall Blake's troops barred the way to Hensham's men, forcing them to leave their weapons outside.

They looked suddenly like a crowd of football supporters whose team faced relegation.

Hensham pulled Blake to one side. 'Don't get any ideas, Colonel. I told you the version. There was an accidental exchange of fire, most regrettable loss of life. There'll now be an enquiry. That's all you have to remember.' He jabbed Blake's arm. 'And I suggest you do, if you want to make it out of here. Don't imagine that the presence of two bloody journalists is going to make any difference.'

The Italian must have heard him, for he turned away from the wounded and approached the two officers, no longer wearing his smile.

'Some more of our colleagues will be arriving tomorrow. We are, how shall I say? The advance guard. We will talk later, yes?'

'Of course. Only too glad to.' Blake smiled genially and turned to Hensham. 'You've obviously brought some supplies for the wounded. I think we'd better see what we can do for them. It isn't going to be an easy night.' He pointed outside to where the snow had begun swirling and scattering as the storm blew in from the east. Already it was covering the helicopters on the clifftop, blanketing the building, freezing the countryside for miles around. As he turned back and stared at the faces in the hall, it struck him that the world outside was a lot more welcoming, and a lot less dangerous.

Upstairs Blake and English held a hurried, whispered conference.

'Keep his men away from the guns. Keep them quarantined and watched, as far as you can, all through the night. I'll worry about Hensham.'

'Listen Tom. It's not an even match. His people are fresh. Ours are tired as dogs. If it goes badly we'll hold 'em for a while – but not that long.'

'Maybe it won't come to that.'

'What are you going to do?'

'Stay calm till the press arrives, then have a news conference and blow the lid off . . . What else can I do?'

'He'll never let it get that far, you know that.'

Blake laid a hand on English's shoulder. 'We just have to stay alive till morning . . .'

'I wish that sounded more likely.'

Suddenly, both men spun round as if caught by a whip, hearing the exact same shimmer of noise behind them, inaudible to an untrained ear.

'Tom.'

'God, Geralyn, what the hell . . . ?'

She had come to look for him, she said, climbing the stairs, sliding quietly along the bare boards. *How much had she heard?* English muttered something and made his way back along the corridor, leaving the two of them alone.

'Aren't you going to say anything?'

'I'm sorry.' He rubbed his eyes. 'A lot's happened since I last saw you.'

'You OK?'

'No. Are you?'

'I'm fine, apart from having to pilot a helicopter in a blizzard – for the first time in six years. Just let me know if I can help. That's all I want to do.'

The silence sat between them for a moment, each uncertain whether to reach out to the other. Only neither moved.

'When did you last eat, Tom?'

'My stomach doesn't keep records that far back.'

She grinned. 'I'll look for something downstairs. Since no one's telling any stories, I might as well fix the food.'

Hensham had chosen his moment well, slipping away, scouting the downstairs rooms, moving below to the basement. Some of the wounded were in corridors, mostly Serbs. Several lay unconscious and beyond help.

But he wasn't interested in them.

Kiro had been locked away in a room at the end of the corridor. The guard let him look inside, before ushering him out again, slamming the door. And then another room with no guard. Hensham entered quietly to find a single figure on a bed, lights dimmed. Special case written all over this one, and yet the face is turned to the wall. He leans over the bed, and he knows the profile, knows the man, knows all he can know about him. The hard, granite profile, the scratched, embattled features, the nose half-mended, like an old leather punch-ball.

'This way Brigadier . . .' English suddenly in the room, poised, his holster open, hand just an inch away from the Heckler & Koch . . .

'I seem to have got lost . . .' But Hensham is well aware who he's found and he can't resist the grin of satisfaction, as he's marched back to the main hall. Jimmy McIlvane. Found you at last, my old son. Sorry you're not feeling well. Come to Auntie. We'll make you better.

Jimmy was as good as dead already.

Chapter Sixty

Sometime after three Hensham began his ploy, striding through the main hall and out into the snowswept grounds, two thugs in attendance. The storm had blown east where it would eventually meet the dawn and die away over Russia. But for now the mountain stood in unbroken darkness, as the clouds swept in low and damp, blacking out the moon.

Tom Blake watched him pick his way to the helicopter and slam the door. Hensham had his own satellite communicator. That was clear enough. But why use it now? Final instructions?

Whichever way you looked at it, this was the night of the last performance. The show was closing. The company dissolved. No encores, no callbacks. You always knew when it happened. The last night always felt like it.

Five minutes later Hensham emerged alone, striding in the thick snow towards him. Blake couldn't help touching his gun to assure himself it was still there. He didn't like the sense of purpose in the man's walk, never trusted him, no one ever had.

The Brigadier stopped a yard in front of Blake, and jerked his head at him.

'Need a place to talk.'

'Talk here.'

'London's changed its mind.'

'What does that mean?'

'Don't push me, Blake. I warn you . . .'

'You wanted to talk, OK? Right! Now talk, or I go inside.'

Hensham shook his head. 'I don't know what the fuck it means, but they seem to be pulling the rug from under everyone.'

'Explain.'

'They've turned a fucking cartwheel or something. Seem to be suggesting you bring Kiro back . . .'

'To England?'

He nodded.

'You're joking . . .'

'At least for now. They want an investigation. I was told . . . if there's sufficient evidence, Scotland Yard's war crimes unit'll put him up for trial.'

'Jesus. I don't believe it.'

'Believe it.' Hensham's right foot kicked at the snow. 'But you have to get out of here now. They don't want any more press running all over the shop and finding you both here. Now, Blake. That's the deal. Isn't that what you wanted?'

'Why should I trust you?'

'Don't then. But if it was left to me, I wouldn't be laying on a helicopter for you, I'd blow your brains out here on the mountain. Far as I'm concerned you're finished, inside the Army and out.'

Blake turned and walked away.

'Twenty minutes. That's all. You and the Serb. Be here.'

Even as Blake climbed the staircase Hensham was moving. Down the steps to the basement and along the corridor. At the end, the guard watching Kiro's door is no longer interested. Hensham knew the type. 'More than my job's worth.' Carried out orders, nothing else. Wouldn't even look up if a jumbo jet crashed in the garden. 'Wasn't my fault, guv. You told me to stay here.'

He was sitting hunched on a stool and half-asleep as Hensham approached.

'Got a light?'

The soldier fumbled in his pocket. As he did so Hensham brought his knee up sharply against the man's chin, cracking bone, slamming his head against the door. He went out fast.

Three doors back now. Left-hand side. And he felt his way inside, sensing the darkness as he eased open the door. In the corner was a tiny candle, almost burned out, and Jimmy lying on his back on the narrow metal bed.

From the waistband of his fatigues he took a Browning 9mm, screwed on the silencer and held it against the man's temple.

The eyes opened half-way, but there was no surprise in them. Jimmy wasn't resisting.

'I thought you'd come, Hensham.'

'Hallo Jimmy.' He bent forward and whispered in the Scotsman's ear. 'You didn't keep to our arrangement, did you Jimmy? That morning in Aldershot – what we agreed. Do the job, but keep it silent. Only that was too much for you, wasn't it?'

'I didn't like the job.'

'So you told him, didn't you? You told Blake all about it.'

'No.'

'You're a fucking liar, aren't you?'

Jimmy grinned. 'Yes, Mr Hensham, I'm a fucking liar and so are you.'

And Hensham raised his hand and shot him through the forehead, but it didn't erase the grin on Jimmy's battered face. He left it behind him in the dying light of the candle, as his final testament.

Which meant that in *his* kind of book, the one that never, ever gets written, he'd acquitted himself just fine.

Chapter Sixty-one

The fight broke out about a hundred yards from the Pumas. Six of Blake's men had sneaked away from the house, anxious to divide up the contraband they had transported by donkey. But the negotiations went badly. Voices were raised. There were threats and insults; and before long a bitter argument had turned into a full-scale brawl, the noise echoing out across the grounds of the main house.

After a minute Hensham's guards wandered away from the helicopters to watch the spectacle – which was exactly what they were meant to do.

Ordered and choreographed by Major John English, the diversion gave him the opportunity he had been seeking for most of the night: to examine the Pumas in detail. What were the weapons Hensham had with him? What communications? It was as well to know such things.

By nature the Major had seldom accepted things at face value. But here, nothing was as it seemed. The Serb invasion was only half an invasion. Hensham's commando assault had turned into a tense standoff. This wasn't war, but a series of war dances that were dangerously distracting. For when the music stopped, the killing always began.

Only rule there was.

By the time the fight erupted English had secreted himself in a clump of bushes some thirty yards from the helicopters. Keeping low and quiet he slid through the snow towards them, tearing open the first of the side panels, crawling rapidly inside.

He didn't know what to look for. From his pocket he took a tiny flashlight and shone it around the cockpit. Nothing. Standard radio equipment, maps, belts, wires – all the basics.

The second helicopter was the same.

Through the Perspex he checked that the fight was still in progress. Christ, he hadn't seen anything like it since Arsenal had lost at Highbury. The boys were at it with a vengeance, kicking, punching, tearing at each other like wolves. For Hensham's men it would be better than a night on the town. Standing on the sidelines they were clapping and cheering as the brawl intensified.

Into the last helicopter now. Still nothing.

Same maps, same radio. So very ordinary. Except for a box below the pilot's seat. English tried to open it, but there was a lock in place. Forcing it would leave traces . . .

He took a quick look through the window and froze. Suddenly the fight seemed to have lost its appeal. At any rate three of Hensham's men were on their way back.

English slipped out through the side panel and flattened himself on the ground, as far down the incline as he could manage.

As the men approached they were laughing, but the laughter was short-lived.

'Better get this old crate started . . . Orders. Supposed to be ready for take-off 0450.'

English strained forward to hear the voices.

'Why just one?'

'Only one lot leaving.'

The men began laughing.

'Listen, just get moving and fuel the fucker.'

'Who's flying?'

'Two of *them*.'

'That's it?'

'What about the pilot?'

'Stripe.'

'Bloody hell. Couldn't fly his way out of a fucking paper bag.'

'Won't have to, will he?'

A moment of silence and they began laughing again.

As they walked away English made his move – fast back to the house, playing and replaying the conversation in his mind. Each time he heard it, he liked it less.

Blake had fetched Kiro himself from the makeshift cell and brought him to the main hall. The man stood sullen and angry, his arms handcuffed behind his back, face swollen and puffy.

'Where we going?'

'Holiday camp.'

'You big piece of shit, Blake. I get out of here, I start talking 'bout you.'

'Look forward to it.'

Hensham led Blake to one side. 'This is the route you've been given. You bypass Skopje and head south for the Greek border. From there you're cleared through to Thessaloniki and you'll get fresh instructions by radio. Pilot's briefed. That's all London's given.' He bit hard into his bottom lip. 'I meant what I said earlier. When this is over, you're finished in the Army . . .'

Blake held up his hand. 'Wrong Hensham, when this is over, you'll be the one taken out and publicly castrated. I know what you did. I know the sequence of events from start to finish. I haven't even begun.'

He turned away and pulled Kiro's arm. 'On our way, fat man. Lots of nice new friends for you. Gonna be a great day.'

Slowly they made their way out into the grounds. Blake had looked round for English but he wasn't to be seen. Damn the man. He needed to talk to him, needed to warn him. All he had to do was hold out till the press came. Just a few hours. Where the bloody hell was he?

As he ran, English knew what it all meant: the conversation, the locked box beneath the pilot's seat. He knew what they had planned.

Bypassing the hall, he took the back stairs three at a time, sprinting for the east wing where Geralyn was sleeping.

He didn't knock on the door, but woke her quickly and quietly.

'You have to get out of here. Get the Huey and get out. You're in great danger. So is Blake.'

'What? I don't understand.'

'You don't have more than a few minutes, believe me. This thing is about to blow . . .'

She didn't need telling again, pulling her coat from the chair, dressing in seconds.

And the drum was beating again inside her. Loud, precise, quite unmistakable.

Running now through the corridors, English leading. Down the back stairs, through the kitchen, straight out into the freezing night. The clouds had parted and the stars were fading fast. To the east the sky carried two faint stripes of blue and orange – signposts to the day ahead.

The Huey had landed on the south side of the building well away from the others, so no one noticed as they crossed the grounds, crunching their way through the frozen snow. English pushed her inside. 'For Christ's sake get it started, take it to lift-off speed and wait. I'll get Blake over to you, but it won't be till the last moment. Whatever happens, whatever you see, don't come back here.'

Again English crossed back to the house, heading for the Puma.

A crowd of soldiers had gathered around it. He couldn't make out if they were his or Hensham's. But then they parted to make way for Blake. It was the third helicopter, the last machine he had checked, the one with the locked box, rotors now turning.

As he ran he could see Blake pushing Kiro inside, looking round, nodding now to a few of the soldiers. Hensham close by. And then he spotted him, and as Blake came forward, English beckoned him away from the crush.

'Tom, listen to me. Don't get on that helicopter . . .'

'You're crazy. I have to. I'm escorting Kiro . . . there's going to be an investigation . . . I . . .'

'Bullshit. That helicopter isn't going to make it. I'm certain it's booby-trapped. You get on it, and you'll die with Kiro. They're closing us down, can't you see that. Get out Tom – the Huey's gonna leave on the other side of the house. Run for it . . . I'll hold them off here. You don't have a choice. For God's sake.' He pulled an envelope from his pocket and gave it to Blake. 'Take Jimmy's tape and get out of here.'

'I can't do that.'

'You have to. If this is ever to mean anything, you have to get out, and tell what happened . . . Please Tom, I've never asked you for anything. Go now . . . God's bloody sake . . .'

'I don't leave you and the others. Can't do that.'

'Then you'll fuck it up and they'll kill us all – and your name'll be damned as the stupidest of bastards for the rest of time . . .' He took Blake's hand for just a second. 'Best commanding officer in the whole British Army. Been a pleasure, sir. Now fuck off.'

And Blake didn't wait any longer, turned and began running through the snow, as the shouts went up behind him and the rotors on the Puma picked up speed.

Calmly, English stuck a grin on his face and walked back through the crowd. 'OK, OK, he'll be back in a second. Wants to kiss the girl goodbye, that's all . . .'

But someone must have heard the Huey. One of Hensham's men started calling from the house. Another rushed towards him. English could see some rapid-fire discussion. They weren't going to buy this for long. He looked behind him, and nodded to his sergeant. It was a nod they had long ago worked out between them and it meant only one thing – a ten-second warning that something truly lousy was about to happen.

It didn't even take that long. At the top of his voice, Hensham began yelling orders and a group of his men set off fast in the direction Blake had taken.

The Major didn't hesitate. Dropping to one knee, he pulled out the Heckler & Koch and fired three shots at them, noting with satisfaction that two of the men went straight down in the snow.

He took aim again and a third buckled. Not bad, he thought, for a pistol shot at forty yards, on a dark night, with a wind going crazy in all directions.

And then he felt a terrible jolt of pain in his shoulder and he knew they'd hit him. Another jolt, but this time there was no pain at all. Instead, he could feel himself falling with his arms outstretched, surprised that the ground seemed so far away, that it took so long to reach, that he couldn't feel the snow or the cold or anything at all.

For a moment the noise of the world grew distant and alien. But even as he lay there, his body slumped and disconnected, the silence shattered and he could hear the terrible beating of wings and the wind rushing over him.

So he knew that Blake had got away.

On maximum lift, the Huey tore off the side of the mountain and dropped fast towards the valley.

Blake had a final glimpse of the world on its side, of tiny, black figures on the snow, some moving, others motionless, their limbs outstretched or buckled beneath them.

'Where to?' she kept asking him, only it was some time before he could answer. He couldn't shake the picture of English's face or the sound of his words, or the knowledge that he had shaken the hand of a brave man for the very last time.

Chapter Sixty-two

Despite the years since Geralyn had last piloted a helicopter, her movements were sure and exact. She *knew* flying, knew what the machine would do. She could plot distances and bearings in her head. And even when the wind picked up and the snow slammed against the side of the machine there was no cursing, no moments of panic.

'The weather's good,' she insisted. 'Might even ground some of the other aircraft in the region. Make it harder for them to . . .' and the sentence was left unsaid, because it didn't need saying.

Using the charts she flew south, low and fast, with the Huey juddering and complaining and the trees so close he could have leaned out and touched them. And then there were open plains and more hills, and the machine rose again using the cloud as cover – the fastest straightest route out of the country, because now they were running. No looking over the shoulder. No sentiment. Not until they were somewhere else. If they made it.

Twenty minutes after take-off she landed the Huey smooth and straight on the edge of a forest about a mile inside the Greek border. And they didn't wait for the rotors to stop, simply got down into the snowdrifts and forced their way to the main road.

He had never run before. Neither in the Army nor out of it. So he didn't know how it would feel. His own side had always been the right side, guardian of the just cause and the moral imperative. And now his own side had sent Hensham to kill him.

You don't know how far they reach. You only know they are desperate. And today or tomorrow they'll come after you again. Because they have to. Now that you know what they did – now that you hold the taped confession from the man who did it.

Thoughts as they ran.

They hitched a ride in a truck that stopped endlessly to deliver food on the road to Thessaloniki, and from there an internal Olympic Airlines flight to Athens. Outside the airport she bought him cheap clothes from a secondhand store – thick woollen jacket and badly made jeans and summer sandals – so he no longer looked the part of a soldier, or a uniformed refugee, or anyone who could get killed.

With her credit card Geralyn purchased two seats on a Pakistani airlines flight to Newark and they sat in the centre of the airport lounge, surrounded by the crying babies who always fly long-distance and the mothers who shout at them, and the bags and boxes into which they distil their lives.

In an airport you become your baggage. Old and travel-worn, or new and sleek, or tatty and casual. So they carried some plastic bags and a bottle of wine and whisky, and a bunch of magazines – because no one travels with nothing. Not if they wish to arrive.

Thirty minutes before the flight Geralyn excused herself and made a collect call to Washington. She had almost lost hope of locating Harrison Drew, but the phone was answered immediately, and although no one spoke she knew he was listening.

'I have Blake with me.'

He was waiting. There was the faint hush of a trans-atlantic line. He wanted more details.

'We're booked on a flight to Newark, leaving now.'

'I see. You must have moved quickly.' Voice a little slower, breathing more laboured. 'Get him to the apartment on 54th Street.'

321

'Just that?'

'Just that. We're pulling out. I don't want you further involved. His own side will take care of him.'

She replaced the receiver and went back into the lounge. Blake smiled and she smiled back, laying her hand on his arm.

'You OK?' she asked.

Only to her, in that moment, it was as if a switch had been thrown and Blake was now a matter of complete indifference.

Harrison Drew looked out over the grey, snow-filled garden in Georgetown and felt the pain seep back into his body. He was tired of the routine – good weeks, bad weeks, always waiting for the jagged knife to slice into his body, never knowing when it would come, dominated and pursued by the cancer.

It wasn't a fair fight.

Drew smiled to himself. The disease came and went and fought when it felt like it. But the result was never in doubt. When it was good and ready, and the terms were right, the final lance would be administered. Till then you simply played the game.

Of course Washington had made him used to that. Game playing, with or without the rules, with or without any players. Only now he was getting out while he still could.

The problem was duty. And his was to safeguard the foreign policy of the most powerful country on earth and extricate it from the damn fool enterprises it got itself into.

Always the same ones, he reflected. They just looked different and came in different packaging. And yet they were all last week's, or last month's expedients – and now they were no longer wanted.

Allies could be allies on Monday. By Thursday they could become major irritants to the happiness of the American people. They had to be jettisoned, and that in itself was an art. Time it right, and you could shake their

322

hands and kick them in the balls in swift, consecutive movements. Time it *really* right and you could even blame the kick on someone else.

Drew picked up the phone and dialled through to the office of Anthony Amesbury in London and told him where he could find Colonel Tom Blake, in the event that he was so minded.

He must have fallen asleep at the desk. For when he awoke, the day had aged and the sky had darkened. And in the corner, on the window-seat, sat Dmitry Kallin, Defence Minister of the Republic of Russia.

'My dear friend, I hope I didn't startle you. The housekeeper let me in . . .'

Drew coughed for a few moments. 'Ask her to get us coffee, if you'd like some, or a drink . . . ?'

'She's gone. I said I'd make coffee if you wanted it.'

Drew swallowed and looked around for a glass of water. His throat was painfully dry and he knew his temperature had risen.

'Please turn down the heating, Dmitry. That switch there on the wall.'

'It's cold, my friend, the heating doesn't seem to be working.'

'Dammit, Dmitry, I said turn it down.'

'As you wish.' The Russian rose to his feet and fiddled with the switch on the wall. 'I'm afraid it's broken, my friend.'

'Jesus Christ, what's the matter . . . ?' He tried to get up but the effort was too great and he sank back into the desk chair. 'Why the hell have you come, Dmitry?'

'To discuss events.'

'Far as I'm concerned there's no event. It's over. We're pulling out . . . from what I hear the Serbs pretty well have the place anyway. Not our concern anymore.' He ran his hand across his forehead. Christ it was hot.

'Dmitry, please get me some water from the kitchen.'

'In a moment, my friend.'

'What the fuck's the matter with you? I need a goddam glass of water now.'

'Of course I shall get it for you. Which way is the kitchen?'

'Quick, fellah . . .' He could feel the heat searing round his body. Any moment now the pain would follow. Only this would be worse. He knew it would be worse. There'd never been a build-up like this before. 'Dmitry, the water. Quick man!'

Suddenly the glass was in his hand, and he held it shakily to his mouth, gulping clumsily, spilling it, forcing what was left down his throat.

'Over there on the sideboard, a bottle of pills. Give them to me.'

Dmitry reached over and in the semi-darkness put the small bottle into his pocket. 'I'm afraid I don't see them, my friend.'

'They're there. Don't be fucking stupid. I always keep them there. Bring them here for Chrissake, Dmitry . . .'

And then, as if from a long distance away, the pain began to climb.

'The pills, you fucker, bring me the pills. Find them. Please . . .'

Dmitry on the floor., kneeling, searching . . .

And in that moment the first of the jabs hit him in the left side. Pain, the way he'd never felt it. An incision with a blunt, burning blade, gouging out his life . . .

'Help me, man . . .' His head shaking, fingers dancing crazily in the air. Only then did his eyes understand. And Harrison Drew, fifty years in the scum-bucket of American politics, shut his mouth and sat stiff and proud in his chair, determined that Dmitry should not feel he had won, even as the pain tore again and again into his body, and his feet scraped uncontrollably on the wooden floor.

'I'm sorry my friend.'

And Harrison Drew died where he sat, without offering the courtesy of a reply.

Chapter Sixty-three

Peter Hensham arrived in London on the early evening flight from Zurich, anonymous, wearing his anger like an open wound.

The sight of Blake taking off from the mountain stayed with him, stinging deep inside.

But, God, had he made the bastard pay!

One by one they had mopped up his men, like the vermin they were, outgunned them in a battle that had lasted more than an hour. On both sides the casualties had been horrendous. Only he and four others had survived, and together they had heaped the corpses into a pile inside the building – Serb, British and anyone else who'd been there – set fire to them, and blown the place up.

Those were the orders.

Only Blake had slipped away. Only Blake was missing from the grand funeral.

Hensham took a taxi a couple of miles to a tourist hotel on the A40, booked a room under the name of Jett, and went out to the phone booth in the street.

Amesbury had been in the bath, he said, getting ready for a cocktail party. The chatty tone shocked Hensham but he didn't drop his guard. You never did that with Amesbury.

'Little messy, wasn't it, Peter?'

'Bloody messy.'

'Pity about Blake.'

Hensham sighed audibly. 'I've put out the word. Within twenty-four hours something'll come back. We know he flew south with that American journalist. I've got every bugger I can muster checking back.'

'Then call them off.'

'What did you say?'

'Call them off.' Amesbury's voice brimmed with amusement. 'Got a pencil and paper handy?'

'What the . . . ?'

'254 East 54th Street, New York. Apartment 612. Did you get that?'

Hensham fumbled for the back of his ticket.

'Where's that?'

'That's where Blake is, Peter. I suggest you have a good dinner and some rest, then take the first flight to New York in the morning. Sound OK? Fellow from the Consulate will meet you and do the necessary. We'll talk when you come back. Bye.'

Not only was Amesbury late for the cocktail party, he was still in his dressing gown when the doorbell rang.

It was not the right attire for unscheduled visitors, not with the red dragons sprawling lasciviously across its lower reaches.

Shuffling to the door, he peered irritably through the spy-hole. At first he didn't recognise the man, but then his memory seemed to clear and he recalled the young fellow with the pony-tail, Dmitry's friend, the one he'd met a hundred years ago at the flat in Docklands. What the bloody hell was his name?

He opened the door a little way and put his head round.

'I'm sorry, I didn't expect visitors.'

Andrei licked his lips and appeared to hunt for the correct English phrase. 'It is me who is sorry, Minister. I have urgent message from Dmitry Kallin, Minister of Defence . . .'

'Yes, I know who he is. You better come in. Can't stand all night on the doorstep.'

He led the Russian through into the living room,

suddenly aware once again of the pungent perfume – the
femininity of the fellow, the liberal sprinkling of powder,
like a French courtesan from an era long past.

'I don't have long I'm afraid.'

'I understand.'

'So please sit down and tell me your message.'

And then a profoundly disquieting thing happened.

Andrei did indeed sit down, but he came and sat on the
arm of Amesbury's chair and placed a relaxed and very
supple hand on his knee.

'I beg your pardon.'

'I am sorry.' The voice was almost a whisper. 'Do you
wish me to stop?'

'Of course I . . .' Amesbury looked at the young man and
something seemed to jolt inside him. A memory of a feeling.
A memory of a memory. Lord! Nothing like that had
happened since the upper third at Marlborough. So long
ago that he'd buried . . .

'You, er, said there was a message . . .'

Andrei's hand stayed where it was. No, it even began to
undulate gently towards his thigh.

'Dmitry asked me to make sure you were happy with
everything . . .' The Russian licked his lips.

Amesbury made a supreme effort and got to his feet, his
breathing suddenly urgent and harsh. What in God's name
was the matter with him?

'Look here . . .' It was difficult to summon up one's
dignity in a black dressing gown, littered with images of
priapic dragons. 'I think you'd better leave.'

'I did not wish to offend . . .'

'Good God, man, if Dmitry had any idea . . .'

'He told me to offer you any assistance you might wish.
We are anxious not to make things more difficult, after the
events yesterday . . .' The voice trailed off into the middle
distance.

'Please thank Minister Kallin, but we have everything
under control.'

'He will be delighted to hear it.' Andrei stood up. 'You have been most kind.'

'Not at all.' Amesbury relaxed. Somehow order and reason had been restored.

Andrei approached to within a foot of the Minister, but his eyes were glistening, as if close to tears.

'You are a fine man, Sir Amesbury. A good-looking man . . .'

'I . . .' Oh God, he thought.

'I will visit again sometime, yes?' He took a step closer and now the perfume was almost unbearable, and Andrei's hand was sliding up his arm, even as he slipped round behind the Minister, massaging his shoulder . . .

And Amesbury never saw the foot of steel wire that flashed out of Andrei's pocket, with the two wooden handles at either end, custom-made in a Moscow warehouse. He hardly saw the glint, coming over his head, his hands jerking upwards as the wire cut deep into his neck, slicing through the skin, severing vocal cords and tissue and windpipe, without even the merest glitch or hesitation. So smooth and practised it was. Honed, you might say, over many years in many different places. Only the best for Sir Amesbury. The very best they had. Made in Russia. For export anywhere it was needed. Of course he should really have been grateful – so little time was there for the terror to register before the air supply was cut and the blinding, screaming darkness of the other world came rushing to meet him.

Chapter Sixty-four

For a while Peter Hensham lay on the bed, reading the newspapers. They hadn't a clue what had happened out at the sharp end. But then they never did. Ignorant pricks! And just as well they were! He picked at the Room Service meal, and stared at the planes and the traffic outside his window.

But he knew what he really wanted. Knew what would slake his thirst and his rage. Knew where she lived.

He rented a car and drove west towards Aldershot. The sky carried a regal moon, surrounded by puffy white courtiers, and there were ridges and mountain ranges, blown and shaped by the wind.

Such a contrast to the miserable, cold streets, and the low semi-detached houses. The life beside the television. People watching other people who did things, never doing themselves.

Christ, it made him livid – all the sloganisers, the armchair politicians and soldiers. Never fired a gun in their lives, but could bloody well tell everyone else how and where to do it.

Such was the mood that took him to the front garden of Sarah Blake's house. This was what he wanted most.

'Jesus, Peter . . .'

'Sarah.'

'I've been trying to contact you for the last twenty-four hours. I've been worried sick.'

'Going to let me in?'

They went into the sitting room. He hated it on sight, the provincial chintz, so cheap, so make-do – the worst of the Army houses with its hand-me-down furniture, half-cleaned and tidied, before the next stupid bastard joined up and got it. God, it all made you sick. People with no style, no pride, never made anything of themselves.

He took the sofa. 'Drink?'

She went over to the sideboard and poured him a whisky.

He watched her back. She was cheap too, when all was said and done. Anyone who let him treat her the way he had was a slut. Blake's slut. Turned out they were well suited.

'I've been worried, Peter. What happened out there? And where's Tom? What's going on?'

'I thought you two were separated.'

'He's still the father of my children, Peter. I want to know if he's safe.'

'Course he's safe.' Hensham took a swig of the whisky and then another, swilling it around in his mouth. 'Any more of this, is there?'

'Should you?'

'For Chrissake woman, give me a fucking drink. I'll pay for it if you want . . .'

She handed him the bottle and sat the other side of the coffee table. 'I was worried. Surely you can understand that.'

'There's been an undercover operation, that's all. Taught the Serbs a bit of a lesson . . .'

'But there were casualties . . . ?'

He poured another half-glass and drank it straight down. 'There are always casualties. Can't you understand anything? War isn't a game of darts down at the pub, where you all score on a blackboard and bugger off home afterwards . . .'

'I didn't think it was. I'm just concerned, that's all. Everyone is. Some of the other wives are almost out of their mind with worry.'

'They'll be told in time. It's highly sensitive.'

'That's not very considerate, is it? We all live with the risks of the job but . . .'

'Come here, Sarah.'

'What did you say?'

'I said come here, over here, now . . .'

'You're joking, surely. I'm talking about casualties among friends and families and you want me to sit on your bloody knee. You're out of your mind. Besides, the children . . .'

Only the scowl had settled on his face, and now the anger and the alcohol were driving him, firing him.

Before she could move, he had lunged across the coffee table, landing half on top of her, pushing her down on her back.

'Stop it Peter, the children are upstairs . . .'

'Shut your fucking mouth.' The face livid above her, eyes bright and wild.

'Don't, Peter. I'll scream . . .'

'You wouldn't dare . . .' And already his hands had torn the blouse, scooping out her breasts, his knee forced between her legs . . .

'Oh God no . . .' Her fist came up and smashed his nose, and in that moment there was blood gushing from his face. A hand reached under her skirt, grasping for her panties, but they wouldn't come away. For a second he stopped and slapped her hard across the face . . .

'Please, God. Oh no, please no . . .'

'Enjoy it, slut. Enjoy the best fuck of your sluttish life . . .'

And suddenly there was a terrible scream that filled the ordinary little room, where the electric candles still blazed down from the cheap chandelier, and the fire fizzled dangerously in the corner – a scream from beside the door. They both turned to see her: the fresh, blonde schoolgirl in fresh blue uniform, hairband and red-apple cheeks, her mouth open in horror and her fists clenched, and the scream forming again in her throat. 'No! No! No!'

'Veronica . . .' Sarah calling out to her, running after her, tripping on the stairs, Hensham, half-undone, staggering to the door, bolting down the path, shirt-tail trailing behind. Tiny, jumbled events in rapid succession.

And upstairs the little girl kept screaming into her pillow, with her world upended and split apart before her eyes.

Two hours passed before she cried herself to sleep. Two hours before Sarah could bring herself to enter the living room.

The whisky had spilled and the glass had smashed, and it took her some time to brush it all away and sponge the carpet.

Chapter Sixty-five

Geralyn had barely spoken on the flight across the Atlantic, and now, as the taxi banged its way over the rutted streets of Manhattan, he could almost touch the coldness between them.

'You can keep the apartment for a couple of days. Belongs to the network.' She stared out of the window at the solid, moving wall of Christmas shoppers. 'Then you're on your own.'

Blake shook his head. 'I'm on my own already. Better that way.'

They got out on 54th Street and she collected keys from the downstairs porter. The apartment was on the sixth floor: cold, unlived-in, full of old magazines and heavy mahogany furniture.

This was transit accommodation. He was used to the feel of it. The dust on the furniture, the stained carpets, the half-cleaned stove. In the Army you spent your life moving home, so the walls were never that important. Your real place was on the road.

'What will you do?' She perched on the edge of the sofa.

'Sleep – then I'll get moving. Don't worry, there's a kind of soldier fraternity around the world. Plenty of people to help. Plenty of them on the run. I know where to go. What about you?'

'Back to the network.' She sighed and raised her eyebrows. She was even more beautiful without her make-up. The hair wild and untamed. The face paler, the eyes enclosed in shadows. 'I'll manufacture some excuse about getting booted out of the country. They'll be pissed at me – but not that pissed.' She tossed her head. 'I'll make it up to the managing editor.'

'That's how it goes, huh?'

'That's how it always goes.' She shrugged and opened her purse. 'There's a couple of hundred for you, to get some clothes and some food. Pay me back when you're rich and famous . . .'

'Geralyn . . .'

'What?'

The word thrown out like a punch.

'What happened? To us, I mean. I thought we had something back there in Skopje . . . or was I mistaken?'

'We were both mistaken.'

'Why?'

'I thought I could be different this time . . .' She shut her eyes for a moment, as if unwilling to show him what they were saying.

'What do you mean?'

'Nothing.' She stood up. 'I have to go now. I'm sorry.'

'Sorry for what?'

'You.'

For a moment her eyes locked onto his, then she stood up and walked straight past him into the hall. A second later he heard the front door shut behind her. Somehow, he felt certain she had left him a message, and it wasn't a pleasant one.

Blake must have slept the clock round, for when he woke, the sun was low again in the sky and New York had a light painting of snow. God, what had happened to him? He should call Sarah, call the children, tell them he was all right, but he knew he couldn't. They'd be listening and watching, and no telephone was safe from surveillance.

In his pocket, though, was the ammunition he'd use to get him home. Jimmy's tape. Jimmy's confession. In the end, that would be his ticket. For all the lives it had cost. For all the friends he'd lost.

In the morning he'd go down to the Village where the headquarters of the network operated. The old soldiers', old boys' network – not good old boys, but the bad ones who'd stamped on too many official toes, crossed too many governments, taken part in operations that never should have happened – and now needed to disappear. There had always been a pipeline, but Vietnam had refined and rebuilt it. Scores, hundreds had passed down it to new lives and new destinations all over the world. You paid your money, and you took your trip.

And now Blake would take his – while he still could.

He lay back on the bed, but it took an hour before he could sleep again.

Even through the shower door, with the water rushing and steaming, Sarah heard the news.

She didn't stop to grab a robe, just ran naked into the bedroom and stood beside the radio.

Christ, something had to leak soon – a report, a comment, a scrap of hard news. But nothing. A sportsman had been suspended for drug abuse, a fire in an old people's home, a minor royal to divorce – again. Such was Britain that December morning.

She dried off and went downstairs. The children had already left for school, Veronica neither crying nor talking. The sounds and images she had witnessed the night before were in a box – and neither she nor her mother wanted to touch them.

As Sarah stared out at the front garden Phyllis Mead appeared at the gate, hair awry, clothes untucked, looking like an unmade bed. She didn't use the bell, just banged on the door till it was opened.

'Thank God I caught you.'

'What is it Phyllis? I'm not feeling very sociable today.'

'They've started visiting the wives.'

335

'What are you talking about? What d'you mean?'

A pinprick of alarm.

'All the families of those out there – with Tom.'

'Christ Jesus! I don't get it. Hensham was round here last night and said everyone was OK.'

They stood staring at each other in the hall.

'What are they being told?'

'Nothing firm. There's been an accident in a remote area, may be casualties. Be prepared. It's highly irregular. They don't normally tell anyone anything until they're sure.'

'Tell me Phyllis. Either they know or they don't.'

'That's what Eddie says. He reckons there's no such thing as a remote area in Macedonia. Whole country's only the size of a bloody tea cozy.'

Sarah led the way into the living room, sat down, then stood up again. 'Christ Phyllis . . . No one's called *me*. Hensham was lying through his teeth.'

'You could call *them* . . .' She bit her lip. 'The other thing is there's a total news blackout on this one. Everybody's been told to keep it shut. Not a word beyond close family.'

'What else does Eddie say?'

Phyllis looked at the floor.

'I want to know what he thinks.'

'I'm sorry Sarah. You don't want to know. You really don't.'

'Tell me.' She took hold of her friend's arm and held it tight.

'He says it's a special operation gone badly wrong. He doesn't think any of them are coming home.'

Chapter Sixty-six

Hensham had looked forward to this day. And now it was his to play with. The events of the night had been trivia. Sarah Blake was trivia. Finally, he was on his way to New York to complete the business once and for all.

His flight left exactly on time from Terminal Four, heading north over the Midlands, turning west over Wales and the Isle of Man, painfully slowly for a man in a hurry.

But get it right, he thought, and he'd really be on his way. Amesbury had a whole basket of treats at his disposal. Troubleshooting around the world, maybe even deputising for the Minister –expediting with speed and discretion, the Whitehall way. And, given time, in the nature of such things, word would be passed, his account would be credited, and there'd come a little mention in the Honours List, the printed name in *The Times*. Brigadier Peter Hensham, OBE for services to his country.

And even more satisfying, the knowledge that he would feed Tom Blake to the dogs. Personally. By his own hand.

When he reached New York there was, as Amesbury had promised, a man from the Consulate to meet him. Stephens, Simmonds, something like that. It wasn't important. The fellow looked more like a chauffeur than a diplomat. Blue suit, blue raincoat, plain blue tie. Probably a blue jock strap. What was the matter with these buggers? And yet he had the package.

Hensham waited till they had pulled onto the Rockaway Boulevard before opening it, weighing it in his hand.

'Seems in order.'

He unwrapped the yellow duster, pointed the Browning 9mm at the floor of the car and squinted down the barrel.

'Silencer?'

'In the holdall.' Simmonds jerked his thumb towards the back seat. He'd been all set to label Hensham 'a silly poser' from London, wanting a gun in case he got mugged in Times Square. But now that he'd met him he wasn't so sure. Fellow was a tough bastard. Looked as though he knew how to use the thing. And Simmonds didn't want anything to do with that.

Turning right off the Parkway, Hensham tucked the gun into the waistband of his trousers and transferred the silencer to his jacket.

'What about keys?'

'We rented an apartment this morning on another floor. There were plenty available. So the porter's not a problem. I got a set of masters from one of the handymen. Couple of hundred bucks still gets things done.'

'I want you to hang around in case things get a bit messy. Stay in the car. You don't have to keep it running. Just be there.'

'Wait a minute, I was told to drop you and leave immediately . . .'

'Well, I'm changing your orders.'

'The hell you are . . .'

Hensham removed the gun and stuck it straight against Simmonds's head.

'You'll do as you're fucking told. Is that understood?'

Simmonds didn't reply.

Fifteen minutes later, he pulled up a block away from the apartment building and pointed it out. The street was still crammed with shopping and rush-hour traffic. Black stretch limousines stood bumper to bumper as the smoke from the hot-air ducts wafted around them.

Hensham got out and made for the front door. The porter was helping an old lady into a taxi, so his entrance passed unnoticed. Lift to the eighth floor. Check out the safe haven. That was the rule.

He opened the front door and closed it behind him. The door creaked badly. He tried it again, moving it more rapidly. No creaks. Would Blake's door be the same?

For ten minutes he memorised the geography of the place, checked the phone, listened for noises from the heating and the water pipes. Every building has its signature tune. He wanted to make sure he knew this one, well before he moved.

When he was satisfied, he changed into rubber-soled shoes and a track suit and took the emergency stairs down two flights to the sixth floor. Just as he reached the landing, a woman stepped out of the lift carrying a screaming child, its face bright red with anger.

'He gets so mad,' she said. 'It's always this way at Christmas. He wanted a bear with a blue ribbon and it was too expensive, and I told him he couldn't have it.'

'That's too bad.' Hensham smiled sympathetically. 'Perhaps next year.'

'I guess. Anyway, you have a nice evening.'

Blake slept badly. The mattress dipped unevenly, the sheets carried indelible stains. There was a sense, he decided, of too many bums in transit. All different sizes. All one-night stands.

He didn't know if it was the scream that woke him. The block was incessantly noisy – all day long there were rows and shouts. People called from their windows, banged doors, hammered nails.

He sat up and listened.

It was as if the whole country was throwing a tantrum. Didn't anyone ever shut up?

And then he remembered what had brought him there, remembered English on the top of a mountain, remembered the flight from Greece.

Knew he had to move.

Outside in the living room the streetlamps threw lights and shadows across the walls. Below him cars were hooting ceaselessly. The city would be at a standstill.

He pulled the plastic bag Geralyn had given him and laid it on the bed. Inside were some fresh clothes, a sweater, gloves.

He'd need them wherever he was going.

For a moment he wondered what Sarah and the children were doing. Probably on their way home from school, stopping at the sweetshop, not knowing . . .

And then his thoughts froze inside his head.

For years he'd listened and watched in silence, for years he'd made decisions that turned on the tiniest, briefest of sounds. So he knew what he'd heard. Knew what he'd felt. It had been the tiniest shimmer of draught, brief and cold, like the sigh of a dying man.

For a moment Hensham stood on the doorstep listening, aware that the next decision he took would be irrevocable. Christ, he'd been lucky.

The door had opened in complete silence, not even a creak. It was a good sign. A good omen.

But when he tried to close it, the bolt resisted. He could force it, no problem, but not without noise, so he left it a half-centimetre ajar.

In the darkness, he fastened the silencer to the barrel of the Browning and smiled at the sound that reached him. From the interior of the apartment, he could clearly make out the sound of deep breathing. Blake was asleep for Christ's sake, kipping just a few feet away. Quite uncontrollably the blood seemed to rush to his head, like a giant wave.

He tiptoed forward on the balls of his feet, thanking God for the rubber soles.

Living room now. No curtains. Just the lights from the street, and the random neon strips in the office blocks that encircled them. Sirens in the distance. Always the same in New York. Never more than a step away from emergency.

So close now, Hensham. So bloody close.

He crosses the main room, testing the rugs, but they don't slide.

Bedroom left, and the snoring is much louder. The man was out like a light. Easy, Hensham. Take it so fucking easy. Take your time.

An open doorway ahead of him to the bedroom. Curtains drawn, but his eyes have grown used to the gloom. He can see the shape on the bed, feel the presence of the one man who . . .

Gun in position now. And he'd made up his mind to fire all twelve bullets. Each one to be sent on its way with maximum hostile intent. Eleven in a row. And the final one, the despatcher. Close up in the nape of the neck.

One step forward and you can't fucking miss.

And then the front door banged hard. Jesus! And the screaming seemed very close, almost as if the child was inside the flat.

Sweet fucking . . .

And Hensham steps back, suddenly aware that there are footsteps very close. He'll have to kill them too. Nothing for it. If the kid comes into the flat. He turns, towards the corridor, but even as he moves two hands clamp onto his gun forcing it down towards the floor, wrenching it from his hand.

Blake!

The gun slammed away from him into the dark corner. He dives for it, but his feet don't move. Something round his neck. Tight around it. Rope. No . . . the hands. Fingers of tensile steel . . .

His own hands now fighting, tearing, but he can't get a grip. There's something slippery on them. Liquid. Blood. Whose blood?

He hasn't come this far just to . . .

'Blake, you're going to die for this . . .'

And still he can't see him. Still there's no sound. Just the fingers going deeper into his neck . . .

341

They're forcing him down onto his knees . . .

Can't hold it. Can't slow it. And in the distance of his mind there's a realisation, gathering pace, a conclusion heading fast towards him, a mad, unstoppable rushing in the ears. Shouldn't be happening. Fight it, man. Get rid of it. But his hands won't tear him loose.

A light has gone on, and Hensham has been dragged into the living room. Still can't see who's behind him. But in his horror and pain he can see the child, who's wandered in, staring in silence, slipped away from his mother, shouldn't wonder, transfixed, mouth open, unsure of what he sees before him.

Watching with innocent curiosity, no malice of any kind, watching the face turn colour. First red, then pale, then a mauvish hue, as the life is squeezed inexorably from the body.

And then the little boy screams again and runs back up the corridor, because this isn't after all a thing of interest or entertainment. Not that he knows . . .

There's something primeval in the act of execution. One man deciding the fate of another, taking a life with his hands in slow and agonising fashion.

Ritual of violence. Curse of the world since time began. And now on the floor of the sitting room, six floors above New York, it's over.

Blake stands up and unclenches his fingers. Doesn't look at the body. Doesn't search it. Doesn't want to touch it or see it, or acknowledge that it was ever there.

Quite calmly, he takes the plastic bag and finishes dressing. Then he walks down the corridor, through the hall and onto the landing. The child has gone and the screaming has stopped.

For both of them, he realises, the shock will come later.

Chapter Sixty-seven

There were three all-night diners. There was coffee. There were padded chairs.

And by seven in the morning the sun was climbing into the sky, beginning work, weak and pale, on another winter's day.

He bought a *New York Times* from a kiosk and sat in a restaurant on Sixth Avenue.

His mind wanted to read, but his eyes wouldn't do the job. Too many other images, too many faces. He could see the past so clearly, but the present seemed to have no shape at all.

Breakfast came to the table and he ate it, unaware what he'd ordered, and what it was.

Outside the window a tiny group of carol singers tried to make itself heard above the noise of the roadworks.

Half-way through his cheese omelette a man in dark blue coat and velvet collar joined his table, said 'hallo' and ordered the same thing. It wasn't till his meal was served that he glanced across to Blake and introduced himself.

'My name's Dmitry Kallin.'

'Pleased to meet you.'

'I am the Russian Defence Minister.'

Blake's eyes narrowed and for the first time there was a glint of recognition in them. He looked round for the inevitable bodyguard.

'Don't be alarmed, Colonel Blake.'

'Why not?'

'You're not in danger from me . . .'

Blake shot a glance behind him. 'Who am I in danger from?'

'I think you know the answer to that.' He put down his fork and pushed the plate away. 'There's a rumour going round – scandalous of course – that you have with you a certain tape . . .'

'And you want it.'

'Me? Good heavens no. I don't want it, Colonel Blake. What use is it to me?' He swallowed a mouthful of coffee. 'But to you it is of great value. You could bring down a government with that tape.'

'If I had such a tape.'

'I sincerely hope you do have it, Colonel. My advice to you is very simple. Don't hesitate to use it.'

'Why do you say that?'

'Use it before they find you. They always do in the end. They have resources you can only dream about. You think you're just one of ten million in this city, but you're very exposed. Very easy to find. Plenty of traces. Plenty of cameras. Plenty of people saw you come in. You passed through Immigration. You're on the computer. They know you're here.' Dmitry called for the bill. 'Amesbury's dead. I think you should know that . . .'

'God . . .'

'And at this moment your wife is one of a group being told that their husbands were killed in an accident in Macedonia. Officially, you died, Colonel Blake. Believe me when I say you don't have long.'

'And if I publish the tape . . . ?'

'It'll be highly embarrassing to your government – and . . .'

'You're a very special kind of bastard, Kallin. Do you realise how many people had to die for the sake of this miserable fucking operation?'

'Ah, the tone of the injured moraliser . . .'

'Better than the tone of an armchair killer, wouldn't you say?'

'And you, of course, Colonel Blake – you never killed for a cause.'

'It's the betrayal, Kallin. The endless, ceaseless betrayal that sets you apart. You kill for policy. Nothing else. Today's or tomorrow's. Doesn't seem to matter, does it?'

Dmitry shrugged and smiled. 'Remember what I said, my friend. You don't have much time. And then there's another factor . . .'

'Someone might change their mind, you mean. New orders? Blake's an embarrassment. Blake's a risk. Do something about him. That sort of thing?'

'How quickly you begin to understand politics.'

'Get out of here Kallin.'

'I was never here, Colonel Blake. Nor were you.' He got up from the table, pulled on his coat and walked away without looking back.

Blake felt in his pocket for the tape Jimmy had made, then he too made his way out of the diner past the carollers, chanting on about joy and triumph, and the season of goodwill.

There was, of course, no such thing.

'I'm sorry to call so late, Mrs Blake.'

'Please come in. I've been expecting you.'

Captain Harry Phillips had donned the thin smile of condolence, a kind of sharing, caring smile that says: I know you are suffering, and I'm suffering too. But Sarah wasn't interested in the niceties.

'Please tell me why you've come.'

'Wouldn't you like to sit down?'

'This is my home, Captain Phillips. If I want to sit, I'll sit. For now I want some information from you.'

He sighed, as if it were all too painful for him. 'I'm afraid I don't have good news.'

'Then I'd better hear it.'

'Very well. We believe your husband's unit came under fire from Serb forces in a remote region of Macedonia . . .'

'When was this?'

'About thirty-six hours ago. We've had reports of serious casualties, I should say fatalities. But the weather is bad in the area, and we have not ourselves verified the reports independently . . .'

'So where do these reports come from?'

'From the Americans and Russians who have a presence in the area. I should tell you that they are on the spot, and the reports have been reasonably detailed. But obviously we must confirm them ourselves as soon as possible.'

'Please tell me what the reports say.'

'Mrs Blake, there were heavy casualties – that's to say on both sides.'

'Let me put this another way, Captain Phillips. Were there any reports of British survivors?'

He paused for a moment. 'No, there were not.'

'So to the best of your knowledge my husband is dead.'

'I very much regret that his body appears to have been positively identified. As I said though, we . . .'

'. . . will be seeking confirmation. I understand.'

She pushed past him and opened the front door. 'Thank you for coming, Captain. I'm sure it's not an easy thing.'

'Mrs Blake . . .'

'Please go. I . . .' And she ushered him through the door and shut it quickly behind him.

She wasn't going to let him see her cry.

Not tonight. Not any night.

Back in the sitting room the phone was ringing and she picked it up slowly and listened.

'AT & T,' said the voice. 'Collect call from New York. Will you pay for it?'

'What?'

'Collect call from New York. D'you want it or not?'

'I suppose so.' She tried to clear her thoughts. 'Who is it?'

Postscript

Tom Blake returned to Britain following a week of uproar in the international media.

He rented an apartment three miles from the family home in Aldershot, from where he gave interviews to the press and television and spoke of the brave men with whom he had served.

Captain Phillips and two former associates of Peter Hensham were summarily court-martialled. A civilian staff member at the Ministry of Defence was fired. The Foreign Secretary was despatched to Macedonia to apologise on behalf of the British Government.

In London a commission of enquiry reported that Amesbury and Hensham had run a renegade operation inside the Ministry of Defence, without any Cabinet sanction – and were entirely to blame for the episode.

There were dark suggestions about the manoeuvrings of foreign intelligence services, but the rumours remained inconclusive. Nothing was known for certain. Nothing was ever proved.

At the inquest on Sir Anthony Amesbury, the police pathologist reported, solemnly and on oath, that he had died of natural causes.

In New York the District Attorney's office confirmed that Peter Hensham had been the victim of a hit-and-run accident. There were no witnesses and no post mortem was conducted.

Under intense questioning in the House of Commons the

Prime Minister insisted there had been a full and frank enquiry into the whole affair.

The fact, he said, that the information had been made available to the public so promptly was living proof that democracy was in safe hands.

Colonel Tom Blake was invited to a special reception at Number Ten Downing Street, but he declined to attend.